To Honor and Trust

This Large Print Book carries the
Seal of Approval of N.A.V.H.

TO HONOR AND TRUST

TRACIE PETERSON
JUDITH MILLER

THORNDIKE PRESS
A part of Gale, Cengage Learning

GALE
CENGAGE Learning·

Detroit • New York • San Francisco • New Haven, Conn • Waterville, Maine • London

GALE
CENGAGE Learning·

LIBRARY OF CONGRESS CATALOGING-IN-PUBLICATION DATA

Peterson, Tracie.
    To honor and trust / by Tracie Peterson, Judith Miller.
      pages ; cm. — (Thorndike Press large print Christian fiction) (Bridal Veil island)
    ISBN-13: 978-1-4104-5538-3 (hardcover)
    ISBN-10: 1-4104-5538-6 (hardcover)
    1. Large type books. I. Miller, Judith. II. Title.
PS3566.E7717T63 2013b
813'.54—dc23   2013004855

Published in 2013 by arrangement with Bethany House Publishers, a division of Baker Publishing Group

Printed in Mexico
1 2 3 4 5 6 7 17 16 15 14 13

To Honor and Trust

CHAPTER 1

Bridal Veil Island, Georgia
January 1913

Callie Deboyer opened the ornate front door of Fair Haven, certain there had been a terrible mistake. Who was this woman? Surely she couldn't be the nanny Mrs. Bridgeport had hired for the children.

With hat askew and mousy brown hair laced with strands of gray jutting in all directions, the woman standing on the other side of the threshold squinted at Callie through the screen door. Did she dare open the door of Luther and Eunice Bridgeport's elaborate twelve-bedroom cottage to this woman?

"Good morning." The woman leaned forward. "I'm Maude Murphy, the new nanny. Are you Mrs. Bridgeport?"

Callie cautioned herself to withhold further opinion. If this was indeed the newly hired nanny, she didn't want to start things off poorly. She didn't want to be accused of judging a book by its cover, but this woman was not what she'd expected. Maude Murphy came with a fine recommendation from one of the former residents of Bridal Veil Island, but this woman's appearance belied someone with years of experience as a nanny to wealthy families. Despite the fact that Mrs. Bridgeport and Mrs. Murphy had exchanged correspondence, they'd not yet met in person, and Callie couldn't help but wonder how their first meeting would go. Would Mrs. Bridgeport be as shocked as she was?

Mrs. Murphy's shoulder sagged a bit to the right, probably due to the weight of the traveling case she grasped by one hand. At the sound of clattering shoes in the hallway, Callie glanced over her shoulder. Five-year-old Daisy stopped behind Callie and peeked around her skirts while seven-year-old Lottie stared at the woman.

Lottie leaned forward until her upturned nose touched the screen. "Who are you?"

Before Callie could correct the girl's unsuitable manners, Mrs. Murphy stooped down and placed her nose near the other side of the screen. Nose-to-nose, they stared at each other for a moment. "I am Mrs.

Murphy. Your new nanny. You must be Lottie."

Lottie took a quick backward step. "You're too old to be our nanny."

"Lottie! You owe an apology to Mrs. Murphy."

Oh dear. So did she. She'd kept the poor woman on the porch now for several minutes. Without waiting for Lottie to beg the woman's pardon, Callie reached forward and opened the door. "Do come in, Mrs. Murphy. I'm sorry to have kept you standing on the porch." Callie gave Lottie's shoulder a gentle squeeze. "What would you like to say, Lottie?"

Lottie coughed as she inched forward. "I'm sorry I called you old, but our other nanny, Miss Sophie, was young like Miss Callie."

Daisy stepped from behind Callie. "Miss Sophie got married." Lottie gave the older woman an appraising look. "Are you going to get married?"

Mrs. Murphy sat her traveling case inside the front door. "I've tried that twice before. I don't think I'll be doing it again."

The children appeared confused, but Callie didn't give them an opportunity to ask further questions. "Why don't you girls run upstairs and tell your mother that Mrs.

9

Murphy has arrived and we'll meet with her in the sitting room."

Lottie coughed as she and Daisy ran up the steps. Mrs. Murphy watched for a moment. "Is the girl sick?"

"No, but she does suffer with a cough some of the time."

Mrs. Murphy nodded. "I see. Well, I don't want to take charge of children in need of constant medical care, if you know what I mean. I'm not good around sickness and such."

Callie peered at the woman, wondering why she would become a nanny if she didn't want to care for a sick child. "All children are ill from time to time, but the Bridgeport children are generally quite healthy."

"Good. Glad to hear it."

The two of them were as different as day and night, clearly separated by much more than their years. Using her own five-foot-six-inch height as a guide, Callie surmised Mrs. Murphy would measure a mere five feet, perhaps a little less. The woman's hair was dull and askew, while Callie's rich coffee-brown hair bore a beautiful sheen and had been carefully arranged. She couldn't condemn the woman for the deep lines that creased her weathered face or for the extra pounds that had settled around her midriff. She'd obviously lived enough years to earn every wrinkle and pound. Still, Mrs. Murphy's outward form proved a stark contrast to Callie's flawless complexion and trim figure. There hadn't been much wind this morning, so Callie decided the woman's rumpled appearance must have come about during her boat ride across the Argosy River from Biscayne. If not, Mrs. Bridgeport might dismiss the woman before she'd even begun her position.

"Would you like to straighten your hat before we sit down, Mrs. Murphy? There's a mirror in the sitting room that you can use." Callie waved the older woman toward a rectangular mirror surrounded by a frame of molded brass and tortoiseshell. The mirror was perfectly centered above an ebony side table. With its spiral-turned legs and carved ivory figurines, the table was a favorite purchase of the Bridgeports, made during their European travels.

Mrs. Murphy stepped in front of the mirror, tucked one loose strand of hair behind her ear, gave the no-nonsense felt hat a tug, and turned around. "That will do for now. I figure the missus is more interested in my ability to care for the children than whether my hat is perched at a proper angle."

She propelled herself across the room with

a short-legged gait and settled on the pale blue upholstered settee. Her feet barely touched the floor, and Callie wondered if this woman would prove capable of handling young Thomas Bridgeport. At twelve years of age, he was already taller than Mrs. Murphy, though she likely outweighed him by at least twenty pounds. Still, Thomas could be a handful — especially if he decided he didn't like someone.

"I understand you've worked as a nanny for several wealthy families in the area, Mrs. Murphy." Callie took a seat in an open armchair near the settee. From the appearance of her work-worn hands and ragged fingernails, Callie wondered if Mrs. Murphy's recent employment had been as a nanny or a housekeeper.

Callie immediately scolded herself for the judgmental notion. She disliked the fact that so many of the women in the Bridgeports' circle of friends judged everything from outward appearance. Shortly after she'd begun to work for the family, Callie realized that she'd taken on some of those same behaviors. Over the past couple of years, she'd been asking God to nudge her when such thoughts crossed her mind. God had been faithful to answer her request. It seemed as though He was prodding her far more frequently than she'd expected.

Mrs. Murphy squared her shoulders. "I sent my letter of reference to Mrs. Bridge-port."

Callie hadn't intended to insult the woman, but Mrs. Murphy certainly appeared offended. "I know she was pleased with the recommendation, or she wouldn't have hired you to work with the children."

Mrs. Murphy gave a firm nod that jostled her hat back to its previous off-centered position. Given the woman's curt reply, Callie couldn't decide if she should mention the hat. Before she could make up her mind, Mrs. Bridgeport sashayed into the room, wearing a pale yellow dress of imported batiste, adorned with wide inserts of French lace. Her ebony hair was fashioned in a perfect Grecian coiffure that accentuated her azure eyes and fair complexion.

Before greeting Mrs. Murphy, Mrs. Bridgeport hesitated and let her gaze sweep over the woman. She clasped a palm to her bodice and flashed Callie a look of concern before returning her attention to the new nanny. "Good morning, Mrs. Murphy."

Mrs. Murphy scooted forward on the settee and bobbed her head. The movement was enough to launch her hat into a graceful pirouette. All three women stared at the chapeau as it came to rest on the patterned Axminster carpet.

Mrs. Murphy jumped to her feet, retrieved the hat, and squashed it atop her head with the flat of her hand. "That ought to hold for a minute."

"I'd be pleased to loan you a hatpin, if you'd like." Callie edged forward on her chair.

"That's not necessary. It will stay put if I don't move my head much."

Callie nodded. "In that case, I'll leave the two of you to your discussion and go upstairs to help the children unpack their belongings."

Mrs. Bridgeport gestured for Callie to remain seated. "I think you should stay, Callie. After all, you spend almost as much time with the children as their tutor and can likely answer some of Mrs. Murphy's questions more easily than I."

Callie sighed and settled back in the chair. She would have preferred to be elsewhere while Mrs. Bridgeport conducted her interview with Mrs. Murphy. Callie knew her mistress well. Being present meant Mrs. Bridgeport would ask Callie's view of the newly hired nanny. If there was one thing Callie didn't want to do, it was give an opinion.

Mrs. Bridgeport sat in a chair opposite Mrs. Murphy. "I don't normally hire anyone without a prior personal interview. However, when I received the superb recommendation from Harriet Winslow, I thought you would be perfect for our children." From the quiver in her voice, Callie guessed Mrs. Bridgeport wasn't truly convinced she'd made the right decision.

"I met your daughters, and I believe we'll do just fine." Mrs. Murphy's lips curved in a half smile. "Your letter said you also had a twelve-year-old boy. I haven't met him yet, but I know boys can be taxing from time to time. 'Course there's plenty for boys to do here on the island, so between his teacher and me, we should be able to keep him from getting into too much trouble." She shot a look at Callie. "Isn't that right?"

"Yes, of course," Mrs. Bridgeport said. "I plan to enroll Thomas in golf and tennis lessons. And he enjoys riding horses, so I doubt you'll find him the least bit troublesome. He's a fine young man."

"Too bad he doesn't have a brother. Boys seem to behave better when they have a brother close to their own age."

Mrs. Bridgeport shifted in her chair. "He has three older brothers. The two closest to his age are in boarding school. Thomas will

15

turn thirteen next year, and he'll then go off to join his brothers at boarding school." Mrs. Bridgeport rang a bell for the housekeeper and requested she bring a tray of lemonade. "Have you worked for any of the other families on Bridal Veil, Mrs. Murphy?"

"No, I haven't, but if you want another recommendation, I could see about getting a letter from one of my other employers. They've moved to Boston, but I think I have their address."

Mrs. Bridgeport opened her fan and flapped it back and forth. "That won't be necessary. I'm sure this will work out just fine." She glanced toward the hallway. "Have your belongings been delivered? I saw only one small case by the front door."

"They should be bringing them up from the dock anytime now."

The housekeeper reappeared with a pitcher of lemonade and three glasses balanced on a silver serving tray. Mrs. Bridgeport motioned for her to place it on the side table. "Mrs. Murphy, this is our housekeeper, Lula Kramer. Lula, this is Maude Murphy. She is replacing Miss Sophie as the children's nanny."

Lula glanced at Callie before she turned and smiled at the new arrival. "I'm pleased to meet you, Mrs. Murphy. I'm sure you'll be very happy here. When you're ready, I'll be pleased to show you to your living quarters upstairs." Maude tipped her head as she thanked Lula. This time her hat slipped forward but stopped just short of falling off. Lula pointed to Maude's head. "Would you like me to put your hat over there with your traveling bag, Mrs. Murphy?"

Maude snatched the hat from her head and finger-combed her disheveled hair. "I'll just hold it. No need to bother yourself."

Mrs. Bridgeport lifted the pitcher to pour lemonade, but before she had finished, Maude jumped to her feet. "I'm not particularly fond of lemonade. I believe I'll take Lula up on her offer to show me to my room." She held her hat in front of her like a shield. "Unless you have some other questions for me, Mrs. Bridgeport."

"No, that's fine. We'll talk more later — after you're settled. I'll want to go over your duties so there are no misunderstandings about my expectations."

Callie didn't miss the concern that deepened the creases in Maude's face. No doubt she was uncomfortable, and who could blame her? Being the new person in a household was difficult. To find one's place within the familial framework without offending the employer or other staff often proved to be a challenge. Callie had been readily accepted by both family and staff, but that was due to the Bridgeports' friendship with her grandmother. There had been no barriers for her to surmount, but she had seen new servants falter under such pressures. Mrs. Murphy appeared confident and strong-willed. Perhaps she could overcome the scrutiny that was sure to come — not merely from the Bridgeport servants but from servants in other households, as well.

Once the two were out of earshot, Mrs. Bridgeport handed Callie a glass of lemonade. "She isn't at all what I expected."

Callie took a sip of her drink. "She seems nice enough."

Mrs. Bridgeport frowned. "Did you see her hair? And that hat? The hem of her dress was frayed. Didn't you notice? Mind you, Callie, I'm not going to judge her abilities on a frayed hem, but she's not what I anticipated. Harriet Winslow is a woman of impeccable taste, and I simply cannot imagine her hiring someone as unkempt as Mrs. Murphy to care for her children."

"The Winslow children are much older now. Perhaps Mrs. Murphy was a little tidier when she worked for them. If she's good with the children, that's all that matters, isn't it?"

Mrs. Bridgeport traced her finger through the condensation on the outside of her glass. "I'm not sure that's true, Callie. If the person charged with teaching a child to be neat and well groomed is unkempt, what does that say to a child?"

"She's likely gone upstairs to refresh herself. The next time you see her, I'm certain you'll be pleasantly surprised."

"Eunice!" The screen door banged, and Mr. Bridgeport strode into the hallway. "There's a trunk being delivered from the dock. The wagon's out front. Where does it go?"

"Upstairs to the nanny's room. Mrs. Murphy has already arrived." She shooed him aside. "I'll direct them."

Spying the pitcher of lemonade, Mr. Bridgeport helped himself to a glass. "Good morning, Callie."

"Good morning, Mr. Bridgeport. Did you have a good hunt?"

A smile curved the man's lips. "Indeed. They'll be serving some of the quail for dinner at the clubhouse tonight." He dropped into one of the chairs. "Nothing like a morning hunt in the great outdoors to revive the spirit."

Callie wasn't sure about the hunt part,

though she did enjoy watching an early morning sunrise on Bridal Veil Island. A sunrise or sunset in the city simply could not compare to those on Bridal Veil. She stretched forward and eyed the front door. "I thought Thomas was with you."

"He is — or he was. I gave him permission to remain at the barn and help curry the horses. He'll be back in an hour or so." Using his thumb as a pointer, Mr. Bridgeport gestured toward the stairs. "How's the new nanny? You think the children will like her?"

"She's quite different from Sophie. Older."

He nodded. "Well, if she passed Eunice's inspection, I'm sure she'll do just fine." He downed the remainder of his lemonade. "I'd best get out of these hunting clothes before Eunice sees me sitting on her good furniture." He turned toward the hallway but stopped as Mrs. Bridgeport and Mrs. Murphy descended the stairs.

For a moment, his mouth gaped open and his eyebrows furrowed as he stared at the two women. "In heaven's name, who are you?"

"Luther, I'd like to introduce you to our new nanny, Mrs. Murphy."

Callie leaned forward and immediately

understood Mr. Bridgeport's puzzlement. Although Mrs. Murphy had changed her dress, she appeared even more rumpled than when she'd first arrived. If she didn't prove to be excellent with the children, Callie feared Maude would soon be seeking another position.

During the few weeks since Sophie's marriage, Callie had managed to act as both nanny and tutor, but to attempt to handle both positions through a full winter would be impossible. Locating, interviewing, and hiring a qualified candidate now that they were in Georgia would prove extremely difficult, if not impossible. Most locals wouldn't want to move north once the family returned home. Callie pressed her hands together and offered a silent prayer that Mrs. Murphy would prove to be a perfect nanny who would shower the children with affection.

CHAPTER 2

Eager to check into his room, Wesley Townsend strode toward the steps of the Bridal
Veil clubhouse. He'd been opposed to coming along on his family's yearly winter
retreat to the South but had eventually
given in to his mother's tearful plea. Now,
after traveling by train from Massachusetts
to Georgia with his married siblings, their
spouses and children, as well as his parents,
Wesley needed some time to himself. Not
that he didn't love his family, but he had
grown exceedingly weary of their constant
talk about his future. Each one of them
seemed to think he or she knew what was
best for him. And all of them agreed that
the first order of business was to find him a
wife. But Wesley had no intention of seeking out a wife at this stage of his life. Too
much had happened over the past few years
and he needed time to discover exactly what
he wanted to do before he thought about

marriage — not the other way around.

"Do slow down, Wesley. This isn't a foot-race; it's a vacation." Blanche Townsend tugged on her son's arm and glanced over her shoulder. "We've left the rest of the family in our wake."

"They're not that far behind, Mother. I'd like to get registered and into my room."

"I think your father will need to take care of the registration, Wesley. We're here at the invitation of Josiah and Margaret Wade. Your father made the arrangements for all of our rooms through Josiah and the hotel director." She glanced about the perfectly manicured grounds. "Use of the facilities on this island is by membership or invitation only. Since the Wades were sailing for Europe, it was most kind of them to offer us their apartments." She squeezed his arm and smiled. "We can wait in those lovely wicker chairs on the porch." She tipped her head closer. "I told Margaret I don't think I'll sail for several years. After the disaster with the *Titanic* last year, I've developed an aversion to ships."

"I don't think you need to fear sailing, Mother. There are train wrecks, yet you still ride trains."

"I know you're right, Wesley, but still . . ." She clasped a hand to her bodice and shook

23

her head. "Those poor people. I do hope the Wades will be safe."

"As do I," he said as they climbed the steps and sat down on the wide porch that surrounded the huge clubhouse and surveyed the lush lawns and ornamental shrubs.

For as long as he could remember, their family had wintered in Virginia at White Sulfur Springs. He'd been astonished when his father had announced the family would visit a new locale this winter, but his surprise had vanished when he learned two textile investors would also be visiting the island. His father would be closing a deal to expand the family's textile mills in Massachusetts as soon as they returned home in the spring, and he likely planned to mix business with pleasure while on Bridal Veil.

No doubt his older brothers, Charles and Daniel, were also in on the scheme. And his sister Helena's husband, Richard Kennebec, who also worked in the family business, had probably been the one to discover the investors would be on the island. Since his marriage to Helena, Richard had used his ability to sniff out such details in order to help the company. Wesley had heard rumors his brother-in-law enjoyed gambling, and he now wondered if Richard gathered his information at the racetrack and gaming tables. For his sister's sake, he hoped this wasn't true, for he had a few friends who had ruined their lives with such pursuits.

His mother stepped to the railing as his father climbed the steps. "When will they bring the luggage, Howard? I do want to freshen up as soon as possible."

Helena and Richard approached the front steps moments later. Richard carried their baby boy while Helena attempted to keep the two girls in tow.

Howard Townsend raked his fingers through his thatch of thick white hair. "I must go inside first, Blanche. Give me a few minutes and we'll get settled." His jaw twitched as he turned and looked at Wesley. "Look after your mother while I take care of registering the family and securing our keys."

Wesley nodded. He doubted his mother needed "looking after," but he didn't argue. The twitch in his father's jaw meant only one thing: The family patriarch was reaching the end of his rope.

"I believe this is going to be a wonderful change of pace for all of us, don't you?" His mother let her gaze sweep from one family member to the next. "It's too bad Charles had to remain in Massachusetts." His mother glanced toward Daniel. "And your father says you'll be staying only a week or so. That saddens me very much."

Wesley didn't comment, but he thought Charles and Daniel were the fortunate ones. He would be here all winter, listening to how his life had taken a wrong turn and that he needed to move forward and make some decisions regarding his future. With the acquisition of several woolen mills due to take place as soon as they returned to Massachusetts, Wes was expected to manage the new mills, or be prepared to support himself with some other form of meaningful employment.

"If Father is going to be away all winter, Charles and I need to be in Massachusetts to take care of the business. Melody may remain an extra week or two, but she doesn't want to be separated for too long." Daniel grinned. "We are newly married, after all. And Father will be working while he's here. He plans to hold several meetings with investors who will be vacationing at Bridal Veil." At age twenty-eight, Daniel had as much charm as a dose of castor oil.

"What happened to my fun-loving brother?" Wes eyed Daniel and scooted to the edge of the wicker chair. "I remember when you enjoyed playing tennis and riding horses."

"The rest of us grew up and learned to work for a living. How long has it been since you've actually done anything useful, Wes?"

The words stung like salt in an open wound. "I'm not sure anyone in this family believes I've ever done anything useful, Daniel — especially you and Charles."

"Now, boys! Let's don't ruin our vacation before it's even begun." Blanche patted Wesley's shoulder. "And we all know how hard you worked in college and medical school. And down in Texas, too."

His sister, Helena, bobbed her head. "And I've commended you over and over for the work you did with those New York doctors, Wesley."

"That's right, Helena. We all have expressed our admiration." His mother glanced at the group with a look in her eye that defied any one of them to disagree. "Haven't we?"

"There's no need to coerce them, Mother. I know what they think. And frankly, it doesn't matter. I don't dictate how they should live their lives, and I'm not going to permit them to have a say in mine."

Daniel shook his head. "We're not attempting to tell you what you should do,

Wes. But you're twenty-five years old. You've said you don't want to return to medicine. If that's the case, you know you're needed in the family business. With the recent acquisition, there's a real need for you to step up and manage the new mills."

The family business was the last place Wes wanted to spend his time. Working in the office of the family textile mills was as unappealing as a toothache, but it appeared this entire vacation would be riddled with pressure for him to take his "rightful place" in one of those mills.

"I have keys!" Wesley's father strode toward them with several keys in his hand. "All of the rooms are adjoining except for yours, Wes. They couldn't manage to get all of us together. I hope you won't mind."

"Not at all. Just hand me my key, and I'll find my room." Wes stepped forward and extended his hand.

His father clamped his hand around the keys. "They have their own way of doing things here at the clubhouse, and we'll be expected to abide by the rules."

Wes exhaled a long breath. "I'm sure there will be ample time to hear the rules later." He hoped his father wasn't going to read a set of regulations before they could go to their rooms.

Mr. Townsend waved the family to silence. "The first rule is that the hotel staff will escort each family to their room. They want to be certain we are properly settled. We are asked to wait in the grand sitting room just inside the front doors or enjoy ourselves here on the porch until our name is called. The hotel clerk said a young lady would be out shortly to serve us lemonade." He extended his arms to Helena's daughters, and both little girls came running to him, each one settling on one of his knees.

Wesley was surprised by the show of affection. He couldn't remember a time in his life when he'd sat on his father's knee. In fact, he didn't recall his father being home much at all during his childhood. When they'd spent winter months at White Sulfur Springs, his father would remain for only a week or so, and then he'd return to his work in Massachusetts. Shortly before their departure for home, his father would reappear to travel home with them. And during his summers in Lowell, Wesley spent most of his time outdoors with his brother or friends. Exploring the woods had instilled an interest in trees and plants that had never left him. While in college, he'd taken a number of botany classes and had enjoyed them so much that he'd briefly considered becoming a botanist rather than a physician. His life wouldn't be in this present state of disarray if he'd become a botanist or landscape architect — anything other than a medical doctor.

The clerk called out his father's name, and both girls jumped down. "Can we come and see your room, Grandpap?"

Any sign of his earlier irritation vanished as he winked at his granddaughters. "As soon as your mother and father give you permission, you can come to our rooms." He leaned down and kissed each of them on the cheek before they followed the hotel clerk.

Wesley reached for his small traveling case and withdrew a book. While his brother and Richard were talking about the textile mill, he read about the art of architectural landscape. Once he had settled his belongings into his room, he planned to begin exploring the island. He was eager to find new floras that were listed in his book. On their short buggy ride from the dock to the clubhouse, he had observed any number of plants he'd never before seen. And the landscaping around the cottages and clubhouse was magnificent — proof that work could be found for good landscape architects.

Helena's husband, Richard, leaned against one of the thick white porch columns. "I hear they have an excellent golf course here on the island, Wes. That should keep you occupied for the entire winter."

Wesley couldn't decide what bothered him more — Richard's arrogant sneer or the sarcasm in his voice. For an instant, Wesley considered mentioning the racetrack as the place where the family would likely find Richard, but such a comment would hurt his sister more than Richard.

"Thank you for thinking of me, Richard. One of Father's friends told me about the course before we left Massachusetts. If it's as good as he said, then you can be sure I'll spend a great deal of time there." He flashed a smile at Richard. "You should give golf a try. The fresh air and exercise might help you."

"Is that what you learned in medical school? A little fresh air and exercise will fix any problem?"

"It won't fix all problems, but fresh air and exercise are proven to aid good health." Wes patted his stomach. "And it appears you've put on a bit of weight."

"I could have told you fresh air and exercise aid good health. It would have saved your father the money he spent sending you to medical school."

"Stop, Richard!" Helena reached for the baby in his arms. "Take the girls and let them watch the croquet game on the lawn."

Once they were alone, Helena took a chair next to him. "Don't let Richard's comments bother you, Wes. He's not happy unless he's irritating someone."

Wesley glanced over the railing at Richard and the two girls. "The girls are growing up. They're good-looking children."

Helena's lips curved in a forlorn smile. "I long for the days when they were much younger and more dependent upon me."

Wes chuckled. "You could always have more. Besides, they're only five and seven. It's not like they've become adults just yet."

"Speaking of children, when are you going to find a girl and settle down? Mother mentioned several young ladies she thinks would be perfect for you." Helena resituated the squirming baby on her lap.

Wes pushed up from the chair and settled against the white wooden railing that surrounded the porch. "I'm beginning to think this entire vacation was arranged to either force me to accept a position at the textile factory or to find me a wife."

"Or both." She grinned at him. "You know Mother and Father. When they come together with a plan, they usually circle around and tighten the ranks."

"So there is a plan?"

She held up her hand. "I was only joking with you. However, you know that Father believes you should be doing something with your future."

He closed his book and tucked it back into his bag. "I'm glad to hear that everyone knows exactly what I need."

"We're your family, Wes. We all want you to succeed and be happy." She swatted a pesky fly away from the baby. "Did Mother mention the masked ball to you?"

"No." He sighed. He disliked the formal events that the resorts seemed to think necessary each season. "Why so soon? Couldn't we enjoy at least a week or two without some formal gathering?"

Helena flashed him a smile. "I believe this is a welcoming ball so that newcomers like us can get acquainted with the other guests. It wouldn't be a welcoming ball if they waited for two or three weeks."

"Maybe I can convince Mother I don't need to get acquainted."

Helena laughed. "You know better than that. The rest of us received our instructions about the teas, card parties, and balls that we're expected to attend before we ever departed Massachusetts. She likely feared you wouldn't come if you'd received the information in advance. You have a few days' reprieve. As I recall, the ball won't be held for three more days. Oh, the clerk just called our name." She jumped up and waved to Richard. "Bring the girls, Richard. They're ready to take us to our room." She patted Wes on the arm. "I'm sure they'll come for you soon."

He nodded. "I'll see you at dinner."

Wes leaned back in his chair and watched his sister and her family as they made their way to the hotel entrance. In some ways, he wished he could be like Charles or Daniel or Helena — that he could be satisfied marrying the proper socialite and working for the family business. But he didn't fit the mold. And he doubted he ever would — not after all that had happened in Texas. In fact, he wondered if he would ever find peace again.

CHAPTER 3

Callie followed Maude into the sunroom, where Mrs. Bridgeport planned to explain her list of expectations. Though Callie had attempted to escape this meeting, Mrs. Bridgeport insisted upon her presence. Once they'd settled in the cushioned wicker furniture, Mrs. Bridgeport unfolded a piece of stationery.

She tapped the piece of paper and smiled at Maude. "I've written these down so I won't forget any of the things we need to discuss concerning the children." Mrs. Bridgeport cleared her throat. "But first I want to address my expectations regarding personal appearance."

Maude snapped to attention. "Last I knew, none of us is able to change the way we look. We're stuck with what the good Lord gave us." She pointed her thumb at Callie. "Not that I wouldn't prefer to look like her — or you, for that matter, Missus

— but that ain't going to be happenin'."

Mrs. Bridgeport arched her brows. "Isn't going to happen."

Maude frowned. "That's what I said."

"I was correcting your grammar, Maude. You should have used the word *isn't* instead of *ain't*. I want the children to use proper English. I'll add that to my list."

Maude's look of confusion remained, but she nodded. "I'll do my best."

"Now, let's return to the topic of personal appearance." Mrs. Bridgeport turned her attention to Maude. "I want our children to be well groomed at all times. And we must lead by example. Don't you agree, Maude?"

The older woman immediately tucked a loose strand of hair behind her ear. "Well, I do think children should be neat and so forth, but I'm all for lettin' them have fun and get dirty, too. Elstwise, there's not much sense in having a childhood, now is there?"

"Childhood is a time to have fun, but it is also a time to instill proper values. Callie takes care of educating the children. They are fluent in both French and English, and they have been equally successful in their other educational skills, as well." She beamed at Callie. "That, of course, is due to Callie's excellent example and dedicated efforts. The children are quite fond of her, yet she sets high standards for them."

Maude reached over and patted Callie's arm. "Good for you, Callie. Sounds like the missus might be preparing to give you an increase in pay."

Callie smiled at the older woman. Somehow, this meeting had gone off the rails and Mrs. Bridgeport was having difficulty getting it back on track.

"I was attempting to make a point that children frequently learn by following the example of others. For instance, when Callie instructs the children to speak in French, she reinforces her request by conversing with them in French."

Wide-eyed, Maude turned toward Callie. "You speak French, do ya? That's mighty impressive. Maybe I could learn a few words if ya have time to teach me." She tipped her head to the side and looked at Mrs. Bridgeport. "To see someone old as me learning to speak French might set a good example for the children, don't ya think?"

Mrs. Bridgeport withdrew a handkerchief from her pocket and blotted her forehead. "Let's not worry about French lessons at the moment, Maude. As the children's nanny, you are the one charged with making certain they are cared for and properly groomed. Unless they are in classes with Callie, the children are under your supervision. To that end, your appearance is very important." She inhaled a deep breath. "You will provide a much better example for the children if your hair is properly arranged and your clothing is clean and pressed."

Maude traced her hand down the wrinkled skirt. "My things have been packed, and I'll see to pressing them first thing, Missus. I doubt I have dresses that will meet the standards you might be expectin'. I hit a spot of hard times and didn't have money for new dresses and such."

"Dear me, I am sorry to hear you've been through difficult circumstances, Maude." Mrs. Bridgeport's face turned as pink as the roses that bloomed in her garden each summer. "I want you to come with me to Biscayne at the end of the week, and we'll find some suitable clothing for you. Had I known of your situation, I would have sent money in advance for you to purchase whatever you needed."

Maude's face lit up like candles on a Christmas tree. She touched a hand to her unkempt hair and leaned a little closer to Callie. "Maybe you can show me how to fix my hair a little more proper. Since it turned gray a few years ago, it's become wiry and hard to manage. I pin it down, but in no time it pops from beneath the pins like corn exploding over a hot fire."

Callie smiled. "I'll see if there's a style we can develop that might be easier for you to manage."

Mrs. Murphy scooted back on the cushioned chair and rested her arms across her waist. "That's mighty thoughtful of you."

Mrs. Bridgeport's features tightened. "Surely you know how to fashion hair, Mrs. Murphy. Our nannies have always styled our daughters' hair, and I assumed that since you had worked as a nanny for Mrs. Winslow, you would know how to fashion and care for the children's hair and clothing."

"Oh, I can take care of the children just fine — unless they have some of this wiry gray hair like my own." She cackled and slapped her leg as though she'd found great humor in her own comment.

Clearly this was not the nanny Mrs. Bridgeport had expected, yet Callie remained certain the woman possessed fine attributes. Why else would she have come so highly recommended? Still, Maude's behavior was a far cry from the refined and proper behavior of their former nanny, Miss Sophie, and Mrs. Bridgeport's frustration appeared to be increasing by the minute.

Hoping to ease her employer's concern, Callie scooted forward on the chair. "Since you have a meeting to attend this morning, Mrs. Bridgeport, I would be happy to show Maude a bit of how we do things here at Fair Haven."

The strained look on Mrs. Bridgeport's face vanished. "I had completely forgotten I was to meet with the ladies to go over plans for some of our personal entertaining this season. Thank you for reminding me, Callie." She flashed a smile at the younger woman. "I'm sure you can more easily explain the children's schedule and show Maude where things are and how I expect items cared for in the children's rooms."

Mrs. Bridgeport strode toward the sunroom doorway, but then stopped and glanced over her shoulder. "And Callie, don't forget that I'm planning on your attendance at the masquerade ball later in the week."

Callie inwardly cringed at the reminder. Even though they weren't related, more often than not, the Bridgeports treated her as a member of the family. "Perhaps it would be better if I refrain from attending any evening events until Maude is more accustomed to caring for the children."

"Nonsense. Maude will be just fine with

the children." Mrs. Bridgeport turned her attention to the new employee. "Won't you, Maude?"

"Yes, ma'am. I believe we're going to get along just dandy."

Mrs. Bridgeport smiled. "There, you see?" She snapped her fan together. "I plan to join Luther at the club for lunch once my meeting ends, so please go ahead with the children's lunch."

Once she'd departed the room, Maude turned her full attention upon Callie. "Appears that you have the job of teachin' me as well as the children. I'm guessin' the girls are upstairs?"

"Yes. They are delightful children, and I'm sure you'll enjoy them very much. When their schedule is interrupted, they go to the spare room upstairs that we use as a schoolroom and playroom. Weather permitting, I try to take them outdoors for some of their lessons each day. And, of course, Thomas enjoys sports, and since he is older than the girls, I do my best to take care of his educational needs while incorporating outdoor sports whenever possible."

Mrs. Murphy eyed a rifle hanging over the mantel. "And I suppose his father takes care of the hunting portion of his education."

Callie nodded. "That's true. However,

Thomas occasionally accompanies us when I take the girls to play croquet or shuffleboard. All three of them enjoy outdoor games. However, because of the outdoor sporting activities for Thomas, there are times when I'll need to leave the girls in your charge. You won't have any problems with them. They're happy playing with their dollhouse or having a little tea party with their dolls out in the gazebo." Callie pointed toward the large gazebo not far from the house. "How many children did you care for when you worked for Mrs. Winslow?"

Mrs. Murphy's eyebrows pinched together. "Depended on the time of year. Some of them went off to boarding school, and sometimes they'd all be home for the holidays and so forth."

"Did they have daughters, or only sons?"

"Some of both." Mrs. Murphy jumped up from her chair as if she'd been hit by a load of buckshot and touched a finger to her eye. "Time's a wasting. Why don't you show me around the house, and then I'd like a look at the children's rooms. Best to know where I'll be spending most of my time, don't you think?"

Perhaps thoughts of her previous charges had stirred poignant memories for Mrs. Murphy. Employment as a nanny or tutor to young children created a bond that was not easily broken. Callie knew all too well, for she dreaded the day when the remaining Bridgeport children would be sent to boarding school and her services would no longer be needed.

She grasped Mrs. Murphy's arm. "I'm sorry. Sometimes I ask too many questions."

The older woman's lips curved in a wavering smile. "No need for apologies. There are times when I've been accused of the same thing. Sometimes I become a bit overwrought when I think of the Winslow children being all grown up. Would be nice to hear from one or two of them, but I'm sure they forgot me the minute they went off to boarding school." Her pale gray eyes clouded when she looked at Callie. "You know how it is — once they get away from home, things are never the same, even when they come back for a visit."

Callie did know. Even though she hadn't been tutor to the three older Bridgeport sons, she'd heard their mother lament the fact that they'd all changed far too much to suit her once they'd gone off to school. Hoping to keep Thomas at home, Mrs. Bridgeport had used that argument with her husband, but to no avail. Besides, if Thomas wasn't permitted to join his brothers at boarding school next year, Callie was certain there would be mayhem in the Bridgeport household. If he'd been given his way, Thomas would have gone off to school even before he turned thirteen, but much to his annoyance, he'd been unable to convince his mother.

Mrs. Murphy glanced about as they entered the small kitchen. "The time passes quicker than ya think — you'll see. In seven or eight years, that youngest girl will be packing her trunk and heading off to boarding school, and then where will ya be?" She turned in a circle. "This is a mighty small kitchen for such a big house. How do the cooks prepare meals without bumping into each other?"

"Most meals are eaten at the clubhouse. In fact, it's very much expected. The kitchen was installed in the house for occasional family meals and for the children when they don't join their parents at the clubhouse for dinner or during the more formal events conducted in the evenings. The children eat breakfast here in the kitchen each morning, as well."

She nodded her head. "From what the missus said, it sounds like you sometimes join them at those fancy doings over at the clubhouse."

"My grandmother and Mrs. Bridgeport's mother were dear friends for many years. I moved to Indianapolis to live with my grandmother when I was fifteen years old, and it was due to Grandmother's friendship with Mrs. Bridgeport's mother that I secured this position after my grandmother's death. In some circumstances, Mr. and Mrs. Bridgeport insist I attend formal events with them."

"Oh, so yar rich, too." Mrs. Murphy put her hand over her mouth, realizing she'd overstepped. "Sorry, of course ya ain't rich . . . not if ya have to work for a livin'."

Callie wasn't at all sure what to say. Her family's financial status wasn't any of the woman's business.

Mrs. Murphy recovered her boldness as they walked down the hall. "You should take advantage of going to parties with those wealthy folks so you can find you a man and make a life of your own. Like I said before, these children will all go off to boarding school, and you'll be left looking for work." She *tsk*ed and patted Callie's shoulder. "Take it from me, finding work when you're old isn't so easy. Folks know it's hard for us old folk to chase after their little ones. They'd rather hire someone young instead of someone ready for a rocking chair."

Mrs. Murphy wasn't old enough to consider a rocking chair, but the woman was correct: Callie did need to make plans about her future — about whether she would heed her parents' wish for her to join them in Africa. The thought caused her to shiver. Unlike her parents and their overwhelming desire to serve in the mission field in Africa, Callie preferred to serve God in the United States.

Callie led Mrs. Murphy to the back staircase, but her thoughts remained on Africa. To travel so far and leave familiar surroundings held little appeal, yet she wanted to help her parents. She wanted to please them, too. For more than a year, she had prayed for God's leading in her life, but her prayers had been shallow. She didn't truly want God to answer her prayers unless He directed her to remain with the Bridgeports. "I've been giving the matter of my future great thought — and a good deal of prayer. Mr. and Mrs. Bridgeport suggested I open a school of my own in the future. However, my decision doesn't need to be made this winter."

"You're right. And you're probably going to keep saying that same thing to yourself every winter for the next eight years." Mrs. Murphy paused on the steep stairway and panted. "So I'm to use these back stairs all the time?"

"No, of course not. The servants in this household use both the front and back stairs — whichever is more convenient."

After inhaling a deep breath, Mrs. Murphy continued climbing. "Well, you know how it is. Some of these rich folks want their servants to be invisible. Never could understand how a person could serve you and remain invisible. Maybe that's why a few of the families I worked for didn't get on with me very well."

The remark caused Callie to glance over her shoulder at the older woman. She hoped Mrs. Murphy would do her best to get along with all members of the family. The Bridgeports weren't difficult employers, but they did expect the servants to meet their expectations. "Was there some sort of problem at your last employment?"

"No. I wanted to get to a warmer climate for the winter, and no matter how cold the weather, the family stayed in Pittsburgh."

"Has it been some time since you worked for the Winslows?"

"A number of years. I'd been in Pittsburgh quite a while, but I knew a reference from Mrs. Winslow would be more important than from the family in Pittsburgh. They didn't know Mr. and Mrs. Bridgeport." She nudged Callie's arm. "Truth is, they weren't what you would call wealthy. They hired me because the missus was a bit feeble in the head and needed someone to stay with her while the mister was at work. Poor woman needed all the help she could get — couldn't remember her name half the time."

"Well, I'm sure she appreciated your kindness." They walked the hallway of the second floor, and Callie gestured toward the doorways as they passed, advising which bedroom belonged to which family member.

"Sure is a lot of empty bedrooms," Mrs. Murphy commented.

"Mrs. Bridgeport usually keeps these bedrooms available for visiting guests. She prefers the children's nanny be close to their rooms, although I know your room is somewhat small. Would you like me to inquire about having you moved?"

Mrs. Murphy gasped. "When I went in there earlier, I noticed it's kind of warm. A bigger room would be nice."

Callie wasn't sure how to answer the woman. During her first winter at Bridal Veil, Mrs. Bridgeport had insisted Callie have a double room on the second floor. She wouldn't hear of Lydia Deboyer's granddaughter being thought of as less than family. *"It's unseemly and I will not hear another word about it,"* Mrs. Bridgeport had insisted. That statement had ended all further discussion of a small servant's room for Callie.

"I can speak to Mrs. Bridgeport on your behalf."

"No need — I'll ask the missus. I don't have a problem speaking up for myself." When the two of them had stopped outside the door to Callie's bedroom, Maude peered inside. A cream satin and chiffon gown embroidered with coral beads and spangles lay draped across Callie's bed. Mrs. Murphy's mouth gaped open. "That the dress the missus was talking about? The one you'll be wearing to that ball?"

Callie nodded.

Mrs. Murphy pursed her lips and arched her brows. "That looks like something the missus should be wearing instead of a tutor. How'd you manage to buy something like that on your wages?"

"Mrs. Bridgeport purchased the gown."

Maude rested a hand on her hip. "I wouldn't mind having the missus buy me a dress like that. I'm thinking I better keep my eye on you, Miss Callie. Looks like you've learned how to make things work to your advantage."

The comment troubled Callie. She'd never attempted to take advantage of the Bridgeports. Instead, she'd done her best to discourage their gifts, but she'd met with little success. Did Maude consider her some sort of scheming employee? "Mrs. Bridgeport is quite generous with her employees. You'll recall she has already offered to purchase you some new clothing, Maude."

"Well, I'm sure anything she buys for me won't compare to that gown on your bed."

Callie cocked her head toward the bewildering woman. One minute Mrs. Murphy seemed confused about her role as a nanny and about suitable etiquette within a proper household, but the next minute she clearly understood the cost of beautiful gowns and the finer things of life. One thing was certain: If she couldn't help Mrs. Murphy fit into the household, Callie's season on the island would be filled with caring for children both day and night. And as much as she loved all three of them, she couldn't see to all of their needs and still act as Mrs. Bridgeport's companion.

Not to mention the fact that Callie's conversation with the peculiar nanny had been a strong reminder that she had a lot of thinking — and praying — to do about her future.

CHAPTER 4

That evening Callie remained alongside Mrs. Murphy while she helped the children through their bedtime rituals. Thomas, of course, insisted he needed no help from anyone and bid them good-night when he strode down the hall to his bedroom.

"Thomas is quite the grown-up young man, isn't he?" Mrs. Murphy glanced toward Callie as she helped Lottie slide her nightgown over her head.

"He feels he's well beyond the need of a nanny, and I suppose that's true enough, though he is still in need of his school lessons. He doesn't take education as seriously as his parents would hope."

Mrs. Murphy picked up Lottie's hairbrush and set to work on the girl's hair. "You said you lived with your grandmother in Indianapolis, so how'd you learn to speak French?"

"I attended a finishing school in Indianapolis and then attended college in Chicago. Grandmother insisted I take French lessons — as well as singing lessons. And I'm glad she did." She nodded toward Lottie and Daisy. "I've begun teaching both of the girls French, along with their other lessons."

"So did your grandmother pass on when you were away at your schooling?"

"No, I had completed my education and begun teaching at a small private school in Chicago. However, I returned to Indianapolis to be at her side. I was gone long enough that the school had to fill my position, so when my grandmother died, the Bridgeports offered me a position as tutor to their children. I've been with them ever since."

"And ya got no regrets?"

"None at all. As I said earlier, they have been extremely good to me. They treat me more like a relative than an employee."

"That's what Lula said while you were gone to dinner at the clubhouse with the family earlier tonight."

Mrs. Murphy smiled, but Callie thought she'd detected a hint of resentment in the older woman's tone. "Dinner is easier for the adults when I'm along. I can easily see to the children's needs while the adults visit."

Daisy leaned her head on Callie's shoulder. "Miss Callie takes me to the bafroom when I need to go. Mama doesn't like to take me."

"It's not that she doesn't like to," Callie corrected. "When your mother is in the middle of a conversation, it isn't always convenient for her to break away."

Daisy lifted her head from Callie's shoulder and pinned her with a wide-eyed stared. "Oh. I thought she didn't like the bafroom at the clubhouse."

"Don't be silly, Daisy." Lottie shot a disapproving look at her sister. "Why wouldn't Mother like the bathroom?"

Callie wagged her index finger back and forth. "Now, girls, there's no need to argue over something so trivial."

Daisy scooted around to look at Callie. "What's a 'trivial'?"

"Trivial isn't a thing, Daisy. It means unimportant. Sisters shouldn't argue at all, but certainly they shouldn't be upset with each other over something that doesn't matter."

"But bafrooms matter, don't they?"

Callie chuckled. At this rate, the topic of bathrooms would continue until Mr. and Mrs. Bridgeport returned home for the night. "They are important, but we're going to end this discussion, and the two of you are going to say your prayers. Then Mrs. Murphy and I will tuck you into bed for the night."

The older woman nudged Callie's arm. "Call me Maude. It makes me feel old when you say Mrs. Murphy. Besides, I think using first names is friendlier, don't you?"

Callie nodded. "Then I shall call you Maude from now on."

The two women listened as the girls said their prayers. They ended with the usual recitation of people for God to bless. "Oh, and God bless Mrs. Murphy, too," Daisy added as the two women were departing the room.

"Thank you, Daisy. That was sweet of you to include me in your prayer."

Daisy inched up on her elbow. "Mama says we can all use as many blessings as we can get."

Mrs. Murphy grinned. "And that's very true. Now off to sleep with ya, and I look forward to seeing your cheery little faces in the morning."

"Would you like to join me downstairs for a cup of tea, Maude?"

"Don't mind if I do. And there might be a few of those shortbread cookies that Lula shared with me earlier today. She brought them from home, and I have to say that Mrs. Bridgeport would be wise to use Lula's abilities in the kitchen as well as cleaning the house."

Callie was surprised that Lula had taken such a quick liking to Mrs. Murphy. She usually kept her distance whenever new help came into the house or when guests arrived for a visit. And Lula was always neat as a pin — a fact that made the friendship seem even more unlikely.

"Lula said she's worked at Fair Haven ever since the Bridgeports had the place constructed, but she says she'd never want to work at the clubhouse. Says there's too many snooty guests who expect ya to bow and scrape to 'em."

"Did she? I didn't know that she'd ever associated with any of the guests in the clubhouse." Callie placed the teakettle on to boil and opened the door of a glass-fronted overhead cabinet. She removed two cups and saucers and placed them on the counter.

"She has four or five friends from Biscayne who ride over on the boat with her every day. They all work in the clubhouse — two as housekeepers and two in the kitchen. Lula said they've told her stories that make her happy she's working at Fair

Haven instead of the clubhouse. Seems it's mighty hard to make all those rich folks happy."

"I find most of the guests quite lovely, but since I've never worked there, I couldn't say how difficult it might be." Callie didn't want to be drawn into gossiping about the guests who visited Bridal Veil — not with Maude or anyone else, for that matter.

Maude rustled through several items in the pantry and finally located the remains of Lula's shortbread cookies. "I found 'em." She held a small bag aloft and crossed the room to the fold-down kitchen table. After opening the cloth napkin, she pointed to the cookies. "You wait till you taste one of these. Don't believe I've ever had better cookies in all my years."

Once the tea had brewed, Callie poured the steaming amber liquid into their cups and carried them to the table. Maude stirred both cream and sugar into her tea and immediately bit into one of the cookies before pushing the napkin toward Callie.

"Go on and try one. You'll not be disappointed."

Callie picked up a cookie, took a bite, and nodded her agreement. "You're right. It is an excellent cookie."

Maude took a sip of her tea and leaned

back in her chair. "Tell me what it's like over there in the clubhouse. I doubt I'll ever get invited to go inside."

There it was again — that slight sound of resentment Callie had detected earlier. "If you'd like to see some of the rooms, I'm sure Mrs. Bridgeport wouldn't mind arranging for you to take a tour someday in the future."

"I think I'd get more than a few stares if I went inside that fancy clubhouse." She brushed her palm down the front of her faded skirt but brightened after a moment. "I'd be pleased if you'd just tell me about some of the ladies and how they look in their fancy dresses and jewels — and what the inside of the clubhouse looks like when it's all lit up for a grand party."

Mrs. Murphy certainly was a woman with a myriad of questions, but everything on the island was new to her. On Callie's first visit, she'd been intrigued by the homes and the people who flocked to Bridal Veil during the winter. She'd soon learned that Bridal Veil could present a few unique challenges for the visitors.

When one of the ladies took a dislike to another or felt slighted by another guest, it was difficult to avoid each other on the island. Guests ate their meals in the huge dining room, and although there was an early and a late seating, trying to change the time when one took one's meals could prove difficult — and usually impossible. A fact Callie wouldn't have realized had one of Mrs. Bridgeport's dear friends not experienced the situation.

"The interior is lovely, although some of the rooms are more rustic than one might expect — largely due to the number of guests who enjoy hunting the wild animals on the island."

"The women hunt, too?"

Callie nodded. "There are a few who enjoy hunting with their husbands. A number of the women are riding enthusiasts, but more of them prefer playing croquet or a game of whist or attending the usual teas. Those events are held inside the clubhouse. Occasionally one of the ladies will host an event at her cottage."

Maude chuckled. "Cottage! The very idea of calling a place like this a cottage. If these folks want to see what a real cottage is, they need to visit the outskirts of Biscayne when they cross the river to do their shopping."

Callie didn't mention the fact that few of the women shopped in Biscayne. Most sent their servants to purchase any necessary items. If the women wanted to purchase items for themselves or their families, they took several days and went to Savannah for a shopping excursion.

"From the looks of the outside of the clubhouse, I thought it would be mighty fancy inside, too."

"Some sections are quite elegant. The dining rooms and entertainment areas where they host balls and such have beautiful chandeliers and furnishings. And though I've never visited any of the suites on the upper floors where many guests have their quarters, I'm told they are lovely — especially the ones that have sun porches with a view of the grounds and the river in the distance."

"I'm guessing they pay a pretty penny to stay in that place. Amazing when you think about the difference in those people and folks like me. Seems it would be fairer if all that wealth was spread out more equal-like, don't you think?"

"I haven't spent a great deal of time thinking about such things, Maude. Whether I think it is fair or not won't change anything."

"I know, I know, but when you see those ladies with all them jewels around their necks and dangling from their wrists, don't it make you think that's just not the way it should be?" She took a gulp of her tea. "They do have lots of pretty jewels, don't they?"

"They do, indeed. Would you like more tea?"

Maude held her cup in the air. "Don't mind if I do."

"You mentioned you've been twice married, Maude?"

"That's right. Neither one of 'em was faithful. After that, I decided I was too old to put up with another man that didn't want to keep his word." She sighed with pleasure as she bit into another cookie. "How is it a pretty gal like you is still single? You never been in love?"

Callie's stomach clenched at the mention of love. "Yes, once. In fact, I was engaged to marry."

The older woman wrapped her hands around the teacup. "What happened? I hope he didn't die."

"No, but it felt almost like a death." Callie paused and inhaled. "We had courted for two years, and I thought he was the man the Lord intended for me. He seemed so perfect — the kind of man every girl wants to marry."

Mrs. Murphy clucked her tongue. "Those are the ones you gotta watch out for. Those smooth-tongued fellows can lead a woman astray. I know. Both the men I married could sweet-talk just about anyone. Land alive! Homer, that's my second husband, could have convinced a man to give up his coat in the middle of winter. So this fellow of yours decided he wasn't the marrying kind?"

"No. He married another woman." Even after two years, Callie's stomach lurched at the memory.

"Well, I say a person needs to look at the bright side."

Callie swallowed the lump that had formed in her throat. Recollections of Matthew still evoked a great deal of pain. She had hoped to recover from the anguish long ago, but the memories continued to haunt her. "Exactly what is the bright side to having your intended leave you for another woman?"

"You could have married him and then have him find another woman that pleases him more than you. That's what happened to me, and that's a whole lot worse. Take my word for it, you're better off to be rid of a cheating man afore you say 'I do.' " Maude picked up her cup and carried it to the sink. "I best wash up these dishes and set to work on some of my mending. Why don't you join me upstairs, and we'll continue our chat."

Once finished in the kitchen, the two of them climbed the back stairs. Callie considered refusing Maude's invitation, but decided her letter writing could wait. There was no denying Mrs. Murphy was an interesting woman, though Callie still thought it odd that such an earthy woman had come so highly recommended by one of Mrs. Bridgeport's cultured friends.

With her needle and thread in hand, Maude began mending a tear in one of her skirts. "You mark my words, one of these days you'll find a good man. There are still some good ones out there. And once you quit your tutoring, you'll need a man to provide you with a home."

Callie shook her head. "I have my grandmother's house. She left it to me, so I don't have that worry, Maude. Besides, I've made up my mind that I'll remain single. I don't want to go through this pain ever again."

Maude waved her threaded needle in the air. "Posh! Once your heart heals, you'll find a man who will sweep you off your feet. When that happens, you'll forget about the past and march right down that church aisle."

Callie didn't argue, but Maude was wrong.

There had been any number of eligible men who had attempted to court her since Matthew had broken her heart. None had been able to break down her defenses, and she planned for it to remain that way.

"So you live in your granny's house when the family's in Indianapolis?" Maude knotted and cut her thread before examining the mend she'd completed in her skirt.

"No, I rent out the house and live with the Bridgeports. Mrs. Bridgeport said it would be foolish of me to live there since I'd be traveling with them much of the time."

"Well, nice it is that you have some extra money to buy the niceties we'd all like to have."

Callie detected a hint of jealousy in the older woman's comment. "Most of the money from rent is used to maintain the home and pay taxes and insurance, Maude. I don't count on the rent money to support myself."

From the look on Maude's face, Callie wasn't certain the woman believed a word she'd said about the rent. In truth, Callie had considered selling the house shortly after her grandmother's death, but Mr. Bridgeport had advised against the idea. He believed real estate to be a good investment, so she'd followed his recommendation. Besides, there was a sense of comfort knowing she would have a place to live should the need arise in the future.

"Miss Callie, where are you?" Daisy's tearful cry was followed by the padding of footsteps in the hallway.

"I'm in Miss Maude's room, Daisy." Callie turned toward the doorway as Daisy rushed into her arms.

"I had a bad dream." Daisy burrowed her face in Callie's shoulder and sobbed.

"It was just a dream, child. Nothing to be afraid of," Maude said. She stood and held out her hand. "Come along and I'll tuck ya back into bed."

"Nooo. I want Miss Callie."

"You go ahead with your mending, Maude. I'll take Daisy back to bed." Callie stroked the child's shoulder. "But you'll have to walk. You're getting too heavy for me to carry."

Daisy scooted from Callie's lap, and together they returned to her bedroom. After tucking her into bed, Daisy reached for Callie's hand. "I don't think I can go to sleep. Will you tell me a story, Miss Callie?" The child's small lips curved in a winsome smile. "Please."

How could she possibly refuse? "Only a

short story. And you must promise to close your eyes while I tell it to you. That way, you'll be more likely to fall asleep."

"I promise." She nestled her head against the feather pillow and promptly closed her eyes. "Make it a story about a girl named Daisy."

Callie grinned. "Once upon a time, there was a pretty little girl with blond curls and a lovely smile. Her parents were delighted when she was born, but they hadn't chosen a name for their beautiful baby. The baby's father said to his wife, 'I think we should name her Geraldine after my mother.' But his wife shook her head. 'Oh no, we cannot do that, for my mother would be unhappy.' "

Daisy giggled. "That's good. Geraldine is an awful name."

Callie brushed a strand of hair from the girl's forehead. "The wife said, 'Perhaps we should name her Matilda after my own dear mother.' Well, the husband wasn't happy with that idea, for he knew his mother would be disappointed. 'Perhaps we shouldn't name her after anyone. Instead, we should select our own special name for the child.' "

Daisy's eyes popped open. "And they named her Daisy!"

"Shh, let me finish the story." Callie

pressed a finger to her lips. "The mother quickly agreed that this was an excellent idea. Even though each of them suggested a variety of names, they couldn't reach an agreement. 'Whatever are we to do?' the father asked. 'The child must have a name.' Then the father said he would take a walk and give the child's name further thought."

"Did he go for a walk?" Daisy's eyes remained closed, but a smile tipped the corners of her mouth.

"Yes, indeed. While the father was out strolling in the gardens, he stooped down, picked a beautiful bouquet of flowers for his wife, and returned upstairs. When he entered the bedroom, his wife opened her eyes and saw her husband holding a lovely bunch of daisies in his hand. He said, 'I brought these for you to brighten your room.' The wife was delighted with the flowers, and she said to her husband, 'We should name our baby daughter Daisy. She will brighten our lives just as the bouquet of flowers has cheered my room.' The father beamed his approval, and they agreed that the beautiful little blond-haired girl would be named Daisy."

"And then what happened?" Daisy peeked at Callie.

"Close your eyes and try to go to sleep."

Callie lowered her voice to a mere whisper. "Each night the mother and father would sit together by the baby's cradle, and they would tell her that she was a special flower in God's garden of grace. That they had waited for her a very long time, and they prayed for her each day. You see, they wanted her to grow up to be a very good and special person, and . . ." Callie remained very still and listened to Daisy's soft snores.

Her heart ached as she looked down at the child, a reminder of all she had hoped for. How she longed for children of her own to love and nurture. But marriage and children would require her to risk her heart once again. The thought of such pain caused a lump to rise in her throat. It would be safer to join her parents, where she would be sheltered from further heartbreak. But was running off to serve God in order to avoid further emotional scars a true commitment to Him or simply an easy escape? Though she'd prayed for God's guidance, His answer had not yet arrived.

She bent forward and placed a kiss on Daisy's forehead before departing the room. Her decision would require more prayer. Would she really be willing to give up moments like this with a child of her own if God called her to the mission field?

Thankfully, she didn't have to decide to-night.

CHAPTER 5

Before she'd gone downstairs for breakfast, Callie considered checking on Maude and the children but finally decided she shouldn't interfere during their early period of adjustment. The children and Maude needed to become accustomed to one another, and if Callie intruded during these first few days, the children would likely continue to seek her out rather than Maude.

After finishing a light breakfast, Callie returned upstairs to the spare room designated as their classroom and prepared worksheets for the girls and Thomas. She wasn't certain if Thomas had gone hunting with his father again. If so, she'd need to speak to Mr. Bridgeport, as the young man was going to fall behind on his lessons if he was absent from the classroom each morning. She'd attempted to discuss the matter with Mr. Bridgeport during dinner last evening, but they'd been interrupted. And she couldn't change his school lessons to the afternoon, since those hours were filled with a variety of riding, golf, and tennis lessons that could not be adjusted. Otherwise Callie would have insisted Thomas complete his lessons after lunch.

A short time later, Maude and all three children entered the classroom. "I'm pleased to see you, Thomas."

"I'd rather be out hunting with Father, but he said I couldn't miss my lessons again today." Thomas settled at the large wooden desk and frowned.

"Your father is a wise man. He knows you need a solid education before you head off to boarding school. How would you feel if you were behind all your classmates?" Callie didn't hesitate long enough for him to answer. "I know you would be terribly embarrassed if you couldn't answer the instructor's questions, and the other fellows might poke fun at you. We don't want that to happen." In an exaggerated gesture, she clasped a hand to the Gibson collar of her white embroidered waist. "And should your parents receive a bad report, they might decide it was due to my inability to train you properly for higher education. They might decide I shouldn't continue as your sisters' teacher."

"Oh no!" Daisy wailed. "You must study hard, Thomas. I don't want Miss Callie to leave us."

"Stop your blubbering, Daisy. Mother would never terminate Miss Callie. She thinks of her as a third daughter." When Daisy didn't relent, Thomas pointed his pen in her direction. "Get busy with your crayons, and I'll see to my work. You don't need to worry about my ability to get good grades in boarding school."

Lottie turned toward her brother. "I know you'll do well, Thomas. You've never failed at anything."

"Thank you, Lottie." Thomas shot a smile in his sister's direction. "You see, Daisy, there's nothing for you to worry about."

Daisy sniffled and picked up her crayons. She didn't appear completely convinced, and Callie silently reprimanded herself for saying something that would upset the child. If Thomas needed further correction, she'd be sure to do it when the two of them were alone.

Maude remained in the room while the children set to work, and Callie stepped to her side. "How are you doing, Maude? Did everything go well this morning?"

"That it did. The girls are quite easy to manage, and young Thomas cares for himself very well. The cook prepared us a fine breakfast of bacon, eggs, and toast. All three of the children ate well." She patted her stomach. "And so did I." She leaned a little closer. "I'm a bit surprised the Bridgeports have a full-time cook, what with them eating most of their meals over at the clubhouse. Jane Nichols must have a great deal of spare time on her hands."

"She helps Lula with the housework when she isn't preparing meals. Then if Jane needs help in the kitchen, Lula steps in to aid her. I'm sure you'll discover we all help each other as needed."

"Did you give any more thought to what I said yesterday?" Maude arched her eyebrows.

They had talked about many things yesterday. Callie frowned as she attempted to recall their conversation. "You mean about Mrs. Bridgeport taking you to Biscayne to purchase dresses?" Callie didn't wait for a response. "I believe she has that on her schedule for this afternoon. You might ask her when she returns from the clubhouse."

"No, not the shopping. Why would I ask you to think about that? This island would be the perfect place for you to find a fellow. This morning Jane told me that there are lots of good-looking single men who come here every year." Maude gently poked Callie's arm. "You need to make an effort to let your heart heal and move on to another fellow. Even if you don't feel quite ready, there's nothing wrong with keeping company with a few of them — see what they have to offer, so to speak."

During the past year, Callie had given thought, and a great deal of prayer, to her future. "I'm really not that interested in a romance. I'm considering joining my parents and teaching at their mission school. Perhaps not right away. I've been praying for God to direct my path. I know Mr. and Mrs. Bridgeport want me to remain as a tutor for the girls, and I've considered going back to teach at the private school in Chicago, should an opening arise, but I'm simply not certain. Using my teaching skills at the mission school would likely prove the most rewarding."

Maude lurched back and stared at Callie as if she'd grown a second head. "Have you lost your good senses, girl?" She grasped Callie's arm. "Now you listen to me — going off to some mission and hiding out is not a place for a young, beautiful woman like you. No, it is not. Those places aren't for women at all, unless, of course, they're unsightly and have little to offer otherwise."

She wagged her head to emphasize her displeasure. "You'll never find a husband worth his salt in a place that needs a mission. Take my word for it, there's nothing but beggars and thieves in those kinds of places. Is their mission in the rundown section of some big city like New York?"

"No — it's in Africa."

"Africa!" Maude shrieked.

Both girls turned in their chairs, and Thomas looked up and stared at them. Callie motioned to the children. "Pay Maude no mind, children. Go on with your lessons." She nudged the older woman. "Please keep your voice down."

"Well, you can't blame me for being surprised. Why in the world would you even think about going off to Africa? That's the craziest thing I ever did hear."

"God calls people to different places throughout the world, Maude. We can't all stay in our comfortable homes. If we all adopted that idea, others would never learn of Jesus."

"If you're wanting to teach school and tell folks about Jesus, you don't have to go off to Africa. You'd be better off in Chicago. There's sure to be plenty of people in Chicago who need to know about Jesus. Have you thought about how lonely it would be? Sure, you'd have your mother and father, but I doubt you'd have many people your age that you could talk to — and once you get over there, I doubt you could come back right away. If I was you, I'd do a lot more praying before setting sail to someplace like Africa. I've got nothing against God or prayer, but I think you need to use some good sense, too."

Callie didn't tell Maude she'd already considered the isolation she would experience in another country. If she hadn't feared the loneliness, she wouldn't have waited to hear from the Lord. She'd have taken matters into her own hands, packed a trunk, and boarded a ship for Africa. At least that's what she'd been telling herself ever since the letter arrived from her parents asking her to consider joining them. And the arrival of a letter from Miss Landry, the supervisor of the school where she'd taught in Chicago, had further complicated the situation. Miss Landry had written shortly before Christmas, saying there would be a teaching position open in September, and she'd offered the job to Callie. However, Miss Landry wanted a decision by the end of May.

Lottie waved her paper overhead. "Will you check my answers, Miss Callie?"

Maude started for the door. "I best get busy and straighten the children's bedrooms."

Callie nodded. "And don't forget to ask Lula if Mrs. Bridgeport plans on your going over to Biscayne this afternoon."

"That I will. You children have a fine day." Maude waved toward the girls before she turned on her heel and strode from the room.

Callie sat down beside Lottie and quickly checked her answers. "That looks perfect. And your coloring is quite lovely, Daisy. I think that picture should be hung on the wall."

Daisy clapped her hands. "Maybe Thomas can make a frame for my picture. Could you, Thomas?"

He shrugged. "If Miss Callie says we can go look for some wood."

"I've planned for us to take the bicycles and ride around the island to look for indigenous plants."

Daisy waved her crayon in the air. "What's an indignant plant?"

Callie chuckled. "The word is *indigenous,* and it means plants that are native to Bridal Veil Island. Plants and trees that we don't find in Indianapolis."

"Like the live oaks? We don't have those

at home."

"Exactly. That's excellent, Lottie. Do you remember why those trees are called live oaks?"

She bobbed her head. "Because they stay green all year long."

"Right! You did a good job remembering what you learned last year."

Daisy pushed her lower lip into a pout. "I 'membered, too, but Lottie said it before I got a chance."

"Well, I'm proud of you, too, Daisy." Callie tousled the younger girl's blond curls as she glanced toward Thomas. "Why don't you girls go downstairs and see if Maude will help you bring the bicycles from the rear garden out to the front of the house? I think Thomas will be through with his algebra by the time you've brought all four bicycles around."

The girls jumped up from their chairs, clearly eager to spend time outdoors on such a beautiful morning. "I'll tell Miss Maude." Daisy elbowed her sister on the way out the door.

"No, I will," Lottie countered, pushing ahead of Daisy.

"No arguing, or we won't be able to go," Callie called after them. All sounds of their bickering ceased, but Callie guessed they'd simply lowered their arguing to whispers.

A short time later, Thomas looked up from his worksheets. "I'm finished. Do you want to check them before we go?"

Callie grinned. "You know I do." She took the paper from him and scanned his answers. "Wonderful, Thomas! I do believe you've gained a good understanding of algebra. And there's nothing like the lure of the outdoors to get you moving along on your schoolwork, is there?"

He nodded and headed toward the door, his long-legged stride outdistancing Callie. "I'd rather be outside than anywhere else. Of course, I'd rather not have the girls along, but if that's the only way I can get out of this classroom, then I won't object."

Callie retrieved her straw hat, and soon the four of them were bicycling along a path that would lead them away from the cottages to a more secluded portion of the island. During their previous winters on Bridal Veil, Callie had explored portions of the island, but with more than four thousand acres on the fifteen-mile-long island, there were places she'd not yet seen. And the children were always interested in discovering new and different areas during their outdoor adventures with Callie. Sometimes they explored the river side of the island and at other times the area that bordered the Atlantic Ocean.

Today, however, Callie thought they would attempt to locate some plants and trees that might be different from any they'd previously discovered. Thomas had taken the lead, with the two girls and Callie following close behind. "Stay on this path, Thomas. I don't want to go toward the ocean."

He glanced over his shoulder. "What about the river path? I don't think there's anything exciting to see out this way."

"If we don't find anything, we'll choose another path, but first I want to try a new area." She knew her refusal wouldn't make Thomas happy, but this outing was part of their school lessons for the day — and she hoped they would make some new discoveries. She'd even brought along paper and pencils for the children to make drawings of their finds. Soon the remaining cottages were behind them and they'd gone a distance further when Thomas suddenly swung his handlebars to the left and brought his bike to an abrupt halt on the side of the path. Lottie followed and Callie swung to the right. Clearly uncertain what to do, Daisy remained on course and rode headlong toward a man who was leaning down, partially blocking the path.

Now on his feet with the bicycle careening straight to him, he reached out and grabbed the front of the handlebars with one hand and scooped Daisy off the seat and into his left arm. Both the man and Daisy stared wide-eyed as the bike toppled to the ground.

Already off of her bicycle, Callie rushed toward Daisy. The man had settled her on the ground and was stooping in front of her. "That was scary, wasn't it?"

"Daisy! Are you injured?"

"Noo." She shook her head and looked up at Callie. "I don't think so." She pointed at the man. "I almost hit him."

Callie grasped a hand to her midsection. "I saw that. I'm very thankful neither of you was hurt." Her gaze settled on the man still stooped down in front of Daisy. "You aren't hurt, are you?"

With a quick smile, he removed his cap. "No. If anything was injured, it would be the bicycle." He motioned to Daisy. "Let's have a look and see if anything is broken." The man leaned over and righted the bike as Thomas joined them and began to examine the tires.

Daisy drew closer to the man. "I'm Daisy. Who are you?"

He raked his fingers through a shock of

sandy blond hair. "My name is Wesley, but you can call me Wes."

"*Mr.* Wes," Callie instructed.

"I'm sorry I almost runned into you, Mr. Wes, but you were in the path, and I couldn't stop." Daisy peered at him as if she expected some explanation.

"The accident was my fault. I shouldn't have been blocking the path, but I wanted a better look at this live oak."

Daisy edged near. "I know 'bout live oaks. We learned from Miss Callie. She's teaching us about indignant stuff."

"Indigenous," Thomas corrected. He rested Daisy's bicycle against a pine tree. "What's so different about this live oak?"

"I don't know that there's anything particularly different, but I stopped to examine the grooves where the dust and leaf mold are accumulating." Wes pointed to a deep groove in the bark of the tree.

"Yeah? So what's so good about that?" Thomas leaned forward to take a closer look.

Wes laughed. "That turns into a type of mulch that provides a good spot for seeds or plants that are blown near the groove to make a new home. That's why you see resurrection fern lining the lower branches of most of these live oaks." He motioned

81

Thomas closer. "And see here? That's a palmetto trying to set up housekeeping."

Lottie shook her head. "Trees don't live in houses." She walked around Thomas and peeked at the groove in the tree. "Did you know live oaks stay green all year?"

"I did know that." Wes glanced at Lottie. "Would you like to know more about these giant trees?"

"I would." Daisy jumped up and down while clapping her hands.

"What about you, Thomas? Are you interested in botany and studying plants?"

"Some of them, but I'd rather look closer to the water. I think there's lots of interesting plants in the marshes around here."

"That's true, but there's a lot to learn about these huge old live oaks, as well as the pines and palmettos on the island. What do you find interesting about these live oaks?"

Thomas studied the tree for a while. "I like seeing the moss that hangs from the branches, but I wonder if it hurts the trees — like a parasite." He smiled at Callie. "Miss Callie taught me about parasites last year in my classes."

"That's an excellent observation. You're obviously thinking, Thomas, but the Spanish moss on these trees isn't a parasite. It doesn't kill by extracting food from the tree. The moss gathers moisture and minerals from the air and dust, and then it manufactures food with the aid of chlorophyll and sunlight."

With that comment, Wesley had gained the children's complete attention, and he gestured for them to sit on one of the thick branches of the live oak that hung low to the ground. All three of them lined up on the sturdy limb while he explained that the moss only borrowed the tree as a place on which to grow. "It just needs a place to hang out."

Thomas chuckled and nodded. "Kind of like we're hanging out on this limb."

Wes grinned. "Exactly, but you won't stay on that limb, and the moss will remain on the tree."

"But what if the tree gets sick and dies?"

"I don't think you need to worry about this tree dying for a long time, Daisy. There's an old saying that a live oak tree takes a hundred years to grow, lives for a hundred years, and then takes another hundred years to die. And did you know there are lots of plants that are used to make medicine and help us become well?"

Daisy touched a finger to the tree. "Does the tree make its own medicine? Is that why it lives so long?"

Wes chuckled. "No, but I'm sure your teacher will agree it's important to know about plants, because while some of them help heal, some are poisonous. You need to learn which ones to avoid and which ones are helpful."

When he looked in her direction, Callie nodded. "That's very true."

"Do you know about the good ones to make medicine?" Daisy drew closer to Wes.

"I've studied a lot about plants, and I do know some that help. Butterbur helps with headaches and coughs." He touched the tip of Daisy's nose. "And there's a plant called aloe vera that can help heal burns."

Callie listened as the man she assumed to be a groundskeeper continued talking to the children. His knowledge of plants surprised her, but it was his quick smile and vibrant blue eyes that drew the children in. As he reached toward the tree, his shirt stretched taut and revealed broad, muscular shoulders. He glanced over his shoulder, and she looked away — but not quickly enough. He'd seen her staring at him, and her cheeks burned hot with embarrassment. He would think she had no manners.

Though it proved difficult, she forced her thoughts away from the handsome man and back to the welcoming ball coming up. If she could think of a good excuse, perhaps Mrs. Bridgeport wouldn't insist upon her attendance. On the other hand, she knew Mrs. Bridgeport was intent upon Callie meeting a proper young man, marrying, and having children of her own. And Mrs. Bridgeport was very aware that the best place for Callie to meet one of those proper young men was at the various balls and parties hosted in the clubhouse.

Callie tried to envision herself in the arms of various unknown strangers, being led onto the dance floor in her cream-colored satin and chiffon gown, but the moment the picture became clear, fear grabbed her in a choke hold. Perhaps if she could skip this first ball of the season, she would feel more comfortable about attending the next one.

But that wouldn't happen. Mrs. Bridgeport would never relent. Callie sighed. She'd simply have to don the dress and make an exit at the earliest opportunity.

She only hoped she could do so before any man asked her to dance.

CHAPTER 6

Wes looked in the mirror and straightened his tie. If he could have his way, he'd forgo these formal dining room dinners with the family, but living in the clubhouse didn't permit him that opportunity. The clubhouse kitchen provided room service, but he dared not attempt to miss the family gathering each evening. It would be a little easier once his brother Daniel returned to Massachusetts. He would be delighted to see Richard leave, as well. It seemed that Daniel and Richard took great sport in finding fault and making him the brunt of their jokes.

The only pleasant time he'd encountered since arriving had been his time alone exploring the island — and meeting that young woman and her students that afternoon. *Callie.* Lovely name. Lovely girl. Probably has a line of suitors a mile long. He strode out of the room and down the hallway.

How he disliked this shallow style of living. He wanted his life to count for something more than owning textile mills and trying to outdo his competitors. The businessmen who frequented these private resorts came to impress their rivals or to make deals with them. And their wives arrived with the idea of wearing more expensive clothing and jewels than their peers. It was all a game of outclassing one another. And whether his father liked it or not, Wes didn't intend to play the game. He might not be prepared for a return to treating patients, but perhaps his love of botany and experience in the laboratory in New York would lead him back to research again — just so long as it didn't take him back into the field where he would be required to actually work with patients. The thought caused his hands to tremble, and he rushed from the room before he could dwell on the idea.

The family was already gathered in the foyer outside the dining room when he walked down the staircase. His mother was fanning herself, as if overcome by an oppressive heat wave.

The moment she caught sight of him, she hurried to his side. "We've been waiting for ten minutes, Wesley. They have a dinner schedule in the dining room. The headwaiter isn't particularly happy that we weren't all here at the appointed time. Your father isn't pleased, either."

He steered his mother back toward the rest of the family. "I'm sorry, Mother, but you should have had the waiter seat you. I could have located the table."

"That's the problem. They won't seat people until their entire party has arrived." She held her fan in front of her lips. "It has to do with creating difficulty for the waiter assigned to a particular table or some such thing." She lowered the fan long enough to flash a smile and signal the headwaiter. "Do express your regrets for keeping the others waiting, Wesley."

"I may have been living away from home for a number of years, Mother, but I still possess a few good manners."

His father stood by the door leading to the dining room with his arms folded across his chest and a frown on his face. "Good of you to finally join us, Wesley."

"My apologies, Father." He glanced around the group. "And to all of you. Time got away from me, and I didn't return as early as I had planned." Wes nodded to the headwaiter. "I'm sorry for any inconvenience to you and your staff."

"We are here to make your stay as pleasant as possible. No explanation is necessary, sir." The waiter straightened his shoulders. "If you will all follow me, please, I'll see you to your table."

Walking single file, they made their way between tables draped with crisp white tablecloths and set with gold-rimmed china and sterling silverware. Candlelight glistened in the crystal goblets like starlight in a midnight sky.

Wes cringed inwardly when he realized he'd be seated between his brother-in-law, Richard, and his father. "I'd be happy to change seats, if you'd like one of your daughters over here by you, Richard."

"No need. They'll be eating their dinner upstairs with their nanny. They raised such a fuss that Helena agreed they could come down for a short time, although I didn't think she should reward their bad behavior."

Helena squared her shoulders. "They'll be here only long enough to eat a fruit cup, Richard. They need to learn to behave properly when we're dining out. This is a good experience for them." She unfolded her napkin and placed it across her lap. "If you care to discuss this further, I'd be happy to do so in our rooms — after dinner."

Wes sighed with relief when their waiter

appeared and broke the uncomfortable silence by detailing the dinner offerings for the evening. After they had completed their order, Richard nudged Wes. "Exactly what were you doing that caused you to be late this evening? An extra game of golf? Or were you availing yourself of the tennis courts provided for the guests?"

"I haven't seen the golf course or the tennis courts, Richard. I haven't seen stables or the racetrack, either. Have you?" Wes immediately regretted his retort. He didn't want to get into a petty argument with Richard. There was already too much tension around the table.

"I did check the racetrack, and I must say it is quite impressive. I didn't believe it could compare with Churchill Downs, but it does." He leaned in and kept his voice low. "Unfortunately, the races won't begin for another week."

"I'm sure Helena and the girls will enjoy having you with them to picnic and explore the beach." When Wesley reached for the water pitcher, a waiter rushed forward and filled the empty goblet.

As the evening progressed, talk among the men became focused upon the textile mills and the increasing price of wool, labor, and machinery. Meanwhile his mother and the other women discussed the latest ladies' fashions. Wesley soon discovered he had nothing to offer to either conversation, so he let his thoughts wander toward the charming young lady he'd met earlier in the day.

"So what do you think, Wesley?" His father, Richard, and Daniel were all staring at him when he looked up from his plate.

"About what?" He forked a piece of baked redfish that had likely been the catch of the day.

"You haven't heard a word we've said, have you?" His father's voice was laced with condemnation.

"No, I must admit that my thoughts were elsewhere, but I'm listening now." He swallowed the bite of fish and wiped his mouth.

"We were discussing the expansion and your coming on board as manager." His father glanced at Daniel. "Daniel has agreed to spend some time showing you the ropes so you'll be prepared by the time we open the mill. I'm sure he'll assist you with hiring procedures and the like, won't you, Daniel?" Their father beamed at Daniel.

"Whatever you decide will be most helpful, Father. We all want the family business to flourish, don't we, Wes?"

Daniel lifted his glass to the gathered family members, but Wes ignored the gesture. His stomach had tightened until he felt as if a vise had been clamped around the center of his body. The delightful fish swimming in buttery garlic sauce no longer held any appeal. Instead, the sight of his remaining dinner caused his stomach to lurch. Why did his father think it necessary to discuss this matter now? Surely his father already assumed Wes wouldn't join the family business, but once again his father had donned imaginary blinders.

The same thing had happened when Wes went off to school. His father had expected him to take courses in business. To the family patriarch, the idea of becoming a physician was nonsensical. After all, physicians didn't command much respect, and they certainly didn't make much money. For someone of the lower class, becoming a physician might be a step up, but not for someone among the upper class. With a jovial pat on the back, his father had remarked that one day he'd end up in the family business. Apparently his father had decided that time was now.

Leaning back in his chair, his father patted his midsection and looked at Wes. "I assume I can take your silence as agreement."

Leaning toward his father, Wes kept his

voice low. "No, Father, you may not. I have no intention of ever joining the family business. And it might be best if we discussed this privately."

"We are talking about the family business. Why would we discuss it privately? Your decision affects all of us." His father spoke loudly enough to capture the attention of the women at their table.

His mother patted his father's arm. "Do keep your voice down, Howard. The people at the other tables aren't interested in your conversation." She glanced over her shoulder, clearly wondering if anyone was looking toward their table. "Remember we are guests of the Wades. They were most kind to offer the use of their apartments for the season, and we don't want to do anything that would create embarrassment for Josiah or Margaret." She pinned him with a warning look. "Even though the Wades won't be here during the season, you can be sure the regular guests will be delighted to notify them of any impropriety on our part."

"For the love of heaven, Blanche, quit worrying about Josiah and Margaret Wade. It's your son who should be causing you concern. Did you hear him say he has no intention of ever joining the family business?" Before she could answer, his father turned to face Wesley. "You best give this more thought, son. Even though I didn't approve of you becoming a physician, I paid for your education. And even though I thought it was foolhardy, I didn't argue when you went off to New York. And I held my tongue when you decided to go to Texas. Beyond that, and at your mother's behest, I agreed I would give you the rest of the winter before insisting that you settle down."

Wes leaned back and nearly toppled his chair. "Settle down? You make it sound as though I've been doing nothing but having fun since I finished medical school."

"As far as I'm concerned, you haven't been doing anything that's going to secure your future, and now it's time to get to work. If you don't join us at the textile mills when we return to Lowell, don't plan on the family supporting you."

Wes could feel the heat climbing up his neck. He needed to keep his temper in check. His jaw twitched when he caught a glimpse of Richard's smirk, and he purposefully pushed back from the table. "Excuse me. I believe I'm through for the night." Weaving among the tables, he strode from the room, his anger mounting with each step.

"Wesley! Do stop — I can't run after you

in these shoes."

He exhaled a frustrated sigh. Why had his mother followed him? Surely she knew that it would only make matters worse. Didn't his father always accuse her of taking Wes's side? Her actions would add fuel to the already raging fire. He continued outside to the porch and waited for her.

"Do come back inside, Wes. He doesn't mean it. You know your father sometimes speaks without thinking."

"That may be true, Mother, but I believe he has given this a great deal of thought and he means exactly what he says. However, he need not worry about supporting me. I may not find a job that he will think praiseworthy, but I won't look to him for support."

"Promise you won't do anything rash, Wes. Just give me time to speak to him."

Wes shook his head. "Please don't, Mother. I don't want either of you to concern yourselves about my future." He smiled at her. "I have an education and good health, and I know that with God's help, I'll find the answers for my future."

Callie waited alongside Mr. and Mrs. Bridgeport in the foyer outside the dining room of the clubhouse. "I do wish we could have secured early seating for the season. They always give preference to those living in the clubhouse, and most of them don't have children. I doubt there will be many evenings when Lottie and Daisy can join us. They'll fall asleep before dessert. Of course, Thomas would have no problem, but he dislikes having to dress for dinner every night and will use any excuse to avoid eating in the clubhouse."

"Perhaps I could have the girls take a nap in the afternoon if there are evenings when you want to bring them along," Callie suggested.

The headwaiter, Mr. Hall, approached with a broad smile. "Good evening, Mr. and Mrs. Bridgeport, Miss Deboyer." He bobbed his head. "It is always a pleasure to have you dine with us. Please follow me."

Mr. Hall turned on his heel and came nose-to-nose with a group of departing guests. "Excuse me, Mr. Townsend, I didn't realize you were approaching. Are you acquainted with Mr. and Mrs. Bridgeport?"

"I don't believe I am." Mr. Townsend extended his hand to Mr. Bridgeport, and the men exchanged pleasantries. "I hope you'll have an opportunity to meet my wife, Mrs. Bridgeport. She had to leave dinner early this evening, but I'm sure you'll see her at some of the social events you ladies share at the clubhouse. We have another son, but he departed earlier, as well. It's a pleasure to meet you folks." He clapped Mr. Bridgeport on the shoulder. "If you have any desire to extend your investments, I'm always interested in gaining the right investors for our woolen mill expansion."

"I'll give it some thought." Mr. Bridgeport glanced toward the waiter. "I believe we're holding up dinner seating. Nice to meet you, Mr. Townsend."

"They were quite a lively group, weren't they?" Mrs. Bridgeport commented as she took her seat between her husband and Callie. "Did you notice the necklace the daughter, Helena, was wearing? That must have cost a fortune."

Callie hadn't noticed the necklace. She had been too preoccupied with watching Mr. Hall dance from foot to foot while he waited for the conversation to end. She was certain he had immediately regretted asking if the Bridgeports knew the Townsends.

Mrs. Bridgeport nodded toward the next table. "Do look at the dress Mrs. Wilson is wearing, Callie. That is absolutely beautiful. I wonder if she had it made when they were in Europe this summer. And her brooch is stunning. Perfect with her dress, don't you think?"

Callie nodded. "It's quite lovely."

"I don't know if I mentioned this earlier, Callie, but when I wrote to enroll Thomas in his golf and tennis lessons, I signed you up, as well."

Callie's mouth gaped open. She'd never before taken lessons with the children. She'd made certain they arrived on time and waited until they finished, but she'd not previously been included. "How generous of you, Mrs. Bridgeport. Though I wouldn't say my athletic abilities will match those of Thomas, I may discover some untapped talents."

Mrs. Bridgeport gazed toward another table before shifting her attention back to Callie. "I'm sure you will prove an excellent student."

"But who will care for Lottie and Daisy while I'm taking golf and tennis lessons with Thomas?"

The older woman arched her brows. "Why Maude, of course. She can't expect to sit idle all day. We're paying her to be a nanny for the children. Besides, learning to play golf and tennis should prove a genuine advantage. Several of my friends have mentioned it is considered beneficial for young women to acquire a measure of athletic skill."

Callie knew what Mrs. Bridgeport meant when she said it was considered an advantage. She dearly loved her employer, but the woman was determined to find her a husband. And now it seemed she'd decided that if Callie could play golf or tennis, Prince Charming would swing into her life. No matter how hard she tried, Callie simply could not convince Mrs. Bridgeport that she didn't want or need a man.

As they completed dinner, Mr. and Mrs. Minton, friends of the Bridgeports, stopped at their table and invited them for coffee on the enclosed porch.

Callie touched Mrs. Bridgeport's arm. "I hope you won't mind if I return to the cottage, Mrs. Bridgeport. I have a few lessons to prepare for the children."

Once she'd secured Mrs. Bridgeport's approval, Callie departed, eager to enjoy a breath of fresh air. Maude greeted her when she entered the house a short time later. "Did ya have a fine dinner over there at the clubhouse?"

Callie nodded. "It was very good, thank you. Are the children asleep?"

"They're in bed, although I'm not positive they've gone to sleep." She took another stitch in the stocking she was darning. "They were good for me, though I had to tell Daisy two stories before she finally agreed she was ready for bed."

Callie chuckled. "Daisy does love stories."

"Can't blame her. I love a good story myself. I'm guessing you could tell a few stories about all those fancy women you see at dinner and such. What were they serving for dinner?"

Callie sat down opposite the older woman. "They had a choice of redfish or quail this evening. Many times the kitchen prepares the game or fish that the hunters and fishermen bring in each day. I had the fish, and it was excellent. No one could ever complain about the food that is served in the clubhouse, but the formality wears thin with me. It seems the only thing that is important is being able to impress one another with their extravagance. And it's not just the women. The men take great pleasure in boasting about their investments and latest business ventures."

"And their wives are right there ready to spend all that money on their gowns and jewels. Am I right?"

Callie nodded. "I think so. I'm not sure what glitters more, the huge chandeliers or the jewels the women wear to their parties."

Maude finished darning and broke off the piece of thread. "Mr. and Mrs. Bridgeport decided to stay and visit longer, did they?"

"Yes. They're having coffee with Mr. and Mrs. Minton, a couple they've known for years. I suppose I should go upstairs. I need to complete some lessons for tomorrow." She hesitated a moment. "I best warn you that Mrs. Bridgeport has decided I should take golf and tennis lessons with Thomas, so you'll be required to look after the girls while I'm with him."

"What?" Maude looked up from her sewing with a startled look on her face. "Did you say you're going to take lessons or that you'll take Thomas to his lessons?" She fidgeted with the piece of thread.

"Thomas and I will both be taking lessons. Mrs. Bridgeport thinks it will be helpful."

Deep furrows creased Maude's forehead. "So you'll be taking tennis lessons?"

"Yes. Both tennis and golf lessons. We begin tomorrow." Callie thought she'd been perfectly clear. She couldn't determine if Maude was truly perplexed or if the older woman was displeased that she'd have to care for the girls while Callie was with Thomas. Then again, perhaps Maude was feeling another pang of jealousy. Not that

Maude would want to take tennis or golf lessons — but that Callie would enjoy the same advantages of a guest rather than being treated as an employee. Callie couldn't be certain what it might be, but it was apparent something hadn't set right with the woman.

CHAPTER 7

Bound for the Bridal Veil golf links, Callie said her good-byes to the two girls on the front porch while Thomas brought their bicycles around the corner of the house. Neither of the girls had been pleased to hear of Callie's plans for the afternoon. They didn't mind in the least if their brother departed, but to have Callie leave them for a few hours was entirely another matter. Had it not been for Maude clutching Daisy's hand, the little girl would still be clinging to Callie's skirts.

Maude inched a step closer to Callie. "So you're off to learn how to play golf, are ya?"

Callie nodded. "I believe we'll begin the tennis lessons later this week. I'll check that schedule before I return home this afternoon." She reached down and stroked Daisy's cheek. "No tears. I left you something special in the playroom, but if you cry, Miss Maude won't be able to give it to you."

Daisy's lip quivered. "I p-p-romise not to cry."

Walking between the two bicycles, Thomas advanced at a slow pace as he tried to keep them upright. Callie hurried toward him. "Let me help you."

He released his hold on her bicycle and immediately straddled his own. "We need to stop by the caddie shack before we go for the lesson. Father said he had my golf clubs taken over there when we arrived."

They waved to the girls and Maude, and once they were at a wide spot in the path leading toward the links, Callie pedaled alongside Thomas. "I do hope they have some clubs that I can use. Otherwise, we may have to trade off."

Thomas smiled. "Maybe the instructor will have some that you can use."

"Maybe. We'll check first thing, but it's your lessons that are most important." There must occasionally be other guests who have decided to take golf lessons but don't own any clubs. Surely a resort such as Bridal Veil would have made arrangements for such an event. Her lack of athletic prowess remained at the forefront of her mind as she swerved around a rut in the trail.

In all likelihood, her inept attempts would provide Thomas with several chuckles. If for no other reason than hearing his laughter, she would enjoy trying the game. At least Mrs. Bridgeport hadn't suggested sailing lessons. With Callie's lack of agility, she might have landed in the middle of the ocean. Still, if Mrs. Bridgeport had declared Callie would take sailing lessons with Thomas this season, she would have done her best. The boy loved sports — and time away from his sisters — and Callie wanted him to enjoy his time at Bridal Veil to the fullest.

Thomas glanced at her, anticipation shining in his eyes as he pumped his legs and raced ahead. He arrived at the caddie shack before she did and was already off his bike and inside before Callie dismounted. Though she normally insisted the children let her take the lead, she couldn't fault Thomas. His excitement had been palpable all during their classes this morning, and she wouldn't restrain him now.

Glancing around as she placed her bicycle next to the wooden structure, she wondered if all of the caddies had already gone out with other golfers. The place looked deserted, yet the door remained open, and Thomas hadn't come back outside. The moment she stepped across the threshold, Thomas turned toward her. The boy looked as though he'd lost his best friend. An older man sat not far away wiping a golf club with a dirty towel.

Callie stepped to Thomas's side. "Whatever is wrong?" She looked from the boy and settled her gaze upon the man. "Are you the golf instructor, sir?"

The man clenched a pipe between his teeth as he pushed up from the chair. "Nope. I was telling the boy that our golf instructor was due to arrive two weeks ago, but I haven't seen hide or hair of him. Every time someone walks through that door, we all hope it will be Bobby McLaren." He shoved the golf club into a canvas and leather bag. "That's the name of the golf instructor — Bobby McLaren."

"If Mr. McLaren isn't available, who is giving lessons? Both Thomas and I were enrolled by Mr. Bridgeport long before we arrived on the island."

"Yup. I see your names down here in the schedule book. Thomas Bridgeport and Miss Callie Deboyer." He withdrew the pipe from his mouth. " 'Course that don't change a thing. If there's no instructor, then there's no lessons."

"What about you?" Callie gestured to the

golf clubs he'd been cleaning.

He chuckled. "I don't golf. These clubs belong to one of the members. I told him I'd clean 'em. The golf links are open. There's men out there golfing right now. There's just no lessons."

Callie sighed — not for herself, but for Thomas and the disappointment she knew he was trying to hide. "Can I assume that someone has attempted to contact this Mr. McLaren you mentioned — or that the officers of the Bridal Veil Island Club are seeking someone to fill the position?"

The man shrugged. "I couldn't tell you what the officers are doing. They've never invited me to attend any of their meetings." His lips curved in a wry grin. "I can tell you that Mr. Nusbaum is the one in charge of the sports and recreation, and he hires the instructors for golf, tennis, riding, and other sporting activities here on the island. The officers of the club don't bother themselves with that — they hire the supervisors and let them take care of hiring the likes of Bobby McLaren."

"Then can you tell me what action Mr. Nusbaum has taken?" Callie's patience had begun to wear thin. This man talked as slowly as he moved.

"We-l-l-l." He drew the word out as

though it had five syllables rather than one. "He's looking for a replacement, but it's hard to find someone once the season has already begun at these resorts. Mr. Nusbaum will be here tomorrow right after lunch if you want to come and talk to him in person." He picked up a pencil. "I'll mark it right here by your name if you want to see him."

"Please do. I'll speak to Mr. Bridgeport. Perhaps he'll come and talk to Mr. Nusbaum. If not, I will be here." She rested her hand on the boy's shoulder. "Come along, Thomas."

They were mounting their bikes when the man appeared in the doorway. "I forgot to tell you that the tennis instructor, Archie Penniman, can take the boy for lessons today instead of next week, if you like. His schedule ain't full, and he's trying to help out until Bobby gets here."

Thomas scooted around on the seat of his bicycle. "I can go back to the house and get my tennis racket and meet you at the court." A glimmer of excitement sparkled in his eyes, and though Callie wasn't excited at the thought of a tennis lesson, she readily agreed.

Thomas took off as though he'd had a fire lit beneath him, but there would be no need for Callie to hurry. Both the golf course and the tennis courts were located north of the Bridgeport home. Depending on how fast he pedaled, it would take Thomas a while to make his way home and back again to the tennis courts.

As she came to a fork in the road, she decided to take a side path that would lead her directly to the tennis courts. Coming around the bend at a good speed, she slammed on her brakes and careened off the path to the right while a figure jumped back to the left. She couldn't believe her eyes. The man she'd nearly struck down was Wes, the same fellow the four of them had nearly hit yesterday.

He appeared as surprised as she felt. "It seems I've become a favorite target for cyclists."

"I do apologize. My thoughts were elsewhere, and I should have braked before rounding the corner." She gestured toward the side of the pathway. "Of course, it would help if they'd trim down some of these high grasses so it would be easier to see around the corners."

He swiped dust from his pants and chuckled. "I don't believe there are enough gardeners on staff to keep the weeds and marsh grasses trimmed all over the island."

He tipped his cap. "Good afternoon, Miss Callie. Where are your young charges on this fine afternoon?"

Callie explained the girls were at home and Thomas had gone to retrieve his tennis racket. "We were prepared for golf lessons, but I'm told the instructor has gone missing. There seems to be some doubt they'll find another one." She pointed to the golf bag on his shoulder. "So, if you're taking those clubs to the caddie shack for a guest scheduled for lessons, there's no need to rush."

Wes patted the bag. "These belong to someone who already knows how to play the game, but I'm sorry to hear about the pro. I'm sure Thomas is disappointed."

"He is, but it may be best for anyone else on the links."

"And why is that?"

"I was scheduled to take lessons with Thomas, but I may have saved some poor soul from being clunked on the head with a golf ball when I made an erratic swing."

Wes chuckled. "If you've never before golfed, it's more likely you'd miss the ball entirely or take out a chunk of the green. I think those other golfers would have been safe having you around."

"Perhaps, but I did offer up a few prayers

for them before we arrived at the caddie shack."

He tipped his head to the side and grinned. "You consider golfing so worrisome that you would ask God to intervene?"

"That probably sounds silly to you, but for years I've asked God to take care of the big as well as the little problems in my life. And if I injured someone, it would be a very big problem." Callie didn't go on to tell him that she would have liked an answer to prayers regarding her future plans as well as her prayer for protection for the golfers.

"I don't think it's silly to ask for God's help. I just never thought of anyone needing to pray before heading onto the links." He pushed his flat-billed cap to the back of his head.

"If you knew my lack of athletic ability, you would think my prayers quite appropriate."

"Point well taken, Miss Callie, but I doubt you're as inept as you say." He pointed to her bike and smiled. "Then again, you are a bit dangerous on that bicycle."

Callie returned his smile and motioned toward the path. "Now that you mention bicycling, I best be on my way. Thomas will arrive at the tennis courts and wonder what has happened to me. Nice to see you again . . ." She hesitated. "I don't believe I know your last name."

"Just call me Wes. I dislike formalities." He settled the strap of the golf bag back on his shoulder and strode off with a wave.

While he continued walking toward the golf course, Wes weighed an idea. No doubt his family would be furious with him, but if the club needed a golf pro, he might qualify. Especially if the club was in dire straits. And from what Callie said, that was exactly the situation. He'd won his share of college and amateur tournaments and had even been approached about becoming an instructor at his alma mater. A fact he certainly had never mentioned to his father.

Wes didn't intend to make a hasty move. First, he'd play the course and give the matter some more thought. He entered the caddie shack, surprised at the lack of activity. "All the caddies out on the course?" he asked the man sitting in a corner smoking his pipe.

"Don't have many working today." He tapped the book on a table close to his chair. "Did you schedule a time to tee off?"

The man looked at the book and then at Wes — they both knew he hadn't. "I've never golfed on this course, but I can go out without a caddie, if need be. I have a stand for my bag and clubs." It wouldn't be his preference, but he could do it.

"If you're not in a rush, there should be a group coming in within the next half hour — unless they got themselves stuck in the sand and marsh grass." He chuckled and shook his head.

"So it's a rough course?"

"Not if you know how to golf, but most of these fellows are too proud to admit they need some lessons. They've played a round or two and think they know it all."

"You play?" Wes noticed the bag of clubs sitting nearby.

"Nah. Golf's not where I take my pleasure. Give me a good horse that can run like the wind, and I'm a happy man. In my younger days, I was mighty good at rowing, but now I leave that to the younger fellas."

"You don't play golf, but you're in charge of the caddie shack?"

He frowned at Wes. "Did I say I was in charge of anything?"

"I just guessed that since you had the registration book, you were in charge."

"I work for Mr. Nusbaum, so I go where I'm told, when I'm told, and I don't ask a lot of questions. Today I was told to come over here and work in the shack; tomorrow

I might be mowing the grass."

"If I wanted to find out information about that golf pro who went missing, I would talk to Mr. Nusbaum?"

"How'd you know 'bout the golf pro?" His eyes suddenly shone with recognition. "You must have talked to that gal who left not long before you got here."

Wes nodded. "Does Mr. Nusbaum frequent the clubhouse?"

"I'm sure he's over there some, but I don't know his schedule except that he's supposed to be over here tomorrow after lunch."

The sound of good-natured voices drifted through the open window of the shack, and both men glanced outside. Wes didn't recognize any of the men in the group, but he hadn't expected to. Bridal Veil was new to him, and so were the people who frequented the resort. He couldn't be sure if that would be an advantage or disadvantage in securing a position.

The older man put two fingers in his mouth and let out a shrill whistle. Two caddies broke from the crowd and ran toward the shack. "Take the one on the right. He knows the course better, but don't tell either of 'em I told you who to choose. The one on the left would never speak to me again, and we don't need no hard feelings."

Wes nodded. "Thanks for the advice."

When the two caddies rushed through the door, Wes signaled to the one on the right. "I could use you out on the course if you're not too tired."

The young man tipped his hat and grinned. "Never too tired to be out on the golf course. My name's Ted." He reached toward Wes's caddie bag.

"And mine's Wes Townsend. Pleased to meet you, Ted. I haven't golfed this course before, so I'm looking for all the help you can give me."

The fellow grinned. "Always glad to give advice, Mr. Townsend."

Wes slapped him on the shoulder. "Then we should get on just fine."

Just as Callie feared, Thomas had already arrived at the tennis court. He had parked his bicycle, and she could see him lobbing the ball across the net — or at least making an attempt. Over the past year, Thomas had taken a few classes at the indoor court at his father's club in Indianapolis, but this was an outdoor grass court and would likely require some adjustment.

Callie strode toward the court and took a position a short distance from the sideline. When Thomas missed the ball and went running to fetch it, the instructor approached her. He was a small-framed man, with dark hair and eyes the color of strong coffee. "Good afternoon. I'm Archie Penniman, the tennis instructor here at Bridal Veil. I don't believe we've met."

"Callie Deboyer. I am tutor to the Bridgeport children. This is the first year any members of the family have been enrolled for tennis lessons. Thomas has probably informed you that he has taken a few lessons in Indianapolis, but he's never before played on a grass court."

"And what about you, Miss Deboyer? I noticed your name on my list of students. Have you had lessons back in Indianapolis?"

He smiled and stepped closer — too close, as far as Callie was concerned. She took a backward step. "No, I must admit that I haven't. The nearest I've come to playing tennis is badminton, and that with the children. I don't have a racket."

"That's not a problem. We keep a number of them available for guests who are taking lessons and might not own a racket."

"Why don't you go on with the lesson for Thomas? It's far more important that he have additional lessons before heading off for boarding school next year. Whether I learn is of little importance."

116

"But you've signed up for instructions." He leaned in. "And I'd enjoy teaching you far more than a young boy preparing for boarding school."

His breath grazed her neck. She frowned and stepped back. "Please keep a proper distance, Mr. Penniman."

"I'm sorry. I didn't mean to offend. It must be your beauty that keeps drawing me toward you." He appeared contrite. "Please accept my apologies."

Mr. Penniman obviously considered himself quite the ladies' man — the type of fellow Callie tried to avoid. She didn't want to misjudge him, but he was much too forward for her liking.

"Your apology is accepted." She glanced toward Thomas, who had stooped down to retrieve the ball. "To be honest, I'm not particularly athletic, so you will find much greater reward teaching Thomas."

"Ah, but the note I received expressly stated that your skill level should reach or exceed young Thomas's. That means I'll need to spend more time with you, for his parents obviously want him to have a strong opponent in order to further build his skills when you return home in the spring."

Thomas ran toward them holding the ball aloft. "Are you ready, Mr. Penniman?"

Callie gestured toward the court. "I shall begin my instruction on our next visit. Please don't disappoint Thomas, Mr. Penniman."

"If that's what you wish. It's my desire to please you."

Callie wasn't certain what to think of Mr. Penniman. Surely he was trustworthy and a gentleman, or the club wouldn't retain him. She glanced up as Thomas laughed and sent the ball flying across the net. For Thomas's sake, she'd find some way to handle Mr. Penniman and his unwanted advances — at least she hoped she could.

CHAPTER 8

After his return from the golf course yesterday, Wes made several inquiries regarding the whereabouts of Mr. Nusbaum. However, the man had proved to be as elusive as the club's absent golf pro. After playing the course, Wes had hoped to speak to the supervisor and secure the position as golf pro. He'd even decided he would agree to take the job on an interim basis. Should Bobby McLaren appear, Wes would immediately step aside. He'd had the proposal ready to present, but Mr. Nusbaum was nowhere to be found. And there certainly was no reason Mr. Nusbaum shouldn't agree to his offer. Wes couldn't accept any pay for the position or he'd lose his current status and be unable to enter further tournaments as an amateur.

Slipping away after lunch proved a bit more difficult than Wes had anticipated. Without his knowledge or agreement, his mother had scheduled a game of family croquet. For once, his brother Daniel and brother-in-law, Richard, sided with him and agreed that the men should not be included in the game. His mother had finally acquiesced but only after reminding them that she would accept no excuses regarding the upcoming masked ball.

They had all agreed they wouldn't dream of missing the event. Had he been able to discover some way to avoid the dance, Wes would have done so, but he knew the other men in the family used such events to broaden their search for possible investors. For years he'd watched his father and oldest brother, Charles, work their way through a room. He disliked the way these men seemed to use each other to advantage. Of course, it wasn't only his relatives — among the wealthy, it had become a customary way of making connections and doing business. Watching these men through the years was one of the reasons Wesley had chosen a profession that would lead him away from the business world.

And though his medical career had proved to be a disastrous mistake, his decision to eschew the family business remained a steadfast choice. He didn't want to be there, and he didn't believe God wanted him there, either. Perhaps working as a golf pro this winter would give him — and God — time to formulate a plan. He smiled, thinking of Miss Deboyer and her prayers for the other golfers. She said she prayed over concerns of both great and small consequence, but he wondered if she'd ever faced a matter of enormous import. Probably not. She appeared to be a young woman who had sailed through life with little difficulty.

Walking toward the golf course, his gaze fell upon several interesting plants, and once again he wondered if he could best use his skills to serve mankind through research. With his love of botany and his strong medical background, that made the most sense. And yet, he remained unsure. As he entered the caddie shack, he pushed aside thoughts of his future career and greeted Ted, the caddie who had accompanied him on the course yesterday.

Two other men were inside the shack, and Ted tipped his cap and pointed his thumb toward one of them. "This here's Mr. Nusbaum. I told him you'd be coming to see him." The young man grinned. "I see you brought your clubs."

"Couldn't come to the golf course without clubs, now could I?"

The caddie motioned to the other man.

"I'm ready to hit the links whenever you are, Mr. Branson."

Mr. Nusbaum extended his hand. "Ted tells me you're quite a golfer — said your name was Wes and you've won a few tournaments. I assume you've got a last name, but Ted said he couldn't recall it."

"Townsend. Wesley Townsend." Wes gripped the man's hand and gave it a firm shake. "Good to meet you."

The supervisor motioned toward a couple of worn wooden chairs. "Sit down and let's talk." He settled on one of the chairs and withdrew a pipe from his inside pocket. "So you're interested in working as our golf pro?"

Though he would have preferred to keep his identity secret, Wes wouldn't dare attempt to hide the fact that he and his family were guests staying at the clubhouse. After explaining that instead of participating in some of the other activities, he'd prefer to work at the golf course, he leaned back and stared at Mr. Nusbaum. "Are you willing to give me a try?"

"To tell you the truth, I'm between the devil and the deep blue sea, and you're making me a good proposition. I like the idea that you're willing to step aside if Bobby should show up, which I doubt at this point. What I don't like is that you and your family are guests at the hotel. It could make some of the other workers uncomfortable. And maybe some of the guests, too." He arched his brows. "Know what I mean?"

Wes nodded. "I do. If you like, I could try to keep it under my hat, but there might be guests who would see me at the clubhouse and recognize me. I think if we tell any concerned guests that I'm not being paid and have agreed to step in and help because of the circumstances, there would be no problem."

"Why would you do that?" He hesitated. "Are you thinking if you don't take pay you could come and go as you please? I can't say that I have a golf pro available and then not be able to count on you."

Wes straightened and shook his head. "I'd do it because I'd prefer to be on the links rather than sitting in the clubhouse, and because I can help. Who knows? One day I may decide upon this becoming my profession."

Mr. Nusbaum took a match to his pipe and puffed on the stem until the tobacco took hold. "Now, why in the world would a fellow from a family of wealthy businessmen consider a future as a golf pro? Makes no sense."

Wes shrugged. "I doubt it will ever happen, but if it does, I'd be pleased to have a reference. Do you golf, Mr. Nusbaum?"

"No. I don't have time for playing sports. I'm too busy trying to make sure the guests are happy." He held the stem of his pipe in the corner of his mouth. "And if I was going to take up a sport, it wouldn't be golf. Can't make much sense of the game, but I know it's become important to folks who frequent resorts." He motioned toward the course. "We've expanded this one — started out pretty small years ago, but now it's eighteen holes and considered a pretty good course around these parts."

"I agree. It's a course that requires a good deal of skill on the last nine holes but is easy enough on the first nine that beginners aren't discouraged."

"Right. That's what Bobby said, too." Mr. Nusbaum removed the pipe from his mouth. "I know what you've told me about your game and the trophies you've won, but if I get complaints from the guests that they're unhappy with your abilities, I'll . . ."

Wes held up his hand. "If you get complaints, I want to know. And if you or the guests are unhappy with my performance, then I'll step aside just the same as I said I would if Bobby McLaren returns."

"I don't suppose there's much more I could ask for, though I do feel that I'm taking advantage of you. We'll see how things work out, and if all goes well and you should need that reference letter in the future, I'll be glad to oblige."

Wes extended his hand. "Then we've got a deal. All I need to know is when I begin and what lessons are scheduled."

"You can begin right now. I'll go up to the clubhouse and see that notices are sent to all of the guests who have signed up for lessons." Mr. Nusbaum clapped Wesley on the shoulder. "Glad to have you here, Mr. Townsend."

"I think you should call me Wes, don't you?"

Mr. Nusbaum chuckled as he knocked the tobacco from his pipe bowl. "You're right, Wes." He tucked the pipe into his pocket. "I'll check in with you tomorrow and see how things are going. If there's an emergency, send one of the caddies running." He stopped in the doorway. "When Ted returns, tell him to inform the caddies I've hired a golf pro, and they'll be back on their regular schedule."

"Yes, sir." Wes waved as he bid the supervisor good-bye.

Once alone, he surveyed the small building that acted as a resting spot where the caddies could gather in between games as well as a storage space for golf clubs and belongings the members didn't want to shuffle back and forth to their cottages or the clubhouse. Though it wasn't grand, there were benches where players could rest, and the few who wore hobnail-spiked shoes could sit on the benches and change. There was an adjacent room he hadn't seen on his previous visit, one with more comfortable chairs and a few tables scattered about. He would be quite happy spending any free time in the small frame building.

"Is anyone here?"

At the sound of a woman's voice in the front office, Wes stepped to the doorway that separated the rooms. Unexpected pleasure swept over him when he caught sight of Miss Deboyer standing in front of the desk. Jagged shards of sunlight streamed through the side window and danced like fireflies on the dark curls peeking from beneath her straw hat.

"Good afternoon, Miss Deboyer. It is a pleasure to see you again." He didn't miss the surprise that shone in her dark brown eyes that were a near match for her hair. "And may I say that I'm doubly pleased there isn't a bicycle involved in our meeting this time." He smiled and hoped his joke wouldn't offend her. When she chuckled, he relaxed and strode to the desk. "Are you here about the golf lessons?"

"Yes. The fellow who was in here yesterday told me that Mr. Nusbaum would be available to give me information about the lack of a golf instructor." She glanced toward the other room. "He said he would be here after lunch. I know I'm a bit late, but I thought he would wait an extra few minutes. Did you see him?"

"Yes, as a matter of fact, I did."

"Did he happen to mention if there'd been any news from Bobby McLaren? Thomas is eager to begin his golf lessons, and I do hope someone is going to make proper arrangements."

"Arrangements have been made. You are speaking to the newly hired golf pro. I am certain teaching you and Thomas will give me great pleasure." He sounded like a foolish schoolboy, but she fascinated him. This young woman combined elegance and practicality in a way he'd never before experienced.

"You? I thought you were one of the gardeners or groundskeepers."

Wesley was momentarily taken aback when he realized she thought he was a club employee rather than a guest. The idea pleased him. She was a refreshing young woman, and if she knew he was a guest, she'd likely become quite formal — and embarrassed. "I have studied botany, but I don't believe I said that I worked as a gardener, did I?"

She frowned. "No, I suppose you didn't. I simply presumed that with your wealth of knowledge, you supervised the landscaping or helped preserve the island in some way."

"I have a genuine love of botany and landscaping, but when I learned the golf pro had gone missing, I told Mr. Nusbaum of my qualifications and he agreed to give me a try. The guests will be unhappy if they're without an instructor for the entire season." He gestured toward the clubhouse. "Mr. Nusbaum is currently delivering notes to guests who had enrolled."

"I see. Well, I suppose . . ." She glanced toward the door.

He could see she needed further convincing. "Once you've had your first lesson, I hope that you and Thomas will decide that golf instructor should be listed as one of my accomplishments. I've won several tournaments, but if you or Thomas find my lessons ineffective, I'll ask that any payment be refunded to Mr. Bridgeport."

A hint of pink colored her cheeks. "No, no. I didn't mean to imply you aren't qualified. I was simply surprised by the turn of events." She fidgeted with her belt, obviously uncertain and perhaps embarrassed that she'd challenged him.

"I completely understand your confusion, Miss Deboyer."

Her shoulders relaxed and she graced him with a cheerful smile. "Since Thomas missed his lesson yesterday, perhaps you have time this afternoon."

Wes glanced at the book. "If you could be back in half an hour, I believe the three of us would have time for nine holes."

"Oh, I don't have clubs, so you should have ample time. I'll walk along with the two of you and watch."

He smiled and pointed his thumb toward the storage area. "There's a caddie bag and clubs with your name on them in the storage area — right beside the ones belonging to Thomas."

She let her gaze rest on the row of caddie bags and grinned as she recalled telling him she feared clunking a player on the head. "I think you should be very afraid, Wes. Teaching me how to golf may prove to be quite an ordeal."

He touched his forehead in a mock salute.

"I believe I'm up to the challenge, Miss Callie."

She turned and headed for the door. "It may take me a little more than a half hour. I need to stop by the tennis courts and tell the instructor that Thomas will be golfing this afternoon."

Wes nodded. "I'll be right here."

Callie pedaled toward the tennis course. Best to stop there first and then fetch Thomas. She was pleased when she spotted Mr. Penniman standing near the court. He waved and shot her an exaggerated smile as she pulled alongside him.

"You're a little early, but we can use the extra time to visit." He reached for the handlebars of her bicycle.

"I'm not staying, Mr. Penniman. I came by to tell you that you could remove Thomas from your schedule for this afternoon. I must get back to the cottage, or we'll be late for his golf lesson."

She lifted her foot to the pedal, but Archie maintained a hold on the handlebars. "I hadn't heard anything about Bobby McLaren returning to the island. Who's giving lessons?"

Callie hesitated, realizing she still didn't know the instructor's last name. "His first name is Wes, but that's as much as I can tell you. I'm sure Mr. Nusbaum could answer your questions." She glanced at his hand. "I really must go or we'll be late."

"I'm disappointed I won't see you this afternoon. I was hoping you would agree to spend the evening with me. Some of the employees are going over to the beach. There will be a bonfire, and we could get to know each other a little better."

"I'm afraid I couldn't, Mr. Penniman. My evenings are usually filled with caring for the Bridgeport children or other family activities. My duties go beyond that of a regular work schedule."

"But surely you must have some free time. Don't the children have a nurse to help care for them?"

Callie placed her foot back on the ground. "How did you know that?"

"I-I didn't know it to be a fact, but most of these rich folks have got a servant to take care of everything from shining the silver to laying out their clothes, isn't that right?"

"I'm sure it depends on each household, Mr. Penniman. Now, if you'll turn loose of my handlebars, I really must be on my way."

He tipped his head to the side and smiled. "You never did answer my question. You must have a bit of free time for some fun."

131

"I never know in advance, Mr. Penniman. Other than during Thomas's lessons, I don't think we'll be seeing each other."

"And during your lessons — let's don't forget that you're supposed to learn the game as well as your young charge."

"We'll see, Mr. Penniman. Now, if you would please re move your hand?"

He released his hold on the bike. "I'm doing as you asked, but not because it's what I'd like."

She rode off before he could think of some other way to delay her. Perhaps he thought his forward attitude was the way to win a girl's heart, but she found his behavior unnerving.

CHAPTER 9

"Where have you been all day?" Daniel strode into Wesley's room with a frown as sour as his tone of voice.

Still holding his black tie in one hand, Wesley stepped back to the mirror. "Good evening to you too, Daniel."

His brother stepped behind him and looked into the mirror. "You didn't answer my question. Where have you been all day? Mother's been worried."

Wes positioned his tie beneath the wing-tipped shirt collar. "I'm twenty-five. I don't think Mother or any of the rest of you need to worry about my whereabouts. However, if it will set your mind — or hers — at ease, I've been at the golf course."

Daniel turned away and dropped onto the brocade sofa. "I knew it. I told Father I was sure we could find you at the golf course."

"I thought Mother was the one concerned about my whereabouts."

Daniel folded his arms across his chest and glared at Wes, looking much like an irate parent. "We were all concerned. Mother realized you were missing when Father inquired if anyone had seen you. Father had hoped to have you sit down with us so that we could discuss your new position."

Wesley sighed. "I've told all of you that I have no desire to become a manager in the mills. What must I do to make him understand that I have no passion for business?"

"Passion? Come on, Wes. We're talking about a job — you know, work. A place where we earn money to live in this manner. And don't argue that you don't have a head for business. It's not as though the rest of us completed college and were prepared to assume our positions. It will take a bit of time for you to become acclimated, but eventually you'll adjust." Daniel traced his fingers along the fabric of the brocade sofa. "Charles and I agree that so long as you continue to avoid coming into the business, you are playing with fire. He wants to continue to grow, and he has promised the investors that he has the right person to lead us forward in this expansion."

"Well, that certainly wouldn't be me. You and Charles have what it takes to work in the mills. I don't."

Daniel frowned. "You could learn if you wanted to. Besides, Father is losing patience."

Wesley turned to face his brother. "I think Father is capable of speaking for himself. You and Charles may be older than me, but I don't need the two of you conspiring about my future."

"We're not conspiring. We're trying to help you."

"When I want help, I'll ask. Your time would be better spent helping your wives and children."

"Listen, Wes, you need to accept your lot in life. You had your chance to go off and do as you wanted, but if you're not going to practice medicine, it's time to contribute."

Wes sat down on the arm of the couch. "Tell me, Daniel, didn't you ever have a desire to do anything other than step into the family business?"

His brother's features softened. "Yes. As a matter of fact, I wanted to be a sailor, but Father pointed out the folly of such a decision."

"Why was it folly? If that's what you wanted to do with your life, you shouldn't have given in to what Father wanted."

Daniel shook his head. "Going off to sea

was no more than a young man's dream. I soon realized Father was right. And you'll do the same if you don't want to ruin your standing within the family. There's a real need for you to help with the business. You're a grown man, and it's time to put aside your selfish desires and focus on what's good for the entire family."

A surge of anger swelled within Wesley's chest. He stood and turned away from his brother before he said something he might regret. Why did all of them think they knew what he should do with his life? And why was he considered selfish if he didn't join the family business?

"Personally, I think you should have at least tried going to sea. If you're completely honest, I'm sure you still wonder what you might have encountered if you'd followed your instincts."

Once again Daniel eyed him with disdain. "Taking my position with the mills was expected of me — just as it was expected of Charles and is now expected of you. The time has come to settle down, take a wife, and assume your position with the company."

"I've heard that tale enough times, Daniel. You can stop repeating it." He buttoned his white waistcoat and straightened the lapels of his black swallow-tail coat. "Let's go downstairs and join the family."

"You might consider the fact that Father would like to look toward retiring from the business and enjoying the fruits of his labor. You know, traveling and such. If you'd step up, he and Mother could relax a bit."

Wes didn't rise to the bait Daniel tossed at him, though he hadn't before heard this argument about his father wishing to retire. If it was true, why expand? Still, the thought that his unwillingness to join his brothers in the family business might hamper his father's retirement pricked his conscience.

Although he wasn't looking forward to the ball, Wes headed to the door. Anything would be more pleasant than arguing with his brother. They stepped outside the room as his parents were departing their suite. His mother wore a peach gown and matching mask. Tiny feathers were attached to the mask and appeared to wave at him as she approached.

"I have a mask for you, too, Wesley." She smiled and handed him a black mask embellished with several rows of black and gold cording. "This one is quite nice, isn't it? I had my milliner create masks for the entire family before we left home. She's such a talented woman."

His father nodded toward the stairs. "Daniel and I will meet you downstairs."

"Oh yes. It's better we don't all appear together. Someone will immediately guess who we are. Wesley and I will follow in a few minutes." His mother gestured for him to put on the mask. "Let's see if it needs any adjustment."

He placed the mask over his head and pulled it down until he could see through the eyeholes. It covered more of his face than he'd anticipated. "It's rather large, don't you think?"

"The idea of a masked ball is to hide your identity, Wesley." His mother patted his arm and spoke in the placating tone she'd used when he'd been a young boy unwilling to follow instruction.

"Since I know very few people, I think I could go without a mask and not be recognized."

Though he thought the idea of a masked ball a bit of silliness, he knew he wouldn't win an argument with his mother. In her estimation, a masked ball could only be outdone by a full costume ball. And she'd already lamented the fact that they wouldn't be wearing costumes for the first formal gathering of the season.

She tapped her fan against the front of his

stiff white shirt. "If you would spend more time with us, you'd become acquainted. The rest of us have already met many of the regular guests staying here at the clubhouse as well as some of those who have cottages on the island." She gave the fan an extra tap against his shirt. "I might add that I've discovered there are a number of lovely, eligible young ladies who would be pleased to make your acquaintance."

Wesley's shoulders stiffened at her final remark. "I have no more interest in striking up an acquaintance with one of these socialites than I do in taking a position in father's business." When her lips trembled, he leaned forward and brushed a kiss on her cheek. "No need for tears, Mother. You have three children who have married and two of them have given you grandchildren."

"And I want to see you just as happy as my other children."

Wes cleared his throat and pointed toward the stairs. He didn't think his brothers and sister were particularly happy with their lives. If so, they hadn't revealed it to him. In fact, they appeared fairly miserable, but he couldn't say such a thing to his mother.

She grasped his arm. "Let's go downstairs. I'm sure you're going to discover some beautiful young lady who will be thrilled to dance with you."

Wes touched his index finger to his mask. "I won't be able to distinguish who is beautiful and who isn't."

"You may not be able to see their faces, but it won't be difficult to discover which ones have excellent manners and the ability to converse. Outward beauty is a benefit, but inward beauty is of greater importance."

They descended the final steps, and Wesley escorted his mother to the doorway of the ballroom. "You are right, Mother. If you will excuse me, I shall see if I can strike out and find a woman of inward beauty."

Before his mother could protest, Wesley made his way toward the edge of the dance floor, carefully weaving around small groups of visiting men and women. After locating a quiet spot beside the doors leading to the outdoor gardens, he surveyed the room. If he remained along the fringes of the dance floor, perhaps after an hour or so he could sneak up the back stairs without being missed. If good fortune was with him, his family members would remain at a distance.

He'd been standing near the doorway for only a short time when a lady drew near. Her sagging jowls, crooked fingers, and thin, wrinkled skin were sure signs she was old enough to be his grandmother.

She smiled and nodded toward the dance floor. "You should be out on the dance floor creating fond memories with a young woman."

His mother caught his eye as he glanced across the room. His stomach clenched when she gestured toward a group of young girls at the end of the room. If he didn't do something, she'd likely march across the room and give him explicit instructions.

Wesley extended his hand to the elderly woman beside him. "Why don't you and I go out on the dance floor? I don't know if we'll create any memories, but I'll do my best to stay off of your toes."

She clasped a veined hand to her bosom. "You want to dance with me? I'm an old woman."

Wesley laughed and took her hand. "It would be my honor to dance with you."

They'd made only one turn on the dance floor when his partner said, "We're not supposed to give away our identity, but I think wearing these masks is pure silliness. It's a wonder someone hasn't fallen down and broken a bone or two. By the way, I'm Margaret Willoughby."

"I thought our identity was supposed to be a secret."

"Oh, stuff and nonsense. If I want to

introduce myself to my dance partner, I'll do so. Besides, my late husband invested enough money in this island that they don't dare say a word to me." She tipped her head back and laughed like a young debutante enjoying her first ball. "But you need not worry. I won't insist upon knowing your name because I'd likely forget by morning."

She continued to laugh at her own humor, and Wes couldn't resist joining her. He thought her delightful as she regaled him with stories about the early days on the island. "Nowadays I'm pleased to pay a young fellow to pedal me around the island in my *chaise roulante.*"

Wes raised his eyebrows. "Truly?"

She chuckled. "There are several in use on the island — the club even rents out a few — but mine is special. My husband had it specially made for me. You'll have to come see it someday. Have you ever seen one?"

"I don't believe I have," Wes said.

"It's a huge wicker chair with wheels on each side and a small wheel at the front end. The rear portion of a bicycle had been attached behind the wicker chair. That's where the young man sits and pedals. It's quite comfortable for me, because I don't have to pedal." She leaned close as he circled near the musicians. "I'm not so sure the young man enjoys it near as much as I do. I'm certain he's exhausted by the time we return to the clubhouse."

"I doubt he is tired at all. You are as light as a feather, Mrs. Willoughby."

"And you, young man, know how to flatter a woman." She sighed as the music came to an end. "I do believe I need to sit down for a bit."

Wesley escorted her back to a chair near the doors. "May I get you something to drink?"

"I don't want to take advantage of your time, but I would be grateful for a cup of that terrible punch they're serving." She shook her head. "You would think with the amount of money they pay the chef, he'd learn to prepare a proper punch, wouldn't you?"

Wes chuckled. "Indeed I would. I'll see if I can locate something that might be more to your liking."

After requesting a glass of lemonade for Mrs. Willoughby, Wes surveyed the room. He narrowed his eyes and watched his father, who appeared to be in deep conversation with another gentleman. A young woman, likely the man's daughter, stood nearby. Without warning, the three of them turned to look at him. For the first time that evening, he was thankful to be wearing a mask. Perhaps they hadn't seen him staring in return. Once the waiter returned with his order, Wes breathed a sigh of relief and zigzagged through the crowd, carefully balancing Mrs. Willoughby's drink.

"Thank you, dear boy. Lemonade is my favorite — how did you know?"

"Just a guess. I wanted to avoid bringing you a cup of that horrid punch."

He glanced over his shoulder and inhaled a deep breath. The musicians were preparing to play their next selection, and his father, along with the gentleman and young woman, was heading toward him. Without a doubt, his father was bringing the young woman to meet Wesley with the hope that he would consider her a suitable candidate for marriage. And with her lemonade in hand, he couldn't very well sweep Mrs. Willoughby back onto the dance floor.

There was little time to waste if he was going to avoid being drawn into his father's plot — and that's exactly how he'd come to think of his family's resolve to find him a wife — a calculated plot to control his life. He scanned the surrounding area for another elderly woman, but the only one he could locate was using a cane. He doubted she'd agree to take to the dance floor. With his entourage in tow, Wesley's father was steadily advancing toward him.

He turned toward a woman partially hidden by the draperies near the doorway. She wasn't elderly, but time wasn't on his side. Taking long strides, he extended his hand as he neared her side. "May I have the honor of this dance?" Behind the mask, her eyes darted from side to side. She looked as if she'd like to turn and run. If so, he could understand, for he felt the same way.

"I-I suppose so, though I don't know that we've met."

Wesley clasped her hand before she had an opportunity to run away and leave him stranded with the woman his father had chosen. Wesley escorted her to the edge of the dance floor and pointed to his mask. "That's the idea of the mask, isn't it? We don't know each other. I believe it's supposed to be rather mysterious and intriguing."

She rested her hand on his shoulder as he grasped her right hand in his left. "I suppose you're correct. I find all of these formal parties rather boring. I was just looking to make an escape when you asked me to dance."

"I thought as much when I saw you hiding behind the draperies." Wesley twirled her away from the edge of the floor, where his father had now positioned himself. The young lady and older man were no longer at his side.

She giggled. "I didn't realize I was so obvious. If I could avoid every one of these parties, I would do so. Unfortunately, that doesn't often occur." She followed his lead with perfection. "As far as I'm concerned, these gatherings are no more than a way for the women to show off their jewels and fashions and for the men to brag about their latest business success." She pulled her lower lip between her teeth for a moment. "I apologize. I shouldn't have said such a thing."

"I don't know why not. I couldn't agree more." There was something familiar about her, yet he hadn't met any of the young socialites since his arrival.

Tipping her head to one side, she looked up at him. "So you're not one of those businessmen hoping to meet just the right investor?"

Wes looked into her eyes and wished he could remove the mask and see her face. "No, I'm not, but it sounds as though you're either the wife or daughter of such a man."

She chuckled. "I am neither. I'm just a

woman who enjoys getting to know people without the pretense. To tell you the truth, I generally prefer the company of servants to that of their mistresses. Though I may not always agree with them, I find them more forthright."

"That's because servants don't attempt to impress one another. On the other hand, most of the people in this room wish to be the most important person on this island." He smiled down at her, surprised by how much they had in common. "Do you find many opportunities to visit with the servants and staff here at the clubhouse?"

"Sometimes. In the past, I've enjoyed the company of several of the maids, and several days ago I met a very nice man who works here as a gardener. No, that's not correct. He's the golf pro and a levelheaded sort of fellow."

His stomach lurched. This had to be Callie, the young woman who had nearly knocked him over with her bicycle. He stared deep into her eyes. Yes, he was sure of it. No wonder she had seemed familiar. "So first he's a gardener and then he's the golf pro? Which is it?"

She quickly explained how she had met the gardener and how he'd become the island golf pro. There was no doubt: He was dancing with the Bridgeports' tutor — and he was enjoying every minute. When the dance ended, he cajoled her into remaining for one more dance. When she agreed, he was filled with an inexplicable sense of pleasure. As they continued to dance, he questioned her a bit. She told him what he already knew: She was a tutor and also accompanied Mrs. Bridgeport to some of her society functions.

"And what of your future plans? Do you intend to remain a tutor?"

Her smile faded. "I am giving great thought and prayer to my future, but I haven't made a decision yet." She went on to explain that her parents were working as missionaries in Africa. "I'm considering the possibility of joining them. The people there are in great need of teachers, doctors, and above all, God. But I've recently been offered another teaching position in Chicago at the school where I previously taught. Of course, I am very fond of the Bridgeport children and am not eager to leave them, so I'm carefully weighing my decision."

This truly was a woman of much deeper substance than he'd imagined. When she refused another dance, he didn't attempt to dissuade her. If she remained with him any longer, he might say too much and reveal his identity. For now, he liked the idea of her thinking of him as no more than one of the help.

CHAPTER 10

Although no written rule existed on Bridal Veil, it had become customary for guests with children to attend ten o'clock worship services on Sunday mornings. Guests who preferred to worship without the possibility of a crying infant or fussy toddler arrived at eleven o'clock. Callie thought the practice of separate worship a disservice to the youngsters. She believed children needed the opportunity to learn proper behavior in all circumstances. And she also believed those without children needed to exhibit greater tolerance for the little ones. However, what she believed didn't change the rules on Bridal Veil, and the separate worship services continued.

Callie descended the front stairs and smiled at the three children who stood in a row near the front door. Maude remained a few inches away, facing them. They looked like little soldiers awaiting orders from their commanding officer.

"Good morning, children. You all look lovely today." Callie came alongside Daisy and traced her fingers through the little girl's hair.

Thomas wrinkled his nose. "I might look handsome, but please don't say I look lovely, Miss Callie."

"You're right, Thomas. You look very *handsome.*" Callie turned and gave Maude a nod of approval. "And you are looking very nice in your new skirt and waist, Maude. It appears your shopping with Mrs. Bridgeport was successful."

"Maybe not as fancy as I would have liked, but I'm satisfied with the new clothes the missus purchased for me." The nanny touched a hand to her hair and smiled. "And after your lessons, I think I've finally mastered my hair a bit. It's not looking as unruly, do you think?"

"You've done a good job with it. I know it takes a few extra minutes, but it is quite attractive."

Maude stared at herself in the hallway mirror. "You're right — it is becoming. And the missus said she thought I looked like a new woman." She squeezed Callie's arm. "I have you to thank for helping me. All these years I've never been able to manage this hair, but it didn't take you long to figure out how to comb and pin it into place. You've lots more talent than most."

"Thank you, Maude." At the sound of footsteps overhead, Callie glanced toward the stairway. "We should be home by noon. We'll go for brunch at the clubhouse after church, so you have plenty of time to attend church and eat at the dining hall if you'd like. Jane attends regularly, and I'm sure she'd be glad to have you go along with her."

"She's already offered," Maude said.

Maude didn't say if she planned to attend, and Callie didn't ask. The hired help were required to attend a separate church service in one of the large dining halls where most of the servants were served their meals. That the servants weren't welcome at the church where the guests and investors worshiped disturbed Callie and went against her personal beliefs and the Bible training she'd received from her parents. Additionally, only privately employed servants, like Maude, Jane, and Lula, had the privilege of choosing to eat at the family cottage or take an occasional meal at the dining hall.

The Bridgeports descended the stairs together. Mrs. Bridgeport grasped Daisy's hand, and Mr. Bridgeport gestured toward the front door. "Come along or we'll be late." Lottie rushed forward and took her father's hand while Thomas and Callie followed behind.

During her first season on the island, Callie had boldly inquired about the practice of having a separate place of worship for the servants. Mr. Bridgeport had hemmed and hawed for a few moments before he told her the edifice wasn't large enough to accommodate both guests and servants. But Callie knew his explanation didn't hold water. She'd seen plenty of open pews in the sanctuary. On her second Sunday at Bridal Veil, she announced she would attend worship services with the servants.

That decision had brought an immediate and resounding no from Mrs. Bridgeport. "You're needed to help with the children. Besides, you're not truly a servant. We consider you part of our extended family. I'll hear nothing more about this subject." And that had put an end to Callie's effort to show her solidarity and gain equality for the servants.

She thought herself a failure and a coward. If she'd been more like her mother and father, she would have argued her cause — or at least made a stand for what she believed to be right. But she hadn't. Since then, she'd dutifully marched off to the separate church services where the guests and investors sang hymns accompanied by their expensive organ. And each Sunday, the manifest hypocrisy greeted her at the front doors.

The six of them took their seats in one of the pews close to the rear of the church — Mr. Bridgeport's choice. He preferred to have a vantage point that afforded him a good view of the congregation. Callie thought he used the time during the sermon to choose whom he would invite to join them for brunch. Instead of enjoying his family during the Sunday morning meal, Mr. Bridgeport discussed business. And though Callie cared deeply for both Mr. and Mrs. Bridgeport, she sometimes thought they placed too much importance on wealth and status. She did, however, remind herself that if it weren't for their wealth and status, she wouldn't have a job with them. And they treated her like family — something she'd not have with any other employer.

After the final hymn had been sung, Mr. Bridgeport gestured to a young couple with two daughters. When they drew near, he greeted them. "Mr. and Mrs. Kennebec, isn't it? We met after dinner a few evenings ago. I had hoped to invite your parents to brunch this morning."

The young woman was holding hands with each of her daughters. "The rest of the family will be attending the late service."

Mrs. Bridgeport stepped to her husband's side and introduced herself. "Your girls appear to be about the same age as our daughters." She patted Lottie's shoulder. "This is Lottie, she's seven, and this is Daisy, five." She nodded toward Thomas. "And our son Thomas, who will soon be thirteen."

"How nice to meet all of you. Our girls are exactly the same age as yours. We have an infant son, but he's with his nanny. I do wish we could join you for brunch, but we had an early breakfast and will be joining the rest of the family when they return." She smiled at Mrs. Bridgeport. "Please call me Helena. I always look for Richard's mother when someone addresses me as Mrs. Kennebec."

Mr. Bridgeport and Mr. Kennebec led the way toward the clubhouse, no doubt talking business. Callie and Thomas followed closely behind Mrs. Bridgeport and Mrs. Kennebec. The four girls skipped ahead of the group, their childish laughter a soft echo on the warm morning breeze.

"I would find it much more to my liking if

we had a cottage rather than rooms in the clubhouse," Helena said. "We're accustomed to wintering at White Sulfur Springs, where we had a great deal more space. I find the rooms in the clubhouse difficult with the children. All the stairs and such."

"Yes, I'm sure that does pose a problem. You'll need to bring the girls over to play some afternoon." She glanced over her shoulder at Callie. "Callie conducts lessons for the children during the morning, but we can arrange a time for an afternoon visit. Do you have a tutor with you?"

"No. They're attending the school here on the island. We had been told that the school was quite good. Should I have brought along a tutor for them?"

Mrs. Bridgeport shook her head. "No, of course not. Callie tutors our children year-round, so she accompanies us when we come to Bridal Veil. Now, tell me a little about yourself, Helena. My husband mentioned your family is in woolens or textiles of some sort. Is that right?"

"Yes. My father owns two woolen mills in Lowell. My husband has joined the family company. Personally, I do my best to avoid their business discussions. I find it all a bit boring."

"I will be certain to extend an invitation

to you and your mother when I entertain some of the ladies for an afternoon of cards." Mrs. Bridgeport glanced over her shoulder. "Callie, please add Helena and her mother to my guest list."

"Thank you. Oh, and if you wouldn't think me too forward, you might consider adding my sister-in-law, Melody. She recently married my brother Daniel. She won't be here for the entire season, but if you'll be entertaining within the next couple of weeks, I'm sure she'd appreciate being included."

As the group climbed the steps to the wide veranda surrounding the clubhouse, Mrs. Bridgeport once again signaled to Callie. "Do add Melody Townsend to the list, as well, Callie."

Callie nodded and remained at a distance while the group bid their farewells. The Kennebecs strode toward the stairway that would take them to their upstairs rooms while Callie and the Bridgeports waited to be seated in the dining room.

"The Kennebecs seem a nice young family, don't you think, Luther?" Mrs. Bridgeport grasped her husband's arm as the waiter led them to their table.

"Nice enough, I suppose, but it was Kennebec's father-in-law that I had hoped to visit with this morning." He brushed the waiter aside and held the chair for his wife. "The Kennebec fellow has no power to make business decisions for the family."

Callie settled the children and sat down between the two girls. For the remainder of the meal, she visited with Thomas and the girls while Mr. Bridgeport went on and on about his business ventures. Callie stole several looks at Mrs. Bridgeport during the meal. Poor woman. It appeared she was as bored with her husband's talk as the rest of them.

The girls waved to Maude, who was waiting on the front porch when they returned to Fair Haven. Callie followed as Maude shepherded the children inside. "Let's get your clothes changed so you don't ruin your Sunday best." Maude glanced over her shoulder at Callie. "I don't know if you've made plans for this afternoon, but it's a lovely day to spend some time on the beach. I do enjoy the ocean."

"Can we go, too? Please?" Lottie and Daisy stopped at the top of the stairs and continued to plead with Maude and Callie.

"Sunday afternoons are free time for the staff," Mrs. Bridgeport told them, patting Daisy's shoulder. "You girls know that. This is when Callie and Maude can spend several hours enjoying themselves."

Daisy's lower lip quivered. "But I want to go to the beach. Will you take us, Mama?"

Mrs. Bridgeport shook her head. "I would love to, but I can't today. I told your father I would plan a dinner party for next week, and I've not yet taken care of the details." She smiled at Callie. "Of course, I won't object if you want to take the girls along with you."

Both girls jumped up and down and squealed. "Oh, please, Miss Callie, say we can go with you."

Callie wasn't certain what to do. Maude had extended the invitation, and she didn't want to ruin her plans. She looked at Maude and arched her brows.

Maude leaned down and wagged her finger. "You can come along, but no more of this pouting. And the first time you do not listen, we'll march you right back home. Am I understood?"

"Yes, Miss Maude," the two of them chanted in unison.

The girls were quick to change their clothes and follow every order Maude issued on the way to the beach. Callie spread a blanket a short distance from the water, and while the girls searched for shells, she and Maude sat down on the blanket and watched the breaking waves roll to the shore.

"A lovely day for relaxing. I've had hardly a minute to visit with you over the last couple of days what with your taking Thomas for all of his lessons, the big doings at the clubhouse last night, and church this morning. I'm thinking you must be exhausted from trying to meet the needs of both parents and children in the Bridgeport household."

Callie chuckled. "It's not so difficult. I've been with them long enough that I've become accustomed to their expectations."

"Does that include giving up your days off whenever it's convenient for the missus?"

"She doesn't ask often. It takes a couple of weeks after we first arrive on the island for everyone to become acclimated to the different surroundings, schedules, and people. Mrs. Bridgeport doesn't usually entertain so soon after our arrival, and I think that's why she wanted time alone this afternoon."

A gust of wind ruffled the blanket, and Maude grabbed the corner and stretched it back into place. "That's good to know. I don't mind this once, but I like having a bit of time to do as I please without the children." She leaned back and stared at the blue sky. "Did young Thomas enjoy his golf and tennis lessons?"

"Yes. I think he preferred the golf instruction over the tennis lessons, and I completely concur with his choice."

Maude frowned. "Why is that? Was the tennis instructor not capable?"

Callie leaned closer. "I believe he's a capable teacher, but he's much too brash a man for me. I didn't like the way he conducted himself when I first spoke to him about the lessons. And I told him so in no uncertain terms." She shivered as she recalled how Archie had behaved. "On the other hand, the golf lessons were much more enjoyable. Thomas liked the instructor."

"And you?" Maude arched a brow.

"Yes. He was kind and well-mannered. I liked him very much. After a few attempts with the club, I finally managed to hit the ball a short distance." Callie laughed as she recalled how Wes had praised her feeble attempts.

"I'm sorry to hear about the tennis instructor. Now that he knows how you feel, perhaps you'll find him more acceptable next time."

"I do hope so." Callie brushed a stray curl off her forehead. "I met a very nice gentleman at the dance last night. He was most refreshing. Unlike most of the men who attend the formal affairs, he wasn't intent upon discussing business or money." She inhaled a deep breath of the sea air. "I become so weary of the never-ending conversations about money, fashions, and industry, but generally that's all these people want to talk about."

"There's nothing wrong with money — without it everything ceases to function. It's a necessity in this world we live in. If I was you, I'd be learning everything I could from those rich folks."

Callie shook her head. "For many years, I lived a somewhat opulent lifestyle. Until my parents went to the mission field, they weren't much different from Mr. and Mrs. Bridgeport. We didn't want for anything. But once they prepared their hearts and minds to preach God's Word, they sold most all of their belongings to help begin their work in Africa."

Maude lurched forward. "You must be joking with me. What kind of parent does such a thing?"

"Parents who love God and want to serve Him. I was moved by their willingness to make such a sacrifice. Giving up worldly possessions creates a sense of freedom, and if I decide to join my parents in Africa, I intend to sell the house and few possessions my grandmother left me."

Though she'd always admired her parents' decision and spoke highly of the sacrifice they'd made, Callie had paid a price she didn't mention to others. While her friends in boarding school went home to parents and siblings during holidays and summer vacations, Callie returned to the quiet home of her grandmother. Not that Granny hadn't been wonderful, but it wasn't the same as having her parents. For Callie, everything had changed when her parents departed — like a ship without mooring, she'd been set adrift in uncharted seas.

It wasn't until Matthew stepped into her life that she turned loose of the fear and loneliness. Slowly he'd stripped away her doubts and said he'd love her forever, but apparently she hadn't been enough for him. Late at night when sleep escaped her, she wondered if she would ever be enough for anyone.

Maude reached forward and patted Callie's arm. "No disrespect, Miss Callie, but that's a bit of craziness you're planning. You need to reconsider what you'll be giving up.

Think about the fine dresses and lovely parties, the comforts you enjoy every day."

Lottie hurried toward them and deposited a handful of shells on the blanket before scurrying back to look for more. Callie stared after the child. "I would miss some of the people I'd leave behind, but not the possessions." She smiled at the older woman. "I would miss you, Maude."

Maude cackled. "Go on with ya. You don't know nothing about me except that I've been married a couple of times."

"I much prefer talking to you than listening to which investor wants to merge his company with another. Why don't you tell me more about yourself? I'd very much enjoy learning about your past."

Maude dipped her hand into the sand and watched as it sifted between her fingers. "That's what my life's been like. A handful of sand that slipped through my fingers and left me with nothing. I had two husbands; neither was worth his salt. I know I shouldn't speak ill of the dead, but I'm better off with them out of my bed and in the ground."

Callie sputtered. She didn't know how to reply to such a comment. "I see. Well, do go on with your story."

"My family came from Ireland two generations back. I worked hard to rid myself of my Irish accent, though I can't say I've been completely successful. My mother encouraged us to try to speak better English. She said we'd get a lot further if folks didn't know we was Irish. I didn't understand back then, but I learned she was right. Back when my mother was young, there were lots of people who disliked the Irish and wouldn't give them work. Truth is, there's still lots of folks that don't like us." She straightened her shoulders and shook her head as if to rid herself of a bad memory.

"But you've overcome all of that and secured excellent employment, Maude."

"I s'pose you're right, but one position with the Bridgeports doesn't make up for a lifetime of being treated with disrespect."

Callie frowned. "But you worked for the Winslow family for a number of years."

"What? Oh yes, the Winslows." She bobbed her head and stood up. "I think I'll go and see how the girls are doing with the shell collecting."

Callie watched Maude amble across the hard-packed sand. The woman appeared to be a walking contradiction. On some days her recollections were clear as a bell while at other times, her remembrances seemed quite blurred. How could Maude forget her years of employment with the Winslows? Surely she didn't believe such a fine family had treated her in a disrespectful manner. Then again, Callie recalled that Mrs. Winslow could be both arrogant and abrupt at times. But for Maude to say such a thing when she knew the Winslow and Bridgeport families were well acquainted was odd. Callie shook her head. One thing was true — Maude Murphy was a strange woman.

CHAPTER 11

"Come along, Thomas, or you'll be late for your tennis lesson." Callie waited near the front door and smiled when the boy appeared from around the corner with a sandwich in one hand and his tennis racket in the other. "You're hungry already? It hasn't been that long since you ate your lunch."

"Maude says it's because I'm a growing boy. She says young fellows my age need lots more food than girls." He chomped another bite from the sandwich and chewed with enthusiasm.

Callie grimaced as he smacked his lips together. "And boys need to chew with their mouths closed, as well."

Thomas chuckled. "Sorry." He waved the remainder of the sandwich toward the bicycles sitting alongside the porch. "Ready?"

Though she would have preferred to walk

on such a beautiful afternoon, Callie didn't object. If they didn't ride bicycles, they would definitely be late. Truth be told, she longed to send Thomas to the tennis courts by himself. After last week's encounter, she worried she might be required to fend off further advances from Mr. Penniman.

Never before had she encountered such forward behavior from a man. She wanted to believe she'd misjudged him and all would go well today. If not, she might speak to Mrs. Bridgeport and ask to be excluded from her lessons. Surely there was some other youngster who would be willing to take her place and practice with Thomas so that she could avoid Mr. Penniman. Of course, once they returned to Indianapolis, she doubted there would be anyone willing to accommodate the boy's busy schedule. If Lottie was older, she could take lessons and act as her brother's opponent. What was it her grandmother used to repeat when Callie would wish for things to be different? *"If wishes were horses, beggars would ride, and if turnips were watches, I'd wear one at my side."* Yes, that was it. She smiled at the remembrance — and the truth of the old rhyme.

She had been employed to teach Thomas and help make his wishes come true. If that included learning to play tennis, she would do so. The boy had pulled several bike lengths ahead of her and was standing waiting beside his bicycle when she arrived. Archie Penniman stood by his side, smiling at her as she applied the brakes and came to a halt.

"I just told Thomas I had begun to worry that you'd forgotten his lesson." Archie drew near and grasped the handlebars of her bicycle. "Let me put that over here for you."

She immediately stepped aside. "Thank you, Mr. Penniman."

"Call me Archie. I dislike formalities and insist that all my students address me by my first name." He ruffled Thomas's hair. "Right, Thomas?"

Thomas smiled at Mr. Penniman as though the sun rose and set on the man's approval. "Yes, Archie."

"I'm afraid his parents' wishes must overrule your request, Mr. Penniman." She turned and looked at Thomas. "You may address Mr. Penniman as Mr. Archie or Mr. Penniman, but you may not call him Archie. Even though he has given you permission, your parents would not approve." She smiled at him before returning her attention to the instructor. "I believe Thomas is ready to begin."

"Have you been practicing at all, Thomas? I don't think I've seen you or your teacher since your last lesson."

"We haven't been back here, but I've practiced my serve in the backyard by hitting against the storage building out back." The boy giggled. "I think you'll see that my serve has improved some." Thomas headed toward the court, his tennis racket in one hand and a ball in the other.

Callie lagged behind, hoping to avoid her lesson, but instead of hurrying to the courts, Mr. Penniman remained near her side.

Archie gestured to a lanky young fellow carrying a racket and approaching the courts from the opposite side. The young man loped toward them. "Thomas, come and meet your partner, Hank."

Hank's broad smile revealed a row of uneven teeth. "Mornin', Archie. I'm ready whenever —"

"This is Hank McGruder. He works here — helps out with lessons and takes care of keeping the courts in good condition. He's going to work with Thomas while I'm teaching you the basics, isn't that right, Hank?"

Hank nodded and tipped his cap. "Right you are. Do you want me to begin with him now, Archie?"

Before the boy could rush off, Callie

grasped his arm. "Perhaps it would be better if Hank instructed me and you helped Thomas. Since his parents want him to excel in the sport, I think he should have the benefit of your training." She forced a slight smile. "You are, after all, the professional instructor."

"I am, indeed, but young Thomas needs work on his serve and return. Hank is proficient with both. I think you'll discover he is quite accomplished. In fact, some of the guests request Hank as a partner. And he connects with the younger boys very well and is patient with them."

The young man beamed as Archie lauded his talents. "I think Thomas and I will get on very well, miss." He dug the toe of his shoe in the dirt. "And I've never instructed a woman. I don't think I'd be very good at it."

A feeling of defeat washed over Callie as she released Hank's arm. It appeared Archie had taken great pains to arrange the lessons in a manner that pleased him. She inhaled a deep breath and silently prayed this would go well.

Thomas and Hank had already begun to lob balls back and forth when Callie and Archie stepped to the court next to them. Archie remained at her side. "First let me

171

see how you hold the racket. I need to check your form." He let his gaze sweep over her. She grasped the racket in her hand, but before she could swing, Archie stepped behind her and, while holding one arm around her waist, placed his hand over hers. "You'll get no power in your swing if you hold the racket that way."

Callie wrenched away from him and pinned him with a glare. "I do not wish to have you take hold of me in that manner, Mr. Penniman. I'm sure you can find some other method of showing me the proper way to hold a racket."

Archie chuckled. "I'm just trying to make sure my students get their money's worth. Seems you're one of those gals that's got her laces fastened tighter than a turkey that's been trussed for Thanksgiving dinner. You need to relax and enjoy life a bit, Callie. And I'm just the one who can provide that enjoyment."

Not wanting to alarm Thomas, Callie withheld her desire to immediately return home. Every hair on the back of her neck bristled as she stared at him. "Please listen carefully, Mr. Penniman. If you do not cease the unwanted and impolite advances you are directing at me, I will report you to Mr. Bridgeport. I have every confidence that he will not only speak to your supervisor, he will demand that you be terminated from your position as tennis instructor." Speaking to Mr. Bridgeport would be her last resort, but she hoped the threat would be enough to frighten Archie.

"So you want to play hard to get." His lips curled in a wolfish grin. "I know how you girls like to play cat and mouse. You want men to chase after you in order to prove we truly desire your company." He tipped his head forward and lowered his voice. "But unlike a mouse, I know you really want to be caught. Just this once, why don't we set aside the games? I'll agree that you're an enticing little morsel, and you can agree that I am both interesting and appealing. With that out of the way, we can begin to truly enjoy our time together." He winked. "I'm sure you understand my meaning."

Unable to restrain herself, Callie clenched her racket and swung. Archie let out a bellowing yelp.

Both Thomas and Hank raced toward them. "Is anyone hurt? What happened?" Hank shouted.

"I was attempting to improve my swing. Unfortunately, Mr. Penniman misunderstood my intent and stepped too close."

Callie directed a furtive smile at Archie and quietly said, "I think the only thing bruised is your ego, isn't that right, Mr. Penniman?"

He gave her a hard look but forced a smile when he turned toward Hank. "I'm fine. Just a whack on the arm. Callie hasn't learned how to control her racket, but I'm going to teach her."

Callie clenched her jaw. "Not today, Mr. Penniman. I think you should take care of that injury to your arm." She placed her hand on Thomas's shoulder. "I'm going to come and watch you while Mr. Archie locates some ice for his wounded ego."

"Huh?" Thomas frowned. "I thought you hit his arm."

"Right. He'll want to find some ice for his arm." She brushed a strand of hair from her forehead.

"Callie, wait!" Archie strode toward her. "I apologize. Please don't report me. I need this job to support my mother."

"You apologized the last time we met, Mr. Penniman, and yet you were even more ill-mannered today. How can I believe you?"

"I can only give you my word and ask that you give me another chance."

"I will give the matter further thought, Mr. Penniman, but it is your behavior that has created this situation."

From his frown, she was certain he'd expected her to immediately capitulate and forgive him. He was a man accustomed to winning his way with a few sweet words. She was a woman who'd heard far too many charming excuses. She would wait and see if Archie's actions matched his words — and then she would make her decision.

Maude had the girls ready and waiting when Thomas and Callie arrived at Fair Haven a short time later.

"Maude fixed my hair, Miss Callie. Do you like it?" Daisy twirled around in front of Callie.

Callie stooped down in front of the child. "It is very nice. You'll be the envy of every little girl at the puppet show this afternoon."

Lottie frowned at her sister. "I think my hair looks better than hers."

"You both look lovely, and I'm very pleased you're ready to go. We must hurry or we'll miss the beginning of the show." She glanced toward the side of the house. "Come along, Thomas. You can leave the bicycles there and put them away when we return."

Thomas remained beside the bicycles. "Do I have to go? Puppet shows are for babies."

"Are not!" Lottie shouted.

"Now, now, we're not going to raise our voices, Lottie." Callie strode to the far side of the porch and leaned over the railing. "I would be grateful if you'd come along. I planned to have you gather ideas about stage construction so you could build a small replica for the girls. I thought it would be fun for them to make up some stories and produce their own shows while we're here." She straightened her shoulders and glanced toward the girls. "What do you say, Thomas? Will you come along and sketch out some ideas?"

He grinned. "Sure. I didn't know you needed my help."

Callie withheld a grin. She could always count on Thomas to agree if he thought she was in need of his help. "I'll go upstairs and get my sketchbook, and then we can leave."

"I'll go and get it. Lottie and Daisy have short legs. I'll catch up to you in no time." He circled around the porch and was in the house before they'd made it down the front steps.

"Have a good time. I'll want to hear all about it when you return." Maude stood on the porch and waved as they departed.

As Callie walked with the girls, she pushed aside thoughts of her displeasure with

176

Archie. Some girls probably found him handsome, but not Callie. His rude behavior made him as unattractive as the overzealous businessmen in the dining hall.

They'd gone only a short distance when Thomas jogged alongside Callie, holding the sketchbook and a pencil. "I told you I'd catch up in no time."

"I think we're going to have great fun this afternoon. I'm not certain if this will be a puppet show or a marionette show, but I think you'll like either one."

Lottie tugged on her hand. "What's the difference?"

"To make a puppet move, you put your hand inside and work your fingers around like this." Callie spread her fingers and pretended that she had slipped a puppet over her hand. "But marionettes have strings that control them, and you must move the proper string to move the character around the stage."

Daisy wiggled her fingers in several directions. "Puppets would be easier, wouldn't they?"

"Yes, and I'm hoping that after you watch the show, the two of you might want to try a puppet show of your own. We can make up some stories, and we'll try to make some puppets out of old socks and such."

Thomas tapped the sketchbook. "And after I have a look at the stage that's being used this afternoon, I'm going to see about building one for you."

The girls' excitement mounted as they entered the clubhouse. For the next hour, the children delighted in the puppet show presented by a small traveling troupe that the recreational director had enlisted. The parents and tutors who had escorted the children gathered at tea tables that had been arranged nearby. Without Mrs. Bridgeport along, Callie was pleased for an opportunity to sit with the group of tutors.

They were exchanging pleasantries when Mrs. Albright, one of the mothers sitting at an adjacent table, gasped and clasped a hand over the fancy brooch pinned to her gown. "I hadn't heard anything about a robbery. Are you certain, Rose? What was stolen?"

"I heard about the robbery, as well," another woman Callie didn't recognize added. "My husband told me jewelry had been taken from one of the cottages."

Grace Wilson waved a server away from their table and poured a cup of tea for Mrs. Albright. "Oh, dear me. That is terrible news. We've never had such problems in the past." She placed the teapot on the table and passed the cream to Mrs. Albright. "I'm thankful we're staying here in the clubhouse, where there's less likelihood of anyone entering our rooms."

Rose Barclay, the initial bearer of the news, elaborated about the items that had gone missing the night of the ball. "This kind of happening puts everyone on edge."

Mrs. Albright glanced toward the puppet stage. "I do wonder if bringing all these outsiders onto the island is a good idea. I know the recreational director wants to provide different entertainment each season, but having strangers skulking about isn't a good thing."

Mrs. Wainwright leaned forward and helped herself to a pastry. "I wouldn't say they're skulking about, Lydia. They're performing a puppet show. I doubt any of the performers who have been here would have enough time or opportunity to locate and enter the cottages." Using the silver tongs, she placed the delicacy on her plate. "And I don't think this is the forum to discuss such a distasteful matter. I am certain the incidents are being investigated and will be resolved in no time." Mrs. Wainwright's admonition brought an end to any further mention of the robbery.

When the puppet show ended, the children were permitted to examine and play with the puppets while Thomas inspected the stage and sketched several pages of drawings.

He handed the sketchbook to Callie. "What do you think?"

"Your drawings are wonderful, Thomas, but now we need to start toward home so we can all freshen up before dinner."

Thomas tucked the sketchbook under his arm. "We could take the trail through the woods. It's faster than going around by the road."

"You're always coming up with good ideas." Her praise caused Thomas to blush and look away. "Why don't you take the lead? You're more familiar with this path than I am."

The sun glistened through the limbs of the live oaks, and the fallen pods that blanketed the trail crunched beneath their feet as they continued onward. A branch cracked behind them and Callie whirled about. Her mouth turned dry, and she clenched her hands as a streak of white disappeared into the brush. The tree branches swayed in the breeze, and a bird flickered overhead. How silly of her. The streak of white had likely been nothing more than a bird roosting in the brush.

She'd nearly calmed her nerves when another noise sounded to the left. Her breathing turned shallow as she strained to listen. Was someone hiding in the woods and following them? Since reading of a child being kidnapped and held for ransom two years ago, she'd worried the same might happen to the Bridgeport children. In the past, her main concern had been when they'd traveled from place to place in the city — on Bridal Veil she'd believed they were more protected and safe from the outside world. Yet harm could come to the children anywhere.

Her heart pounded a rapid beat, and perspiration dotted her forehead. For the sake of the children, she must remain calm, but if someone was out there, she wanted to know. She developed a rhythm of looking to the right and to the left and then glancing over her shoulder.

Fear took hold and prickled the hair on the nape of her neck. As she twisted to look over her shoulder, her foot lodged beneath a tree root. Pain shot through her ankle, and she dropped to the ground, her arms and legs flailing helter-skelter.

Thomas rushed to her side and grasped her arm as she attempted to stand. "Are you injured, Miss Callie?"

"I think I twisted my ankle." Even as she spoke, she could feel the swelling in her shoe, but she had to get the children safely home. "Let me see if I can walk." She allowed Thomas to help her to her feet, but when she attempted to take a step, she grimaced in pain. "I don't think I can do it, Thomas."

He straightened his shoulders. "I can run for help. Shall I take the girls with me?"

The girls would slow him down. If someone was after them, he'd be more vulnerable with them along. Yet how much protection could she offer if someone attempted to take the girls from her? She'd fight to the death for them — that much she knew. She couldn't linger over her decision.

"Run for help, Thomas. I'll keep the girls with me. And if anyone attempts to stop you, keep running. Don't stop for anyone, do you understand?"

He appeared confused but nodded his head. "I'll be fine, Miss Callie, and I'll be back in no time."

The boy took off like a runner sprinting for the finish line. She motioned to the girls to sit down beside her. "We can use this time to start our story for the puppet show."

While the girls talked in soft voices about a wicked witch who would be mean to a fairy princess, Callie listened to every swishing bush, every rustling leaf, and every crackling branch.

With every sound, she twisted in one direction and then another until Daisy stood and placed her tiny hands on Callie's cheeks. "Are you listening to our story, Miss Callie?"

"Yes, I'm listening, but I'm also watching for Thomas to return." Her heart was beating so loud within her chest that she marveled the child didn't hear it.

Soon she heard pounding footsteps, and Thomas appeared with the golf instructor. "Look who I found. I told Mr. Wes what happened, and he said he would come and help."

Wes tipped his hat and stooped down in front of her. "Is your ankle sprained or broken?"

"I'm sure it's a sprain."

"Maybe I should take a look, just in case."

"No." Heat infused her face. "That's not necessary."

"Well, Thomas tells me you're unable to walk, so I think there's nothing left to do but this." In one swift motion, he encircled her body and lifted her into his arms.

"Mr. Wes!" She wrapped her arms around his neck instinctively. "I do appreciate your willingness to help, but I think if you would simply lend support, maybe I could walk."

He shook his head. "Nonsense. You're light as a feather, and it's my pleasure to help a damsel in distress."

There was something about this man that created a sense of peace within her, and she longed to simply place her head on his shoulder and enjoy these moments. The fear she'd felt for the last half hour vanished in Wes's presence. He was the kind of man who made you believe you'd always be honored and cherished.

This was the kind of man she thought she'd found in Matthew. She stiffened at the remembrance and reminded herself that trusting a man would only lead to pain and disappointment.

"Here we are." With a broad smile, Wes gently lowered her into a chair on the front porch while Thomas and the girls rushed inside to find their mother.

"Thank you so much for your help. I don't know what we would have done if Thomas hadn't come upon you. I don't think Maude or Mrs. Bridgeport could have carried me."

Wes chuckled. "It was my pleasure, and I hope you'll soon be up and about. If you'll excuse me, I need to return to the links to give a golf lesson." He started toward the front steps. "Be sure to put some ice on your ankle."

"Wait!"

He turned. "Yes?"

"Where did Thomas find you?"

"I was in the woods. You recall I enjoy botany."

She nodded and waved good-bye, but a weight settled in her stomach. Had Wes been the one following them in the woods? And if so, why? The thought caused a shiver to course down her spine.

Could not even a man like Wes be trusted?

CHAPTER 12

For two days, Wesley had attempted to come up with a way to contact Callie — a way where he wouldn't need to reveal his true identity. Returning to the cottage meant he might be seen by Mr. or Mrs. Bridgeport. And though he'd not yet been introduced to the couple, it would be impossible to avoid making their acquaintance at some social function in the near future. Since he didn't want Callie to view him as a socially elite sort of fellow, he hadn't reached a point where he wanted to take a chance on being recognized.

His intent was not to lie or trick her, but he wanted more time to get to know her without any pretenses — without her thinking of him as a member of the social set. He had enjoyed their comfortable conversations and hoped for more time with her before disclosing that in addition to acting as the golf pro he was a guest at the club-house.

Wandering along a path near the common gardens, Wesley stopped to admire some of the flowers. He glanced up when one of the gardeners approached and gestured toward the array. "There are more varieties in the greenhouse. Guests are welcome to pick a bouquet any time they'd like."

The gardener had solved his problem: He'd pick a bouquet of flowers and have them delivered to Callie. After the gardener handed him a pair of shears, Wesley selected a variety of flowers he thought she'd enjoy. He realized she might not be able to swing a golf club for another week or so, but he hoped she'd be able to accompany Thomas for his next lesson.

He stepped into the greenhouse, amazed at the wide selection of flowers. The sweet scents of the mingling blooms greeted him. He turned to the gardener, who remained nearby to answer questions or meet any request. "You have an astonishing array from which to select. And all of them are beautiful."

"Only the best for the guests of Bridal Veil Island." The old man gave him a lopsided grin. "That's our motto here at the green-house. We try to keep everyone happy."

"From what I see around here, I doubt anyone could complain."

"To tell you the truth, I don't think we've ever made it through a season without a few complaints, but we keep trying." He chuckled. "Never can tell, this year may be the one."

Wes studied his bouquet for a minute. "I don't see how I can improve upon this any further, do you?"

The gardener took a closer look, stepped across the greenhouse, and returned with several clippings from a cinnamon fern. "If you place these fronds around the outer edges of your bouquet, it may add to it a bit. See what you think."

Wes nodded. "It does. Thank you for your help. If I write a note to go along with the bouquet, do you have someone who could deliver it for me?"

"We do. I need your name and where you're staying to log into my book, and I'll attach a card with the required information."

Wes tightened his hold on the bouquet. "What information?"

"I need to put the name and address of the person you're sending it to, and I have to include your name and address on the card, as well. Something new they started a couple years ago."

"Why?"

"I don't make the rules, mister. I just do what I'm told." He reached for the flowers, but when Wes didn't hand them over, the old man frowned. "You want them delivered or not?"

Wes shook his head. "On second thought, I think the young lady would be pleased to have me deliver them in person."

The gardener tucked the shears into a sheath on his belt. "Probably right. I hope she likes them."

Wes held them up a few inches as he turned to leave. "I'm sure she will."

"Come back anytime."

Wes strode away and didn't stop until he was sure the gardener couldn't see him. He stared at the bouquet. He wasn't going to personally deliver the flowers, and he couldn't let anything so pretty go to waste. Unable to come up with another plan, he turned toward the clubhouse. His mother would appreciate the flowers.

He'd gone only a short distance when he heard someone call his name and a bicycle wheeled up beside him. "Thomas! What are you doing over this way?"

"I talked Mother into letting me ride my bicycle down to the river for a while. Since

Miss Callie still isn't walking very well, Mother said she'd let me go by myself this once, but I have to be back on time, or she'll never let me go again." He glanced toward the sky. "Do you know what time it is?"

Wes pulled his watch from his pocket. "Fifteen past three."

The boy sighed. "I've got fifteen minutes before I'm late, but I can make it back in ten if I pedal fast." He lifted his foot onto the pedal.

"Wait a minute, Thomas." Wes extended the bouquet toward the boy. "Do you think you could carry these flowers and still manage your bike?"

Thomas straightened his shoulders. "Sure! I can carry lots of things and still ride without any trouble."

"Would you take them to Miss Callie and tell her that I hope she's feeling better and I look forward to seeing her at the golf course very soon?"

"I can, but why don't you come along and give them to her yourself? I'm sure she'd be pleased to see you. She was real sorry you took off so quick the other day. And my mother wanted to meet you." He nodded his head toward the road. "Come with me."

"I can't. I've got some other matters that I need to attend to right now, and I'd hate for these flowers to wilt before I can deliver them."

"Okay. I'll take them, but I better get going or I'll be late."

The boy wrapped his hand around the bouquet and sped away. At the rate he was pedaling, Thomas would make it home in far less than ten minutes.

Earlier in the afternoon, Callie had enlisted Maude's help. Together with the girls, the four of them had gathered on the front porch to create puppets. They were in the midst of cutting and sewing when Thomas, flowers in hand, rounded the front fence and skidded to a stop a few inches from the porch steps.

He held the bouquet aloft. "Look what I brought, Miss Callie. Get-well flowers from Mr. Wes." After resting the bike against the porch railing, he ran up the steps and presented her with the bouquet. "Mr. Wes said he hopes you're doing much better and that you can attend lessons next week."

The words caused an unexpected tingle of excitement. She hadn't experienced such pleasure since receiving flowers from Matthew. She sniffed the bouquet. *Be careful. You still don't know if you can trust him any more than you could Matthew.*

"That was most kind of him. The flowers are beautiful. Would you take them to the kitchen and ask Lula to put them in water, Thomas?"

Thomas took the flowers and headed for the door. "If Mother comes looking for me, I'll be out back working on the puppet stage."

The moment Thomas entered the house, Maude tapped Callie's arm. "So you've got you a beau, have ya? I knew all that talk of not trusting a fella and going to Africa wouldn't last, once the right man came your way."

Callie didn't want to discuss Wes with Maude or with anyone, for that matter. He was a nice man and she enjoyed his company, but she barely knew him. And she wasn't interested in a beau. But trying to alter Maude's opinion would likely result in failure. Better to change the subject than try to convince the nanny. Though she hadn't known Maude for long, Callie had already discovered the nanny seldom adjusted her opinion.

She tipped her head toward the older woman. "I haven't had an opportunity to mention this before, but when I took the children to the puppet show the other day, I heard talk of valuables being stolen from one of the cottages."

Maude ceased her stitching. "Is that so? What kind of valuables did they say?"

"A diamond bracelet and a jeweled hair clasp, along with some other valuable pieces. I hope they find the culprit. It makes me uneasy to think there might be thieves roaming about." She kept her voice low to prevent the children from hearing.

"I can't say as I'm too surprised."

Callie dropped her sewing to her lap. "Why? Do you know something about the incident?"

" 'Course not, but I doubt those jewels will ever be seen again. This resort is full of haves and have-nots. With the number of poor folks working as servants, I'd think there would be plenty of thievery." Maude dipped her needle into the fabric and continued to embroider a bright red nose onto one of the puppets.

Callie frowned. "That hasn't been the case in the past. I think if any thefts had been reported, Mrs. Bridgeport would have mentioned it to me. Most of the servants and workers have been here for years. I'm sure the help is carefully scrutinized before being hired."

"You may be right, but when folks get into dire circumstances, there's no telling what they'll do. The money from selling a few pieces of expensive jewelry would go a long way." She hiked a shoulder. " 'Course that's just one old woman's opinion."

"You're not old, Maude. And you may be right about the jewels, but I hope not."

A memory of the noises in the woods on their way home the other day flashed through her mind, and Callie shivered. Could that have been the thief? She shook her head. What a silly thought.

She pushed the idea from her mind, and when they'd finished sewing, the two women went inside. Callie stopped in the hallway. "I believe I'll take some time and write to my parents while you see to the children, Maude."

Callie hadn't expected to hear from her parents while at Bridal Veil. A letter had arrived shortly before their departure, and her parents knew she'd be gone for the winter. If her mother did write, she'd send her letters to Indianapolis for fear they might not reach Callie on the island. They had both learned that mail deliveries to and from Africa were not something one could count upon for swift or correct delivery.

Her letter wasn't particularly long. She told her parents about the children and the activities at Bridal Veil. She didn't mention her injury — they would only worry. And though she knew they wanted to hear she was planning to join them, Callie ended her letter by saying that she was still praying for God's direction and asked that they do the same. She decided against telling them about the job offer in Chicago, but she continued to weigh her options. She'd been happy teaching there, and during her time in Chicago, she'd become acquainted with Jane Addams and even taught English classes at Hull House several evenings a week. The experience had been gratifying, and with the expansion of Hull House, there would be an even greater need for teachers and volunteers. Wasn't that work as important as the work in Africa? Her decision would be much easier if God would whisper in her ear or perhaps drop a note from heaven.

She smiled at the idea as she signed her name and then reread what she'd written. The leisure pastimes at Bridal Veil likely sounded quite mundane to those who were serving God on another continent. Yet her parents' letters expressed interest in her pursuits with the Bridgeport family. Besides, her parents had once enjoyed the same activities, and if she didn't write about such things, there would be nothing to fill her letters.

Day by day, Callie's ankle continued to
heal, and so long as she used a cane, she
was able to move about fairly well. She'd
informed Mrs. Bridgeport she could once
again accompany Thomas to his lessons. If
his golf lesson had been scheduled for today
rather than tennis, she would have been
much happier. But since she wouldn't be
able to take a tennis lesson, there would be
no reason to worry about Archie.

Mr. Bridgeport had rented a wheeled
chaise, though Callie wished he would have
arranged for a carriage. She still thought it
would be too great a task for Thomas to
wheel her about, but he'd been practicing
for several days and vowed he was up to the
task.

She settled in the wicker seat. "It's going
to be more difficult with me as your pas-
senger, Thomas. I weigh more than your
sisters." He'd been pedaling his sisters during his practice sessions.

He climbed on and began to pedal.
"There's not much difference."

Callie chuckled. "We've only gone a few
yards. Let's see how you feel once we get to
the tennis court. I doubt you'll have enough
energy for your lesson."

Thomas proved her wrong. When they arrived at the tennis court, Thomas had more than enough energy for his lesson.

After they finished, Archie strode over to where Callie stood watching. "He's improved, don't you think?"

Mrs. Bridgeport had accompanied Thomas to several lessons, and Callie had to admit there was marked improvement since she'd last seen him play.

Thomas beamed at the compliment. "I've been practicing with Hank most every day."

"And with me," Archie said.

"Right. And with you." Thomas ran inside the small storage building to put away his tennis racket.

"Let me help you to your chaise." Archie grasped her elbow.

"I'm much better simply using the cane, but thank you for the offer."

Archie frowned, but he removed his hand. "Thomas tells me that you've been giving them lessons about the plants and wildlife on the island. I'd be pleased to take you on a carriage ride and show you some places where you could take the children for some of their studies."

"I believe I can locate enough unique places to show them on my own, but thank you, Mr. Penniman."

Once Thomas returned, Archie grasped Callie's arm and helped her into the chaise. "Do you know where to find the giant sea turtles that come up on the beach to lay their eggs?"

"No, but I don't —"

Thomas came around the chaise, his eyes wide with excitement. "Have you seen them, Mr. Archie? I heard they're huge and look like giant sea monsters."

Archie chuckled. "They're big all right, but I don't think they look like monsters. They come up on the beach at night and lay their eggs, and I know where to find them."

"Oh please, Miss Callie," Thomas pleaded with wide eyes.

"I can come by for you at eight o'clock in the morning. I'll show you where they are, and then you'll know where to take the children when you have a chance at some later time. We can be back in time for my first tennis lesson." Archie grinned. "I'll bring a carriage so you'll be comfortable."

She didn't attempt to hide her irritation when she looked at Archie. He was a manipulative man who would use anything to gain an advantage.

"Have you forgotten that we have lessons in the morning, Thomas? I'm sorry, but I don't think it will be possible, Mr. Penni-man."

"But we could change them to the after-noon. I'm sure Mother wouldn't care one bit if we switched the lessons to the after-noon this one time. Won't you at least ask her?" Thomas had become as persistent as Mr. Penniman.

"The best I can offer is this." She turned to Archie. "I will speak with Mrs. Bridgeport and see if she is willing to have me change the schedule. You may come by at eight o'clock tomorrow morning, but please know that if Mrs. Bridgeport doesn't find the ar-rangement acceptable, we won't be going."

"I'm more than willing to take my chances. I'll see you in the morning." He winked before he turned and strode back toward the tennis court.

Callie settled back in the chaise and sighed. Hopefully, Mrs. Bridgeport would deny the request to change the day's sched-ule. If she didn't, Callie would need to ar-rive at some other plan to avoid Archie Pen-niman and his carriage. Right now she longed to have a shell like one of those large sea turtles. What a wonderful place to hide from the likes of Archie Penniman.

They'd gone only a short distance when Thomas wheeled the chaise to the side of the path and came to a stop. "Mr. Wes!" The boy yanked off his cap and waved it overhead before glancing over his shoulder at her. "Mr. Wes is heading our way. He motioned for me to stop. Is it okay?"

She chuckled. "Since you've already stopped, I think it would be rude to commence pedaling before he's had a chance to say hello."

Moments later Wes jogged to the side of the chaise. "I hoped to see you soon. How's the ankle doing?"

Thomas pointed to a nearby wooded area. "If you two are going to talk, can I go and see if there are any new plants over there?"

Callie nodded. "Yes, but stay close enough that you'll hear me when I call."

Thomas took off as though he'd been granted a supreme gift. Strange how she liked the idea of spending time alone with Wesley, while thoughts of being alone with Archie Penniman caused her stomach to roil. And though both of them had shown interest in her, they were complete opposites, especially in their behavior.

"I'm glad to see you, as well. I wanted to thank you for the lovely bouquet of flowers you sent." The ribbons of her straw hat flapped in the breeze, and she pushed them aside. "You could have brought them to the house, you know. I would have been delighted to have them delivered in person."

The moment the words escaped her lips, she wanted to snatch them back. He'd likely think she was in the habit of encouraging men's attention. She felt the heat rise in her cheeks and wished she could make a quick escape.

He leaned on the side of the chaise, their faces close enough that she could see the glint in his eyes. "I'm glad you liked them, and I'm sorry I couldn't deliver them in person, but I had to get to the golf course. I did select them myself, though."

"Truly? I don't believe I've ever received flowers that have been personally chosen by someone. Unless we're picking flowers from our own garden, I think most of us rely on the florist." She beamed at him. "You did an excellent job. I thought the colors magnificent."

His eyes shone with appreciation. "I must admit the gardener over at the greenhouse made a few suggestions. We should go over to the greenhouses one day. Just walking through there is a pleasure." When she didn't immediately reply, he continued. "Of course, with my love of flowers and plants, I found the place quite amazing. I'm sure there are other things you'd rather do in

201

your spare time."

"No, not at all. I'd enjoy a visit to the greenhouse. I love flowers." She pointed to her ankle. "It would have to be after my ankle heals, of course."

She wanted to tell him he could come by the house when he wasn't busy with golf lessons, but she'd already appeared far too forward.

CHAPTER 13

Thomas chattered endlessly about the sea turtles as he pedaled the chaise back to Fair Haven. By the time they arrived at the house, guilt had taken hold of Callie. She didn't want to disappoint the boy, yet she simply could not accept Archie's invitation. Perhaps with all of his exploration around the island, Wes had discovered where the sea turtles nested. She'd ask him, and if he had spare time one day, he might be willing to show her. Later, she could take the children there. As long as Thomas knew he'd eventually visit the nesting area, his disappointment would be short-lived.

The girls raced down the porch steps to greet them. "Miss Maude is helping us make another puppet." Lottie grinned. "She's using one of Papa's socks. She said it was a spare, so he wouldn't miss it."

Callie had eased out of the chaise and leaned heavily on the cane when Daisy grabbed her around the legs. "Come see, Miss Callie."

"I will do exactly that, but first I need to speak with your mother." She held tight to the rail as she ascended the porch steps. "I'll come back to the porch as soon as I've spoken to her."

"She's not here," Lottie said.

Callie looked at Maude. "Mrs. Bridgeport is gone? I didn't recall she had any invitations for this afternoon."

"She and the mister have gone over to Biscayne with a group of folks. I don't think the missus was too pleased with the last-minute plans, but Mr. Bridgeport insisted. I gathered it included some sort of business talk among the husbands."

"Why didn't they simply have dinner at the clubhouse? They could have talked there."

Maude arched her brows. "Seems one of the wives wanted to have dinner at the fancy hotel over in Biscayne. Said she needed to see something other than the clubhouse dining room."

Lottie held up the latest sock-puppet creation and smiled.

"Very nice. Miss Maude is becoming quite good at making puppets."

"It needs hair," Daisy said. "Miss Maude

said you'd take care of that. Will you, Miss Callie?"

Callie nodded. "Yes, of course." Keeping her gaze fixed on Maude, she stroked the child's blond curls. "Did they say when they would return?"

Her stomach clenched as she awaited the answer.

"The mister said they wouldn't be back to the island until late. Captain Fleming said he'd return to the mainland for them at ten. But the missus said that if the men got involved in talking business, they might want to go to the clubhouse, and if that happened, she doubted they'd get home before midnight." Maude inhaled a deep breath. "Either way, she said we should all go to bed and not worry about their return."

The news hit Callie like a blow to the midsection. She leaned against one of the ornate porch pillars and withdrew a handkerchief from her skirt pocket. Patting the beads of perspiration that had formed along her upper lip, she tried to calm herself. Truth be told, she felt as though she might faint. Of all days, why must Mrs. Bridgeport be gone today? What if she didn't have an opportunity to speak with her before Archie arrived in the morning? Not only did she not have another way out of the turtle trip, but Mrs. Bridgeport would likely be unhappy if she changed the schedule without permission. Her mind whirled and worry settled on her shoulders like a heavy weight.

Maude's features tightened and she jumped to her feet. "Are you not feeling well, Callie? You're white as a sheet. Let me help you to one of these chairs." She motioned to Lottie. "Please ask Lula for a glass of water, child."

With Maude's help, Callie lowered herself into one of the wicker chairs. "I'll be fine, Maude. I had hoped to speak with Mrs. Bridgeport about a matter as soon as I returned. I think it was merely the surprise of hearing she won't be home until late."

"I don't know why something so simple as that would cause you to turn white and perspire like a summer rain." Maude's frown deepened. "Did ya have some sort of trouble over at the tennis courts?"

"I put the chaise back in the shed like Papa told me." Thomas loped around the side of the house and onto the porch. "We had a good time today. I played very well, and Mr. Archie even complimented my progress, didn't he, Miss Callie?"

"Indeed. You played very well."

Thomas beamed at Maude. "And guess what else?"

Callie wagged her finger. "You promised you wouldn't say anything just yet, Thomas."

He bowed his head. "Sorry. I forgot."

On the way home, Callie had convinced Thomas they shouldn't share information about the sea turtles until final arrangements had been made with his mother. The girls would be as excited as Thomas, and refusing Archie's offer could become even more difficult.

"Tell us. Secrets aren't nice." Lottie forced her lower lip into a pout.

"This is a surprise, and if we tell you, then it will be ruined." Callie lifted the girl's chin with her forefinger. "You need to pull your bottom lip back in before a bird comes and roosts on it."

"I'd like to have a bird." Daisy shoved out her bottom lip and walked to the edge of the porch. Moments later, she turned around. "How long will it take before they see me?"

Maude laughed and shook her head. "Miss Callie was joking. There aren't any birds small enough to sit on your lip. Or anyone else's, for that matter." She pointed to the crayons and paper lying nearby. "If I'm to keep making these puppets, you need to get back to making the scenery."

For the remainder of the afternoon and evening, Callie considered her options. It hadn't taken her long to realize they were few. When she finally went upstairs, she sat down at her desk and penned a note to Mrs. Bridgeport stating she would like to speak to her first thing in the morning. She'd considered waiting up, but worried she might fall asleep and fail to hear Mrs. Bridgeport come upstairs. Besides, she doubted the woman would want to discuss sea turtles after a long evening of socializing. After placing the note beneath the Bridgeports' bedroom door, Callie returned to her room and prepared for bed.

Of course Callie's note was no guarantee Mrs. Bridgeport would be dressed for the day and downstairs before Archie arrived. When staying out late for social functions, the mistress was known to remain abed until after eight o'clock. Because she hadn't wanted to alarm the older woman, Callie had carefully worded her message. She could only pray Mrs. Bridgeport would awaken early.

And pray, she did. Sleep eluded her for several hours, so she had used the time to ask God's help. To those like Wesley, it might seem farfetched to ask God to intercede and awaken Mrs. Bridgeport, but to

Callie it was quite normal. She needed help and she believed God would provide what she needed. As a child, she'd learned that's what the Bible said. Of course, she'd also learned that her desires and God's plans didn't always align. Still, she believed God wanted only the best for her. In this particular case, she believed God would agree with her: Archie Penniman wasn't God's choice for her. And unless God intervened and changed him, Callie doubted Archie would be God's choice for any woman.

When the morning sun peeked through the windows, she dressed as quickly as possible and stepped into the hallway. She waited a moment, hoping she might hear or see some sign of life appear from the room at the end of the hall. But she didn't. Cane in hand, she descended the front stairs, where Thomas greeted her with a bright smile.

"Mama already talked to Mr. Archie and said you can go with him."

"What?" She grabbed for the railing to maintain her balance. How could this be? She gasped a breath of air. Thomas must have been mistaken. "Mr. Penniman isn't due for another half hour, and I didn't think your mother had come downstairs yet."

He danced from foot to foot. "She did —

she's outside talking to Mr. Archie now. She said locating the sea-turtle nests was a wonderful idea, and she thanked him for being willing to take you out there on his time away from work."

"Did she? Do you think you could ask her to come inside and speak to me?"

"Sure."

Thomas started for the door, but she grasped his arm. "Thomas, would you stay outside with Mr. Penniman and talk to him? I want to speak to your mother privately in the sitting room."

He nodded and grinned. "I have lots of questions I can ask him about the sea turtles."

She stepped into the sitting room while formulating exactly what she wanted to tell Mrs. Bridgeport. Although she disliked Archie's behavior and didn't want to spend time with him, she didn't want Mr. Bridgeport going to Mr. Nusbaum, who would likely discharge him. She knew how such matters were handled. His discharge would cause the gossip to fly. Guests who played tennis would be angry they'd lost their tennis pro, and she would be in the midst of the firestorm. Even worse, Mr. and Mrs. Bridgeport might be ostracized. Guests didn't like their resort life disrupted, and they'd already been inconvenienced by Bobby McLaren's desertion as their golf pro. Further interruption would cause no end of displeasure.

Wearing a cream and white linen day dress, Mrs. Bridgeport swept into the sitting room with a bright smile. "Good morning, Callie."

Callie greeted the older woman and gestured toward the stairs. "Did you see the note I left under your bedroom door last night? I asked to speak to you this morning."

"No." She frowned. "Luther probably brought it downstairs and put it on the side table where we place the mail." She glanced toward the other room. "Well, I suppose all is well that ends well. I'm here and we can talk." She glanced toward the front door. "I must say that Mr. Penniman is quite a charming young fellow, isn't he?"

Callie cringed and shook her head. "Not exactly. To be honest, Mrs. Bridgeport, that's why I wanted to speak to you. He has been overzealous in his attempts to keep company with me."

Mrs. Bridgeport clasped a hand to the ruffles that adorned the bodice of her dress. "Dear me. Why didn't you say something? I would have had Luther speak to him. In

211

fact, I will say something this very moment."

Callie clasped Mrs. Bridgeport's hand. "Please don't. I've given the matter great thought." It didn't take Callie long to explain her position and the possible consequences.

After hearing her thoughts, Mrs. Bridgeport agreed. "I suppose you're right. I hadn't considered the ramifications. Still, we don't want you in a situation where anyone would attempt to take advantage. The very thought angers me." She rubbed her arms. "I think we should go outside, and I'll tell Mr. Penniman that I've reconsidered and don't believe you should go. I do wish I would have waited and spoken to you before I agreed."

Callie wished she had, as well, but she didn't want to cause the woman further distress. "I have an idea. When we go outside, why don't you tell Mr. Penniman that you've decided the children should accompany us? I would feel quite safe if Thomas and the girls are along, and that way they won't have to wait until a later date to see the turtle nests."

Mrs. Bridgeport beamed. "I do believe that's a perfect solution. Let's go talk to Mr. Penniman right now."

Archie did his best to appear pleased when

Mrs. Bridgeport explained the change of plans, but Callie noticed a distinct tick in his jaw. The older woman smiled and placed her hand on Thomas's shoulder. "I know this will prove to be a delightful adventure for the children."

Archie gestured toward the buggy. "I don't believe there will be adequate room for all of the children, Mrs. Bridgeport."

She frowned and glanced at Callie. "I suppose that's true, but it's large enough for Thomas to join you. He can go along and help Callie remember the location for future visits with the girls."

Thomas stepped forward and directed a generous smile at Archie. "Miss Callie does have trouble with directions from time to time, and I'd be most pleased to join the two of you."

Callie would have preferred all three children, but having Thomas along would provide as much protection as she would need. And there would be little opportunity for any unseemly comments in the buggy. Thomas would easily hear every word that was spoken.

Had Thomas not peppered Archie with questions about the sea turtles and other animals that inhabited the islands, the ride would have been unusually silent. Archie told Thomas how he'd learned to play tennis while in school at New York, but later he said he'd learned while living in Georgia. Callie gathered Archie was one of those men who had trouble keeping his stories straight. He'd likely told so many different ones, he'd lost track of the truth.

"I think we'll have to stop here. I can't take the buggy to the area where the turtles nest." Archie stepped down from the buggy and extended his hand to Callie. Once she had reached the ground, he wrapped his arm around her waist.

"Please remove your arm, Mr. Penniman." Callie pushed on his arm until he released his hold.

Archie pointed to the west. "We need to go down the beach about half a mile. It shouldn't be too bad once we get through this loose sand and onto the hard-packed area of the beach."

Callie did her best to follow Archie and Thomas in the loose sand, but after only a short distance, she realized such a walk could easily reinjure her ankle. "I think it would be best for me to wait at the buggy. You take Thomas and show him. He'll be able to direct us back once my ankle is completely healed."

Archie stepped closer. "I would be delighted to carry you."

"No thank you, Mr. Penniman. Either take Thomas to the turtle nests or take us home." She turned toward the buggy. "And that is my final word on the matter."

"Suit yourself." He waved toward Thomas. "Come on, then. We're on our own to see what we can find."

Callie settled in the buggy and removed a book of poems from her bag. After searching for the turtle nests, she had planned to sit on the beach and read. Instead, the buggy would have to do.

She'd been reading for a short time when she glanced up to see Archie returning. She pushed herself up a bit to see if she could spot Thomas, but he was nowhere in sight. Fear gripped her as she continued to scan the area for any sign of the boy. "Where is Thomas?"

Archie pointed toward the beach. "No need for alarm. He's examining the turtle nests and doing quite fine. There's nothing to harm him." He grinned as he stopped beside the wagon. "I told him I thought I should come back and make certain that you're all right."

"I'm fine."

He hoisted himself into the buggy beside her. "I couldn't agree more. As far as I'm

215

concerned, you're the most handsome woman on all of Bridal Veil Island. I know we got off to a bad start, but I truly am a gentleman. I'd like to court you properly, if you'll agree. I'd be more than pleased to show you the beach in the moonlight."

"How many times must I tell you that your forward behavior is unwelcome?"

"I'm not so sure you mean that." He leaned toward her and chuckled when she pushed him away.

Her heart hammered and bile rose in her throat. She needed to keep her wits about her. Lifting her hand to strike him, she stopped short when she heard someone whistling a familiar tune.

"Thomas is coming. Get away from me."

"What are you doing back so soon, Thomas?" Archie jumped down from the buggy.

"I started feeling sick to my stomach. Is it okay if we go home, Miss Callie?"

Callie nodded and welcomed him into the carriage. God had answered her prayers. Never before had she been thankful for an ill child.

CHAPTER 14

A loud knock startled Wesley. His stomach knotted at the sound. Few people visited his room, especially so early in the morning. Yesterday his mother had complained of not feeling well, and concern for her mounted as he hurried across the room. He swung open the door, surprised to see his father, a frown on his face.

Gesturing toward the sitting area, his father said, "We need to talk." He strode across the room and dropped into one of the brocade-covered chairs. "I see you're dressed for another day at the golf course." He shook his head. "I hope you're not planning on wearing that garb into the dining room."

Wes looked down at his clothing. "There's nothing inappropriate about what I'm wearing. Many of the men wear tennis or golf clothes into the dining room. I've even seen a few come in their hunting attire." He chuckled. "I don't think it will hurt their digestion."

"I'm not concerned about their digestion. It's more a matter of how a person is perceived, Wesley. People judge such things all the time." He brushed his hand down the front of his jacket. "With the expansion of the mills, I've been required to take out substantial loans. It would be beneficial to Townsend Mills and to our family if we could entice some of the men here to invest in the mills. Having a son who consistently appears to have nothing better to do with his time than play golf doesn't breed confidence or build a desire to invest in our company. I've told them this is a working vacation for the men in our family, but your attire tells them the opposite."

"I'm baffled by what you've told me, Father. I haven't agreed to come on with the mills, so you shouldn't have given anyone that idea." His mind whirled at the possibility. Was that truly how these powerful men conducted business? Surely not! Then again, perhaps they did. He really had no idea how such choices were made. His business knowledge would fit into one of his mother's sterling thimbles.

"I don't mean to sound disrespectful, Father, but I truly do not understand how my golf attire could adversely influence any possible business investors. You should advise those men that I'm not involved in the business. That should set their minds at ease."

"Quite the contrary." His father sighed. "If I attempt to explain a son who is uncertain about whether or not he wants to enter the family business, it will only give rise to further concern. As for explaining your past — well, that would be entirely another story."

"You can state the truth in a simple manner. Tell them I have given up the practice of medicine and am using the winter months to make some decisions about my future. They may then draw their own conclusions." Wes sat down in a chair opposite his father.

"I don't think you understand the gravity of this matter, Wesley. If I don't find several investors, it could create deep financial concerns for the family. We do need to impress them. And let's not forget that telling investors that I have a son who chose to become a doctor will not impress them. The fact that you've left the profession will hold more sway with those men."

"I'm sure they share your ideas on the medical profession, Father. And I heard enough about that when I went off to school. I think we'll have to agree to disagree on the subject. While doctors don't make much money, they do reap the benefit of helping others." Wes leaned forward and rested his arms on his knees. "It grieves me to know that you've taken such a financial risk, Father, and I do want you to find the investors you need, but —"

"But it doesn't grieve you enough to do your part and join me in the business. These men want a definitive plan regarding operations, and I can't give them one at this point because my son won't make a decision to manage the new mill."

Wesley didn't want to argue with his father, but he simply couldn't give him the answer he wanted to hear. Not yet.

His father sighed. "Would you at least get out of those golfing togs and attend some meetings with me over the next few days?"

"I'm afraid that won't be possible, Father. I won't have time for meetings."

His father's deep frown returned. "And why is that?"

"I've accepted the position as golf pro for the season."

His father jumped to his feet as though he'd been jabbed with a hot poker. "You must be joking. I'll not have any son of mine working as a hired hand at a resort. I don't need additional embarrassment."

His father's words reopened wounds that had barely begun to heal. He'd heard that same accusation when he'd departed for medical school and later when he'd returned from Texas. Why must his father believe that Wesley's every decision was made to humiliate the family?

"Please sit down, Father." He waited until the older man reclaimed his chair. "I accepted the position as golf pro because the vacancy was creating a problem for the resort and because I was qualified. Besides, I knew it would help to fill my days with something I enjoy."

His father tugged on his vest. "It is beyond unseemly that my son is among the hired help on this island. I insist you quit immediately."

"I won't quit, Father, but if it eases your feelings about it, I'm not being paid. I volunteered to take the position because it would help the club. Perhaps your business friends would be more accepting if they knew your son was merely stepping in to help the resort maintain the level of sporting instruction they've come to expect at Bridal Veil. Without a golf pro, there would be no instructor to help golfers improve their game, and it would mean the annual tournament would not be recognized." Wesley leaned a bit closer. "I'm certain some of those business acquaintances of yours play golf."

His father shrugged. "I really don't know. Some of them hunt, but —"

"More and more wealthy men have begun to golf, Father. I'm sure Mr. Nusbaum could confirm that fact. And from personal knowledge, I can tell you that there is a great deal of business conducted on the links nowadays." Wesley leaned back in his chair. "You might even want to consider taking up the game, Father."

"Richard says the racetrack is where he makes his contacts, you say the golf course, and Daniel thinks it's the hunting lodge. I still prefer doing business after dinner with a glass of brandy and a good cigar."

Wes glanced at the clock. He didn't want to be late to the golf course, yet his father didn't seem to be in any rush to leave. Instead, he leaned back and appeared as though he might be settling in for a lengthy stay.

"I told your mother I was not leaving this room until we had matters settled, and I intend to keep my word. So you might as well quit looking at the clock."

"Exactly what matters, Father? I need to be at the links in less than an hour."

"Then we'll have a message delivered that you'll be late. Unless we're able to quickly come to a meeting of the minds. Since you pretend to be unclear about what I plan to accomplish, let me make it very clear. First, before we leave this island, I want your word that if you have not decided upon some other future plans where you will earn a living, you will come to work for the textile business."

"I don't —"

"Let me finish, and then you can have your say. Second, you need to be making a concentrated effort to find a suitable wife. If you don't want to go through the selection process on your own, I know your mother is eager to help. We would, of course, like the young woman to be someone who would be, shall we say, an advantageous choice for the family."

Wesley bit his tongue, but if his father continued down this path, he would soon interrupt. In fact, he might walk out of the room.

"I don't find this third point as pressing, but your mother would be most appreciative if you would at least make an appearance at some of the social functions." He cleared his throat. "And if you are to find a wife, there is no better place than Bridal Veil. Your mother and I have met any number of eligible young ladies who clearly meet our requirements."

Wesley choked. "Your requirements? And were these same requirements placed upon my brothers and sister? Was Richard Kennebec your first choice for Helena? If I recall, Mother was aghast when Charles declared he planned to marry Anna. Didn't Mother weep for days over his choice, saying her family didn't meet proper social standards for a Townsend?" He arched his brows. "Yet those marriages both took place without interference by you or Mother."

"That's true enough, but there was no choice with Charles. You're well aware they secretly married and didn't tell us until months had passed. I still disdain what he did, but the past is past. And it is true Richard has developed a bit of a gambling problem, but he makes excellent contacts, and I believe he's devoted to Helena."

From what Wesley had heard and seen, Richard was far more devoted to racehorses than to his family or the textile business, but his father wasn't interested in discussing his siblings or brother-in-law.

"I have been giving my future plans a

great deal of prayer as well as a great deal of thought. I have some ideas, but I am waiting to see what God might reveal to me over these next few months."

His father arched a brow. "Perhaps if you'd confide some details about the possibilities you're considering, it would help me understand."

Wes knew it wouldn't help, but if he was going to get to the golf course, he had little choice. "I'm considering the possibility of using my medical degree in the research field. You know I've always loved botany, and while in New York I helped in the laboratory on a limited basis. I found the work fascinating, I could use my education, and I wouldn't have to deal directly with patients. My other thought would be to use my love of botany to find work doing some sort of advanced landscape architecture. I've checked into it, and more professionals are needed." He leaned back. "Or there's always golf." He hoped his father had heard the lighthearted tone in his final words.

His father swiped his palm across his forehead. "I'd like you to add work at the textile mills to that list of considerations, Wesley. You should remember that God helps those who help themselves, and it's time you started helping yourself." His

225

father stared into the distance for a moment. "If you'll give me your word that you'll have a definite plan by the time we leave here, I won't interfere with the golf situation you've arranged for yourself. Properly explained, I think guests will agree that the donation of both your time and ability is quite generous."

"I don't want to be badgered into finding a wife. I will not agree to have you and Mother seeking out women that please you. I know where that will lead." Wes disliked agreeing to any part of his father's ultimatum, but this conversation would never end unless he made some concessions.

"Hopefully it would lead you down the aisle."

"Down the aisle with a daughter of some investor you hope to finagle into signing on with the mills."

"It's as easy to fall in love with the daughter of an investor as it is to fall in love with the daughter of a poor man."

"I've said that I'm hopeful I'll have a decision about my future by winter's end, but we both know I'm not suited for a position with the family business. Once I have made my decision, I'll let you and Mother know." He paused and inhaled. "As time permits, I will attend a few of the social functions to please Mother. I do not want either of you making arrangements for me to escort anyone to the events. If you do, you'll be sorely disappointed, and quite embarrassed. I know you don't want that."

His father stood and brushed imaginary lint from his lapel. "I cannot say I am pleased by the outcome of this conversation, Wesley."

"Neither am I, Father. However, I think I've heard it said that when neither party is happy over the outcome, it has been a rather fair negotiation. And since we are discussing my future, I'm sure you didn't expect me to submit to your every request."

For the first time, his father smiled. "You wouldn't be a Townsend if you did."

At the moment, Wes would have preferred to have been anyone but a Townsend. In fact, he envied men like his old school chum Andrew Hart. Men who had come from nothing and had made their own way in the world. Andrew's family had been proud to have a son who'd become a doctor. A brief visit in Andrew's home several years ago had revealed a great deal to Wesley. Andrew's family cared little about the material things of life. They found pleasure in helping others and living their beliefs. It was on his visit to Andrew's home that Wes had drawn closer to the Lord. After seeing the way they lived and observing their faith, he wanted the same thing for himself. They were a family who lived with peace and contentment — something he'd never observed within his own family.

"You need only ask," Andrew's father had told him. "God is willing to pour out His blessings and show you the way to a happier life if you but ask."

Wesley had asked God to give him all of those things. In truth, he couldn't say he'd found the same peace and contentment, but he continued to ask and search and pray that God would show him what he was to do with his life. Now he must pray God would answer on the timetable issued by Howard Townsend. He chuckled at the thought and wondered if God was laughing, as well.

CHAPTER 15

As the days passed into February, Callie's ankle healed, and though she and the children had not yet returned to the turtle nesting area, they had completed the necessities to perform their first puppet show. Callie and the girls had written the play, and all of them had worked hard on making the puppets and the scenery for the stage that Thomas had constructed, with a bit of help from one of the gardeners. All three of the children were delighted and filled with a sense of pride as they practiced and received applause from Callie, Lula, Maude, and other servants or workers who happened to be around during their rehearsals.

Callie consistently bolstered the children with enthusiasm and praise, and her approach had proved valuable. The children remained excited about the project and had worked together admirably. Now that they were well prepared, she hoped to reward their hard work with a proper audience. However, the recreational director at the clubhouse had been less than enthusiastic about having the children perform there.

Callie understood the director's decision. After the professional troupe's performance last month, an amateur production might not hold the other children's interest. But Callie remained determined to find a receptive audience for the puppet show.

A tap sounded on the door as the children were completing their schoolwork. Callie straightened from helping Thomas with a math problem as Mrs. Bridgeport stepped inside. She, Maude, Lula, and Jane had been downstairs preparing for an afternoon card party and tea.

"You should finish quickly, Callie. I want you to attend the tea. We'll need you to make a fourth at one of the tables. I've told Maude she's to escort the children down to the beach."

Callie pressed her hand down the front of her skirt. "I'm not dressed to attend the party. Why don't I take the children? I'm sure Maude is tired from helping prepare. Surely you can find someone else to sit in as a fourth."

"I'm afraid not. When I extended invitations to Blanche Townsend and Helena

Kennebec, I also invited Melody Townsend. However, I received word she's already returned home." Mrs. Bridgeport smiled at Callie. "Besides, you enjoy the ladies, don't you?"

Callie didn't enjoy the idle gossip and would have preferred the children's company, but she knew such an answer wouldn't please Mrs. Bridgeport. While she loved both Mr. and Mrs. Bridgeport, she didn't like the pretentious attitudes she encountered with their friends — at least with most of them.

"Look, Mama." After shoving one of the puppets over her hand, Daisy jumped up from her chair and skipped across the room. "This is the princess puppet. Her name is Princess Daisy. Isn't she beautiful?"

"Yes, dear. She's very pretty. And I'm sure she has a handsome prince who plans to marry her."

"She does, but lots of stuff happens before he can marry her. Want to see our play?"

Mrs. Bridgeport stooped down in front of her daughter. "I would like to, Daisy, but I have guests coming this afternoon."

"We could show it to them, too." The child looked up at Callie. "Couldn't we, Miss Callie?" Daisy's face shone with expectation and delight.

"Why, that's a wonderful idea, Daisy. You could perform your puppet show at your mother's tea party. I'm sure the ladies would be charmed. What do you think, Mrs. Bridgeport? The play takes only fifteen minutes. The ladies could watch while they enjoy their tea before the first round of cards."

"Well, I don't know. We've never before done anything like this. They may find it . . . odd."

Callie could sense the older woman's hesitation. She worried far too much about what other people might think. Her children were staring at her with excited anticipation. Instead of concerning herself with what her guests might think, Mrs. Bridgeport needed to concentrate on her children and what they needed.

"I believe they would find it a delightful change. Who knows? You may set a new precedent. All of the other women might attempt to outdo you once they see the delightful presentation by the children."

Callie gave a sideways glance toward the children. She hoped the subtle gesture would remind Mrs. Bridgeport her children were listening. "Thomas and I can go downstairs now and set up the stage."

"Oh, I don't know about a stage. It might

interfere with the tables and seating arrangements. Lula and Jane need to serve the ladies without having to move around something as large as a stage."

Thomas shook his head and pointed across the room. "It's not so big. And we can put it in a corner where it won't get in the way. You and Miss Callie can pick out a spot, and I'll set it up without any help." He hesitated. "Well, I might need some help getting it down the stairs."

Mrs. Bridgeport appeared more resigned than enthused, but she gave a slight nod. "Don't move anything until Callie and I go downstairs and check the space. I'm not giving a definite yes until we see how much room is left."

The children whooped and hollered as though their mother had uttered a resounding yes. And in their minds, that's what her simple nod meant to them. They hadn't heard a word she'd said about available space. So if Callie had to completely rearrange the room, she was determined to locate adequate space for the puppet show.

After making a few alterations to the arrangement of the tables, she helped Thomas carry the stage downstairs and, along with the girls, arranged the puppets in proper order behind the structure.

"You must go upstairs and be very quiet until time for your presentation." Callie tucked a strand of Lottie's hair behind her ear. "I'll come upstairs to get you, but if you make a lot of noise before then, your mother may change her mind and send you off with Maude."

Thomas agreed to take charge, and all three of the children promised they would be quiet. Callie arranged paper, pencils, and crayons on the table to keep them busy before she hurried to her room and changed into a white dress of fine lawn. After quickly arranging her hair, she hurried down the hallway. The guests had already begun to arrive when she descended the staircase.

"Would you show the ladies to their proper seats while I continue to greet here at the door, Callie?"

She'd attended enough social activities on the island that the ladies accepted her as one of them — at least they'd accepted the fact that Mrs. Bridgeport would bring her along whether they approved or not. None of the other women ever brought tutors or maids with them, and Callie's sense of discomfort never diminished while among the women. Truth be told, the more Callie was around them, the more she understood why her mother had written that she had no desire to return to the life of a society matron.

Unfortunately, Callie didn't feel any more comfortable in the company of the servants. Some of them disliked the idea that she received what they called "special privileges." And though she considered mingling with the guests a chore, there were some on the staff who envied her.

Perhaps by the end of winter, God would show her where she belonged. With each passing day and each uncomfortable social function, she wondered if God was calling her to leave this materially comfortable life and join her parents in Africa.

Lydia Albright grasped Callie's hand as she took her seat not far from the puppet stage. "Whatever is that thing sitting in the corner?"

"It is a stage, Mrs. Albright. We have some special entertainment for you ladies this afternoon." Callie smiled at the woman.

"But I thought we were going to play cards. Didn't our invitation state this would be an afternoon of cards and tea?"

Callie sighed. She hoped she wouldn't have to go through this with every one of the guests. "There will be tea, and there will be cards, as well, but Mrs. Bridgeport thought you ladies might enjoy some additional entertainment while you enjoy your tea." The woman appeared totally flummoxed by the possibility of any additional entertainment, but Callie patted her arm and smiled. "I'm sure I can depend upon you to spread the word that you ladies will enjoy an exciting treat this afternoon."

"Well, of course. You can depend upon me." Armed with the idea that she would be the bearer of special news, Mrs. Albright's disposition immediately improved, and Callie hurried off to seat the other guests.

There was only a smattering of applause when Mrs. Bridgeport announced the children would be entertaining the ladies with a puppet show. After the less than enthusiastic response, Callie began to worry she'd made a mistake. After all, several of the women had been present at the professional show, including Mrs. Albright. She could only pray the women would be kind and encouraging. Once she had the children arranged behind the stage, Callie greeted the ladies.

She forced a generous smile. "The children have worked very hard on their presentation. They created the stage and the puppets, and they even wrote the play. I hope as you watch their show, you will be reminded of your childhood days and the delightful world of make-believe."

She stepped to the side of the stage and leaned down to make sure the children were ready before opening the small cloth curtains. While the children commenced with the puppet show, the women drank their tea and ate their sandwiches and cookies. Callie surreptitiously watched the women's reactions. At first they appeared more interested in their tea, but soon their attention was drawn to the stage. By the time the children completed their show, the women were standing and applauding.

"Absolutely delightful," Mrs. Albright called to the children.

"Indeed. You children did a wonderful job." Vanetta Brown glanced about the room and led the ladies in a second round of applause while Callie signaled for the children to take another bow.

Callie had never been so proud of them. "You were wonderful," she whispered as Maude entered to take them for their outing to the beach. "Did you hear the ladies saying how much they liked the show? They were very impressed with your production."

Daisy and Lottie bobbed their heads and smiled. Callie waved to them as they departed out the back door. The children had worked diligently, and she was pleased to see their hard work rewarded with praise from the ladies.

Soon the usual chatter commenced. Though the women were there to play cards, they were also interested in any tidbits of gossip that might be passed from table to table.

The ladies had exchanged a few comments, mostly about the women who weren't present, when Margaret Willoughby tapped her fan on the table. "Ladies, I'm not one to stir things up, but I think you all know that we have a thief running amok on this island."

There were muffled gasps along with numerous murmurs of agreement.

Blanche Townsend glanced about the room. "Has anything like this happened before? I assumed there was adequate security to prevent criminal activity."

"We're told there's security, but one wouldn't know it exists if such happenings can occur," Margaret replied.

"Must we discuss such an unpleasant topic when we're supposed to be having an enjoyable afternoon, Margaret?" Vanetta Brown wrinkled her nose and curled her lips as if she'd smelled something quite foul.

"Of course we must. Something needs to be done about this thievery. If something is stolen from your home, I'm sure you'll adopt a different attitude, Vanetta." Margaret slapped her fan on the table.

Mrs. Brown narrowed her eyes and looked directly at Mrs. Willoughby. "This isn't something a group of guests can resolve. Any criminal activity requires the attention of Mr. Crocker. As superintendent, it's his responsibility to unravel this issue. In my opinion, that's what he is paid to do."

Lydia Albright waved her fan in the air. "I was told that most of the thefts seem to happen when families are busy at the lodge or are gone from their homes to attend special events."

"I think that's true. Our cottage was robbed while we were at the horse races yesterday." Frances Daly touched a lace-edged handkerchief to her eye. "My favorite brooch, a ring, and two necklaces were taken." A collective gasp filled the room. "When we built our cottage, I told my husband he should have a safe installed like the one at our home in Pennsylvania, but he said there was no danger of theft on Bridal Veil." Mrs. Daly daubed her other eye. "Now he knows I was correct, and he's going to take my advice."

Vanetta Brown *tsk*ed. "As I said, this isn't something we can solve, but it seems your husband has decided to lock the barn door after the horse has already been stolen, Frances."

Mrs. Daly's lips drooped into a downward position that formed deep creases along the sides of her mouth. "Well, at least he's doing *something,* which is more than I can say for Mr. Crocker or any of the other staff."

"No need to take umbrage. I'm merely speaking the truth, Frances." Mrs. Brown straightened her shoulders and directed a haughty look across the room.

"I understand Mr. Crocker and the board of directors met, and there is a general consensus that a team of law enforcement officers will be hired." Jeanette Osbourne looked around the room as she made the statement.

"Well, you should know, Jeanette. Your husband is on the board, isn't he?" Mrs. Willoughby arched her brows.

"Yes, but don't mention I've told you. I'm sure a formal announcement of some sort will be made." Mrs. Osbourne's eyes clouded. "My husband wouldn't be pleased to know I've divulged what happened at the board meeting, but I wanted to set your minds at ease."

"Quite right. We shouldn't breathe a word, ladies. Jeanette has been kind enough to take us into her confidence, and we need to show our appreciation by keeping our lips sealed." Mrs. Willoughby gazed about the room, a defiant look in her eyes.

In spite of Mrs. Willoughby's warning, Callie knew that the minute they departed, each one would be looking for someone to tell. These women delighted in being the first to pass along a tidbit of gossip. Callie was certain Mrs. Osbourne's news wouldn't remain a secret for long. And Mr. Osbourne would likely discontinue his practice of sharing any board meeting information with his wife in the future.

Mrs. Brown waved her fan in Mrs. Osbourne's direction. "We're going to be leaving the island early this year, Jeanette. We've been invited to attend the president's inaugural in March."

Every woman in the room swiveled in Vanetta's direction. She beamed at the reaction.

"Truly? You're going to the inaugural ball?" Jeanette's eyes were as large as two saucers.

"No. Mr. Wilson has elected to do away with the ball. He thinks it too frivolous for such a solemn occasion." She lowered her voice. "However, we've been invited to a dinner party the following evening. I must

say I'm somewhat disappointed he's canceled the ball, but my dear husband says we
must take heart that we've finally elected a
good man to take the helm and lead this
country."

"We're thrilled for you, Vanetta, but do
remember that we don't discuss politics at
our gatherings," Mrs. Albright said.

Vanetta looked as though she'd had the
wind knocked from her sails, but she soon
regained a smile when Mrs. Willoughby
leaned close and congratulated her on the
inaugural invitation.

When they were completing their final
game of bridge, Mrs. Daly inquired about
plans for the Valentine's ball. "Who is on
the committee this year? Last year's ball was
splendid, and I, for one, am hoping for a
repeat."

"The social director is taking care of all
the arrangements. No need for concern. I
believe it will be a lovely affair, Frances."
Mrs. Bridgeport briefly looked at Callie
before turning back to Frances. "Is your son
arriving in time to attend?"

Callie knew that look: Mrs. Bridgeport
considered Aaron Daly a suitable catch. She
didn't wait to hear Mrs. Daly's reply.
Instead, she excused herself from the table
then strode through the kitchen and out the

back door. She didn't want to be offered up as a sacrificial date for Aaron Daly. Mrs. Bridgeport might find him suitable, but Callie wasn't interested in a date for the Valentine's ball or a "suitable" husband.

Keeping a steady pace, she walked toward the beach. Maude and the children should still be there. Callie would much rather spend the next hour with them than listen to the women continue their discussion of the Valentine's ball and other upcoming social events — especially since Mrs. Bridgeport typically used these gatherings to seek out possible prospects for Callie. Much as she loved the woman, she disliked her employer's never-ending attempts at match-making.

When she neared the beach, she glimpsed the two girls building some sort of structure in the sand while Thomas appeared to be scouring the sand closer to the water's edge, likely seeking some special shell for his collection. Maude sat hunched over on a piece of driftwood.

Maude waved and jumped to her feet as Callie drew near. "Land alive, but it's good to see you." She rubbed her hand down her back. "I'm tired of sitting on this uncomfortable piece of wood. Can we go home now?"

"The ladies will probably be there for a

while longer, but they've finished playing cards. You can go back to the house if you'd like. I'll wait a while longer and bring the children home with me."

Maude brightened at the offer. "If you're sure you don't mind, I'd be grateful to get out of this sunshine. I'd rather be helping Lula and Jane than sitting out here."

Callie laughed. "Then it works well for both of us. I'd rather be out here on the beach than back at the house."

After Maude departed, Callie examined the sand castle the girls were building. Then she joined Thomas to see what special shells he'd collected. She was examining one of the shells when she heard Lottie call to her. She turned to see Wesley strolling toward her.

He waved and smiled. "Find anything unique?"

Thomas reached into his pocket. "This is my favorite, but it's not a shell." He held out his hand.

"Looks like you found a shark's tooth. I'd say that's a keeper, for sure." Wes looked at Callie. "And what have you found, Callie?"

"I arrived only a short time ago, so I haven't found anything. I thought maybe Thomas could direct me to the turtle nests, so I could show them to the girls."

Wes frowned. "The sea turtles nest during the summer months, usually from June to August, so I doubt you'll see much of anything at this time of year." He tousled Thomas's hair. "But if you want to go and see where they usually come in, I can show you."

Callie tried to recall what Archie had told them about the sea turtles. Thomas had asked a number of questions on their way to the beach that day. Perhaps Archie hadn't actually said they came ashore at this time of year, but he'd led her to believe they did — and he did tell her that he had left Thomas on the beach examining turtle nests. But she and Thomas had never discussed whether he'd seen anything. He'd been too ill at the time, and later she'd simply forgotten to ask.

"Is that why I never found anything when Mr. Archie brought me to look for them? But he said —"

Wes nodded. "Sorry, Thomas, but you won't see much of anything unless it's summer."

Thomas tipped his head back and looked up at Wes. "But Mr. Archie has been working here for a few years. He should know when the turtles lay their eggs, shouldn't he?"

Wes smiled at the boy. "He should, but maybe he was just confused."

Callie knew better. Archie Penniman hadn't been confused — not in the least.

CHAPTER 16

While her ankle healed, Callie had attended and watched both tennis and golf lessons with Thomas, but she'd been unable to participate. During the first week she'd been able to avoid Archie, and during the lessons that followed, he had accepted her requests to maintain his distance. For that, she'd been very grateful. And now that the time had arrived for her to resume her own lessons, she felt a bit more at ease.

As she and Thomas pedaled toward the tennis courts, her thoughts drifted to the two instructors. Not that one should compare, but it had been impossible for her to refrain from doing so over these past weeks. While Archie's behavior toward her had improved, he maintained a certain edge that bothered her. Perhaps because he was accustomed to having girls flock to him, her refusal of his advances had increased his determination. Maybe he was a man who enjoyed the challenge of pursuit, and once a girl accepted his advances, he lost interest. She thought the idea held some merit, but she would never test her theory. Such an experiment could lead to disaster. She shivered at the thought.

Meanwhile, she'd found Wesley the exact opposite of Archie. His comments were kind, yet unassuming. Even when alone with him, she never feared he might attempt to take advantage. His laughter filled her thoughts as she rode.

"What are you smiling about?" Thomas glanced around as though he expected to see something on the road or in the brush that might have created her good humor.

Callie inhaled a deep breath, enjoying the ocean scent carried on the breeze. "Just a few private thoughts. I'm happy to have regained the ability to pedal my bike and join you in your lessons."

She wanted to say "golf lessons," but Thomas might question her if she omitted the tennis lessons. And she didn't want to do or say anything to convey her dislike of Mr. Penniman. Her attitudes were often adopted by the children. She didn't want that to occur in this instance, for she'd seen far too many children fail in their studies and activities due to misunderstanding or conflict with an instructor. Thomas enjoyed tennis, and she'd seen great improvement in his game, so she didn't want to undermine his progress in any way.

The boy lifted one hand from the bicycle handlebars and pushed his flat woolen cap back on his head. "Mr. Wesley likes you."

"Really? You think Mr. Wesley likes me?"

"Yep. I sure do." Thomas continued to steer his bike with only one hand.

Callie tried to hide her smile, but she couldn't deny the surge of pleasure that pulsed deep within. If the boy had said he thought Mr. Archie liked her, she wouldn't have been surprised. But Wes had never done anything to indicate he wanted more than her friendship. Why had the simple remark caused her heart to pound a new beat? She had promised herself she would never again become captivated by the charms of any man. Thomas was probably mistaken. He knew nothing of attraction between a man and woman.

"What makes you think so, Thomas?"

"He said so."

Callie tried to suppress the excitement bubbling in her chest. "Exactly what did he say?"

Confusion clouded the boy's eyes as he glanced at her. "He said he liked you."

"Oh." One word was all she could manage. While at least ten questions rested on the tip of her tongue, she knew better than to ask. Thomas already appeared perplexed by her question. If she inquired further, he might say something to Wesley — something that could prove embarrassing to both of them.

Besides, Wesley's remark had likely been no more than a simple comment. She pictured the golf instructor asking Thomas if he liked his tutor. Thomas would have replied that he liked her very much. In all probability, Wesley would have then said that he liked Callie, too. The remark had nothing to do with Wesley caring for her beyond a casual friendship. That's what she told herself. And the thought should have pleased her. She was, after all, a woman who didn't want a beau. How strange that disappointment should assail her rather than relief.

She pushed aside the thought as they wheeled to the small building near the tennis courts.

Archie stepped outside as they arrived and glanced at her bicycle. "So, the ankle has healed. I'm glad to see you'll be able to continue your tennis lessons today. I heard you went golfing last week." He grinned.

"Of course, golf doesn't take much strength."

She wanted to argue the point, but such a discussion would waste valuable time when Thomas should be playing tennis. Once Thomas took off toward the courts, Archie stepped closer. "I think if you'd let go of the past, you'd discover I'm worthy of your affections."

Startled by his remark, she frowned. "What do you know about my past, Mr. Penniman?" Had Archie been inquiring about her past? She tightened her hold on the tennis racket. Just when she thought the man might have changed, he did something else to create mistrust.

"I don't know anything specific, Callie, but I do know women."

She arched her brows. "Do you? And what does your vast knowledge tell you about me?"

He leaned against the doorframe and assumed a casual air. "You're a beautiful woman, so I believe you've had your share of suitors. Either one of those gentlemen broke your heart, or you're waiting for someone of a higher social class to take notice so that you can enjoy a privileged life. Personally, I believe some cad broke your heart and now you're afraid of men."

The truth of his bold statement annoyed her. "My reason for remaining single is none of your concern, Mr. Penniman."

"As I said before, if you'd let go of the past and trust your heart, you'd find me worthy of your affections."

When he took a step toward her, she lifted the tennis racket. "We've had this discussion one too many times, Mr. Penniman. I told you I would tolerate no further advances from you." She motioned toward the tennis court. "You have a student waiting."

Mrs. Bridgeport had insisted upon buying several new gowns for Callie before they'd departed Indianapolis. Callie had protested the purchases, but Mrs. Bridgeport had prevailed. Callie disliked the fancy parties and balls, but Mrs. Bridgeport counted it her moral obligation and duty to find a suitable man for Callie — whether she wanted a suitable man or not. For the Valentine's ball, Mrs. Bridgeport had selected a fabric the seamstress referred to as peony red. Mrs. Bridgeport declared the color pure perfection. Callie thought quite the opposite. It would be impossible to hide in the bright red confection. At least the older woman's attempts to arrange an escort had proved unsuccessful. For that, Callie was thankful.

Callie looked over her shoulder when Mrs. Bridgeport tapped on the door and entered. "Your dress looks lovely, dear." The older woman rubbed her forehead. "Of all days for sickness to overtake the household. I cannot believe both Lottie and Maude are ill." Mrs. Bridgeport rubbed her forehead. "Next it will be Daisy and Thomas."

Callie smiled at the woman's exaggeration.

Mrs. Bridgeport sighed. "I wonder if I could convince Lula or Jane to stay until we return from the ball."

"There's no need for either of them to remain. I'm more than happy to stay here and take care of Maude and Lottie as well as Thomas and Daisy. Lula and Jane aren't accustomed to caring for the children. It will be much easier for me to stay at home." Callie didn't add that it would also be much more to her liking. She would have been willing to care for an entire household of sick family members if it meant she didn't have to attend the Valentine's ball.

Mrs. Bridgeport clasped her hands together. "I am so disappointed. If only I could think of some other solution."

Callie shook her head with such zeal a hairpin dropped to the floor. "This is where

I am needed. Please don't worry yourself any further."

"Much as I dislike the idea of having you miss the ball, I suppose you're right. I must get dressed and there's not time to make any other arrangements." The older woman's shoulders drooped in defeat as she departed the room, but Callie sighed with relief. In no time, she'd changed out of the dress and hurried down the hallway to check on Lottie.

Once Mr. and Mrs. Bridgeport said their good-byes, Callie returned upstairs. By bedtime, Lottie was feeling much better, and after preparing the children for bed and listening to their prayers, Callie went to check on Maude.

She tapped lightly on the door and waited. "Maude, are you awake?"

"That you, Callie? Come on in."

Maude's voice sounded weak. Callie opened the door and stepped inside. Maude was lying down, her complexion as white as the bedsheet.

Callie studied the woman. "Lottie's feeling much better, so I was hoping you'd regained some strength, too." Callie saw a tray sitting atop the chest of drawers and went over to examine it. "You haven't touched your food. You'll not regain your strength if you don't eat."

Maude placed her palm across her stomach. "I don't think my stomach is ready for food just yet. Maybe tomorrow." She forced a smile. "I'm glad to know Lottie is feeling better. It gives me hope that I'm going to recover. For a while, I wasn't too sure. My insides hurt so bad I thought it would be easier to just go on and die."

Callie returned to Maude's beside. "I'm truly sorry you're so ill. I wonder if you and Lottie ate something that made you sick."

"Don't know what it would be. We didn't have anything other than what the rest of you had for lunch and supper yesterday." She hesitated a moment. "Aren't you supposed to be at the Valentine's ball tonight?"

Callie nodded. "Yes, and I have you and Lottie to thank for saving me another boring evening."

Maude shook her finger. "You need to quit talking like that, Callie. I know you don't like the parties and such, but Mrs. Bridgeport is trying to give you an opportunity to meet someone so that you'll have a good life. I don't want to insult you, but many young ladies your age have already married. The older you get, the fewer chances you'll have."

Callie knew Maude's comments weren't

intended to hurt her — and they didn't. She simply wished she could make others understand that she didn't believe marriage was her only option. Why did a woman need a husband in order to be accepted in society? None of this had seemed important when she'd been engaged to Matthew. But nowadays everyone appeared determined to save her from the possibility of spinsterhood — whether she wanted to be saved or not.

Maude grasped Callie's hand. "Surely you meet some nice fellows when you're out with Thomas and the girls."

Callie shuddered. "The one I was around today wouldn't be considered nice. I think I mentioned Mr. Penniman, the tennis instructor, to you before." She frowned and met Maude's gaze. "I believe he's the most disagreeable man I've ever encountered. He will not take no for an answer. I plan to speak with Mrs. Bridgeport tomorrow. If she can't find someone else to take Thomas to his lessons, I hope she will consider withdrawing him from future classes. I don't want to be around Mr. Penniman again."

Maude appeared lost in thought for a moment but then inhaled a deep breath. "You can't let a few bad apples spoil the barrel. There are lots of good men out there. You just need to find the right one. I think if you'd look around a little and open your heart, there would be many opportunities for someone with your beauty and intelligence."

"Thank you, Maude. That's very kind." For a moment, she considered telling the older woman about Wesley but changed her mind. She knew what would happen. If she dared to mention Wesley's attributes, Maude would assume far too much. Better to keep thoughts of the handsome golf instructor tucked in the back of her mind.

Mrs. Bridgeport had been sympathetic to her complaints regarding Mr. Penniman. She wanted to speak with Mr. Bridgeport and have the matter brought to the attention of Mr. Nusbaum or Mr. Crocker, but Callie had objected. She didn't want the man terminated, but she did want to avoid further contact with him. Because she feared Archie's behavior could prove to be a poor influence upon Thomas, his mother decided to offer him additional golf lessons.

Mrs. Bridgeport sat on the sofa and beamed at her son. "What do you think, Thomas? If Mr. Wesley has time for a daily lesson, would you object to giving up your tennis lessons for the remainder of the season?"

Thomas glanced back and forth between his mother and Callie. "Why? Did I do something wrong?"

Mrs. Bridgeport shook her head. "Not at all, but I believe the additional golf lessons will prove beneficial, and being on Bridal Veil provides an excellent opportunity."

The boy appeared confused, but he didn't question his mother's decision. "If you think it's best, I don't mind. I like Mr. Wes and he's a good instructor."

Mrs. Bridgeport sighed. "Then it's settled."

Once Thomas left the room, Callie shook her head. "Not quite."

"Whatever do you mean, Callie?"

"We don't know if Wesley has enough free time to offer Thomas lessons every day."

The older woman stood and gestured toward the door. "Then you should go and ask him."

"Now?" Callie arched her brows. She had planned to take the children to the beach.

"As my husband likes to say, 'There's no time like the present.' " She hesitated on her way to the other room. "I'll tell Maude to look after the children while you're gone."

Callie doubted Maude would be happy with that piece of news. The nanny had become accustomed to spending her afternoons with Jane and Lula. She didn't know how much help the woman actually provided, but she did enjoy their company and the tidbits they shared about their own lives. If Callie hurried, she could be back in half an hour.

She had almost reached the golf course when she considered the fact that Wes might be out on the golf course when she arrived. If so, there was no telling when he might return, and she certainly couldn't wait around all afternoon. Maude would be more than a little unhappy. If she couldn't speak to anyone, she'd have no choice but to leave a note — provided the caddie shack was unlocked.

Relief washed over when she wheeled her bike alongside the wooden structure. The door stood wide open. She strode inside and immediately spied an old gentleman cleaning his golf clubs. "I was hoping to speak to Mr. Townsend. Do you know where I might find him?"

The man looked at her from beneath bushy eyebrows. "You might try turning around."

She spun around to see Wes grinning from the doorway. "Were you looking for me, Callie?"

"I was. I mean, I am. I mean, yes, I need

to speak to you." A burst of heat flooded her cheeks. Why was she acting like a silly schoolgirl?

"Why don't you follow me outside, and we'll sit on the bench near the live oak? There's a nice breeze."

She followed him but didn't answer for fear she'd once again sound like a blathering fool. Using a towel he carried in his pocket to clean a ball or club when needed, he wiped the bench and waved his hand for her to be seated.

"What can I do for you? I didn't miss a lesson time, did I?"

His generous smile caused her heart to flutter. What was wrong with her? Her mouth turned dry, and she wondered if she could speak.

He narrowed his eyes. "Are you ill?"

"No." She croaked out the response and cleared her throat. "I-I've come to ask if you could possibly provide Thomas with golf lessons every afternoon instead of three days a week." She sighed. Finally she'd been able to respond as though she hadn't lost her senses.

"I thought he was taking tennis lessons three days a week and golf lessons on the alternate three days. I think he'll be too tired for both golf and tennis three afternoons each week, don't you?"

"Mrs. Bridgeport has discontinued his tennis lessons."

Wes rubbed his jaw. "I see. Any particular reason? Thomas said he'd been improving with his tennis."

"I'm not at liberty to discuss the reason." Mrs. Bridgeport hadn't given Callie specific orders not to tell, but it didn't seem proper to tell him the real reason.

"If you're willing to bring him at a different time on those extra three days, I could take him. We'd need to begin at three o'clock on those days, and we could stay right after lunch on the other three days — unless you want to switch and have them at three o'clock every day."

"No. The alternating time is fine. I'm . . . I mean, we're . . . I mean Thomas will be pleased to know you can work with him every day."

Wes chuckled. "And what about you?"

"Me?"

He nodded, a glint of mischief in his eyes. "Are you pleased, too?"

She stood and smiled at him. "Yes, I believe I am."

CHAPTER 17

When Callie had requested daily golf lessons for Thomas, Wes had been delighted. Ever since dancing with Callie at the masked ball, he'd hoped to find some way to become better acquainted with her before he revealed his identity. Not that he'd given her a false name or told untruths about himself, but he hadn't been forthcoming about the fact that he was a guest at the clubhouse and a member of a wealthy family. Right now, he and Callie treated each other as equals, and he wanted it to remain that way. If she discovered his background, she would likely shy away from him. Worse yet, she might believe his desire to spend time with her was for less than honorable reasons.

Unlike some of his friends, Wes disliked the social distinctions that came with wealth. He'd known far too many men who used their money and position to mislead young women. Should Callie ever believe such of him, she would never speak to him again. And he needed more time with her. She was unlike any woman he'd ever met. With Callie, he could be himself. If he wanted to talk about golf, or botany, or his future, or God, she listened. Of course, he hadn't discussed his family or his past. And he'd been careful to avoid asking questions about Callie's family or past, as well. When the proper opportunity arose, he would discuss those things with her, but right now he took pleasure in hearing about the Bridgeport children and her life in Indianapolis and whatever else she offered to share with him. Before he revealed the truth, he wanted to be certain they were on firm ground.

On the other hand, he worried she might discover his identity through a guest who knew him as the son of Howard and Blanche Townsend. For now, Wes counted himself fortunate that he and Callie had never encountered one another at the clubhouse. While the possibilities of that happening were endless, at least the Bridgeport and Townsend families had been scheduled at different seating times in the dining room. And since he'd taken the position of golf instructor, Wes had been able to avoid many of the social functions. That, in itself, was payment enough for his job as acting golf pro.

He strolled toward the caddie shack, his gaze fastened on the path. A smile formed the moment he caught sight of Callie and Thomas. Though he sensed there was always something that caused her to maintain a certain distance, she captured his interest like no other woman. On occasion, she would forget and drop all reserve. It was on those occasions that he could imagine spending his life with her. Over and over, he'd told himself he must temper his dreams of a future with Callie. Still, he hadn't forgotten her words when she'd requested additional lessons for Thomas. She'd told him she would be pleased to spend more time with him. Then again, her comment could have been an offhand courteous remark. Besides, once she knew of his past, she wouldn't want him. What woman desired a man who had proved himself a failure before he'd reached the age of thirty?

Callie parked her bicycle near the caddie shack and strode toward him. "A penny for your thoughts."

Had he not known better, he would have thought she'd somehow been able to read his mind. He chuckled and shook his head. "I wouldn't consider taking your hard-earned money to hear my thoughts."

"So you'll tell me for free?"

He wouldn't tell her exactly what he'd been thinking, but maybe he could use this opportunity to advantage. "I was wondering what attributes young women find desirable in a man."

She stared at him for a moment and then chuckled. "If you would have asked me to guess what you'd been considering, that particular thought would never have crossed my mind." She pushed a curl behind one ear. "I can't speak for other women, but I think the most important thing for a man or a woman is truthfulness. How else can you build trust in a relationship?"

Her answer hit him like a blow to the midsection. The response wasn't what he'd expected to hear. He was hiding the truth — but for all the right reasons. At least that's what he told himself. Would Callie find his reasons as altruistic?

"Look what I've got, Mr. Wes." Thomas climbed off his bike and extended the club toward Wes. "My father was over in Biscayne. He said that since I'm taking golf lessons every day, I should have a sand iron."

Wes turned to the boy, thankful for the interruption, for he didn't have a good answer to Callie's question.

"Have you been telling your father that you've been having a bit of trouble in the bunkers over the past week?"

Thomas bobbed his head.

"Well, I'm pleased he bought you a sand iron, but I'm hoping you'll avoid the bunkers as much as possible." Wes placed his arm across Thomas's shoulder. "You're going to be a fine golfer by the time you go off to boarding school. You need to get a little more loft to your ball at times, but so do I. We'll put that sand iron to work a little later. Right now, I'm going to help you and Miss Callie with your putting. Why don't you go inside and get your putter so we can begin?"

Thomas ran inside, and Callie stepped closer and smiled. "What about you, Wes? Do you think truthfulness builds trust in a relationship?"

He swallowed hard, wishing he'd never raised this topic. "I do think it is very important. I also believe that until you know someone quite well, it isn't necessary to divulge everything about your past."

Her smile faded, and she appeared to contemplate his remark. "I suppose that's true enough. Except with dear friends, I don't share all of my deep, dark secrets." She chuckled. "Still, if I wanted to develop a relationship with someone, I wouldn't lie."

He hesitated. "Well, no. Not an outright lie, but if a question isn't asked, there's no need for an answer, right?"

"It would depend upon the relationship and the importance of the information, I suppose." She tipped her head to the side. "For instance, if I had an interest in a man and he had an interest in me — and let's say this man had . . ." Callie hesitated.

Wes nodded. "Yes, go on."

Her shoulders stiffened. "And let's say this man had already pledged his love to another woman. Whether asked or not, don't you think he would have an obligation to reveal the truth? After all, it would impact both of the relationships."

"In that instance, I would definitely agree he should be forthright."

When Callie appeared to relax, Wes wondered if something similar might have happened in her past. Yet, with her charm, abilities, and beauty, what fool would ever turn loose of her?

"I'm ready." Thomas returned with his putter and headed for the links.

"Not out there, Thomas. There's a putting green down this way. We'll use that for practice right now."

After they'd arrived at the putting green,

Wes removed a putter from his bag and looked at Thomas. "Watch carefully. Once you have your grip, keep your eyes directly over the ball." He looked up. "You should align the ball with your nose, and you can decide if you want to stand straight or crouch over a little, but remember, your arms must swing freely."

Thomas assumed a position with his putter. "Like this?"

"That looks good. Now, when you get ready to stroke your putt, think about the pendulum in a clock." Wes straightened and relaxed his stance. He moved his arm in front of him, mimicking a pendulum. "Like that pendulum, you want to keep your swing absolutely straight."

Thomas nodded.

"Now, watch how I get ready and swing." Wes addressed the ball, swung, and the three of them watched the ball as it dropped into the hole.

Thomas cheered. "My turn. Right?"

Wes nodded and placed the ball in position. "Remember, you need to judge your speed. The grass is very short on this putting green so that means your ball will travel faster."

Thomas aligned his body, glanced at the cup, and swung. The ball rolled directly toward the cup, teetered on the edge, and finally dropped into the hole. Thomas looked at Wes and grinned.

"Excellent! Now let's see if Callie can do the same." Wes waved her forward and watched as she spread her feet apart and hunched forward. "You need to straighten a bit or your arms won't swing free." She nodded, straightened a bit, glanced at the hole, but then returned to her former position. "Wait, don't swing."

Callie relaxed and waited as he approached. "I can't seem to find the proper position. I prefer bending more."

Wes chuckled. "I noticed." He stepped behind her. "Don't be alarmed, but I'm going to stand behind you and hold you in the proper position."

A slight gasp escaped her lips when he placed his arms around her body and leaned forward to cover her hands.

"I hope you're not uncomfortable, but I think this will help." He hesitated a moment. "Keep your eye on the ball, but straighten your back and shoulders until you are leaning against me."

Although she held herself in a rigid line, she followed his instruction.

"You need to relax a little."

"I'm trying." Her voice was no more than

a whisper.

"I'm going to guide your arms in a straight line, and we'll hit the ball."

"I'll try."

"We'll do it together." Wes could feel her discomfort as he guided her arms through the swing, but she didn't pull away.

The ball stopped far short of the cup, but Thomas applauded. "You did good, Miss Callie."

She shook her head. "I'm afraid I didn't do all that well, Thomas."

The boy pointed to another hole. "Let Mr. Wes show you again. I'll practice over here."

"I think it's far more important you spend your time with Thomas. He's the one who truly needs to be well skilled when he goes off to boarding school." She lowered her voice. "I know he hopes to make the golf team."

"Thomas is doing quite well, and I am certain that by the time the season ends here on Bridal Veil, he'll be far superior to any of the boys his own age." Wes pushed his hat back on his head. "On the other hand, you need a lot more attention than young Thomas."

Her lips curved in a demure grin that set his heart racing. "Then I suppose I dare not refuse your assistance."

On several occasions, Callie warned herself to take care. She'd grown increasingly fond of Wes. Each night she told herself it was nothing more than friendship and a shared interest in Thomas and his golf lessons. But deep down, she couldn't deny that she enjoyed his company and looked forward to seeing him each day. If she let her thoughts wander, she could even imagine more — much more. But then she would recall Matthew and the pain she'd suffered. When that occurred, she could push aside any idea of a future with Wes. Or with any other man, for that matter.

During their lesson today, Thomas had invited Wes to join them on an outing after their golf lesson. The boy hadn't requested Callie's permission to invite Wes, so there was little she could do about the arrangement. She could hardly withdraw an invitation she hadn't extended. Besides, the two girls liked Wes, and whenever he was with them, they learned some new lesson about nature.

Wes walked beside her as they returned to the caddie shack after she and Thomas had completed their golf lessons. "Did you make plans to go anywhere special with the children today?"

"They mentioned the beach."

"What about heading toward the more forested area so they can see some of the wildlife? Do you think they might enjoy that for a change?"

His idea pleased her. The children had asked about going to look for deer and wild turkey, but maintaining oversight of all three children in the denseness of the wooded areas had proved difficult in the past.

Lula was sitting on the front porch with the girls when Thomas and Callie returned home. Callie glanced toward the screen door. "Where's Maude?"

"She was feeling poorly. Said she had a headache. I knew you'd be home soon, so I told her to go and rest."

"That was kind of you, Lula. Has Mrs. Bridgeport returned from her luncheon?"

The housekeeper gestured for Callie to sit down. Leaning close to Callie's ear, Lula maintained a watch on the front door. "She was all aflutter. Seems there's been some more of those robberies going on at the cottages. I told her she didn't need to worry none 'cause there's always someone here, but that didn't seem to set her mind at ease."

"Did she say who had been robbed?"

Lula shook her head. "She didn't offer to tell me and I didn't ask." Lula swatted at a fly that landed on her arm. "I got to agree that it does make a person nervous knowing there's a thief prowling around the island."

"I'm sure we have nothing to worry about, Lula, but if you see any strangers, you let Mr. Bridgeport know." Callie patted the housekeeper's hand. "And please don't mention this where the children can hear. Such talk might frighten them."

Lula tapped her finger against her lips. "Mum's the word where the little ones are concerned. You best be off. They're prancing around, eager to be on their way."

Wes was waiting between the two live oaks that bordered a path leading into the woods. From past experience, Callie knew the path ended soon after passing beneath the moss-covered branches of the trees.

They headed off, with Wes cautioning them to be as quiet as possible as he took the lead and Callie followed behind the three children. Along the way, he pointed out brown thrashers whirring through the trees, several buntings calling to one another, and a large red-headed woodpecker hammering its beak into a tall oak.

Wes waved the children forward. "Let's

see if we can find some interesting plants while we're out here."

Lottie immediately pointed to a small white flower. "That's a pretty flower."

Wes drew near and stooped down. "Ah, you've found an early bloomer. That's called bloodroot, and the flowers don't usually begin to bloom until March. See how the thick veiny leaves protect it? And look here on the ground. Just below the surface you can see the roots where it stores a red sap."

"I see them," Daisy shouted. "Can we dig 'em up and squeeze out the red stuff?"

Wes chuckled. "No. Let's leave them in the ground and see if we can find some other plants." He pointed to an area not far off. "Soon those green plants will have pretty purple blooms on them. They're called purple coneflowers, and sometimes doctors use a medicine made from them to help tummy aches."

Daisy giggled and patted her stomach. "What are these?" She pointed to a spot beneath a tree.

Wes grinned and ruffled her hair. "I think those are called weeds."

Callie settled on a low-hanging limb of a huge live oak tree and watched the children as they continued looking for plants and birds in the nearby clearing. The dank, musty smell of the woods surrounded them, and she inhaled a deep breath.

Wes stepped toward her and motioned toward the thick branch. "Mind if I join you?"

"No, not at all." She patted the solid branch. "You certainly know your birds and plants. I'm impressed."

"Thank you, but when something is fascinating, I want to learn all I can." He sat down on the limb while keeping his gaze trained on the children. "There's something I've been wondering about ever since we talked earlier today."

"What's that?"

She attempted to recall what all they'd talked about, but the only thing she could remember with clarity was the rush of excitement she'd felt when he put his arms around her during the putting lesson.

"You said that if a man had already pledged his love to a woman, and then became enamored with another woman, he should reveal that information." He frowned. "Or something along that line, right?" He arched his brows, obviously seeking confirmation.

"Yes, something like that." She clasped her hands in her lap. "Are you preparing to tell me that you are pledged to marry someone, Wes?" Her breathing turned shallow as she waited for his reply.

"No. There's no woman in my life. But I wondered if you'd experienced what you spoke of earlier today? Did a man betray you?"

She bit back the tears that threatened. To cry would have him think she remained in love with Matthew — and that wasn't the truth. Her love for him had vanished, and in its place mistrust had taken root.

There was no reason to hide the truth from Wesley. She didn't dwell on the intricacies of her heartbreak. Instead, she gave him the simple statement she'd learned to repeat. "I was engaged once, but my fiancé ran off with another woman. Unfortunately, all of the wedding plans had been completed before he decided he no longer loved me." She forced a smile. "I'm not the first woman to endure such pain, and I won't be the last."

Wes shook his head. "The man was a fool."

She toyed with the lace corner of her handkerchief. "I appreciate your kind words, but I've learned that men cannot be trusted. They declare their love and propose marriage, and still they prowl about looking for someone better. If nothing else, I have learned that men are liars."

"I hope that you haven't included me in that sweeping statement."

She hadn't given proper thought to her words before she blurted out her thoughts. Just when she thought she was beginning to get over Matthew, her anger took hold again. "Do forgive me. I wasn't including you. You're not a man. . . . Well . . . you are a man, but . . . you're different."

"It's true I am a man, but in what way am I different?"

"You aren't overbearing, trying to steal kisses, and so forth." She shivered as she recalled Archie's unseemly behavior.

He chuckled. "That doesn't mean the thought hasn't crossed my mind from time to time." After pushing up from the tree limb, he turned and stood in front of her. "You are a beautiful woman, Callie. I don't know any man who wouldn't enjoy stealing a kiss from you." He extended his hand. "Come along. We should see if the children would like to try to locate a few deer before we return." When she didn't reach for his hand, he smiled at her. "I promise I won't try to steal a kiss."

She grasped his hand, and as the warmth of his fingers clasped hers, she wondered what it would be like to kiss him. The truth was, Wes wouldn't need to steal a kiss. She'd give him one if he only asked.

CHAPTER 18

There hadn't been time to linger over thoughts of kissing Wes, for as soon as he'd taken hold of her hand, thunder rumbled overhead and the skies darkened. "I need to get the children back home before it begins to rain." She attempted to pull away from Wes, but he held tight to her hand.

"They're children. A little rain won't hurt them. I agree we need to return, but they won't melt."

She shook her head and pulled him forward. "You don't understand. Lottie has been suffering with a perpetual cough ever since we arrived, and being in the rain will only make it worse."

"Has a doctor ever suggested she might have asthma?"

Callie stopped and stared at him. "I don't believe so — at least not that I've been told. Mrs. Bridgeport has always referred to it as a chronic cough. Why do you suggest asthma?"

"I've known people who suffer from asthma. Has she been worse since arriving at Bridal Veil?"

"Yes. She always seems to suffer more when we're here during the winter."

Wes matched her stride as they walked toward the children. "The dampness along the coast, coupled with the heat and humidity in this part of the country, can prove difficult for those with asthma. Their breathing can become even more impaired when the humidity levels increase for long stretches of time."

He knelt down beside Lottie and placed his palm on her back. Callie stood nearby as he leaned close to the child. Twisting around, he looked up at Callie. "I can hear her wheezing, which makes me think this is more than a chronic cough. Is she ever like this when you're at home?"

"Yes, but she's usually somewhat better during cold weather. From what Mrs. Bridgeport has told me, Lottie has had various lung problems since she was a very young child. Asthma does make sense." Callie frowned. "I wonder why the doctors have never considered that possibility."

"Who can say? Maybe Lottie's doctors have never treated anyone with asthma, so the possibility didn't occur to them, or maybe they think she's too young to have it. Perhaps Mrs. Bridgeport should mention it to Lottie's doctor when you return to Indiana." Another round of thunder clapped overhead. "I suppose we'd better hurry." He pointed to his shoulders. "Lottie, we're going to be walking fast, and since you're having trouble breathing, why don't you wrap your arms around my neck and I'll give you a piggyback ride."

Daisy curled her lip in a pout. "What about me? Do I have to walk?"

Wes grinned at Daisy. "I'll carry you next time. How's that?"

"You promise you won't forget?"

"I promise. And since I won't be able to walk quite as fast while I'm carrying your sister, let's have Miss Callie tie my handkerchief to a long stick, and you can wave it overhead like a flag. That way, we won't get separated or lost."

Daisy immediately agreed and could barely contain her excitement as she marched ahead of them waving her small flag.

Callie walked alongside Wes as they headed out of the woods. "Have you always been good with children?"

"I don't know if I'm good with them, but

I very much enjoy their innocence and natural curiosity. Of course, there are some who would tell you that I haven't yet accepted being an adult — perhaps that's why I enjoy being with children so much."

There was an ache in his laughter that caused Callie to look at him. His eyes appeared clouded with pain.

"And who would tell you such a thing?" Callie wasn't certain she should ask, but she'd told him a little of her past. Maybe he hoped she would question him.

"My family — mostly my father and brothers, who want me to quit doing things like playing golf. My mother and sister are intent on seeing me married. I don't think they care if I love the woman, just so long as I have a wife." He bounced Lottie a little higher onto his back. "I don't think they care if I'm happy. They just want me to conform to what they think is best."

"I understand." Callie lowered her voice so Lottie couldn't hear. "Mrs. Bridgeport is determined to find me a suitable husband, even though I don't want one."

"Ever?" He arched his eyebrows.

"That's how I feel at the moment." She gave him a sideways glance. "Of course, one can never say what will happen in the future, but I don't ever again want to experience the pain I went through after Matthew."

"But not everyone is like Matthew. It doesn't seem fair to tar all of us with the same brush."

"Perhaps not, but it will take something akin to a miracle to change my mind."

He grinned. "Well, it's good to know there's at least some possibility."

His words caused an unexpected thrill. He was truly a kind man, good with children, slow to anger, and extremely patient. In some ways she thought he might be too perfect. How could a man who possessed such rakish good looks and so many fine qualities still be single? Yet, here he was in the midst of her life. If she was going to protect her heart, she'd need to remain vigilant.

They continued on, but when they neared the house, Wes stopped and lowered Lottie to the ground. "I'm going to head over to the golf course." He stooped down in front of Lottie. "You feeling some better?" She nodded her head. Once again, he held his head close as the child breathed. "Don't forget to mention the asthma to her mother. She's still wheezing."

"Don't you want to come inside and meet Mrs. Bridgeport? I'm sure she'd be interested in hearing this medical information from you."

Wes waved toward the road. "You can tell her. I need to take care of some things at the links."

Callie watched him head off. How odd. What did he hope to accomplish with a storm moving in? As lightning cracked overhead, she hurried the children along the path and up the front porch steps. They'd barely entered the front door when fat raindrops began to splat on the walkway. Booms of thunder pounded overhead, and soon rain poured from the sky in thick sheets. She walked the children upstairs and wondered if Wes had found refuge before the storm hit.

Mrs. Bridgeport stepped to the doorway of her bedroom as they reached the top of the stairs. "I'm glad to see you and the children have returned, Callie. I was beginning to worry you'd be caught in the storm." She sighed. "Unfortunately, it seems to be raining everywhere." She motioned for Callie to follow her and spoke to the children. "Why don't the three of you go to your playroom, and Miss Callie will join you soon. I need to talk to her for a moment."

The children continued down the hallway,

and Callie followed the older woman into the sitting room that adjoined the bedroom. Mrs. Bridgeport sat down in one of the brocade-covered chairs.

Mrs. Bridgeport's features were pinched with worry when she looked at Callie. "A letter arrived from Gertrude today."

The fact that the housekeeper in Indianapolis had taken time to write a letter could only mean one thing — a problem. Gertrude made no secret of the fact that she didn't like to write letters. The last time she'd written had been two or three years ago when the gardener had injured himself while shoveling snow. Since Gertrude had been required to shovel the snow during the gardener's period of incapacitation, she had written to inquire if he was due any wages. And that couldn't have truly been considered a letter. The few lines had been scribbled on the back of a grocery list.

"She says the *Indianapolis News* has reported everything from tornados and floods to fires stretching from Nebraska to Illinois. They say storms and flooding are expected to move through Indiana." Mrs. Bridgeport thrust the letter toward Callie. "I simply can't bear to think what will happen if the White River and Fall Creek overflow their banks."

Callie quickly scanned the scrawled handwriting. "I don't think we should become overwrought. She doesn't say that it has even begun to rain in Indianapolis. The weather is fickle, and storms change course all the time."

"Perhaps, but it doesn't sound good. Luther has gone to Biscayne to wire the servants and have them secure the house. He's also wiring one of his business partners so that he can get additional solid news." She sniffled as she withdrew her handkerchief. "And to make certain he'll keep watch on the house. Dear me, I can't bear the thought of floodwaters ruining all our belongings."

"Is Mr. Bridgeport troubled by the letter, as well?"

Mrs. Bridgeport touched the handkerchief to her eyes. "He didn't take it so seriously at first when the letter arrived this morning, but he mentioned it to Mr. Wainwright, who said he'd heard reports there was already some flooding in parts of Indiana."

Callie didn't want to press the subject and further distress Mrs. Bridgeport, but the home she'd inherited from her grandmother was located further north and east of the Bridgeport home — an area that could be flooded should the storms hit.

"If Mr. Bridgeport is worried enough to take precautions, I wonder if I should try to have Grandmother's house secured."

"I'm sorry, dear, I should have mentioned that Luther is going to have the servants go and see to your grandmother's home, as well. I was sure you'd want to do whatever you could to protect it. After all, it's all you have left."

Callie withheld a smile. If she lost her grandmother's home, she wouldn't consider herself a pitiable vagabond. She hadn't lived in the house for years, and if she decided to go to Africa or Chicago, she planned to sell it. Good investment or not, she didn't want to deal with the problems of home owner-ship when she no longer lived in Indianapo-lis. Money from the sale would cover ex-penses required to establish her in whatever new life she decided upon. If the home flooded, any insurance money she received would be far less than a sale would provide. But unlike Mrs. Bridgeport, Callie didn't consider her grandmother's home the only thing she had left. Should she lose the house, she still had her parents. They may be living in Africa, but she knew they loved her. In addition, her faith remained intact, though admittedly somewhat shaky since the breakup with Matthew.

But family and faith weren't what the Bridgeports counted when they listed their assets — or anyone else's, for that matter. They were both wonderful people, but Callie had watched possessions become far too important in their lives. The same thing had happened to her parents years ago — before they decided to give up everything and go to the mission field. She doubted that would ever happen to the Bridgeports, but who could say? No one had ever imagined that her parents would sell their belongings and go off to spread the gospel, either.

Two days later Callie was going over lessons with the children when Maude came upstairs. "The missus wants you downstairs. She says I can stay with the children. There's men down there that want to ask some questions."

"Questions about what? Do you know who they are?" Callie pushed up from her chair and walked toward the doorway.

"Something to do with the stealing that's been going on. I think they might be some kind of special police that's been hired." Maude wrinkled her nose. "They spoke to me for a minute, but the missus told 'em I'm always here at the house and my time can be accounted for."

"Goodness! Do they think one of us had something to do with all of this?"

Maude shrugged. "Who can say? They probably figure they've got to do something to earn the money they're being paid, so they're going cottage to cottage asking their questions."

"You're probably right." She hurried down the hallway and descended the steps. Mrs. Bridgeport and two strangers sat in the front parlor.

"Do come in, Callie. These gentlemen want to speak with you. They are investigators who are attempting to apprehend whoever is responsible for the thefts taking place on the island."

A rotund bald man and his lanky partner sat on the couch. Neither one of them stood or even smiled when Mrs. Bridgeport introduced Callie. They waved for her to sit down.

"I'm Fitch and this is Jensen." The rotund man pointed to himself and then at Mr. Jensen.

"Pleased to meet you." Callie sat down beside Mrs. Bridgeport. "How can I help?"

"We've been speaking to owners of the cottages and some of the folks who live in the clubhouse, as well. There's something strange that's come to our attention, and we thought we needed to visit with everyone who lives in this house."

Mrs. Bridgeport straightened her shoulders and glared at Mr. Fitch. "What do you mean, something strange?"

Mr. Jensen leaned forward, his spindly torso extending toward them like a snake preparing to strike. "In talking with the owners of the other cottages, we've discovered that most of them have been entered and robbed, yet nothing has happened here at your house." He craned his neck toward them. "Am I correct?"

"Yes, I mean, I really don't know. I do know we haven't been robbed, but I didn't realize thefts had occurred at most of the other cottages." Mrs. Bridgeport frowned. "Exactly what are you intimating, Mr. Fritz?"

"Fitch. And I'm not suggesting anything, Mrs. Bridgeport. I'm just stating a fact. But it does seem odd that your house would be overlooked." He glanced around the room. "From the looks of things, this house would interest a thief, don't you think?"

"I have no idea how a thief thinks, but I do not like your attitude, sir."

Mrs. Bridgeport's haughty tone didn't seem to bother Mr. Fitch in the least. He merely shrugged and looked at Callie.

"What about you, Miss Deboyer? Any idea why a thief wouldn't enter this house?"

"Probably because Mrs. Bridgeport's jewels are kept in a safe and because the family has live-in servants. There is someone in the house all of the time."

Mrs. Bridgeport nodded. "I am extremely careful to place my jewels in the safe — unless I'm wearing them, of course. I know many of the families who own cottages have never installed safes because we've had little reason to worry about thieves. Have you discovered that it is only the homes without safes that have been robbed?"

The detective shook his head. "We don't give out information regarding our investigation, Mrs. Bridgeport. Word travels too quickly and can spoil our leads. I'm sure you understand."

Mrs. Bridgeport squared her shoulders and raised her head higher. "I am not a gossip, Detective. I was merely curious if you'd considered the possibility."

"We have, and thank you. Now, you say you have servants in the house at all times. Is that right?"

"Yes, what Callie has told you is correct. Many of the other owners don't employ live-in servants. They either use servants hired by Mr. Crocker — he's the superintendent of Bridal Veil —"

"I know who he is," Mr. Fitch said.

"Or they hire part-time staff that live in Biscayne and travel back and forth." Mrs. Bridgeport turned searing eyes upon Mr. Fitch. "I might add that I do not appreciate being interrupted when I am answering your questions. We are under no obligation to speak to either of you, and if you intend to be rude, I will ask you to come back when my husband is present."

Mr. Fitch leaned back, and Mr. Jensen scooted to the edge of the couch. "Please excuse him, Mrs. Bridgeport. We're used to dealing with hardened criminals and sometimes forget our manners."

"Your apology is accepted. Now, what else do you wish to know?"

Mr. Jensen stretched his lanky legs in front of him. "We've spoken to the other servants alone." He glanced at Mrs. Bridgeport. "Would you mind if we spoke to Miss Deboyer? Privately?"

"Callie isn't a servant; she's our children's tutor and considered a member of this family." The older woman reached for Callie's hand. "Do you want me to remain while they talk to you?"

"It's not necessary." Callie looked at the

investigator. "But there's nothing I have to say to you that I wouldn't say in front of Mrs. Bridgeport."

"I understand, but we think most people are more comfortable without others around when we're asking questions." He looked at Mrs. Bridgeport. "So, if you don't mind, ma'am?"

From the look on the older woman's face, Callie knew Mrs. Bridgeport did mind, but she departed without further comment.

Mr. Jensen waited until he was certain Mrs. Bridgeport was out of earshot. "Could you tell me a little more about your role in the family? I know she said you're the tutor and they consider you one of them, but I'm sure it's not really like you're one of *them* in every sense."

Callie explained her duties and assured the man that the Bridgeports treated her quite well. "I couldn't have asked for more caring people when my grandmother died."

"That's nice. But before you came downstairs, Mrs. Bridgeport mentioned you'd come from a wealthy family. Have you found it hard to work for her? I mean I think it would be tough to grow up in a place like this and then have the tables turned."

Mr. Fitch agreed. "Yeah, one minute you're part of a family that's invited to fancy balls and the next minute you're on the outside looking in." He nodded toward the doorway. "Helping someone like Mrs. Bridgeport and teaching her kids can't be what you expected from life, right?"

Callie stared at the man. Was he implying she might somehow be involved in the robberies? "I don't know if anyone can anticipate what the future holds, Mr. Jensen, but I am quite content tutoring the Bridgeport children."

"And what kind of social life do you enjoy, Miss Deboyer? I know some of the servants frequent the horse races during their time off work, and we understand there's gambling among the servants at their card games. What about you? Do you enjoy gambling?"

Callie tried to suppress the anger rising in her chest. "I do not gamble, I do not attend the horse races, and I had nothing to do with any of these robberies. If I wanted to accumulate wealth, I wouldn't gamble or steal to attain such a goal. I am offended by your questions."

"Right." Mr. Fitch twisted his thin mustache between his finger and thumb. "With your good looks, I'm sure you could convince one of these wealthy fellows to marry you."

Callie folded her arms across her chest. "I am not interested in marriage or any of the wealthy men on this island."

"That's strange, because Mr. Jensen was told you've been seen keeping company with one of them." Mr. Fitch glanced at his partner. "Isn't that right, Jensen?"

The man bobbed his head. "Yep. That's what I was told." He narrowed his eyes. "You want to change that story you just told us?"

Callie hesitated. "The only man I've been with is the golf pro. He teaches Thomas and me golf, and he's accompanied the children and me on outings to the beach and forests. He has a vast knowledge of botany and has been helping me to teach the children about the wildlife as well as —"

"And his name is?"

"Wes, Wesley. As I said, he works at the golf course."

Mr. Fitch gave his partner a sideways glance and they both stood. "You don't want to change anything you've told us before we leave?"

Callie shook her head. "No. Nothing."

"And everything you've told us is the truth?" Jensen leaned closer.

Uneasiness assailed her. She'd told the truth, so why did these men make her feel as though she'd been lying?

Standing, Callie gave the men a dismissive nod. "I'm sorry, gentlemen, but I know nothing that will aid you in your search. I'm afraid you'll have to find the thief on your own."

CHAPTER 19

Wes strode down the stairs of the main clubhouse and quickly surveyed the dining room. When he'd returned to the clubhouse last evening, he'd discovered a note from his father beneath the door to his room. The message was brief. "Join me for breakfast at seven o'clock tomorrow morning in the main dining room." His father hadn't signed the note, a fact that wasn't lost on Wes. This was a command, not an invitation.

At least his father had scheduled the breakfast meeting early enough that it wouldn't interfere with his schedule at the links. However, the fact that his father wanted to meet with him had been enough to set Wes's thoughts racing. He truly did not want to begin his day with an argument.

He hoped this would only be a reprimand for his failure to connect with the family. Since taking over as golf pro, he'd been able to avoid eating in the dining room and had successfully circumvented any matchmaking plans. A fact that no doubt annoyed both of his parents.

As soon as he entered the dining room, he spotted his father. After weaving through the mostly empty tables, he pulled out a chair and sat down. "Good morning, Father. You're looking well."

His father snorted. "It's been so long since we've seen you, I could be dead and buried and you'd be none the wiser."

Hoping to relieve the tension, Wes chuckled. "I think Mother would have sent word had there been such a tragedy."

"Speaking of your mother, she's been worried about you. The least you could do is manage to eat a meal with us once a day."

Wes removed his linen napkin from the table, shook out the folds, and placed it across his lap. "I can't leave for the noonday meal, and by the time I get done in the evening, there's not enough time to clean up and properly dress for the dining room."

"So where do you eat?"

"There's a dining room for the employees not far from the links. I usually go there. The food is good, and I can get in and out quickly and don't have to worry about my attire." Wes took a sip of his coffee. "Is that why you wanted to meet? To set Mother's mind at ease about my eating habits?"

"Of course not. I told your mother you wouldn't starve to death." His father leaned back in his chair as the waiter placed breakfast in front of them. "I took the liberty of ordering for you since you're always in such a hurry. I hope it meets with your approval."

"Bacon, eggs, toast, and fruit — how could anyone complain about such a feast?"

While his father uttered a brief prayer of thanks for the food, Wes bowed his head and silently prayed the remainder of their conversation would go well.

His father slathered a piece of toast with strawberry jam. "Here's the thing, Wes. I've met a fellow who's very interested in making some new investments. We've talked at length. However, he isn't completely convinced he'll reap the most benefit from investing in the woolen and cotton mills."

"I'm sorry to hear that." Wes took another a bite of his scrambled eggs.

His father narrowed his eyes. "You can help."

Wes's stomach tightened around the scrambled eggs. Instinctively he knew he didn't want to hear anything more. He longed to jump up from the table and depart, but that wouldn't solve anything.

"How is that, Father?"

His father leaned closer and lowered his voice. "This investor has a daughter."

Wes inhaled slowly and shook his head.

His father jutted his chin and glared at him. "Hear me out, Wesley."

Wes pushed his plate away, his appetite now ruined by his father's announcement. "I'll listen but don't expect me to agree to whatever you and Mother have contrived for me."

"She is a lovely young woman. Perhaps not the beauty you would choose, and she may not be particularly bright, but she comes from an excellent family and very much wants to marry and have children."

Wes stared at his father. "If you were hoping to entice me with your description, you failed. Really, Father. From what you said, I can only guess that this poor young lady is as homely as the day is long and that she doesn't have the sense to come in out of the rain." He shook his head. "Even so, I believe you expect me to say cheerfully that I can scarcely wait to meet this ugly duckling who hasn't a brain in her head."

With a clang, his father dropped his fork on his plate. "That is a gross exaggeration of what I told you. It would be helpful if you'd show some loyalty."

Wes arched his brows. "For me, being loyal does not mean that I am willing to marry a woman I do not love in order to further the expansion of Townsend Mills."

"Love can come after marriage as well as before. Do you think every man who takes a wife is smitten by love before he takes his vows?"

The scoffing tone of his father's words pained Wesley. "You didn't love Mother when you married her?"

"I didn't say any such thing. This conversation isn't about me and your mother. It is about you making a proper choice."

Thus far his father had been successful in his efforts to see their children marry and enter the family business. Wes remained the only holdout. Since his mother hadn't joined them for breakfast, he could only hope she was opposed to his father's choice. He would like to count his mother an ally, but even if she stood with his father, Wes would not agree to such a sham.

"I don't —"

His father held up his hand. "The Dundreys have agreed to join us for dinner on Saturday evening. There is more than enough time for you to tell Mr. Nusbaum you need to leave the golf course early. And if you don't do so, I will." Lifting his coffee cup to his lips, his father eyed him over the rim. "Have I made myself clear?"

Wesley nodded. "Very clear. I know your expectations, and I believe you know mine." He pushed away from the table and stood. "Now, if you'll excuse me, I don't want to be late."

No matter how many times his father said he would give Wes time to make a decision, the older man continued to steam forward and push his own agenda.

His father looked up with a satisfied smile on his lips. "Then we can count on you for Saturday night?"

"I didn't say that, Father. I said I understood your expectations." Without waiting, Wes strode from the room.

Even with family, his father used every advantage. The older man had known Wes wouldn't create a scene in public. That's why he'd ordered Wes to meet him for breakfast instead of stopping by his room. No doubt there would be a message from his mother when he returned to his room this evening. She would meet with him privately and issue a tearful plea. In addition to taking his meals in the servants' dining room, maybe he should inquire about sleeping quarters, as well.

Jumbled thoughts crossed his mind as he

walked to the golf course. He was nearing the links when he was struck by what he must do. He must speak to Callie — tell her the truth about himself. Be open and honest and ask if she could ever consider him as more than a friend. If she declined, it wouldn't change his decision to refuse a marriage of convenience, but he could honestly tell his parents he cared for another woman and planned to do everything in his power to win her heart. Of course, if she accepted, they would need to consider the future. If Callie decided to go to Africa, could he accept such a decision and go with her? Or would she be willing to change her plans and support his idea of using his medical education to do research? There would be much to consider — for both of them.

Still, the realization freed him from the heavy weight that had settled on his chest. As soon as he entered the caddie shack, he checked the day's schedule. Nothing had been penciled in for him following his lesson with Thomas and Callie.

Wes waited near the live oaks leading into the forested area where he and Callie had agreed to meet. She'd been preoccupied during the golf lesson earlier in the afternoon, but when he suggested they meet and take the children to the woods later in the afternoon, she'd readily agreed. When he saw the foursome approaching, his chest tightened. He hoped he could find the right words to express himself. On his way to meet her, he'd prayed that she wouldn't be angry that he hadn't already revealed his identity and the truth of his past. His concern mounted as she drew near.

"I hope you're hungry. The children insisted on a picnic, even though we've already eaten lunch."

He smiled. "I'm always ready for an extra meal or two." Nodding toward the basket, he extended his hand. "I'll carry that for you."

She handed him the basket while the three children ran ahead of them. Callie cupped her hands to her mouth. "Not too far. I want to be able to see all three of you."

The children slowed their steps but continued through the trees, with Thomas taking the lead. Wes glanced at her. "You appear worried. The children are within sight."

"I am worried. Not regarding the whereabouts of the children, but so much that's happened in the past weeks — and none of it good."

Wes arched his brows. "This is supposed

to be a winter retreat away from cares and worries. What has happened that's so terrible?"

"Have you heard about the jewelry thefts taking place on the island?"

He nodded. "I've heard a little about it. Why do you ask?"

"There are detectives questioning various employees about the robberies. Recently, they came to Fair Haven. There were two detectives who questioned me at length. They said it was strange that Fair Haven hadn't been robbed while most of the other cottages suffered some sort of theft. It made me feel as though they were pointing a finger at one of us."

"That's terrible. I didn't know there were detectives investigating."

"So they haven't talked to you?"

"No." Wes glanced at her. "Why should they?"

She shrugged. "I don't know, but they said they had heard I'd been keeping company with a man. I said the only man I'd been with was you. They appeared to know who you were."

"That's strange. I haven't talked to them, and none of the caddies has mentioned a visit from any detectives."

Callie tucked a curl behind her ear. "Wesley isn't a particularly common name. Mr. Crocker probably furnished them with a list of the workers, and I suppose they recalled your name."

"You're probably right. Since they know I'm at the golf course most of my time, they shouldn't have much trouble finding me if they want to talk."

From what she'd said, the detectives hadn't mentioned if they knew he was a Townsend or that the family was staying at the clubhouse. And before they did, he needed to tell Callie the truth about himself. He was still considering the detectives and their behavior when Callie touched his arm.

"The other reason I'm worried is because Mr. Bridgeport has received word of flooding in Indianapolis." She brushed aside a low-hanging branch. "There have been terrible storms in the states adjoining Indiana. We had hoped they might subside before reaching Indianapolis, but that hasn't happened. Mr. Bridgeport received news today that the levees are sure to break, and disastrous flooding is expected to occur."

"I'm so sorry to hear this, Callie. Do the Bridgeports fear their home will be damaged should the rains continue?"

"It's difficult to know. Indianapolis isn't well protected against flooding, but their home is further away from the river." She sighed. "My grandmother left me a small house, and I'm sure it will be destroyed. It is situated fairly close to Fall Creek, where it will surely be inundated by the floodwaters."

"I'm so sorry, Callie. I wish I could say or do something that would help."

"Thank you, Wes, but there's truly nothing that anyone can do. If the house is lost, I'll be sad because it belonged to my grandmother and I shared happy times in the house with her."

"Had you planned to live there someday?"

She gave him a wistful smile that tugged at his heart.

"I don't know. My plans for the future are uncertain. I've been considering several ideas. I've thought about returning to teach in Chicago or possibly joining my parents in Africa."

"I know."

"You know? How is that possible?"

"I believe you told me." His mind raced and fear clutched his throat in a tight grip.

She shook her head. "I don't believe so."

"Then maybe it was Thomas. I heard someone mention Africa." He hoped she wouldn't question him further, because he suddenly remembered that it was while he'd been dancing with her at the clubhouse during the masked ball that she had mentioned Africa.

"No, the children don't know I've given thought to going. I didn't want them to worry I might leave."

He didn't miss the quizzical look in her eyes as she shook her head.

"Miss Callie! Mr. Wes! Come quick!" Thomas was standing near Daisy, waving his arms.

Wes placed the basket on the ground and both of them rushed toward the children. Wes arrived a few paces before Callie and stooped down in front of Daisy. She was holding her hand on her leg and crying.

"What's wrong, Daisy?" Using the pad of his thumb, Wes wiped a tear from her cheek. "Did you scratch your leg?"

"No." She shook her head. "I know I wasn't supposed to take off my stockings, but I was hot." She looked up at Callie. "I sat down on the branch, and while I was rolling them up, a spider bit me."

"Would you let me see?" Wes gently lifted her hand from her leg. The area had turned red and begun to swell. "Did you see the spider?"

Her lip quivered. "I tried to smack it, but it bit me before I could kill it."

Callie stooped down alongside Wes and Daisy. "Can you tell me what color it was?"

"Dark brown or black." Daisy's lips curled into a pout. "I don't like spiders."

Wes smiled. "I'm not very fond of them myself. And since this spider decided to nibble on your leg, I think we should take you to the infirmary and have the doctor look at the bite and see what he thinks."

Callie motioned Wes away from the children. "Do you think this could be dangerous?"

"I'm not familiar with all the spiders that might be on this island, but I know there may be a few that are poisonous. I think the doctor will be better able to look at the bite and treat her."

Fear scaled Wes's spine as he watched the rapid swelling of the bitten area. Had he been able to look at the bite and offer a genuine medical opinion, Wes would have told Callie. But even with his knowledge of botany and a medical degree, he couldn't be certain about this spider bite or the best way to treat Daisy. He had no instruments or medicine, so a local doctor, familiar with common insects in the area, would be Daisy's best chance. And if his instincts were correct, she'd need all the help she could get.

Wes lifted the child into his arms and hurried down the path toward the infirmary. Callie sent Thomas home to tell his parents what had happened.

"What about our picnic?" Daisy's voice was no more than a whimper.

"We'll have our picnic another day. Right now, it's more important we see to your leg." He didn't like her pallor or the sheen of perspiration that had spread across her face. "Daisy?"

"Huh?"

"Just keep talking to me, honey. Just keep talking."

CHAPTER 20

They hadn't been at the infirmary for long when Mr. and Mrs. Bridgeport rushed inside, their features pinched with fear.

Mrs. Bridgeport clasped Callie's arm. "Where is she?"

"In the other room with the doctor." Callie glanced toward the doorway. "He asked us to wait here."

Mr. Bridgeport motioned to his wife. "You go on in, Eunice." He turned his attention back to Callie. "Exactly what happened, Callie? We have always trusted you with the children, but when Thomas came to fetch us, he said they were playing in the woods and that she was bit by some animal." He shifted his gaze toward Wesley and frowned.

Thomas shook his head. "That's not what I said, Dad. I told you —"

Mr. Bridgeport waved the boy to silence. "I want to know what happened to Daisy."

"We took the children to the woods, where

Wes has been teaching them about the different plants and trees. He knows a great deal about —"

"I don't care what he knows about plants and trees, Callie. Tell me about Daisy."

A tear rolled down Callie's cheek, and Wes touched her arm. "If you don't mind, Mr. Bridgeport, I'll explain. Callie is very concerned about Daisy — as am I, but it may be easier . . ."

Mr. Bridgeport waved his hand in a circular motion. "Go on, go on."

With as much speed and clarity as he could muster, Wes told Mr. Bridgeport what had occurred, Daisy's description of the spider, and his decision to bring her to the infirmary.

"Thank you for the explanation. I'm sorry to be so abrupt. But . . ." The older man peered toward the other room.

"I understand you're worried about your child. No apology is needed, sir." Wesley remained beside Callie. "I'm sure the doctor wouldn't mind if you went in. He'll understand your concern."

While Mr. Bridgeport strode into the treatment room, Callie, Wes, Lottie, and Thomas sat down in the waiting area. Thomas leaned forward on his chair. "I told my dad that it was a spider bite, Miss Callie, but he was so busy shouting at my mother to hurry that he didn't listen."

"It's fine, Thomas. Don't worry. I know everyone is worried and upset. You did exactly what I told you. Your parents are here to make any necessary decisions about Daisy's care, and that's what's most important."

His thatch of brown hair fell across his forehead. "Yeah, but Dad sounded like he was mad at you."

Callie reached across Lottie and patted his arm. "Instead of worrying about your father being angry, I think we should all pray for Daisy."

"You think Jesus will make her better, Miss Callie?" Lottie pinned her with a blue-eyed stare that demanded an answer.

"I don't know for certain. I only know that the Bible tells us that we should cast our cares upon Him because He cares for us." She enveloped Lottie's hand in her own. "When someone cares about us, they want the very best for us. But sometimes, because we're human, we don't know what's best. Only God knows for sure, and that's when it becomes very important to trust Him, no matter how our prayer is answered."

Lottie wrinkled her forehead. "Daniel trusted God in the lion's den."

Callie smiled as she ran her fingers through Lottie's hair. "Daniel was very brave, wasn't he?"

Lottie bobbed her head. "And God didn't let him die. So if I pray and ask God to make Daisy better, then He won't let Daisy die, either. Right?" Her eyes glistened with anticipation.

Callie sighed. "Not exactly. Our prayers aren't always answered the way we want."

The anticipation in Lottie's eyes was replaced with a cloud of confusion. "Why?"

"Because God knows it isn't the right answer." Callie squeezed Lottie's hand. "Sometimes it's very hard to continue to trust when we don't get what we want, but we must always remember that God knows much more than we do."

Lottie's lower lip quivered. "But Daisy's my sister. I don't want her to die."

"Come here, Lottie." Wes motioned for the girl to come sit on his lap. Once she was settled, he glanced at Callie. "Let's not talk about dying. I'm sure the doctor will be able to help her. Why don't we pray that Daisy will feel better and the doctor will know exactly how to help her?"

The four of them had completed their prayers when Mrs. Bridgeport stepped into the waiting room. "The doctor thinks we should take Daisy to the hospital in Biscayne. She's having acute pain in the area of the bite along with abdominal pain and muscle cramps. He can't be certain, of course, but he thinks the spider may have been a black widow. He says the bites cause more severe medical problems for the elderly and for children." Tears rimmed her eyes, and she looked away as she lifted a handkerchief to her cheeks.

"I feel terrible, Mrs. Bridgeport." Callie hastened to the older woman's side. "The children were in my care and now —"

"It's not your fault, my dear. Accidents occur all the time. She could have been bitten by a spider just as easily while sitting on the front porch. These things happen." Her lips quivered. "The doctor is hopeful and thinks she'll recover quickly. He simply wants to have another opinion. When Luther told him we were planning to leave for Indiana, he thought it best if we made certain all was well before we departed for home."

"Leaving? I don't understand."

Before she and the children left Fair Haven to go to the woods, nothing had been said about leaving. News of the flooding had been frightening, but Callie hadn't imagined the Bridgeports would decide to leave

315

Bridal Veil on such short notice.

Before his wife could answer, Mr. Bridgeport joined them. "Eunice and I will take the children and Maude to Biscayne. Callie, I'd like you to remain and, with the help of the other servants, close up the cottage and then join us in Biscayne. Providing all is well with Daisy, we'll leave as soon as possible."

She nodded her agreement but couldn't seem to move. It was all happening so fast that she felt like a child attempting to jump from a merry-go-round that hadn't yet stopped.

Mrs. Bridgeport reached for Callie's hand. "I'm going to stay here at the infirmary with Daisy. You and Maude pack enough of our belongings for a few nights, and Luther will bring them when he returns for Daisy and me. He'll need to make arrangements for Captain Fleming to take us to Biscayne. You can pack the rest of the personal belongings and have them delivered to Biscayne when you join us. Lula and Jane can help you close the house. I know it will be more rushed than usual, but at least you've helped before."

Callie forced a smile that she hoped would assure Mrs. Bridgeport. But truth be told, Callie wasn't at all certain she remembered everything that needed to be done in order to close the house. She could only hope Lula or Jane could provide her with a list of instructions.

While Mr. and Mrs. Bridgeport were speaking with Thomas and Lottie, Callie turned to Wes. "You should probably go back to the golf course. We'll be so busy that there won't be time to do anything but pack."

"I don't want you to leave until we have an opportunity to talk. I'll come by the house later."

Callie glanced at the Bridgeports and then turned back to face Wes. "Wait by the live oak behind the house. We can meet there."

Once they returned to Fair Haven, Mr. Bridgeport accompanied Callie into the parlor. "After you left with the children, we received another telegram from home." He cleared his throat and hesitated. "I hate to be the one to give you bad news, but your grandmother's house was destroyed in the flood. It's completely under water." He patted her shoulder. "I'm so sorry, Callie. I know the house was important to you."

"What's most important is Daisy and her recovery. Losing grandmother's home

317

doesn't worry me as much as Daisy's health."

Had loss of the house meant God was removing all other choices so that she would go to Africa or move to Chicago? Loss of the house could certainly mean she should leave, but where was she supposed to go?

"You are a brave young lady, Callie." Mr. Bridgeport squeezed her shoulder. "I can always count on you to remain steadfast in times of crisis. I don't know what we would do without you."

Tears stung her eyes and she looked away. Mr. Bridgeport's kind words created greater emotion than the news regarding her grand-mother's house. And now, thoughts of leaving the children tugged at her heart. How could she go anywhere with this family dependent upon her? Callie pushed the questions from her mind as Maude scurried into the room.

"What's happened? Thomas told me something about leaving for Biscayne within the hour?"

Mr. Bridgeport nodded his agreement and began to explain, but the more he talked, the more unconvinced Maude appeared. By the time he'd completed the explanation, she was shaking her head back and forth like a petulant child.

"No."

Mr. Bridgeport's mouth dropped open, and he stared as though stunned by the woman's objection. After a moment he regained his composure, straightened his shoulders, and glared at her. "No, what?"

Maude didn't flinch. "I don't think what you're suggesting is the best idea. Things would go a lot faster if I stayed here with Callie and helped. We can bring the two children with us when we join you tomorrow. Thomas and Lottie won't have anything to do, and I won't be any help sitting at a hospital in Biscayne. At least here, I can be useful."

Mr. Bridgeport studied her for a moment. "I suppose that does make more sense. What do you think, Callie?"

"I agree. Mrs. Murphy would be good help, and the children will be more content."

"Then it's settled. I'll go and speak to Captain Fleming and return for our small trunks."

Callie nodded. "I'll see to packing them right now."

The remainder of the afternoon continued in a flurry of activity. Maude sat on her heels awaiting another gown to pack. Once Callie had carefully folded each item,

319

Maude placed it in the proper trunk.

Callie handed one of Lottie's dresses to her. "I am so thankful you suggested staying here. You've been such a big help. I doubt I could have managed without your assistance." She smiled at Maude. "It would have taken me at least another day or so to finish what we've completed this afternoon."

"I'm happy to help. That's what friends are for — to be there when we need them. Isn't that right?"

"Yes. And I'm glad you consider me a friend. Once we return to Indiana, I know it will be difficult for you, and I want to help you adjust to your new life. With the flooding, it's going to be hard on all of us, but once life returns to normal, I think you'll very much enjoy life with the Bridgeports."

Using the trunk to balance herself, Maude pushed to her feet. "I'm sure I will. I've never been to Indiana, so you'll have to show me about."

Callie stopped folding and stared at the woman. "But the Winslow family lived in Indiana years ago."

Maude cackled. "Right you are, but I was living in Pittsburgh for so long that I completely forgot. And I'm sure things have changed a lot after this many years." She gestured toward the hallway. "I think I heard

320

someone knocking downstairs. I better see who it is."

Callie hadn't heard anyone knock, but she didn't argue. If they were going to be prepared to leave tomorrow, she needed to keep working.

Maude tucked a stray hair behind her ear as she returned to the upstairs a short time later. "Sorry I was gone so long. Guess I was hearing things. There was no one at the door, but Jane needed a bit of help. Are you coming along, or should I go downstairs and help? Jane said she needed to stop cleaning and prepare a bit of supper for all of us. She didn't think you'd be going to dine at the clubhouse."

"Eating here would be best. I don't want to use valuable time dressing for dinner. Besides, the children would much rather eat here." Callie glanced about the room. "You go ahead. I'm about done packing the children's belongings."

When she had finished, Callie strode down the hallway to the large room where she conducted lessons each day. She should take along some of the supplies to help entertain the children on the journey home. And if Daisy didn't recuperate as quickly as the doctor had anticipated, they might need to remain in Biscayne for several days. She uttered a silent prayer for the girl as she placed crayons, pencils, and paper in a large satchel.

"Dinner's ready, Miss Callie." Lottie coughed and pointed downstairs. "Miss Maude says you should come down now."

"I hope you're not getting sick, Lottie." Callie stood and placed her palm against the girl's forehead. "Do you feel ill?"

"I've just been coughing again." She took hold of Callie's hand. "Miss Jane says to hurry or the food will get cold."

Callie and the other women, along with Lottie and Thomas, gathered in the small kitchen. Jane placed a tureen of soup and a plate of sandwiches on the kitchen table. "Not much, but the best I could do on short notice." She smiled at the children. "It's going to seem strange being without work so early in the year, but it was kind of Mr. Bridgeport to pay us for the entire season."

Maude ladled soup into a bowl for each of the children. "Indeed. I'm sure there's nothing like having enough money to hand it out as you please, while others must work until the day they die."

Callie frowned, annoyed by Maude's inconsiderate comments. What was wrong with her? Jane and Lula had been hired to work until the end of April, and they wouldn't be able to secure employment anywhere else at this late date. Did Maude think it unfair that he'd paid them, while she would be required to work for her pay? One minute the woman was the epitome of kindness, and the next she exhibited a harsh edge that Callie didn't understand.

They'd finished the evening meal and were clearing the dishes when Maude turned toward Callie. "I think I see someone out in the back who's waiting to see you."

Callie stepped to the window and caught a glimpse of Wes leaning against the live oak. Her stomach knotted at the sight of him. "I won't be long, Maude. Watch after the children."

Maude chuckled. "Now, don't you go out there and make any plans to elope with that fella."

"Maude!"

Maude hiked a shoulder. "It could happen. I eloped with one of my husbands. He was a sweet talker that could convince me of most anything." She shook her head. " 'Course the sweet talking quit once we was married, so you be careful. I've seen the way that man looks at you, and you never know when a man's going to get the notion to get hitched."

Callie's heart tilted. Surely that wasn't

what Wes wanted to speak to her about. But he had said he wanted to speak to her before she left.

She laid one hand on the cold doorknob and pressed the other hand to her midsection, where butterflies seemed to be having a tennis match. If he brought up the subject of a future together, what would she say? Would she give up the children or working in Africa or helping immigrants in Chicago to marry a man like Wes? If only she knew for certain she could trust him. Maybe then she could consider a life with him.

Silly woman. She'd allowed Maude's ramblings to give her notions that were not grounded in fact. Yes, he'd shown an interest in her, but that was a far cry from a marriage proposal, and more importantly, a far cry from love. But she had to admit she'd felt that emotional tug on her heart. Did Wes feel it, too?

Hiking up her skirts, she started to cross the yard. Wes hadn't spotted her. Her insides jellied. The man had no business looking so handsome. Maybe she didn't love Wes, but she certainly liked him.

She liked him very much.

CHAPTER 21

Wesley stood beneath a thick limb of the towering live oak that shaded the rear porch of Fair Haven. He leaned against the tree and watched for any sign of Callie. He'd spent the last hours weighing the future, considering what it might hold and what concessions he would be willing to make. He'd gone from thinking Callie might believe she must go to Africa to wondering if she would put aside the idea and consider a life as the wife of a research doctor in this country. It was doubtful she'd be accepted for a teaching position once she married, yet there were many charitable institutions where she could volunteer. If the two of them went to Africa, she could teach — it wouldn't matter there if she was married. But his chances of conducting research would be nonexistent. There would be no laboratories or funding. He would need to return to treating patients. Could he do that? With Callie by his side, he thought it might be possible. But first he needed her agreement to marry him.

He pulled out his pocket watch and glanced at the time. Being late to the clubhouse was going to create major problems with his father. Wesley could picture the patriarch of the Townsend family pounding on the door of Wes's room at the clubhouse right about now.

He'd known when he made the arrangements to meet Callie that he was taking a risk. Even more than a future together, he worried that she might say she wanted nothing to do with him once he revealed the truth. What if she believed he was no different from the man she'd been engaged to marry? She'd been clear: She wanted a man she could trust. Would she think him untrustworthy because he hadn't told her about his past?

"It's too late now." He muttered the words and pitched a pebble across the yard. "She'll either accept me or reject me, and I have no one to blame but myself."

"Are you talking to an imaginary friend, or is someone hiding behind the tree?"

He startled and looked up to see Callie approaching. "Neither. I was talking to myself. Thinking out loud."

Her lips curved in a beautiful smile. "Care to share your thoughts with me?"

"That's exactly what I want to do."

She gestured to the Adirondack chairs near the tree. "Why don't we sit down?"

He sat on the edge of the chair, his chest tight with anticipation. Had she heard what he'd said about accepting or rejecting him? "You know I care for you, and because I do, I want you to know the truth about me." Fear sparked in her eyes and he smiled. "Don't worry. I'm not a murderer or a thief, but on a couple of occasions you've asked about my family."

"And you haven't told me much." Her lips curved in a sweet smile. "I haven't held that against you. I know questions regarding family members can sometimes be difficult to answer."

"That's true enough. In my case, it's because I've always been a disappointment to my family. I haven't been the man they wanted, and my father, particularly, frowns upon the decisions I've made. Though he hasn't said it, I know he considers me a failure." He straightened his shoulders. "It's not that I haven't tried to be the kind of man he hoped for, but it just hasn't worked out."

"I'm sorry, Wes. Feeling that you've disappointed your parents can be heartbreaking. I know I've felt the same way from time to time."

"Because you haven't gone to Africa?"

"Yes. I know they think it should be a simple decision, because it was easy for them."

"Exactly! That's the way it is with my father, as well. Just because certain decisions came easily to him, he thinks it should be the same for me. But we aren't all the same."

"They don't realize that our lives aren't exactly as theirs were when they made their decisions. My parents were already married, and I was away at boarding school when they decided to go to the mission field. They were much older than I am now, and yet they think the decision should come easily for me."

Wes nodded his agreement. "I don't think anyone has ever understood my feelings the way you do, Callie. My mother understands a little, but she tends to take my father's side in order to keep peace. Being with you these past months has been the best time of my life."

A blush colored her cheeks, and she glanced away. "I'm sure there have been other young ladies who have valued your ideas."

"Not like you. Most of them were more interested in a fancy home and large sums of money than in my thoughts about life."

"Then you must have been calling on the wrong kinds of girls, because there are lots of young women who are interested in more than money."

"You're probably right, but they didn't cross my path." He reached forward and clasped one of her hands. "The other night I was thinking about all the things I admire about you, and the list got mighty long."

Her eyes sparkled. "That's very kind of you to say, Wes."

"Well, it's true. I love your candor and honesty — you're not afraid to say what you believe, yet you do it with a kind and gentle spirit. You have a sweet nature, and I admire the way you treat everyone with consideration — including the servants and other workers. I never hear you speak to them in a demeaning way, and you're always quick to offer help to others."

He released her hand as she scooted back in the chair. "My family had servants while I was growing up, but my parents taught me that God desires all of us to have a servant's heart. I think that's why I always wanted to teach. It's my way of serving and helping others. When I was younger, I brought my schoolbooks home, and every evening I worked with two of our servants who didn't know how to read." She stared into the distance as if transported back to another time. "We always treated those who worked for us as members of our family. And they rewarded us with loyalty and love in return."

Wes couldn't believe his good fortune. He'd fought against coming to Bridal Veil for the winter. Now he realized that if he hadn't given in to his mother's pleas, he would never have met Callie. Surely God must have been directing his path to this woman.

"I hope you won't think me bold, but I must tell you how I feel before you leave Bridal Veil." He moved from his chair and stooped down in front of her. "I'm declaring my love for you, Callie. I know we haven't known each other very long, but I do know you are the woman God intended for me."

His heart pounded as he waited for her response.

"I've come to care for you as well, Wesley. To be honest, it has been very hard for me to admit to myself that I was beginning to fall in love with you. I had promised myself that I would never again be hurt by a man."

"And I won't hurt you — you have my word." Wesley gathered her hands in his own.

Callie cast her gaze upon their hands. "Matthew said similar words to me." She lifted her head and looked at him. "I don't want to constantly compare you to Matthew — it isn't fair to you or to our relationship, but you must understand that it will take time for my trust in you to take hold. After being betrayed and so deeply hurt, I guard my heart even when I don't think there's a need." She smiled at him. "But it's your openness and honesty that have begun to break down the fence I'd built around my heart, and I'm thankful you've saved me from myself. I don't want to go through life without the ability to trust the people I love."

His voice faltered. "I hope you count me one of those people you love."

"I do, Wesley. And in time, I know you'll destroy any remaining doubts I might have about the love between a man and a woman."

Wesley massaged his temples, trying to stave off the threatening pressure. He must reveal his past as well as his true identity to

Callie. Waiting any longer to reveal his biggest secret could destroy her mounting trust in him. On the other hand, if he told her right now, would she order him out of her life? He already knew the answer. She was leaving tomorrow — he must tell her before she departed.

He inhaled, trying to dispel negative thoughts. "There are some things about me and my past that I haven't revealed to you. Matters that might cause you to believe me dishonest."

"You just declared your love, and now you tell me that you've lied to me?" She withdrew her hands, and he could see the pain in her eyes.

"Please don't jump to conclusions. It has nothing to do with us or how I feel about you. This is about me and my background, as well as some things in my past. I'm not who you think. I'm not a wandering golf pro. I've enjoyed a life of privilege. My family is quite wealthy." He reached for her hand, but she pulled away. "Please, Callie. Just listen to what I have to say. There are reasons why I didn't divulge these things to you earlier."

She stared at him. "Honesty isn't something you pick and choose for the proper time, Wes. If you care about someone, you should be forthright at all times." Tears rimmed her eyes. "I truly thought you were such a man, but once again I've been wrong."

"No, you aren't wrong. Let me explain. After I've told you everything, I think you'll understand my position."

"That remains to be seen, but I wouldn't be so —"

"Callie! Hurry! Come quick!" Maude stood near the back door, waving frantically in their direction.

Wes jumped to his feet and followed Callie to the house. Why now? Just when he'd gathered courage to tell her the truth.

Callie raced toward the back door, not certain whether she was annoyed or pleased by the interruption. Wes had been keeping secrets. Her heart felt as though it had been torn into pieces. She'd been overcome by feelings that spanned every imaginable emotion: anger, curiosity, confusion, fear, despair, suspicion, surprise, grief, hate — but as she reached the porch stairs, she realized there was one thing she hadn't felt — the desire to forgive. Yet even as the thought crossed her mind, she shoved it away. Knowing how much truth meant to her, still he had lied.

"What is it, Maude?" Callie panted for breath as she awaited the nanny's reply.

"Lottie. She's having trouble with her breathing again. I can't get her to stop crying, and the crying makes the cough worse. She —"

Lottie pushed around Maude's skirts, her eyes red and swollen. She held a handkerchief to her mouth as she coughed and then tried to draw in a ragged breath. She wheezed and her eyes grew large at the attempt to gain enough air.

Callie leaned down and rubbed the girl's chest. "You must quit crying and calmly breathe."

While Lottie continued to wheeze and gasp for air, Wes drew near. "Does she have any medicine that might help?" He reached for Lottie's arms and held them above her head.

Callie glared at him. "What are you doing?"

"It helps ease the spasms. Hot peppermint tea would help, too. There are properties in the tea that help open the bronchial passages. The steam will also help. And if you have a jar of honey, hold it beneath her nose and have her smell it. Sometimes that helps, as well."

Still fighting her anger at him, Callie

shifted around and glared at Wes. "Let go of her. Unless you've become a doctor in the past few minutes, I don't need your suggestions or advice."

He released Lottie's arms and took a backward step. "I was only trying to help."

Callie immediately regretted her harsh words. She might be angry at Wes, but acting the shrew was uncalled for and unbecoming. "I'm sorry, but I think you should leave. I need to see to Lottie."

"Let me come in and lend a hand. If you don't need my assistance with the children, I'm sure there are other things I can do to help." He touched her shoulder. "I need to talk to you, Callie. I want to settle matters between us before you go."

Callie shook her head, tears threatening to spill. "I don't have time. Right now, I must see to Lottie. After that, there are other things needing my attention." She dropped her gaze. "And I think you've already said more than enough."

Placing an arm around a rasping Lottie, Callie hurried across the back porch of Fair Haven. As she crossed the threshold, a tear slipped down her cheek.

He'd said he loved her. Was that a lie, as well?

■ ■ ■ ■

The image of Callie's pain and anger remained in his mind as Wes returned to the clubhouse. He had hoped to go to his room and sort out his thoughts. Instead, his father was already there and greeted him with anger flashing in his dark eyes.

"Where were you? Do you realize how embarrassed I was when you didn't show up for dinner this evening?"

Wes stood inside the door of his room still wearing his golf attire. "I apologize, Father, but I had an unexpected matter arise, and I couldn't make it back in time. I doubt the fact that I went missing for the evening meal will influence the outcome of the negotiations with your investor."

His father's neck reddened beneath the stark whiteness of his stiff collar. "Don't presume to tell me what will or will not affect a possible investor, Wesley. The fact that you didn't appear at dinner created great embarrassment for the young lady. Can you imagine for a moment how she must have felt?"

Wesley nodded. "I will send a note of apology, Father, but please remember that I didn't make these arrangements, and I did not agree to become your pawn in a match-making scheme. If you'll be honest with yourself, you'll recall that I have told both you and Mother that I do not wish an arranged marriage and will not agree to it."

"That's true, Howard. Wesley has told us how he feels." His mother stepped around the two men and sat down.

Wesley's father directed a stern look at his wife. "I don't need you taking his side, Blanche."

"I am not taking Wesley's side. I'm simply saying that he did say he didn't want us to interfere. That doesn't mean I don't think he needs to find a wife and settle down."

His mother pursed her lips and met his father's stern look with one of her own. If he didn't step in, this could turn into an ongoing disagreement between his parents. After his unsatisfactory meeting with Callie, he didn't want to listen to the two of them quarrel about whom he should marry and why he hadn't attended dinner this evening.

"The two of you seem to believe I'm the one in the wrong, so I'll leave the two of you to claim victory." His father gestured toward the hallway. "I do expect that note of apology, Wesley." His father turned on his heel and slammed the door on his way out of the room.

"Your father was quite discomfited when you didn't appear this evening." His mother stared at the closed door. "However, I think you made a wise choice staying away. Madelaine would not have been to your liking."

"Madelaine is the young lady?"

"Yes." His mother touched a finger to the curls along the side of her head. "Not very bright. I tried to engage her in conversation, but I don't believe she managed to convey one intelligent thought." She wrinkled her nose. "And she's quite horsey looking, as well." She hesitated. "But so is her father." His mother shook her head. "Poor girl. It's good her family has money. Otherwise I doubt she'll ever find a husband."

"That is sad, Mother, but —"

"Now then, where were you this evening?"

His mother adjusted her skirts and leaned back. Obviously she was planning on an extended conversation. He knew that determined look in her eye: She wouldn't leave until she'd received the answers she wanted. Besides, she wouldn't want to return to her room until after his father was asleep. That way she could avoid further confrontation.

He considered repeating that he'd been delayed but knew his mother would push for further information. And right now, he needed someone to talk to — a woman who might understand how best to approach Callie and convince her that he hadn't set out to intentionally deceive her.

"I was with Callie Deboyer. She's the governess for the Bridgeport family. Have you met them?"

His mother's forehead wrinkled, and then her eyes brightened. "Yes. I did meet them once — I believe it was at the Valentine's ball. They seemed quite nice. You say this Miss Deboyer is their governess?"

Wesley sat down beside his mother. "Yes. And I'm in love with her."

His mother's eyebrows arched high on her forehead. "In love? Why, that's wonderful news. Why haven't we met her? Were you worried we wouldn't approve because of her lack of social standing?"

"No. I'm not worried what anyone would think of her. She's a lovely young woman who cares little about society's frills and rules, although she was born into a wealthy family."

"Then why is she working as a governess?"

Wes explained that her parents had chosen to give up their worldly possessions and had gone to the mission field. "I think it was admirable of them. Callie lived with her grandmother and finished her schooling. There was some connection between the Bridgeport family and Callie's grandmother, which led to her position with them."

"So she isn't well positioned, but you've fallen in love with her and desire our blessing. Is that it?"

Wesley chuckled. "Not quite, Mother. I don't want to sound disrespectful, but I am a grown man, and if Callie doesn't meet with the family's approval, it will not change my heart. She is kind, witty, and compassionate, a perfect woman for me in every way."

"I see. Well, it sounds as though you've made up your mind. May I ask if you've proposed marriage to her?"

"No. Not yet. You see, there's a problem."

His mother folded her hands in her lap. "Why don't you tell me about it? I'm in no hurry."

Wesley inhaled a deep breath. He needed to gain another woman's perspective, and his mother would be fair. While his father cared little about the subject of love, when it came to marriage, his mother remained a romantic. He hoped she could provide him with some insight.

After gathering his thoughts, he outlined his first meeting with Callie and explained how she'd assumed he was a worker on the island rather than a guest. "I liked the idea and didn't correct her."

His mother held up a finger. "Mistake number one, but go on." After admitting he'd danced with Callie at the masquerade ball and hadn't revealed his identity, his mother held up two fingers. "Mistake number two, but go on."

He explained that they'd spent a great deal of time together during the golf lessons and later on the beach and in the woods with the children, that she'd told him about her parents and their work on the mission field in Africa.

"She's attempting to decide if she should join them. They've written and told her there is a dire need for teachers and doctors."

His mother clasped a hand to her chest. "She knows you're a physician, and she's trying to convince you to go to Africa, Wesley. The girl wants to help her parents and believes that she will please them by securing a doctor for their work. Dear me — did you really not see through this?"

"Mother, stop! Callie isn't like that; she would never —"

"You are inexperienced when it comes to women, Wesley. I am loath to admit it, but there are some devious women in the world, and I think this young woman —"

"This young woman, as you call her, doesn't even know I'm a doctor, so your assumptions are completely mistaken." Wesley pushed up from the sofa and paced the room.

"So you never told her you're a doctor? She doesn't know what happened in Texas?"

He shook his head.

His mother held up three fingers. "Mistake number three, but go on." She shifted. "No — perhaps you shouldn't tell me any more. I'm afraid I'm going to run out of fingers before you finish."

He didn't heed her comment but continued pacing as he explained that Callie had been betrayed by another man and now she feared trusting men because of what had happened in the past.

"And knowing this, you still didn't reveal your past?" She held up four fingers. "Mistake number four, but go on."

"I tried to tell her this evening. That's why I was late coming back to the clubhouse, but we were interrupted. She heard only enough to believe that she had misplaced her trust in me."

His mother gestured for him to sit down. "I must say it appears you've botched things rather horribly. However, I don't want you to give up on love. You need to speak to Callie before she leaves the island — even if it means waiting at the dock and detaining Captain Fleming from leaving." She clasped his hand. "More importantly, you need to pray and seek God's guidance in this matter. If it is His will for the two of you to be together, I believe it will happen." She squeezed his hand. "But that doesn't mean God won't expect you to put forth some effort. I suggest you pray for divine intervention!"

CHAPTER 22

Shafts of sunlight streamed through the bedroom window and slanted across the carpeted floor. Callie cracked one eye and attempted to force herself from the foggy haze of a restless sleep that had been fraught with dreams of Wesley and Matthew — of deceit and lies that had been more nightmare than reverie. Shifting her weight and turning in the bed, Callie caught herself and pulled back before she tumbled to the floor. The near fall jarred her fully awake. This wasn't her room, and it wasn't her bed. No wonder she'd almost upset onto the floor. While trying to comfort Lottie during the night, she'd fallen asleep in the child's bed.

Callie smiled as she spotted the child. Lottie had inched her way farther down and lay curled in a ball with the sheet pulled over her head. Callie's back protested when she stood up, evidence that she'd spent several hours in a twisted position. She rubbed her lower back and padded around to the foot of the bed. Leaning close, she listened to Lottie's breathing and smiled. No wheezing. Wes's suggestions of breathing the honey and drinking peppermint tea had truly helped. She would let Lottie sleep a while longer, for she hadn't rested any better than Callie.

After returning to her own room, she heard noise downstairs. It sounded as though Maude was giving orders of some sort. If so, Lula and Jane would likely be in a foul mood. They didn't mind Maude's help, but they didn't want to take orders from the children's nanny. A fact they'd mentioned to Mrs. Bridgeport on more than one occasion.

Callie brushed her hair and skillfully piled curls atop her head before departing her room. She stopped at the top of the steps. Was that Archie Penniman pacing in the front parlor? Surely not. She thought she'd made it clear she didn't want any further contact with him, but one look and she was certain that Archie was in the parlor.

He turned as she descended the steps. "What are you doing here, Archie?" She truly didn't want to deal with the likes of the tennis pro today.

Her harsh tone didn't appear to bother

him. He smiled and stepped toward her as though he'd been invited to tea. "Callie, it's good to see you. You look as lovely as ever."

She cringed at his unctuous behavior. "Please, Archie. I'm not interested in your flattery. I want to know why you've come here."

"What happened to the sweet, kind young lady who first came to the tennis courts a few months ago?" He grinned and looked around the room as though looking for someone else. While he seemed to think his behavior endearing, his actions had the opposite effect on her.

"The sweet young lady you met disappeared when you treated her in a rude and churlish manner. I don't have time to waste, Archie. Please tell me why you've appeared at Fair Haven without an invitation."

He sighed and clasped a hand to his chest. "I've come because I heard young Daisy had been injured and was taken to the hospital over in Biscayne. I wanted to say I was sorry to hear the sad news and extend my wishes for a speedy recovery."

"Thank you, Archie. That's thoughtful of you." She wondered how he'd heard about Daisy, but during her first year at Bridal Veil, she'd learned that news traveled fast — especially among the servants. News passed quickly at the guests' card parties and gatherings, as well. No doubt Archie had heard at one of the tennis matches.

He stepped a little closer, but when Callie took a backward step, he stopped. "Please don't be alarmed. I don't intend to lay a hand on you." He shoved his hands into his pockets. "With Daisy's illness, I guessed that you probably would be leaving the island and doubted the family would return for the remainder of the season."

Callie nodded. "You're correct. Once Daisy is able to travel, we'll return to Indianapolis."

"That's what I figured, so I wanted to be sure and see you to offer another apology for my forward actions toward you at the tennis courts." He glanced toward the parlor. "Could we sit down?"

"No, Archie, we cannot. As I told you, there's much to do before we depart. You've said your apology and —"

"Please. Let me at least finish what I came to say. I don't want you to leave here thinking me a total cad."

Callie sighed. The man was as persistent as a hound dog sniffing prey. Her scalp tingled at the thought. Was Archie the hound dog and was she his intended prey? If so, she'd need a way to escape. Keeping her gaze fastened on him, she slowly inched toward the front door.

"Make it quick, Archie. You're wasting time, and time is valuable to us right now. We have a great deal to complete before we depart."

"I have always behaved under the belief that young ladies wanted to be pursued — that they enjoyed a man who showed his interest in a more, uh, forward way. So I'm sorry for my actions toward you. I know you were offended. I plan to change my ways with women, and you're the reason for that change. I wanted you to know that."

This was taking far too long. She cared little about what Archie planned to do, but it seemed the only way to get him out of the house was to indulge him for a few more moments.

"I appreciate the fact that you listened and you plan to change your ways. Thank you for coming by to tell me." She stepped closer to the door. "I think you'll have much greater success with the ladies if you treat them with respect."

"Miss Callie, I need you in here to help me." Maude stepped around the doorway leading to the dining room.

Archie moved toward the dining room. "I'd be more than pleased to help you with any baggage and other chores. It's the least I can do."

Callie shook her head. "I don't think —"

"Don't be so quick to turn down an offer of help, Callie." Maude waved toward the rear of the house. "There's horse races going on today, and we'll not get a driver to take the baggage to the dock. They're all busy with the extra visitors attending the races. Had Mr. Bridgeport not arranged for the wagon before they left for Biscayne, we'd be without wagon or horses to haul the belongings."

Callie frowned. "I'm sure he arranged for someone to help us load the wagon."

Maude propped her hands on her hips. "The young fellow who brought the wagon yesterday said he wasn't going to be back — he'd been assigned to work the racetrack weeks ago. When I asked about someone else, he said there wasn't anyone to help us load."

Callie disliked accepting Archie's help, but it seemed she had no other choice. They might be able to handle the bags by themselves, but the trunks were far too heavy to load without a man's strength.

She gave a faint nod. "We accept your offer with our thanks, Archie. You can begin with the baggage by the steps. The trunks upstairs should be loaded after that. I can show you when you've finished with these."

With an impatient look in her eyes, Maude drew closer. "You need to open the safe, Callie. None of Mrs. Bridgeport's jewels have been packed."

Callie arched her brows. "I can do only one thing at a time, Maude. If Archie is to help us, he needs some direction. I can take care of the jewelry later. There's no hurry. Why don't you go up and help Lottie. She was still asleep when I came downstairs, and it's more important that she get up and get dressed."

Maude frowned, but she marched upstairs without further argument. The back door slammed and Thomas appeared with beads of perspiration dotting his forehead. "I put the bicycles in the storage shed and made sure it was locked."

"Thank you, Thomas. That's very helpful."

"Has there been any word about Daisy?"

Callie rested her hand on his shoulder. "No, nothing, but I'm hoping we'll be ready to depart within an hour. Our first stop will be the hospital."

"Maybe she's already left the hospital. What will we do then?"

"If she's been discharged, she'll be with

your parents at the hotel, and we'll go there. I know where they're staying." Callie squeezed his shoulder. "There's no reason for concern. Everything is going to be just fine."

"Even Daisy?"

"I hope so, Thomas. I've been praying for her." She didn't want the boy to dwell on his sister's illness, so she pointed to an empty case near the steps. "Why don't you bring me your mother's small case and come with me? I need to pack her jewelry."

After the pair had entered the dining room, Callie opened the wall safe. "I'll hand the jewelry to you and you can place it in the bag for me." One by one, she handed him the velvet cases and silk pouches, and Thomas carefully placed each one into the bag.

By the time Maude returned downstairs with Lottie, Callie and Thomas had completed packing the contents of the safe. She placed the bag where she'd be able to keep it in plain sight, and then took the children into the kitchen for a late breakfast of fruit and croissants that Jane had picked up before coming to the island. While they ate, Maude directed Archie to the trunks and other bags that had been left upstairs.

Several birds chirped outside the window,

and Callie glanced toward the live oak behind the house. Would Wesley reappear and try to speak with her again? She'd been harsh with him, but from what he'd told her, he'd been pretending to be someone he wasn't. Surely he expected she would be wounded. And though she didn't want a man she couldn't trust, she longed to know exactly what other secrets lay between them.

Perhaps it hadn't been anything as horrid as she imagined. And if she professed to live her faith, shouldn't she have given him an opportunity to tell her what he had hidden? Didn't God's Word instruct her to extend grace, just as it was extended to her? Her conscience told her she'd been wrong, yet she assuaged herself with the knowledge that she'd suffered for extending grace and trusting in the past.

But didn't I die for you? Is it asking too much for you to listen to his explanation? The thoughts plagued her as she finished breakfast.

Lula entered the kitchen and placed several dishes in the sink. "I've closed all the shutters on the front of the house, Callie. Once you and the children are gone, I'll send word to have workers come by next week and close the upstairs shutters. The place will be safe and sound in case of any storms."

"Thank you, Lula. There are some extra croissants." Callie pointed to the platter. "Help yourself."

"I ate before I came this morning, but thank you." Lula ran water in a dishpan and picked up a cloth. "We'd like to hear how little Daisy's doing. You'll send word to us, won't you?" She dipped the cloth in the water. "I stopped by the hospital early this morning before I came over on the launch."

Callie perked to attention. "Lula! You didn't tell me. What did you find out? Is Daisy improving?"

The maid shook her head. "They wouldn't tell me anything except that she's still in the hospital. I asked if I could go up and see her, but they said it wasn't visiting hours."

"Did you ask if Mr. or Mrs. Bridgeport had stayed with her?"

"No. The lady at the desk made it clear she wasn't going to answer any more of my questions. I was wearing my uniform, so I think she knew I wasn't family." The maid's lips curved in a lopsided grin.

"It was kind of you to stop, Lula. I had hoped to hear that Daisy was already discharged." Callie frowned. "This means she must be worse than the doctor at the infirmary initially thought."

"Is Daisy gonna die?" Lottie's eyes filled with tears.

Callie cradled the child's face in her hand. "Let's don't think such sad thoughts. There are very good doctors in Biscayne, and I'm certain they're doing everything they can to help Daisy get well. You just wait and see — soon we'll all be on the train to Indianapolis."

"I want to go and see Daisy when we get to the hospital." Lottie broke off a piece of her croissant and popped it into her mouth.

"We'll see what the doctor says. Now, finish your breakfast so we can be on our way."

Callie turned at the sound of knocking on the front door. "I'll go, Lula; you finish the dishes." She glanced at Lottie. "You and Thomas keep eating."

She strode toward the door, perplexed when she noticed Maude and Archie in the dining room. If the knocking hadn't been so insistent, she would have stopped and asked the nanny why she hadn't answered the door.

Arriving at the door, Callie stopped short when she saw Detectives Fitch and Jensen peering through the screen at her. She rested her hand on the inside handle. What were they doing here? She'd told them everything she had to say when they'd been here previously.

"Gentlemen? How may I help you? As you can see, we're in the midst of preparing to depart the island. I hope you don't plan to detain us."

"May we come in, Miss Deboyer?"

Though she would have preferred to send them on their way, Callie could hardly refuse them. "Step inside, and do tell me what this is about."

The detectives glanced around as they entered. "We're here to arrest Maude Murphy and Archie Penniman for theft."

Callie couldn't believe her ears. "What? Maude is the Bridgeports' nanny. I don't understand." She turned as the sound of footsteps pounded through the rear of the house. "That's ridiculous. Maude —"

The detectives pushed past her and ran toward the rear door. Callie followed and stopped in the kitchen. The children and Lula appeared stunned.

Callie grasped Lula's arm. "What happened?"

"I . . . I'm not sure. First Maude and that Archie fellow came racing through here and nearly knocked me over. I'd just regained my senses when those detectives that had questioned all of us came running in here. One of them nearly knocked me to the floor when he pushed past me. All of them went running helter-skelter through the back-yard." Lula wiped perspiration from her brow. "What in heaven's name is going on, Callie?"

She shook her head. "I don't know, but I think we'll soon find out."

CHAPTER 23

Callie sat wringing her hands in the office of the clubhouse superintendent. The two detectives, as well as Mr. Crocker, sat in a semicircle facing her. She'd been in the office for only a few minutes, and already she felt like a condemned criminal.

Her stomach tightened as she looked around the group. "Could someone tell me why I was brought here?"

"We'll get to that in just a minute. For now, we're the ones asking the questions, Miss Deboyer." Detective Fitch looked at a pad of paper. "When did you first become acquainted with Maude Murphy?"

"When she came to work for the Bridge-port family this year. She arrived on Bridal Veil shortly after the rest of us had arrived from Indianapolis. She was hired to take the place of the former nanny, who got married."

Fitch twisted his mustache. "And what

about Archie Penniman? How long have you known him?"

Callie couldn't imagine why the detectives were asking these questions. Nothing seemed to make sense. "I met him at the tennis courts. Thomas Bridgeport and I took classes for a short time."

"How come you stopped the lessons? Afraid you'd be connected to him somehow?"

"I don't know what you mean by that question." She folded her hands tight in her lap. "I asked Mrs. Bridgeport if we could discontinue the lessons because Mr. Penniman had been quite forward with me. I became uncomfortable in his company. I think it would be appropriate if you told me why you're asking these questions."

Detective Jensen nudged Fitch. "I'll take over." The lanky detective took the pad of paper from his partner. "Here's the thing, Miss Deboyer — and I think you already know this, but during our investigation we discovered that Maude Murphy is Archie Penniman's mother."

Callie gasped as a sick feeling washed over her. Archie's mother? There had to be some kind of mistake.

Several moments passed before Callie could gain enough control to speak. "That isn't possible. They don't even know each other." Her thoughts raced and she massaged her temples, trying to recall the events of the day. Archie had already entered the house when she'd arrived downstairs earlier in the morning. And Maude had agreed to accept his offer of help carrying the luggage, but there had been no sign of recognition between them. Had they even spoken to each other? She couldn't recall. Their names were different, but Maude had said she'd been married previously.

"They do know each other, Miss Deboyer, and they are mother and son. As a matter of fact, the two of them have been in cahoots stealing from the guests on this island."

Callie's mind spun as she attempted to make sense of what the detective was telling her. For a moment she felt as though she might faint. "Mrs. Murphy came highly recommended to Mrs. Bridgeport by Harriet Winslow. Mrs. Murphy worked for the Winslow family for many years as their nanny."

"Did she?" He tapped his notepad. "Not according to our information."

Callie slumped like a wilting flower in need of a drink. "But I don't understand. I saw her deliver the letter to Mrs. Bridgeport, who accepted the recommendation of her friend. Mrs. Murphy told me about her service with the Winslow children. I don't understand any of this or why you're questioning me."

The lanky detective clucked his tongue. "I suppose we might just as well be forthright with you, Miss Deboyer. We have certain concerns that you may have assisted Mrs. Murphy, Mr. Penniman, or both of them in the jewelry thefts."

The blood drained from Callie's face as a loud rush of sound whirled in her ears. She leaned forward and gasped for air. If she fainted, she would slip to the floor in a giant heap. Though she didn't want to make a spectacle of herself, the cool tile against her cheek would be most welcome right now.

"Are you feeling ill, Miss Deboyer?" Rotund Detective Fitch was leaning forward and peering at her.

She stared into his dark piercing eyes. "I'll be fine in just a moment."

He stood and she heard his retreating footsteps. Soon he returned and waved a folded newspaper in front of her face. "Get a cool cloth from someone. It's warm in here, and she's been caught unaware by all of this."

A chair scraped against the floor, and she

heard Mr. Crocker call to one of the club-house servants. Soon she had a cool cloth and a glass of water. Regaining her composure as best she could, Callie held the damp cloth to her forehead.

"I had nothing to do with any thefts on this island or elsewhere, gentlemen. I don't know how you arrived at such an assumption, but your accusations are without merit. I have never stolen anything in my life."

Callie adjusted the cloth from her forehead to her right temple. If only the throbbing in her head would cease. A sickening fear assailed her. Did these men truly think she was a thief?

Detective Fitch continued to stare at her while pulling on the end of his mustache. "I have a list, Miss Deboyer. We'd like you to tell us your whereabouts for the times and dates on this paper."

He thrust the paper in her direction. She struggled to focus as her trembling fingers took the paper from his hand. She tried to calm her nerves, but the paper rattled between her fingers as she scanned the dates and times that had been penned in a scrawling script.

"These appear to be times when I would have been on outings with the children or when I stayed with them at Fair Haven during the evenings. Often I went with the family to dinner at the clubhouse and then would accompany the children back to the house."

"From what we've been told, the other servants left in the evening, and it was just you and Mrs. Murphy there during the nighttime hours with the family. Is that correct?"

"Yes. The other servants remained overnight only if Mrs. Bridgeport was entertaining and they were needed until late into the evening. Those occasions are quite rare, since most socializing takes place here at the clubhouse."

Mr. Crocker gave a firm nod of approval. "We do encourage the guests to host their events here — that's why these beautiful facilities were constructed, after all."

The detective appeared uninterested in the superintendent's comment — his gaze remained fixed upon Callie. "Here's the problem, Miss Deboyer. With no one to vouch for where you were on these dates and times, and with the information we've gathered, we cannot eliminate you as a suspect."

"But the children would have been with me. Do you think I could take three children, furtively enter a cottage, and steal

362

jewels? That doesn't make any sense."

"If you can account for your time and prove you had the children with you, I'd tend to agree." Detective Jensen appeared more convinced than Detective Fitch.

"She's already said that she can't." Fitch glared at his partner. "I'm not going to take the word of children. After all, she's likely already coached them on what they should say if they're ever questioned about where they've been."

Callie couldn't believe her ears. This man was convinced she was a thief. "If you would speak to Mr. and Mrs. Bridgeport, I know they will vouch for my character as well as my whereabouts on the dates in question." She took a long slow breath in an effort to calm down. "Mrs. Bridgeport was always informed of my outings with the children."

"Then maybe we should talk to her." Detective Fitch gestured to his partner. "Why don't you see if you can locate Mrs. Bridgeport."

Callie shook her head. "That will be impossible. Mr. and Mrs. Bridgeport left for Biscayne yesterday, which is where I should be right now. Their daughter, Daisy, is in the hospital and could well be at death's door. That's where we were going when you arrived at Fair Haven. Please tell me: What must I do to convince you of my innocence?"

Before either of the detectives could answer, a burly man with a bulbous nose and wearing a shabby suit filled the doorway to the superintendent's office. "I think you'll want to see this, Detective Fitch." The man stepped into the room and placed a small trunk on the superintendent's desk.

Callie scooted to the edge of her chair. "That belongs to me. Why do you have it in your possession?"

Keeping his gaze fastened on the small trunk, the man leaned down and whispered into the detective's ear. Then he backed away and stood by the door without offering Callie a reply. Fitch stood and lifted the lid of the trunk. His eyes opened wide as he peered into the trunk and then glowered at Callie.

"If this is your trunk, then it appears you've been lying to us." He turned the trunk toward her and tipped it slightly.

Callie's mouth dropped open at the sight, and her heart raced a new beat. "Th-those are not mine." She attempted to lick her lips, but her mouth had turned dry. "I don't know how they got into my trunk."

Fitch pressed his lips into a thin, tight line

as he lifted jewels from the trunk. "I'm sure they aren't yours, Miss Deboyer, but you've already said this is your trunk. Why don't you tell me how these expensive pieces of jewelry happened to find their way into *your* trunk?"

"The only persons who could have put them in there would be Mrs. Murphy or Archie Penniman. Both of them had access to the trunks, but I couldn't tell you who put the jewelry inside. The only thing I can say for certain is that I have never seen those pieces before, and I did not put them in my trunk."

Detective Fitch leaned back in his chair. "This isn't looking good for you, Miss Deboyer."

"You've already told me that, Detective. It is my opinion you should be questioning Mrs. Murphy and Mr. Penniman rather than wasting your time with me."

His lips curved beneath his mustache. "Since there is no doubt of their guilt, they are being detained, and I can question them at any time. You, however, are a different story. Once you leave Bridal Veil, I'm told you will depart for Indianapolis. Attempting to question you after your departure would prove impossible."

"I have told you everything I know —

which is nothing. I didn't even know Maude and Archie were related — a fact I still find difficult to believe."

He pointed to the trunk. "Please consider the information we have at hand, Miss Deboyer. You cannot account for your whereabouts during at least some of these robberies; you know both Mrs. Murphy and Mr. Penniman; the jewelry that has gone missing is in a small trunk you've admitted belongs to you, and . . ."

When he didn't complete his final remark, Callie frowned. "And, what?"

"And both of them have told us you were involved."

"What? How dare they?" Callie sucked in a breath of air. "Well, I suppose I can believe they'd say anything to save themselves, but I'm astonished you would take their word over mine. Exactly what involvement do they claim I've had in these evil deeds?"

He arched one brow. "They say you helped them locate homes where they could steal jewelry, that you told them when there would be opportunity to enter the homes, and they said you agreed to carry the jewels in your trunk." Tapping his notepad, he peered at the paper. "And Mrs. Murphy said you agreed to see that the jewels were sold at a tidy profit when you returned to

Indianapolis."

Callie couldn't believe her ears. "Why would they entrust that jewelry to me, Mr. Fitch? Why wouldn't Mrs. Murphy take the jewels in her own trunk?"

Appearing unconvinced by her remarks, the detective hiked a shoulder. "I have no idea why any of you did what you did, Miss Deboyer. It would help if you could at least account for your whereabouts. Try to think. Is there no one who can vouch for you?"

"The golf pro was with me on some of the afternoons you've listed there. He was helping Thomas with his science and botany lessons, and he went with us to the beach and to the woods on many of those afternoons. Could you send someone to fetch him?"

"You're speaking of the golf pro, you said?" The detective crossed his legs.

"Yes." Callie glanced out the window, where the earlier rain shower had steadily worsened into a downpour. "You could probably find him at the workers' quarters since he wouldn't be able to give lessons in this rain."

Mr. Crocker peered at her as though she'd lost her senses. "The workers' quarters?" He shook his head and turned to the detectives. "I believe you'll find Mr. Townsend in

367

his suite upstairs or perhaps in the dining room."

"No. There must be some mistake. I'm speaking of Wesley, who teaches at the golf course. He is an employee, not a guest."

"On the contrary, Miss Deboyer. Mr. Townsend agreed to assist us by acting as the golf pro, but he and his family are guests in the hotel. I don't know how you came to the conclusion he was living in the workers' quarters."

The room seemed to swirl around her, and she massaged her temples. Wesley was related to Blanche Townsend and Helena Kennebec, two of Mrs. Bridgeport's acquaintances who were staying at the clubhouse? "Are you absolutely certain we're talking about the same man?"

Mr. Crocker nodded. "Absolutely. In fact, I'll go and fetch him right now."

Callie clutched her handkerchief in her palm. Her heart shattered. He'd said his family was wealthy, but she hadn't imagined they were here on the island — staying in the clubhouse. He'd obviously been toying with her affections. No wealthy family would allow any bonds between a governess and one of their sons. And he knew that as well as she. How could she face him now? "I don't know if I want to speak with him at this moment, Mr. Crocker."

Detective Fitch uncrossed his legs and leaned forward to rest his forearms across his thighs. "It really doesn't matter what you want, Miss Deboyer. I want to question Mr. Townsend and see what he has to say about the dates and times you allege he was with you."

Callie couldn't grasp what was happening. Only hours ago she'd been packing to depart for Biscayne. Only hours ago she'd believed that Maude Murphy was a strange but kind woman who cared about her and the Bridgeport children. Only hours ago she'd believed Wesley was a golf pro living in the workers' quarters. Only hours ago she'd thought he loved her.

Her head throbbed and her mind spun like a top. Was her whole life simply one big lie?

CHAPTER 24

Callie's breath caught in her throat when Mr. Crocker returned with Wesley close on his heels. While the superintendent moved to his chair, Wesley stepped close to her side.

Callie's eyes traveled from Wesley's dark brown sack coat and matching waistcoat to his perfectly creased beige trousers with turnups that revealed matching spats. Judging from his appearance, Mr. Crocker had been correct. Wesley Townsend wasn't a mere golf pro.

"Callie." Wes whispered her name, and when she didn't look up at him, he grabbed a straight-backed chair and placed it beside her. He dropped to the chair and leaned close. "Mr. Crocker didn't tell me you were here. Are you all right? What's going on?"

She looked straight ahead. "I might ask you the same thing, Mr. Townsend." She spoke his name with intentional harshness.

"Callie, my family and I being guests at

the clubhouse is part of what I was trying to explain to you when you rushed into the house to care for Lottie."

"That's enough!" Detective Fitch interjected. "We brought you in here because we need to speak to you, Mr. Townsend, not because we hoped the two of you could settle some lovers' quarrel." Fitch picked up his notepad. "We have questions for you."

Callie gasped and Wesley snapped around on his chair. "I don't know who you are, but if you want me to answer any questions, you'll use a civil tone with both Miss Deboyer and me."

"I'm Detective Fitch and this is Detective Jensen. We've been hired by the owners of Bridal Veil to investigate the jewelry thefts that have taken place on the island. We've been working on this case for some time now, and there are still some loose ends. It's those loose ends we need to discuss with you, Mr. Townsend."

"Am I to assume you're discussing those loose ends with Miss Deboyer, as well?"

The detective nodded and pushed his notepad across the desk. "I'd like you to look at these dates and times and tell me if you can recall where you might have been at those particular times."

Wesley picked up the notepad and

scanned the dates. "Do you have a calendar I might look at, too?"

Mr. Crocker jumped to his feet and scurried around the desk. He thrust his calendar at Wesley. "Please use mine, Mr. Townsend."

Callie frowned at the superintendent's ingratiating tone and behavior. He certainly hadn't rushed to *her* aid. Of course, she wasn't a member of the Townsend family.

Wes glanced back and forth between the calendar and the list while tracing his finger down the page. "I believe I would have been with Miss Deboyer and the Bridgeport children during all of the times you have listed here, Mr. Fitch."

"Really? Strange that you could devote so much time to them while acting as the golf pro."

Wesley straightened his shoulders and glared at the man. "Are you questioning my word, Mr. Fitch? Why would I lie about such a thing?"

For the next fifteen minutes, the detective detailed their investigation and the involvement of Maude and Archie. He then added his belief that Callie might be involved due both to her inability to prove her whereabouts and to the statements from Mrs. Murphy and her son.

Wesley started to get up and gestured for

Callie to do the same. "Now that I've explained, there shouldn't be any further concerns regarding Miss Deboyer."

Detective Fitch motioned them back to their chairs. "Not quite yet."

Wesley stopped short. "And why not? I've told you Miss Deboyer was with me."

"I know you're a reputable fellow, Mr. Townsend, but being a detective means I can't let that interfere with getting to the truth." He cleared his throat. "Since I've heard tell, and it does appear that there may be a bit of an ongoing romance between you and Miss Deboyer, I can only assume you might — please note I said *might* — lie for her."

Callie sparked to attention. "There is no ongoing romance between us, Detective."

Wesley's jaw twitched. "If you weren't going to take my word, Detective Fitch, why did you bother to ask me about her whereabouts?"

The detective shrugged. "I have to check out every possible lead. That's my job. And the fact that Miss Deboyer didn't even know who you were is somewhat bothersome and could make me question your honesty, Mr. Townsend."

"I didn't tell Miss Deboyer who I was because I didn't want to be governed by the strictures society places on people of different classes. I quickly discovered Miss Deboyer is much like me — unimpressed with the trappings society considers important. I feared she would reject me if she knew I was a guest at the hotel."

"I won't argue with you, but I don't know many women who would be displeased to learn their suitor is wealthy, Mr. Townsend." Fitch tapped the notepad with his pencil. "Can you think of any other way I can verify what the two of you have told me, Mr. Townsend?"

"Perhaps you could quiz Thomas. I spent much of my time teaching the children about botany, particularly young Thomas. He doesn't know anything about what is happening in this room. If you take him aside and ask him, I'm sure you'll be satisfied. I could even write down a few questions you could ask him about the flora and fauna of the island."

Detective Jensen leaned over his rotund belly. "Flora and what?" He nudged his associate. "Are those more women?"

Wesley sighed. "No. I'm speaking of the plants and animals here on Bridal Veil Island."

"Oh, right, right." The detective's face turned a deep red. "I misunderstood."

Wes nodded. "There seems to be a good deal of misunderstanding in this room." He looked at Callie. "Where is Thomas? If the detective thinks he can take the word of a thirteen-year-old, I'll go and get him."

"Not necessary. We wouldn't want him to speak to you before we talk to him." The detective shifted his attention to Callie. "Where would we find the boy, Miss Deboyer?"

"Both Thomas and Lottie are at Fair Haven with Jane and Lula, the Bridgeports' servants. At least I hope that's where they are. Since I've been here in this office with you, I have no way of saying for certain, Detective."

Callie teetered between anger and fear, but her patience had grown thin as time passed, and she simply wanted to be on her way to Biscayne.

Detectives Fitch and Jensen spoke to each other, and soon Detective Jensen departed, presumably to get Thomas. She hoped he wouldn't frighten the children — or the servants. Poor Jane and Lula had been beside themselves with worry when Callie had been summoned to the superintendent's office for questioning. No telling how they would react when Detective Jensen reappeared at the front door.

Wes leaned close. "You look pale. Are you sure you're okay?"

"Physically, yes."

"Is there any word about Daisy?"

Callie shook her head. "I've heard nothing directly, although Lula stopped at the hospital before coming to work this morning. Daisy was still a patient, but they wouldn't give her any information since she isn't a member of the family."

"I had hoped to hear Daisy had been released." He rubbed his hands together. "I do hope it wasn't a brown recluse spider bite. They are quite dangerous and difficult to treat."

"How do you know? More of your botany studies?"

Her tone was sharp, and his eyes clouded when he looked at her. "It's information I learned in school. We need to talk as soon as you're permitted to leave here. There's a great deal I need to tell you."

"That has already become obvious." As soon as she'd spoken the words, Callie silently reprimanded herself. She didn't want to sound like a shrew, but how could Wesley think she would want to talk to him? Even though he'd known how much she valued trust, he had betrayed her.

When Wesley attempted to explain further,

the detective silenced him. "I don't want you two talking any more until we've questioned the boy."

Callie folded her arms across her waist and stared at the detective. The entire matter was a waste of time — time that could be used to sit with Daisy and give Mr. and Mrs. Bridgeport a reprieve from what must be a worrisome and tiring experience, especially with no help traveling with them. The moment she was free from this office, she'd gather the children, see to the luggage, bid Lula and Jane farewell, and be on her way to the hospital in Biscayne. Thoughts of sweet Daisy suffering from the spider bite renewed Callie's concern, and she bowed her head and prayed for the child.

"Doesn't appear Miss Deboyer's too worried. Looks like she's gone to sleep." Detective Fitch chuckled.

A short time later, Callie opened her eyes and raised her head. "I wasn't sleeping, Detective; I was praying."

The detective narrowed his eyes. "If I was in your situation, I'd be praying, too."

"I was praying for Daisy Bridgeport, not for myself. And I have no reason to fear anything you might discover about me, Mr. Fitch." She gave Wesley a sidelong glance.

"I am quite trustworthy."

Wesley's jaw tightened, but he remained silent and stared straight ahead. He obviously wanted to say something, but the detective was watching him — probably eager to offer another reprimand.

A short time later, Lula, Detective Jensen, and Thomas appeared in the office. Lula's eyes shone with fear as she brought Thomas into the room. "He said I was to bring Thomas over here. I hope I did right, Miss Callie."

"Of course you did. There's nothing to worry about. Is Jane with Lottie?"

"Yes, miss. The luggage is ready. We can close the house and see you on your way as soon as all this is over." The maid glanced at the detectives and then turned back toward Callie. "Are you all right?"

Callie forced a smile that she hoped would encourage Lula. "I'm fine, Lula. If you want to wait outside, I don't think it will take long for the detective to speak with Thomas."

Lula backed out of the room, and the detective gestured to Thomas. "Hello, Thomas. I'm Detective Fitch and I'd like to talk to you. Would that be all right?"

Thomas glanced at Callie before slowly nodding his head. "I guess so."

"Mr. Townsend tells me that he's taught you all about the different plants and animals on the island. Is that right?"

Thomas quickly agreed, and before the detective could ply the boy with more questions, Thomas offered a plethora of information that he'd learned from Wes. "He spent time with us during the afternoons 'cause most everybody wanted to take their lessons in the morning or early afternoon. He would come with us after lunch. You should see some of the shells we found down at the beach."

Although the detective tried to stop the boy's litany several times, Thomas continued telling him about the variety of snakes, deer, birds, and other plants and animals Wes had helped them identify.

Thomas inched closer to the detective. "I have a notebook that tells all about the different plants and animals. I even drew some pictures to help me remember. I could show it to you."

Detective Fitch finally held up his hand. "I believe that's enough, Thomas. If you'd like to go out and wait with the maid, we should be done here shortly."

The moment Thomas exited the room, Wes leaned forward. "I assume that you have enough information to release Miss

Deboyer, as well?"

The detective rubbed his jaw. "I suppose I do, but I'm still not sure why Mrs. Murphy would put those jewels in Miss Deboyer's trunk."

"I think it's quite simple to understand." Wes folded his arms across his chest. "Mrs. Murphy did it because she knew her actions would cast Miss Deboyer in a suspicious light should anything go amiss before they got off the island. She and her son left no stone unturned. They knew they might be caught and planned for that event by arranging to implicate Miss Deboyer." Wes glared at the man. "And you bought into their ridiculous story hook, line, and sinker."

The detective returned Wesley's glare. "It is our duty to investigate every possibility, Mr. Townsend. Your high opinion of Miss Deboyer does not prove her innocence."

"No, it does not. But you have received much more than my opinion. Miss Deboyer's whereabouts have been confirmed by me, and my word has been tested by speaking to young Thomas. I believe you've received enough information to disprove the lies told to you by Mrs. Murphy. And I'm certain Mr. and Mrs. Bridgeport would vouch for the honesty of Miss Deboyer."

"Since we've recovered the jewels and apprehended Mrs. Murphy and Mr. Penni-man, and it doesn't appear Miss Deboyer was involved, I suppose you can leave." Detective Fitch pushed to his feet. "But if we should discover any further evidence against you, I will personally come to Indianapolis and apprehend you."

Callie stood and waved toward her trunk. "If you would please remove the jewelry from my trunk, I'd like to take it with me. I hope the belongings I had packed in there are beneath the jewelry." She looked at Detective Jensen. "Or did you remove them?"

"I dunno, but you can take a look once I get the jewelry out." After removing the jewels, he beckoned her forward. "Looks like there's a few things still in there."

Callie peered into the chest. She wasn't certain all of her belongings remained inside, but she wasn't going to stay any longer than necessary. She closed the trunk and started to lift it from the desk, but Wes reached around her and grasped the handles.

"Let me take that for you."

If she hadn't been so eager to depart, she would have fought to carry the trunk her-self. And she didn't want to argue in front of the detectives. When they stepped into the foyer, Wesley insisted upon carrying the trunk and accompanying them home. No matter what Callie said, he refused to remain behind.

She pushed ahead and walked with Lula and let Wesley follow behind with Thomas. When they arrived at the house, he placed the trunk in the wagon alongside their other belongings and grasped her arm.

"I'm not going to let you leave until I talk to you. I need to explain why I wasn't forthright earlier. You heard me explain to the detective why I hadn't revealed my family background . . ."

She wheeled around. "I don't consider that an explanation for lying to me about who you are. I may have been concerned about your social standing, but I'm not someone who would have brushed you aside because of such a thing. You've given a poor excuse for living a lie — an excuse I won't accept." She stepped toward the porch.

"Wait! There's more I need to tell you. Please!"

She glanced over her shoulder. "More lies?"

He grimaced. "You may call them lies, but I call it withholding a painful past."

She stiffened her shoulders. "What else is there that I don't know? Do you have a wife secreted away at the clubhouse, too?"

"No. I have no wife, and I'm not betrothed or interested in any other woman. But, Callie, this is much worse."

She clenched her hands. "You've been convicted of a crime and have spent the past years in prison?"

"No criminal record, although I sometimes think serving a prison term would be easier than the self-incrimination I heap upon myself." He shook his head. "And not unjustly. You see, I'm responsible for the deaths of many people — not intentionally, but they are dead all the same."

She gasped and dropped to the front step. "What are you saying?"

"I'm not a botanist or a golf pro. Along with medical courses, I took classes in botany and played golf during my college years. During my vacations, I golfed at amateur tournaments." He wrung his hands together. "The truth is, I'm a doctor."

"A doctor?" Her mouth gaped open. "You are a doctor and you didn't help Daisy?"

"I did help — I took her to the infirmary. I had no idea what kind of spider bit her, and there was nothing I could do other than rush her to get proper medical attention. Had there been anything I could have done to help, I wouldn't have hesitated." Pain glistened in his eyes. "Please don't hold what happened to Daisy against me. She needed more help than the doctor at the infirmary or I could give her. And I did help with Lottie, remember?"

Callie nodded. "I know you're right, but hearing that you're a doctor — my thoughts immediately went to Daisy."

"I know, and I wish I could have done something to help her."

She hesitated a moment. "Did you become a doctor because of the people you mentioned who died?"

"No. Quite the opposite. They died because I was their physician, and that's why I no longer practice medicine. My family didn't want me to become a doctor." He gave her a lopsided smile. "As you know, physicians aren't well paid or well thought of among the members of higher society."

In spite of his lies, compassion squeezed her heart. "There is no shame in selecting a profession in which you can help others, Wesley."

"But that's just it. I didn't help. My treatment caused the deaths of my patients."

She leaned forward, unable to stifle her interest. "How so?"

Wesley gazed heavenward. "I was working in New York at a research laboratory with several physicians who had been developing a serum to help in the cure of cerebrospinal meningitis. There had been an epidemic in New York years earlier, and these men had hoped to discover a cure. Although they were confident their discovery would help, it hadn't been widely tested before an epidemic broke out in Texas. In four months, over eight hundred cases were diagnosed in Dallas alone."

Wide-eyed, Callie stared at him. "And these doctors were asked to come to Dallas and help?"

"Yes. I was one of the physicians who went to help train the medical staff in how to properly perform the lumbar punctures to inject the serum." Wes inhaled a deep breath. "Everything was going pretty well, and we were seeing good results, but another outbreak occurred in a smaller community outside of Dallas. The doctor in charge sent me."

She wanted to ignore everything he was saying and run inside the house, but her curiosity and the feelings of love for him that had grown during the past months held her in place. The pain he continued to suffer was obvious in his words.

Wes momentarily closed his eyes. "I wish I didn't have to tell you all of this, but I need to make certain you know the truth about me before you leave. I don't want you to discover anything about my past from someone else." His voice cracked. "When I arrived at that small town, there were so many sick people, and even though I attempted to get someone to help me — someone I could train — no one was willing. So I gave the injections myself." He inhaled and blew out a deep breath. "Most of them died."

"And you blame yourself?"

The minute she asked the question, she saw the bewilderment that shone in his eyes.

"Of course I blame myself. Only a few of those who'd been injected in Dallas died, while it was the opposite this time." His voice cracked and he looked away.

Her emotions battled within. "There must have been something wrong with the serum, or perhaps it was a different strain of the disease." Callie realized she was doing her best to excuse him and thought to stop, but something in her heart pressed her to continue. "There could be any number of things that caused the deaths to occur. I don't think you should blame yourself when you were trying to help."

He nodded. "They may have had a greater chance of recovery if I'd never appeared in their little town. I will always be tormented by the possibility that I did more harm than good." Wes gave her a weak smile. "Of course, it reinforced my father's belief that I should never have considered becoming a physician. He still thinks I should join the family business, and he's given me these few months while we're away from Massachusetts to make up my mind about the future."

His explanation tugged at her heart. She recalled the Townsend ladies visiting Mrs. Bridgeport and speaking so unkindly about Wes. So much pressure from his family and so much pain and guilt to live with. She ached to ease it somehow.

But she pulled away when he reached for her hand. She had to guard herself against a man who had chosen to lie to her. She could not sympathize with him. He'd lied to her about everything — who he was, what he was, and why he was on Bridal Veil. Wes Townsend would have to tend to his own wounds just as she'd have to tend to the ones he had left on her heart. She couldn't trust him, and she could never love a man she couldn't trust.

"I want you to know how sorry I am, and I promise I'll never again lie to you."

Hot, angry tears escaped down her cheeks.

She stood and turned toward the door. "I know you won't, Wes, because I don't plan ever to see or speak to you again."

CHAPTER 25

Though Lottie and Thomas enjoyed the ride across the river, they were more intent on getting to the hospital and seeing Daisy. Captain Fleming agreed to have all of the trunks delivered to the hotel, and he hailed a hansom cab to take the three of them to the Biscayne hospital, a rather nondescript brick building constructed with a view toward the river.

After entering a double set of wide oak doors, Callie headed toward the large wooden reception desk. Her shoes clicked on the shiny tile, and a matronly woman with a tight bun at the nape of her neck looked up from the desk when Callie approached with Thomas flanking one side and Lottie the other.

"We're here to see Daisy Bridgeport."

"We're her brother and sister." Lottie beamed at the woman.

"Children aren't permitted to visit hospital

patients. It's against the rules." The woman's lips drooped into a frown. She pointed to a list fastened to the wall not far from her desk. Much like the matronly woman, the bold, black rules printed on white pasteboard presented an unwelcoming impression. "The children can wait down here with me while you go up. Daisy is on the second floor."

Callie hesitated, uncertain what to do. If Maude hadn't turned out to be a criminal, she'd be here to look after the children while Callie went to check on Daisy and speak with Mr. and Mrs. Bridgeport.

Thomas straightened his shoulders. "I can look after Lottie, Miss Callie. If you'll leave your case with the crayons and paper, we'll keep busy. Won't we, Lottie?"

Lottie shoved her lower lip into a pout. "I'd rather go visit Daisy. I know she'll feel better if she can see me."

Callie stooped down in front of the child. "I know it would make her feel better, too, Lottie. But we must follow the rules. You draw a picture for Daisy while I'm gone, and I'll take it to her later today."

Once the children were situated, Callie strode to the stairs at the end of the hallway and climbed to the second floor. When she arrived at Daisy's room, she stopped outside the door. Daisy appeared to be either asleep or unconscious, she wasn't certain which.

"Callie!" Mrs. Bridgeport jumped to her feet and sent a book tumbling to the floor. "It is so good to see you. When you didn't arrive yesterday, we became worried. Are Lottie and Thomas downstairs? Are they well?"

"Yes. They're fine." Callie nodded toward the bed. "What about Daisy? She doesn't appear to be making much progress."

"The doctors were more encouraged today. They've been using some sort of carbon or charcoal on the wound — I'm not positive, and I don't ask many questions. Luther talks to the doctors, and he says they're optimistic. I did look at the wound, and it's looking better."

Callie lowered her voice. "Is she unconscious?"

"No. Just sleeping. They've been giving her some sort of medicine that makes her sleepy and helps with the pain. I think it's laudanum, but Luther —"

"I know." Callie patted her arm. "Mr. Bridgeport has talked with the doctors."

Mrs. Bridgeport could organize major social events and act the perfect hostess for her husband, but when her children were ill, she lost all ability to cope. Illness in her children created a deep fear in the woman. And little wonder, for she'd lost her first-born child when he'd been only three years old. She said it was due to her inability to provide proper care. Callie doubted that was true, but Mrs. Bridgeport no longer trusted her motherly instincts when one of her children was sick.

"I will be forever thankful to Wesley for rushing Daisy to the infirmary. The doctors here at the hospital told Luther it was the quick action in getting her here that made all the difference. They couldn't be certain, since we didn't have the spider, but they think it was a brown recluse." She clutched Callie's arm. "I've already told Luther that I want to give Wesley a monetary reward."

The irony of the situation nearly caused Callie to laugh aloud. "You can do whatever you'd like, Mrs. Bridgeport, but Wesley Townsend doesn't need your money. While I thought he was simply a golf pro who had learned a great deal about botany, I've learned he is a member of the Townsend family, who are staying at the clubhouse. The family that owns the textile mills in Massachusetts."

Mrs. Bridgeport stared at Callie as though she'd lost her mind. "We met Howard and Blanche Townsend and some of their children. I don't recall ever seeing Wesley in their company."

"I'm not surprised. He dislikes social functions, so when he wasn't at the golf course, he did everything in his power to avoid the club activities." Callie inhaled a deep breath. "You'll be even more surprised to learn that he's actually a doctor. He helped us with Lottie when she had another coughing spell. He believes she may well have asthma."

"Is Lottie all right?" The worry in her tone was evident.

"She's fine. Mr. Townsend's advice worked wonders."

Mrs. Bridgeport shook her head in relieved wonder. "He's a doctor? Well, no wonder he moved so quickly to get Daisy to the infirmary. And God bless him for knowing how to help my poor Lottie." Deep ridges lined her forehead. "I'm sure the Townsends weren't happy with his decision to become a doctor. Mr. Townsend seemed quite obsessed with his business when we joined them for dinner one night. In fact, he tried to convince Luther to invest in his mills."

"Really? Did Mr. Bridgeport agree?"

She shot a look at her husband. "I don't believe so. He mentioned that he thought

Mr. Townsend was pushing too hard. I think he feared they might be having some sort of financial problems because he was pressing for investors at every turn."

The comment surprised Callie. It seemed odd Wesley's father would pressure his son to come into a business if it were failing.

Mr. Bridgeport folded his paper and walked to Daisy's bedside. "The Townsend Mills aren't failing, Eunice. I misspoke. Seems they're expanding. They want additional investors, but I'm still not interested."

Both women stared at him. Without giving any indication, Mr. Bridgeport had obviously been listening to their entire conversation.

"It is rude to eavesdrop, Luther." Mrs. Bridgeport pursed her lips.

"Good heavens, Eunice. I'm sitting in the same room while the two of you are talking. Am I supposed to put my fingers in my ears? I wasn't eavesdropping." He glanced at Daisy. "Is Maude taking the children over to the hotel?"

Callie had hoped to avoid the topic of Maude for a bit longer, but she supposed it was best to tell them while the children were busy downstairs. "Maude isn't with us any longer."

"She quit?"

Callie swallowed hard. There would be no easy way to tell the Bridgeports what had happened. Best to be forthright.

"Not exactly. Both she and her son, Archie Penniman, the tennis pro, were arrested for stealing jewelry from Bridal Veil guests. You recall the investors hired investigators?"

Mrs. Bridgeport reached for the chair and slowly lowered herself onto the hard seat. For a moment Callie thought the older woman might faint. "Her son? Theft? But she came highly recommended by Harriet Winslow."

Mr. Bridgeport poured a glass of water for his wife. "Drink this before you end up in a hospital bed next to Daisy."

He gestured to Callie. "Go on with what you were telling us, Callie."

"The detectives said they have been working on this case for some time."

Mr. Bridgeport tugged on his waistcoat. "Indeed. I recall hearing they were hired after the second or third robbery had occurred."

"They didn't give me all of the details, but when I was brought in for questioning —"

"What?" Mrs. Bridgeport turned as white

as the tile floors. "Why did they question you?"

Mr. Bridgeport looked at his wife. "If you keep interrupting, she'll never be able to explain, Eunice." He nodded at Callie. "Go on."

As best she could, Callie explained that the detectives thought she might have been working alongside Maude and Archie to steal the jewelry. "At first I didn't believe what they said about Maude — I mentioned her recommendation from Mrs. Winslow and that she'd worked for the family for many years."

"And?" Mrs. Bridgeport gave her husband a sideways glance.

"When the detectives questioned Mrs. Murphy about her background and her whereabouts over the past years, she told them she'd been employed by Mrs. Winslow and showed them her reference letter. The detectives wired Mrs. Winslow and discovered the letter was a forgery. Maude never worked for the Winslow family."

Mrs. Bridgeport clasped a hand to her bodice. "Dear me! We had a criminal living in our house, Luther. And I employed her. From the moment I saw that woman, I didn't think she appeared quite right." Mrs. Bridgeport lifted her fingers to her hair. "All that messy hair of hers, and she didn't know how to properly care for the children. Her grammar left much to be desired, as well. I wondered that Harriet would hire someone with such poor skills, yet the reference letter was glowing." She looked at Callie. "Wasn't it?"

Callie nodded. "Yes, it was." It was clear Mrs. Bridgeport needed affirmation she'd made a decision based upon a sound reference.

Mr. Bridgeport leaned against the metal-framed hospital bed. "So this mother and son had been involved in other nefarious behavior before arriving at Bridal Veil?"

"Yes. The detective told Wesley Townsend that they concentrated on resorts, moving north during the summer season and south during the winter season. Archie would arrive first and hire on as the tennis pro or in some other capacity and then arrange for his mother to join him. From what I'm told, this was Archie's second season at Bridal Veil, but it seems his mother couldn't find work last year."

Mrs. Bridgeport sighed. "I gave her access this year. I feel simply terrible."

Callie patted her hand. "Don't blame yourself. Last year the two of them managed to steal from guests at the Ayers Hotel here in Biscayne, where Mrs. Murphy had secured a position in the kitchen during the season. During their investigation, the detectives learned that Maude would discover information regarding guests and Archie would sneak into the rooms and steal. The two of them were quite a team."

Mrs. Bridgeport shivered. "That's very sad. To think that a mother would encourage and participate in crime with her son is incredible. And to think she was around our children."

"I don't think you need to worry on that account, my dear. Had she done or said anything outlandish, they would have told you or Callie." After gracing his wife with a sympathetic smile, Mr. Bridgeport looked at Callie. "This has been quite an eventful time, and it continues with our little Daisy still suffering."

From the dark circles that rimmed their eyes, it was obvious neither Mr. nor Mrs. Bridgeport had rested since arriving with Daisy. "I would be happy to remain here with Daisy if the two of you would like to take the children to the hotel. You could rest for a while, and I could call the hotel if anything should change with her condition."

"I'd like to talk to you a little more before I leave." Mrs. Bridgeport smiled at her husband. "If you'd like to go, Luther, I'll join you and the children in a little while. We can go to dinner before we return to the hospital, and then Callie can go stay with them."

He nodded and picked up his hat from atop the window ledge. "Don't be too long, Eunice. I know you want to visit, but you need to rest, too."

A middle-aged nurse entered the room and looked at the clipboard attached to the end of Lottie's bed before she examined the child. Callie and Mrs. Bridgeport watched in silence, both of them staring at the woman until she finished.

"Any change?" Mrs. Bridgeport's voice held a note of expectation.

"Her temperature is up a bit, but it's probably nothing to be concerned about. From her chart, it appears to fluctuate some." She brushed past Callie and exited the room as quietly as she'd entered.

"I wanted to hear a bit more about Wesley. Even though you hadn't talked to me much, I didn't miss the fact that you had begun to look forward to the outings with him in the afternoons. There was little doubt you enjoyed his company." She nudged Callie's arm. "It's easy for one woman to see when another woman is falling in love. And even though you said you'd never again trust a man, I was sure you had feelings for Wesley." Her lips curved in a generous smile. "And now that I hear he's a Townsend, it's all the better. After all my efforts to find you a suitable match, you've unintentionally taken care of the matter for yourself."

Callie shook her head and slowly explained Wesley's deceit. How he had lied about his family and the fact that he was a physician and bore a great deal of guilt over the death of patients in Texas. "For a while, I did think he was the perfect man for me. I had grown to trust him, but that has all been destroyed by his lies."

"Really? It doesn't seem to me that he actually lied. He withheld information from you because he feared you would reject him. And nothing about his family or his profession is repugnant in any way." She snapped open her fan and waved it back and forth in front of her face. "Of course, he'd do better to go into business with his father than return to the practice of medicine. Doctors simply are not paid enough money to support a family properly."

"But withholding information is a type of lie."

"Is it? I'd venture to say most of us have

withheld information at some time in our lives. I don't condone the behavior, but if it is a lie, then you're as guilty as Wesley."

"How so? I was honest with him."

"But you've withheld information in the past when you thought it to your advantage. You might recall that even though I'd expressly told you I wanted a governess who could give the children piano lessons, you didn't mention you couldn't play. Nor did you tell me you'd spoken with Mary Deitweiler about a position as her personal assistant prior to our interview — a fact that nearly caused a permanent breach in my friendship with Mary."

"You're right." Callie's stomach tightened at the remembrance. "I should have told you before I interviewed for the tutoring position. Though I apologized to both you and Mrs. Deitweiler, I still regret I wasn't forthright."

"I know, my dear. Mary and I have healed any ill feelings that arose out of the incident. I'm merely pointing out that you didn't tell me. I know you didn't do it with any thoughts of malice, but you need to remember that we all make errors in judgment. I believe that's what happened to Wesley — he made an error in judgment."

"But I told him about Matthew and how I

struggled with trusting others. He should have told me rather than let me believe he was an entirely different person."

Mrs. Bridgeport leaned forward and clasped her hands. "You're right. He should have, but he seems to be a young man who has suffered a great deal of personal pain through the tragedy that occurred in Texas. And having met his father, I'm sure he's putting pressure on Wesley, as well." She squeezed Callie's hands. "I don't believe he was deceiving you in order to hurt you. I think he feared he would lose you if you learned the truth about his past."

Mrs. Bridgeport released Callie's hands and stood. She walked to the bed and kissed Daisy's cheek and then turned toward Callie. "I believe I'll go and join Luther and the children. Think about what I've said, Callie. I believe you'll come to agree that I'm right."

While Daisy continued to sleep, Callie considered her conversation with Mrs. Bridgeport. She *had* judged Wesley unfairly. Though he could have been more straightforward about his family, she had made it clear that she wasn't interested in becoming a member of the social set — along with numerous other comments that likely had given him pause. Little wonder he hadn't divulged his parents were the Townsends of Townsend Mills. And she'd shown little sympathy for the trauma he'd suffered in Texas. Granted, she'd told him he couldn't hold himself responsible, but she didn't consider what it must have been like to see all those people die and to feel he'd somehow caused their deaths. Instead of offering Wesley comfort, she'd turned on him — told him he wasn't acceptable, that he hadn't passed her test.

In her concern to protect herself from further pain, she'd forgotten grace. She bowed her head, and with tears streaming down her face, she begged God to forgive her for her callous behavior. If only she could have the opportunity to ask Wesley's forgiveness, as well.

CHAPTER 26

Wesley sat on the screened balcony of his suite that overlooked the croquet lawn of the clubhouse. He leaned forward to watch the children playing and was once again struck by the fact that Callie was no longer on the island. A young boy, who looked much like Thomas, ran across the lawn carrying a croquet mallet, his laughter floating on the breeze like a joyful song.

Wesley inhaled slowly and closed his eyes as the scent of freshly mown grass filled his nostrils. Like a swarm of worker bees, gardeners arrived each morning to manicure the lawns and hedges that surrounded the clubhouse. Mr. Crocker demanded perfection for the guests of Bridal Veil. Whether in the opulent dining room, the lavish suites, or the surrounding grounds, he made certain the workers provided that expected perfection. The same was true at the golf course, where workers daily arrived to care for the greens and rake ridges into the sand.

On any other morning, Wes would already be at the golf course, but this was Sunday. The guests golfed in the afternoon, but they attended church at the island chapel every Sunday morning. He startled when a knock sounded at the door to his suite. Pushing up from his chair, he returned inside and strode across the sitting room.

"Father." Wes failed in his attempt to smile as he backed away from the door to permit the older man entrance. "I thought you'd be down at breakfast."

His father frowned. He'd obviously sensed Wesley's displeasure at the unexpected visit.

After stepping inside, his father strode further into the room. "I plan to go down in a little while, but I wanted to speak to you first. May I sit down?"

"Yes, of course." Wes gestured toward the two overstuffed chairs flanking the marble fireplace. He had hoped for a peaceful hour to clear his thoughts and pray about his future before attending church services with the family, but it appeared that wasn't going to happen.

"Your mother and I had a lengthy talk last night." His father inhaled a deep breath. "About you."

Wes grasped the arms of his chair and

braced himself for an onslaught. How long would it take before his father accepted the fact that he could not control all of his children? Granted, he'd been successful with the others, but Wesley remained determined to stand his ground and make decisions for himself. He was not going to let his failure in Texas give his father a toehold to gain control over his life.

"I'm sure you and Mother have more important things to discuss than me." He forced a smile. "After all, you're in the throes of expanding the mills."

His father nodded. "That's true enough, but nothing is more important than our children."

"I'm not a child any longer, Father, and I —"

"Just hear me out, Wesley. Your mother told me about this young lady that you've met. Callie Deboyer, I believe that was her name?"

Wes nodded. "Yes, that's her name."

When he'd talked to his mother, he hadn't anticipated she would relate their conversation to his father. Then again, he hadn't asked her to hold their conversation in confidence. She hadn't betrayed him, yet her behavior surprised him. He'd always believed she kept their conversations confidential. Maybe he'd been wrong.

"Your mother says that even though Miss Deboyer has left the island, you are determined to win her heart or some such thing." He tugged on his vest. "I didn't listen very well when your mother began using flowery words and speaking of love, but I did listen to the rest of what she said. Afterward, I did some genuine soul-searching and had a long conversation with the Lord."

Wes arched his brows. There had always been prayers at meals, regular church attendance, and Bible reading in their home, but Wes had never considered his father a man who conversed with God or regularly sought God's direction. The idea somehow seemed foreign to him because his father had always presented himself as a self-made man who thought goals could be accomplished only through hard work and tenacity. And life's problems could be solved in much the same way. Now to hear his father say that he'd spent time speaking to God was difficult to comprehend.

"I'm surprised." Wes longed to say something more profound, but at the moment words escaped him.

His father grinned. "That I didn't listen to the love part or that I had a conversation with the Lord?"

"That you would seek God's guidance."

His father's smile faded. "You don't think I seek God's help from time to time?"

Wes leaned toward his father. "I'm sorry, Father. I didn't mean to offend you, but I've never seen you spend much time in prayer or heard you talk much about looking to God for help."

"Just because you don't see me praying or hear me talk about a need for God's help doesn't mean that I've gone through life without seeking divine guidance." He stared at the floor for a moment, as if to gather his thoughts. After clearing his throat, he looked at Wesley. "As I was saying, I did some soul-searching, and it has become clear to me that I should quit interfering in your life. You are the one who must decide what you want for your future. I am not going to try to persuade you to enter the family business any longer. It is not what you want, and I will honor your decision."

Wes loosened his grip on the arms of his chair. "You mean it? There are no hard feelings?"

"No hard feelings. If, in the future, you should have a change of heart, then I will welcome your decision, and there will be a job waiting for you at Townsend Mills." His lips curved in a lopsided grin. "However, I don't believe that will ever happen. I wish you well in whatever decisions you make for your future, but remember that you must decide upon something. While I won't force you to work for me at Townsend Mills, I will not support you while you sit idle. Understood?"

"Understood. I don't expect you to support me, Father."

"Then you have a plan?" There was an expectant gleam in his father's eyes.

"I wish I could tell you that everything is settled, but that wouldn't be true. First, I must find out if Callie will forgive me for withholding the truth from her. If she'll forgive me, then it is my hope to marry her."

"Without any means of supporting her? I think you're putting the cart before the horse, Wesley. You need to decide upon future employment and then consider marriage. I think any young woman would look upon a prospective husband more favorably if he were gainfully employed, don't you?"

"In most cases, I think that is true, Father. But if Callie will have me, I'd like her to join me in making decisions about the future. Shortly after we met, I learned that she has been struggling with plans regarding her own future. I feel I must first win her heart and her trust. Then we can discuss what's ahead for both of us."

"So long as we are clear that I will not support you once we return to Massachusetts, then I'm fine with whatever you decide." His father pushed to his feet and clapped Wesley on the shoulder. "I know I've been hard on you since your return from Texas, but I thought the best way for you to get over the tragedy you'd experienced was for you to find a new profession and keep yourself busy."

Wesley followed his father to the door. "Thank you, Father. Even though you may not agree with me, I am thankful you've decided to let me make my own choices."

Wes returned to the sitting porch. The children had returned inside, likely to eat breakfast and prepare for church. Soon he'd need to do the same. But for now, he looked out toward the river and thanked God for the change in his father's heart. He prayed God would change Callie's heart, as well.

Mrs. Bridgeport returned to the hospital during the evening and stayed with Daisy while Callie went to supper and rested. After sleeping for an hour, she stopped by the Bridgeports' hotel rooms. Mr. Bridgeport answered the door, and she stepped inside, where the children were busy playing a game of checkers in the sitting room.

He gestured toward Thomas and Lottie. "I thought a game might keep the children occupied. I saw the checkerboard in the lobby, and the clerk said we could bring it to the room."

"That was an excellent idea. I'm sure it helps keep their thoughts off of Daisy." She grinned at Thomas. "Are you winning?"

"I'm not sure. Lottie's pretty good."

"Then you best keep a sharp eye on the board." She winked at Lottie and then turned to Mr. Bridgeport. "I'm going over to the hospital. I'll encourage Mrs. Bridgeport to come back here for the night."

"Thank you, Callie."

Callie arrived at Daisy's room a short time later, and after only a few minutes, the doctor and a nurse appeared. He checked Daisy and then urged them to return to the hotel for the night. "There is nothing you can do for her. The best thing is to let her rest — and you need to do the same."

"Her fever has returned, and she hasn't wakened during the past several hours. I think she's taking a turn for the worse." Mrs. Bridgeport wrung her handkerchief between her hands.

"I mentioned yesterday that you can expect to see some of these fluctuations,"

411

the doctor replied. "We had hoped she might have a quick recovery, but that doesn't often occur. I do think you should both return to the hotel for the night. Your prayers will do the most good right now." He waited and when neither of them moved, he glanced at the nurse. "Why don't you stay here with Daisy while I walk Mrs. Bridgeport and Miss Deboyer to the stairs."

"Yes, of course, Doctor." The nurse pulled a chair near the bed and sat down.

Mrs. Bridgeport and Callie followed the doctor. "Do get some rest, ladies. We'll see you in the morning." He turned and headed back down the hall.

Halfway down the stairs, Callie stopped. "I forgot my purse in Daisy's room. Why don't you go ahead, Mrs. Bridgeport, and wait for me in the lobby. There are chairs down there. I won't be long."

Callie turned and hastened up the stairs. She was about to enter Daisy's room when she heard voices inside and stopped.

"I don't think she'll make it through the night. You should check on her frequently and follow the orders I've written. If need be, you can send for me."

Callie gasped and, with her hand still covering her mouth, stepped into the room and circled the partition.

The doctor caught sight of her and sighed. "Those comments weren't meant for your ears, Miss Deboyer."

Callie glared at the doctor. He seemed as distant and cold as the stark hospital room. "You lied to her mother. How could you do such a thing? It's cruel and it's wrong. If these are to be Daisy's last hours, Mrs. Bridgeport will want to be with her. To tell her to go back and rest when you know her child might not live until morning is beyond belief to me. What kind of man are you?"

He took Callie's arm and led her across the room. "I am a doctor who cares about his patients and also cares about the families of those patients. If Daisy's condition continues to worsen — as I expect it will — then she will likely suffer terrible convulsions and bear extreme pain in the coming hours. If her parents are here, those images will be burned into their memories for a very long time, perhaps forever. How do you think they would prefer to remember her, Miss Deboyer? As they've last seen her today, or in a raging convulsion?"

"I doubt they would want to see her suffer, but I can't speak for them. And I can't lie to them."

"I'm not asking you to lie, but you need not tell. Her mother won't question you any

413

further. She's already spoken to me and won't expect another report from you." He frowned. "Why are you back here, anyway?"

"I forgot my purse."

He glanced at the windowsill, picked up her purse, and handed it to her. "I think you should keep this information to yourself."

Callie stared at Daisy's bright red cheeks. Such a sweet and innocent child. Callie couldn't imagine watching the little girl suffer any more than she had already. She was certain Mrs. Bridgeport would come back upstairs if she told her what was expected during the night. And the sights and sounds would likely be more than Daisy's mother could bear. Yet hadn't she condemned Wesley for withholding the truth about himself? She recalled the conversation she'd had with Mrs. Bridgeport only a night ago. Callie had railed against Wes's behavior, yet now she was being asked to do the same thing. Worse yet, she was now considering that it might be the right thing to do.

Fighting back tears, she turned to the doctor. "I won't tell Mrs. Bridgeport."

"Good. I think that's the right thing to do. Now, come along, and I'll —"

Callie held up her hand. "You didn't let me finish. I won't tell Daisy's mother, but I

414

will tell Mr. Bridgeport. I'll leave it to him to make the final decision."

After placing a kiss on Daisy's warm cheek, she hurried from the room. Stopping at the top of the stairs, she dabbed away her tears, straightened her shoulders, and forced a smile.

She held her purse aloft as she approached the older woman. "It was right where I left it."

The two of them joined arms but remained silent as they returned to the hotel. Callie was lost in thoughts of how she might get Mr. Bridgeport alone to tell him the sad news. No doubt Mrs. Bridgeport was lost in her own thoughts and fears. When they reached the door leading to the Bridgeports' suite, Mrs. Bridgeport turned to bid Callie good-night.

"I thought I might come in and see Thomas and Lottie if they're still awake. I haven't had much time with them these last few days."

Mrs. Bridgeport nodded. "Of course. Do come in."

"Mama! Miss Callie!" Lottie jumped up and hurried toward them. "How is Daisy? Can we go see her soon?"

"Not just yet, dear. She's still not well enough, but when the time is right your father will make arrangements so the two of you can slip up to her room for a few minutes." Mrs. Bridgeport glanced toward her husband. "Won't you, Luther?"

"I'll do my best."

Mrs. Bridgeport removed her hat. Her shoulders sagged, and the hollows beneath her eyes revealed a tale of sorrow. She turned to her husband. "I believe I'll go in and lie down for a few minutes, if you don't mind."

"Not at all, my dear. You rest as long as you like. We'll be just fine." Once she'd closed the bedroom door, Mr. Bridgeport motioned for Callie to sit down. "I took the children to Lula's home here in Biscayne this afternoon. She's going to come in the morning and stay here at the hotel to help with the children as long as Daisy's in the hospital."

Lottie turned from her drawing. "We're going on the streetcar tomorrow, and Lula's taking us to the park, isn't she, Papa?"

He smiled and nodded. "That's right."

Callie shot a nervous look at the bedroom door. She needed to gather her courage and tell Mr. Bridgeport, but she'd need to be careful the children didn't overhear.

"Did the doctor come to see Daisy while you were at the hospital?" Mr. Bridgeport asked, scooting forward on the couch.

"Yes." Callie glanced at the children and gestured to the other side of the room. Keeping her voice low, she told him that Daisy had been fitful and they hadn't been able to control her temperature. "The doctor didn't tell Mrs. Bridgeport, but I overheard him tell the nurse that Daisy probably wouldn't live through the night." The words choked in her throat as she relayed the doctor's prognosis for Daisy's remaining hours. "I didn't tell her, Mr. Bridgeport. I'm leaving that decision to you. I don't know what is best."

Pale and shaking, he pulled a handkerchief from his pocket and blotted beads of perspiration from his face. "I thought Daisy was doing a little better earlier today." His voice was a hoarse whisper. "Did Eunice not see how much change had taken place? Perhaps she's aware but doesn't want to admit it to herself."

"The doctor encouraged her to come back to the hotel. I believe she took that as affirmation that Daisy would be all right during the night. Of course, she didn't actually say that, so I can't be certain."

He dropped to a chair and rested his head in the palm of his hand. "I truly don't know what to do, either. Perhaps the doctor is

417

right. More than anything, I think we must pray. You go on to your room, Callie. If I change my mind and we decide to go to the hospital later tonight, I'll come and get you so you can stay with the children."

Callie bid the children good-night and slowly trod the short distance to her room. Once inside, she knelt at the side of her bed and prayed. Sometime later, she moved to the overstuffed chair and continued her prayers. She prayed for Daisy. She prayed for Thomas and Lottie. She prayed for Mr. and Mrs. Bridgeport. She prayed they would all have the strength to accept God's will, no matter the outcome.

CHAPTER 27

The following morning, Callie trudged to answer the door. She'd remained awake to pray throughout most of the night, and this morning she longed for a few hours of sleep. Mrs. Bridgeport's greeting bore a mournful quality that matched the look in her eyes.

The older woman reached for Callie's hand. "We're quite a pair. I believe you look as tired as I feel, and I look as tired as you feel."

Callie grinned. "You're probably right. I was up praying most of the night. Has there been word from the hospital?"

"No, but Luther and I are preparing to leave. Lula hasn't arrived yet, so I wondered if you would take the children down to breakfast. We don't want to wait any longer."

"Yes, of course. Just give me a minute and I'll be down to your room." She closed the door and hurried to the dressing mirror. After quickly arranging her hair, she pinned a large hat over her curls and hoped it would hide the fact that she'd spent little time on her coiffure.

As she picked up her gloves and purse, Callie's stomach again tightened with worry. What news would the Bridgeports receive when they arrived at the hospital? Selfishly, she was glad she wouldn't be with them. Her tears would only make matters worse, and she doubted she'd have the strength to comfort them. She'd never had a child of her own, but she was overcome with physical weakness when she thought of losing Daisy. How would the family ever cope with such a loss?

Callie understood they would need to rely upon God rather than their own strength. They would need prayer and all the support their friends and family could muster. Callie inhaled a deep breath. And if the worst should happen, she would need to gather strength and courage to do her part to help them. Tears pricked her eyes. But how would she ever do that when her own heart throbbed at the very thought of losing the little girl?

She had so many questions about what was happening to Daisy. If only Wes were here. Her heart pounded harder, and she ached to fold herself in the strength of his embrace. Shaking her head, she turned toward the door. No. She couldn't think of Wes. She couldn't think of her needs. She needed to focus on Daisy and the Bridgeports.

She hastened down the hallway, and soon after Mr. and Mrs. Bridgeport departed, Callie tied blue ribbons in Lottie's hair and led the children downstairs to the hotel dining room. She handed each of them a menu.

While the children were perusing the menu, Callie signaled to the waiter to bring her coffee. After taking a sip, she looked over the rim of the cup. "What would you like, Lottie?"

"I want the orange pancakes." She looked up from the menu. "Do you think they're good?"

Callie smiled. "I'm sure they are delicious. What about you, Thomas?"

"Scrambled eggs, bacon, and toast." He placed the menu on the table. "And I'll have orange juice, too."

The waiter returned to the table, poured Callie additional coffee, and took their orders. "Milk for the children?"

"I want some." Lottie smiled at the waiter.

After the waiter had taken their order, the children peppered Callie with questions about Daisy and when they might see her.

She did her best to answer honestly but was thankful when the waiter finally delivered their food. She didn't want to alarm them, yet she wanted them to be aware that their sister's condition had taken a turn for the worse. Lottie didn't seem to understand — or at least acted as though she didn't — while Thomas put on a brave face and had little to say once he heard the news.

They'd swallowed only a few bites when Lula arrived and joined them at the table. "You two ready to take the streetcar to the park?"

Lottie stuck out her lip and Thomas shrugged.

"Why the long faces?" Lula lifted Lottie's chin.

"Last night Daisy wasn't doing very well." Callie did her best to keep her voice calm. "I'm not sure you should take the children away from the hotel until we know how she is this morning." She tipped her head to the side, hoping Lula understood but praying she wouldn't begin crying and upset the children.

Lula nodded. "I see. Are Mr. and Mrs. Bridgeport at the hospital?"

"Yes. They left just before I brought the children down for breakfast. I thought I would go over as soon as you arrived. Then

I can send word back, and you'll know whether to take the children to the park."

Lula glanced at Thomas and Lottie. "Maybe we should all go over there. The children and I can wait in the lobby until you send word down to us."

"Yes, yes. Let's do that." Thomas bobbed his head enthusiastically, and soon Lottie added her excited agreement.

Callie inwardly groaned. If Daisy hadn't made it through the night, Mr. and Mrs. Bridgeport would be distraught. To have Thomas and Lottie see their parents in such a state of distress couldn't be good for them. She wished Lula hadn't made the suggestion in front of the children, but it was too late now.

"I suppose that would be all right." She gave both children a stern look. "But once we get to the hospital, don't ask to go up and see your sister. You must stay in the waiting room and mind Miss Lula. Understood?"

"Yes, Miss Callie." Their voices combined in singsong unison.

On the way to the hospital, Lula touched Callie's arm. "You angry with me, Miss Callie? You haven't said a word since we left the hotel."

Keeping her voice low, Callie explained

her concerns. "I want to protect the children from as much sorrow as possible. I fear having them at the hospital may prove a mistake."

"I'm sorry, Miss Callie. I didn't realize. I can try and talk them into going back to the hotel if you want."

"No, Lula. We're almost there, and without telling them of my concerns for their sister's health, I wouldn't know how to explain sending them back."

Once inside the hospital, the children and Lula settled in the waiting room. Callie produced a tablet, pencils, and crayons. She passed the items to Lottie and smiled. "I think Daisy's room might need some new pictures."

As soon as she was out of their sight, she hurried up the stairs and down the hallway, her gaze focused on the white tiles. She stopped short and looked up when a pair of dark shoes appeared in front of her. Her breath caught in her throat.

"Wesley! How — when — why are you here?"

He smiled down at her. "I'll answer those questions in a moment, but first come with me." Taking hold of her hand, he hurried toward Daisy's room. "I have something to show you." Stepping inside the doorway, he moved aside. "See who is sitting up in bed."

Daisy beamed at Callie. "Miss Callie. You came to see me."

Tears pooled in Callie's eyes and ran down her cheeks as she rushed to the child's bedside and embraced her. "Oh, Daisy! I'm so happy to see you awake."

Daisy's eyes clouded. "I wake up all the time, Miss Callie."

"Yes, of course you do. I should have said that I'm happy to see you feeling much better."

"Then why are you crying?"

Callie wiped the tears from her cheeks. "Sometimes big people cry when they're very happy. I know that sounds silly, but we do. Just ask your mama and papa. They'll tell you I'm right."

Mrs. Bridgeport drew near the other side of the bed. "She's exactly right, Daisy." The older woman looked at Callie. "Can you believe the difference?"

"I'm amazed. Has the doctor given any explanation for the change in her condition?"

Mr. Bridgeport shook his head. "He's as astounded as we are."

"Answered prayer," Callie whispered.

Wesley moved to her side. "I agree. After looking at her medical chart and reading the doctor's notes, I believe there's no other explanation for her recovery." He reached for Callie's hand. "She isn't completely recovered, but I believe she's going to be fine and the worst is over. Daisy's doctor agrees."

Mr. Bridgeport looked outside for a moment. "Did Lottie and Thomas go with Lula?"

Callie explained they were waiting downstairs for some word of Daisy's condition. "I know they would be thrilled to see her, but the rules —"

"Wesley spoke to the doctor and managed to convince him that a brief visit from her brother and sister might do Daisy more good than any medicine." Mr. Bridgeport tugged on his waistcoat. "I'll go down and get them. And I believe you two should find someplace private to talk." He winked at Wesley. "Don't you agree?"

"Indeed I do." Wesley smiled at Callie. "There's a private waiting room down the hall. Why don't we see if it's empty?"

Callie walked alongside Wesley, her heart thumping, her stomach churning, and her thoughts skittering around like leaves on a windy autumn day. The minute they entered the room, she turned to him. "Please, let me speak first. I want to apologize for my harsh behavior."

Wes pressed a finger to her lips. "There's no need for you to apologize."

She pulled his hand away. Her eyes misted. "Please, Wes, I need to tell you this.

"Over the past couple of days it has become abundantly clear that I was wrong to pass judgment on you. I now realize that most of us get caught up in withholding information for protective purposes from time to time. I'm not saying I believe it's the proper thing to do, but I do understand that you weren't attempting to mislead or hurt me when you didn't immediately tell me certain things about yourself. I hope you can forgive me."

"Of course I forgive you. It pained me that I had hurt you." He cupped her cheek in his palm and thumbed away a tear on her cheek. "And I hope that you've forgiven me. I was wrong. My motives were selfish. I was afraid you would reject me if you knew the truth. And when you left the island, I feared all was lost."

"What changed your mind?"

He chuckled. "My parents."

"Your parents? Honestly?"

Pulling her closer, he laughed again. "Yes, honestly. Remember, no more lies. They agreed that if I let you go without pleading my case, I'd never forgive myself. I knew they were right. I decided to follow you, even if it meant going to Indiana, and even if you rejected me — I couldn't let you go without trying to make you understand that I realized what I'd done was wrong, but it was because I cared for you so deeply that I'd followed the wrong path."

Callie's heart soared at the adoration sparkling in his eyes. How could it have been the wrong path if it led her to his arms? Hadn't God had a plan all along?

Wes grasped her hands. "If we're going to have no more secrets, then there's one more thing I need to tell you."

Her breath caught. *No. Please. Not another secret.*

He flashed her a heart-tilting grin. "Callie Deboyer, I want us to be together always."

His words resonated in her heart. A life with this warm and caring man was more than she'd dared imagine. Her smile broadened until her cheeks hurt.

Then she gasped. Her heart plummeted. Last night she'd made a promise to God.

"Callie, what's wrong?"

"I don't think it's possible for us to be together." She lowered her eyes to his chest, now heaving under the weight of her words.

He loosened his hold on her hands and

stepped back. "So you forgive me but you won't consider me for a husband? Is that it? You still don't believe you can love and trust me?" Pain shone in his eyes.

She shook her head. "No, that isn't it. I do love you, and I do believe I can trust you, but —"

"But what?" His voice rose, anger lacing his words. "If we love and trust each other, we can build a strong marriage."

"Where will we build that marriage? In Massachusetts? With you working at your father's textile mill? I can't do that."

His voice softened. "Is that all? We don't need to live in Massachusetts. I can find work. I'm educated. I can support you anywhere you choose."

"You don't understand." Her heart ached. Was this a final test from God? She swallowed the lump in her throat. "Last night when I prayed for Daisy, I made a promise to God."

He nodded. "Go on."

"I promised Him that if Daisy got well, then I would go to Africa and help my parents on the mission field." She forced a smile. "This morning I discovered that God has answered my prayer, and now I must willingly do as I've promised."

"But God doesn't make deals with people.

429

He wouldn't hold you to that."

"But I hold myself to it. I made a vow to Him."

Wesley stared at her for several moments and then stood. He walked to the window and stared outside for several minutes. "If I remember correctly, you told me there is a need for doctors as well as teachers in Africa."

What was he saying? Her heart pounded like a kettledrum. "Yes. That's what my parents have told me."

"I know I don't want to work in the textile mills. I've already told my father that I won't join his company." He sat down beside Callie. "I've prayed for God to show me where I belong and what He would have me do with my future." He took her hand in his. "I believe He has shown me."

Callie gasped. "Truly? We'll go together?"

He smiled. "As husband and wife."

"But what about your fears? Do you think you'll be able to practice medicine once again?"

"I won't know unless I try, but I do believe God can equip me if this is where He would have me serve. I believe all of this has happened for a purpose that I will probably never understand. But I do know that I don't want to live the rest of my life without you at my side."

Wesley stood and drew her into his arms. "I love you, Callie. I want to hold you in my arms for the rest of my life. I want to honor you with my whole being. Will you marry me?"

With her hand on his chest, she felt his heart beating beneath her hand — a heart she truly trusted to cherish her own. "Yes, I'll marry you, Dr. Townsend."

His eyes darkened as he lowered his head and met her lips with a lingering kiss.

Chapter 28

Over the next two days, Daisy's condition steadily improved, and last night the doctor left word he would meet with the family this morning. Mr. and Mrs. Bridgeport, as well as Callie and Wesley, gathered in Daisy's room to hear the doctor's report. Wesley anticipated the doctor would release Daisy from the hospital today. If that occurred, he wasn't certain what it would mean for him, for Callie, or for their relationship.

These past two days had given them time alone to sort through their feelings and hopes for the future. Neither of them doubted their love for the other, and they were in agreement that they should go to Africa and work alongside Callie's parents. Yet neither was certain how they would make all the arrangements. Callie didn't want to leave the Bridgeports without someone to take her place, and Wesley disliked the idea of leaving the guests at

Bridal Veil without a golf pro for the remainder of the season. And their marriage would need to take place before they could leave the country. There would be much to decide.

If Callie left for Indianapolis in the next day or two, Wes doubted they could wed before summer, and they would be away from each other during the intervening months — a thought he intensely disliked. After wrestling with the thought last night, he decided that he'd follow Callie to Indianapolis. With Mr. Bridgeport's help, he could find work until after they married and were prepared to depart for Africa. And he'd do his best to help Mr. Crocker find a replacement at the links, though he doubted that would be possible.

"You appear worried." Concern shone in Callie's eyes as she reached for his hand. "Is there something in Daisy's appearance that concerns you this morning?"

The two of them were seated near the doorway leading into Daisy's room, while Mr. and Mrs. Bridgeport had each pulled a chair close to the child's bedside.

He shook his head. "No. She looks even better than yesterday. I think the doctor will release her."

Callie immediately brightened. "Do you?

That's wonderful news, isn't it? I don't understand why you look so glum if you think we'll get a good report."

He forced a halfhearted smile. "Because I've been thinking about what will happen when she's released."

Her countenance turned somber, and Wesley knew that the realization of what it would mean to them had taken hold. She glanced toward the bedside. "What will we do? I can't leave them just yet. I love you, Wesley, but —"

"I know. Let's wait and see what the doctor says before we try to make any decisions."

He didn't tell her he'd been up most of the night attempting to come to some solution. His worry was enough for both of them. And his own feelings aside, he knew Daisy's return to health was a miracle. The child should not be alive, yet she was now sitting up in her bed, coloring a picture and talking to her parents. God's hand had been at work in the child's recovery, and Wes prayed God's hand would smooth the details of their future, as well. Wes didn't have the answers, but with God's help, the two of them would overcome the mounting obstacles that remained in their path.

They all turned toward the door when

they heard the doctor arrive. A nurse accompanied him into the room, carrying papers in one hand. The doctor smiled and greeted them.

He drew near the bed, his eyes fastening on Daisy's leg. "And how is my favorite little girl?"

Daisy smiled up at him. "Good." She picked up her drawing and held it out to him. "I made you a picture."

The doctor took a moment to examine the child's gift. "And it is a lovely picture. I'll put it in my office. Is that all right with you?"

Daisy giggled and bobbed her head. "Can I go home today?"

"I'm going to look at your leg, and then I'll tell you." He unwrapped the bandage and, after checking the wound, gave the nurse instructions. The doctor brushed a curl from Daisy's forehead. "You may go home today, Daisy." The child squealed with delight, and the doctor smiled before turning to Mr. and Mrs. Bridgeport. "I don't think it would be wise for you to leave for Indianapolis yet. Daisy is much better, but a long train trip and the flooded conditions in the city could complicate matters should she need additional medical attention. I would guess the doctors and hospitals in the city have their hands full right now."

Mr. Bridgeport frowned and nodded his head. "I see. You're probably right. You think we should remain in Biscayne?"

"You need not stay in Biscayne. You can return to Bridal Veil Island. If there should be any change in Daisy's condition, you can bring her back here. I don't anticipate a problem, but I would feel better knowing she's fully recovered before you return home."

Mr. Bridgeport looked at his wife. "I'll get a wire sent home telling Mrs. Hanson of our change in plans, and we'll follow up with a letter of instructions. It's the best we can do under the circumstances." His frown deepened. "Of course, you could remain here with the children, and I could return home and see to things."

Mrs. Bridgeport shook her head. "I'd rather you didn't do that right now, Luther. If Daisy continues to make progress and we hear there's a need for you to go home ahead of us, then we can decide. I don't like the idea of the family being separated, especially when we don't know what conditions we'll find in Indianapolis."

Callie squeezed Wesley's hand. "So we'll all remain at Bridal Veil?"

"Yes. I think that would be best." Mrs.

Bridgeport smiled at Wesley. "I'm certain that decision will please you, as well. Won't it, Wes?"

"I know you have concerns about your home, but I wouldn't be telling the truth if I said I wasn't pleased with your decision to remain at Bridal Veil. And I'm sure my parents will be pleased to have an opportunity to get to know Callie."

Callie hadn't yet had a chance to speak to the Bridgeports about the future, but from the look on Mrs. Bridgeport's face, she'd already deduced what lay in store. "I hope the two of you aren't making any impetuous plans."

Wes met Mrs. Bridgeport's inquiring stare. "Not impetuous, but we have made a few decisions. Right now, I think you have more important matters that require your attention. Is there anything I can do to help you either at the hotel here in Biscayne or at Fair Haven?"

The older woman sparked to attention. "Since Fair Haven has already been closed for the season, it would be helpful if it could be reopened. Dear me, it is such a shame. The cottage was closed less than a week ago and now we'll be reopening it. Yet, I suppose that's the way of things." She leaned forward and kissed Daisy's cheek. "I'm so

437

thankful to have Daisy well that I shouldn't even mention anything so trivial." Mrs. Bridgeport turned her attention to Callie. "Shall we see if Lula and Jane can return for the remainder of the season? I don't see how we can get by without their help."

Callie nodded. "Wesley and I can go speak to Jane, if you'd like. And I'm sure Lula will be pleased to return. Only this morning she mentioned that she didn't know what to do with herself and she hadn't been able to find any work."

Both Mr. and Mrs. Bridgeport agreed they would stay at the hospital and see to Daisy's discharge while Wes and Callie located Jane and saw to matters at the Biscayne hotel. Callie grasped his arm as they descended the hospital stairs. "Perhaps I should go to the hotel and begin packing. Lula can help me. If you locate Jane, we can return to the island by late this afternoon and open the cottage. Mr. and Mrs. Bridgeport could remain in Biscayne and return on the launch later this evening. I'm sure Captain Fleming would agree to come over before sunset, don't you think?"

Wes nodded. "I don't know why he wouldn't. The Bridgeports own a cottage on the island, and it's his job to see to their transportation needs. I think you've come up with an excellent plan. I'll stop at the hotel and see if Lula knows Jane's address. I'm sure the children will be delighted to learn Daisy will be discharged."

"Indeed. And I'm sure they'll be delighted when they hear we're going to return to Bridal Veil. Thomas wasn't happy about forgoing the remainder of his golf lessons."

As they arrived at the bottom of the stairwell, Wes pulled her close. "And what about you, Miss Deboyer? Were you un-happy that your lessons had come to an end?" He dipped his head low and stared into her eyes.

Her lips curved in a delicious smile. "Not unhappy the lessons had ended, but un-happy I'd no longer be spending time with the instructor."

His heart soared at her words. Lowering his head, his lips grazed the tender spot along the side of her neck. "I don't think you'll need to worry about being separated from me again." He wrapped her in a warm embrace and captured her lips in a slow, passionate kiss, thanking God for providing a way for them to remain together. He could never have let her go to Indianapolis without him. Not in a million years.

Wesley's hands turned damp as he approached the front door of Fair Haven. He had hoped to wait a bit longer before asking Callie to meet his family — an experience he feared might send her running away from him rather than into his arms. But his mother had been insistent. She'd waited long enough and wanted Callie to join them for dinner this evening. He hadn't revealed his plans to marry Callie and join her on the mission field, and he doubted the family would agree with their decisions.

At least Callie wouldn't have to deal with Charles or Daniel. They were both in Massachusetts, but Richard might prove difficult, and who could say how Helena would react? In the past, she'd proclaimed that he should be looking for a wife, so she should be happy. Then again, his sister could be as changeable as the weather.

He strode up the steps to Fair Haven and knocked, surprised when Thomas greeted him. The boy stepped aside and invited Wes inside. "Jane and Lula were busy, so I told them I'd answer the door." He glanced toward the stairs. "Are you here to see Miss Callie?"

Wes nodded. "I need to speak to her for a few minutes, but I promise I won't keep her for long."

While the boy raced up the stairs, Wes

waited below, trying to think how he should word the dinner invitation. He wanted to warn Callie that his family could be difficult, yet he didn't want to frighten her so much that she'd refuse to come. It would likely be best simply to be forthright. After all, they needed to have this meeting sometime, so he'd try to convince her it was best to get it over with as soon as possible. But that sounded rather ominous. He'd need to place the invitation in a more positive light, or she'd never agree to accompany him. He startled when Callie greeted him from the upper hallway.

She giggled as she descended the stairs. "I didn't mean to frighten you. Were you so lost in your thoughts you didn't hear me?"

"That's exactly right." He gestured toward the front porch. "Could we go outside and talk for a few minutes?"

"Of course, but I'll need to return upstairs shortly or Lottie won't finish her math." She led the way out the door and sat down on one of the wicker chairs. "What's wrong? Has something happened?"

He dropped to the chair beside her, the sweet scent of jasmine drifting on the breeze. "My parents would like you to join us for dinner tonight. They've arranged for a small private room — so everyone can get to know you. I know it's very short notice, but they are eager to meet you."

"It is short notice. Without Maude, we'll need to make other arrangements for the care of the children. Mrs. Bridgeport is upstairs. I'll ask her if it would be possible."

Wes scooted forward on the chair. "I would pay Jane or Lula extra wages if one of them would be willing to stay." He rubbed his jaw. "Or if you know of someone else who might be willing to help."

She traced her finger along the ridges in his forehead. "Don't worry so. We'll get something arranged. Let me speak to Mrs. Bridgeport."

Wes leaned back in the chair, and though Callie wasn't gone long, it seemed an eternity. He wished his mother hadn't made the arrangements before speaking to him. The family wouldn't understand that Callie couldn't be available at their beck and call.

Callie reappeared with a bright smile curving her lips. "All is arranged. Lula said she'd be happy to stay overnight, and there's no need for any extra pay."

"That's kind of her. I'll properly thank her when I come to pick you up this evening. Seven o'clock?"

"I'll be ready. I look forward to meeting your family, Wes. If they are as kind and loving as you, it shall be a wonderful event."

"You may find a few of them a bit difficult, but I'll be there to protect you." He laughed, hoping to take the edge off his words.

Callie giggled. "I can't imagine they will be anything but kind."

Wes inwardly groaned. "You may find them somewhat overbearing, but together we'll manage the evening." He grinned. "I won't let them eat you alive."

Callie donned an informal dinner gown of pale blue silk with a dropped waistline, white ruching along the neckline, and bejeweled capped sleeves. She would have preferred something a bit less fancy, but Mrs. Bridgeport had insisted. In fact, Mrs. Bridgeport would have preferred Callie wear a formal brown and white chiffon gown, but she had refused to relent.

When Callie appeared downstairs, Mrs. Bridgeport shook her head. "I still think the chiffon was the better choice. You know Mrs. Townsend will be wearing a formal gown, and I'm certain her daughter will follow suit."

"I truly don't care what they wear. I'm more comfortable in this dress, and I know Wesley will think it is perfect."

"Yes, but he is a man in love. He thinks anything you say or do is perfect." Mrs. Bridgeport rearranged the ruffles atop one of the dress sleeves. "If they don't treat you well, you tell them they'll have to answer to Luther."

Callie chuckled. "I think they might fear you more than Mr. Bridgeport."

"Perhaps they should. They'd best be kind." She glanced toward the front of the house. "There's Wesley. Do have a nice time and remember — you're from a fine family. Don't let them intimidate you."

Both Mrs. Bridgeport and Wesley seemed to think she had something to fear at this dinner meeting, yet Callie remained calm as she walked into the private dining room holding tight to Wesley's arm. A silence fell as they entered, and she squeezed his arm.

"Callie, I'd like to introduce you to my family." One by one, he went around the room and made the proper introductions; then he inhaled a deep breath. "Callie and I are engaged to be married."

A cacophony of gasps filled the room. Helena frowned at her parents. "Did you know, Mother?"

"No, I didn't." Mrs. Townsend dropped to one of the chairs and snapped open her fan. "You should have told us, Wesley. I knew you cared for Callie, and I encouraged you to court her, but I didn't know you had already asked her to marry you. Why didn't you tell us?"

"I thought it best to tell everyone while we're together. We can answer all of your questions, and there won't be any misunderstandings. This way no one feels left out." He glanced around the room. "Am I right?"

"Well, I imagine Charles and Daniel will feel left out," Helena said. "I truly can't believe you are engaged to marry, and this is the first time we've set eyes on your fiancée."

Callie smiled. "I believe I met you at one of the tea parties. I was with Mrs. Bridgeport."

Helena ignored Callie's reply. "You two barely know each other, and you've already decided to marry. It seems preposterous." She shook her finger at Wesley. "I hope you're planning a very long engagement. Most couples know each other at least five or six years before they decide to marry. Richard and I knew each other for five years before he proposed, and then we were engaged for another two years."

Wesley narrowed his eyes. "And all that waiting provided you with what, Helena? A perfect marriage?"

"What does that mean? Richard and I are quite happy. Aren't we, Richard?" She didn't give her husband an opportunity to respond. "It is a well-known fact that if you want a marriage that lasts, you should know your partner well."

"I disagree, Helena." Mrs. Townsend slapped her fan on the table. "You are talking utter nonsense. Charles and Anna didn't have a long engagement. Your father and I knew each other only two months before we knew we were perfect for each other, and we married less than a month later."

"Mother!" Helena paled and sat down. "I cannot believe you would reveal such family scandal in public."

"Oh, do get over yourself, Helena. What is scandalous about two people running off to get married when they're in love?"

Helena frowned. "I don't recall you adopting that attitude when you found out about Charles and Anna."

Mrs. Townsend waved the comment aside. "That was years ago. Charles and Anna are now quite happy in their marriage." Mrs. Townsend looked at her husband. "And we're quite happy, as well. Aren't we, Howard?"

"Yes, Blanche, that's right." Mr. Townsend smiled at his wife and then turned to the others. "Blanche didn't want a big wedding."

Mrs. Townsend bobbed her head. "It's true. I didn't. However, I now believe one should create wonderful memories when possible. I'm going to speak to Eunice, and we're going to make certain you and Wesley have a gorgeous affair. I know there's been flooding in Indianapolis, so perhaps we should plan on having the wedding in Massachusetts. Don't you think that's best?"

"I don't know, but I think I should speak to Mrs. Bridgeport. Wesley and I haven't —"

"We don't plan to wait, Mother. Callie and I would prefer to be married here at Bridal Veil. If all goes according to plan, we won't be going to Massachusetts."

Helena picked up her mother's fan and waved it back and forth with increasing vigor. "This is becoming more and more scandalous. You barely know each other, yet you've become engaged and now you're planning an immediate wedding. You do realize people will talk. Oh my. What next?"

Wesley smiled at his sister. "Since you've asked — we'll be going to Africa."

There was a loud gasp before Helena slipped from her chair in a faint.

CHAPTER 29

After a brief interlude that required the use of smelling salts and damp cloths, Helena roused. She'd been back in her chair for only a moment when she glared at Wesley. "This is your fault. You know I am prone to fainting when I receive bad news."

"I wasn't aware you would consider my marriage plans bad news, Helena, but you're typically the first one to complain when you haven't been included in family happenings. I was doing my best to keep from hurting anyone's feelings." He shot her an ornery grin. "At least we were in a private room when you took your tumble."

Callie lightly nudged his arm. Rather than a celebration, this dinner was turning into a debacle. While Callie had anticipated there might be some rancor from Wesley's parents, she was surprised at Helena's attitude. Wesley had indicated he and Helena had been quite close until her marriage to Richard

Kennebec, a man for whom Wes held little respect. After her marriage to Richard, the bond between brother and sister had weakened. Even though Helena had attempted to force a friendship between the two men, neither was interested. Was Helena now going to heap disapproval upon Callie to get back at her brother? Callie shivered at the thought.

They wouldn't be remaining in the country for long, but Callie didn't want to begin her marriage on a sour note with any member of Wesley's family. Yet from the look in Helena's eyes, she might not have a choice. And now Mrs. Townsend's complexion had taken on a pasty color, as well.

Callie tugged on Wesley's sleeve. "I think your mother may not be feeling well. She's quite pale."

"Mother? Are you feeling ill?" Wesley pointed to her glass. "Perhaps a drink of water?"

She gave a slight shake of her head. "I recall a conversation with you regarding Africa, Wesley. I believe you said Callie wasn't trying to convince you to go there."

Callie opened her mouth to answer, but Wesley gently touched her hand. "Callie hasn't convinced me to go, Mother. Rather, we both believe God is leading us to the mission field, where we can best use our talents."

"Forevermore, Wesley. I don't know what has come over you." Helena directed another stern look at Callie. "When we arrived on Bridal Veil, you told us you didn't ever want to practice medicine again. Now you tell us God has directed you to put your medical education to use in Africa? Excuse me if I say that it sounds as though Miss Deboyer is the one doing the leading — not God."

Callie winced at the remark. "I'm sorry you feel that way, but I have not attempted to influence Wesley in any of his decisions."

"Don't pay Helena any mind. She just doesn't want to lose her brother." Richard winked at his wife. "She got used to having him nearby when he returned from Texas, and now she has to give him up again." He nudged his wife's arm. "Isn't that right, Helena?"

"You must admit that going to Africa isn't the same as telling us you're going to live in another state." Helena dabbed her eyes. "We'll probably never see you again."

"Oh, that isn't true at all. My parents come home on furlough every five years."

"Five years!"

Helena's shriek was loud enough to bring

450

the waiter scurrying into the room, but Richard shooed him away after assuring him everything was fine.

Wesley's mother still hadn't regained her full color, but she waved her fan at Helena. "Please restrain yourself, Helena. If your father and I can accept Wesley's decision, then I believe you should be able to do the same."

Helena turned a wide-eyed stare at her parents. "You're going to agree to this?"

Mr. Townsend traced his index finger beneath his starched white collar. "It wouldn't be my first choice for any of my children to go off to some foreign land, but Wesley is an adult and is capable of making his own decisions. Besides, who are any of us to argue with God? If Wesley believes this is what he's to do, then I won't stand in his way." Wesley's father pointed a thick finger at his daughter. "And your childish behavior will only cause ill feelings between you and your brother, Helena. I don't think that's what you want to happen when he's going to be gone for a number of years, is it?"

"No, but I . . ."

Mr. Townsend shook his head. "There is nothing else to be added, Helena. You will miss your brother and so will the rest of us,

451

but when the time arrives for him to depart, we will wish him Godspeed and best wishes with his new life."

"Yes, Father." She turned toward Callie and Wesley. "I'm sorry for my unkind words and rude behavior, but you both must realize what a shock this is for all of us. I hope we will at least have an opportunity to get to know you, Callie, a little better before you leave the country."

Callie smiled. "I hope so, as well, Helena."

Mrs. Townsend straightened her shoulders. "Tomorrow I'll meet with Eunice, and we'll set things in motion for the wedding, but first we must plan an engagement party. I'm certain Mr. Crocker will be happy to assist us in arranging everything. If not, we can have the party at the lovely hotel in Biscayne. Of course, if the weather is nice, we could have the party outdoors."

"But you can't depend upon the weather, Mother." Helena glanced at Callie. "What about the Bridgeports' cottage? Do you think it's large enough to host an engagement party? Would Mrs. Bridgeport prefer the event be at their cottage rather than the clubhouse?"

Suddenly Helena had set aside her concerns about Wesley leaving for Africa and had become swept up in her mother's excitement of planning an engagement party. Callie didn't know what to think of the sudden change, nor did she have any idea what Mrs. Bridgeport might desire. In fact, she didn't know if Mrs. Bridgeport wanted to be included in any of the wedding preparations. They'd not had a chance to discuss the matter.

"I can't speak for Mrs. Bridgeport." She glanced at Wesley. "I don't believe either of us is desirous of elaborate parties or a large wedding. We'll be pleased —"

Mrs. Townsend waved her fan — this time in Callie's direction. "*Tut, tut.* No Townsend is married without a proper wedding."

Callie frowned. "But you said you and Mr. Townsend had a small ceremony and —"

Once again the older woman brandished her fan. She waved it overhead like a flag flying in the breeze. "That's true, and since we're here at Bridal Veil, I'm afraid anything we plan will be attended by fewer guests than if we were hosting the events in Massachusetts. But that doesn't mean we can't manage something every bit as grand." She graced Callie with a bright smile. "I will admit that later in life I had a few regrets that I didn't have a magnificent wedding — not because I would be any more married, but because of the memories and the joy it brings to other people when they are able to plan and attend beautiful weddings."

Mrs. Townsend snapped her fan together and used it as a pointer. "And I know neither of you wants to rob us of our joy."

Callie pressed her lips together and swallowed her rebuttal. She didn't desire an elaborate wedding. But after Helena's fainting spell, Callie didn't think this would be a good time to argue about wedding plans. Instead, she would discuss the matter with Mrs. Bridgeport first thing tomorrow. With her experience handling difficult social situations, perhaps Mrs. Bridgeport could provide an idea or two of how to best handle Mrs. Townsend and Helena before the wedding turned into an extravaganza of sorts.

Mr. Townsend signaled for the waiter to begin serving their meal. It wasn't long after they'd completed their soup course that Richard leaned Callie's way. "I understand the nanny who was working for the Bridgeports was involved in the thefts taking place on the island, and the detectives investigating the case even attempted to implicate you."

Wesley frowned at his brother-in-law. "And how did you happen to learn that piece of information? To my knowledge, there were few people who knew anything about those details."

"Your father pays me to keep abreast of news in the textile industry and of possible investors. You'd be amazed how much other information is gathered during the course of doing business."

When Wesley bristled at the remark, Callie reached for his hand while directing a sweet smile at Richard. "I am certain the detectives spoke to many people during the course of their investigation, but your informants were correct in what they told you. However, since I'm not in jail with Mrs. Murphy and her son, it is obvious they were incorrect in their assumptions."

Callie took heart when Richard's shoulder drooped. She'd obviously deflected his accusations. Wesley was correct about his brother-in-law: The man did enjoy stirring things at every opportunity. Once the discussion about the wedding had settled, he appeared intent upon finding another subject that would create tension and disharmony.

Richard sniggered. "You should have stopped by the jail while you were over in Biscayne. I'll bet Mrs. Murphy would have been more than a little surprised to see you."

Callie folded her hands in her lap and stared at Richard. "If I thought it would have given Mrs. Murphy comfort, I would have gone to see her. To be frank, I feel a great deal of sadness regarding Mrs. Murphy. She was a strange woman at times, but she could be quite kind and caring, as well. I don't know what possessed her to aid her son in such horrendous criminal activity, but it doesn't change the fact that she was good to the children and generally kind to me."

Richard pointed his bread knife at Callie. "Well, I'm not so sure the people she stole from believe she's such a saint. And if she'd stolen your expensive jewels, I doubt you'd be so forgiving." He placed the knife on the bread plate. "Then again, you didn't need to worry since you don't own any expensive jewels. Isn't that correct?"

Wesley pushed away from the table. "I've had enough of your tasteless behavior, Richard."

"No, Wesley. It's quite all right. I'm pleased to answer his question. The fact is that I'm not wealthy, Mr. Kennebec, so I don't need to worry about jewels being stolen. I was, however, sympathetic to the guests and the distress they suffered because of Mrs. Murphy's actions. But it is my understanding that all of the jewelry was recovered and has been returned to the proper owners. And while I don't consider Mrs. Murphy a saint, I do believe she is a child of God who deserves forgiveness. All of us sin, and all of us need forgiveness." Callie shifted in her chair and met Richard's stare. "Don't you agree?"

Mrs. Townsend tapped her fan on the white tablecloth. "I know I agree — and I know that's enough talk about robberies and other unsavory topics. I doubt I'll be able to digest my dinner if this discussion continues."

Later, while they were finishing their after-dinner coffee, Mrs. Townsend excused herself from the table. She returned a short time later, walked to the head of the table, and placed one hand on her husband's shoulder. "I have spoken to Mr. Crocker, and we will host the engagement party here at the island. With my direction and assistance, he assures me that all can be in readiness whenever we decide to have the party."

"But I —" Callie stopped short when Mrs. Townsend snapped open her fan.

In no time at all, Callie had lost control of her wedding plans.

Throughout the days that followed, Mrs. Townsend and Mrs. Bridgeport became as alike as two peas in a pod. What one said, the other agreed to and vice versa. Callie had done her best to try to dissuade Mrs. Bridgeport, but to no avail. The older woman was certain Callie's objections were due to the cost involved with the engagement party and a sumptuous wedding. Wes and Callie acquiesced and decided to wed on the third day of May.

Once the young couple set the date, Mrs. Townsend and Mrs. Bridgeport wasted no time scheduling the engagement party for one week prior to the wedding. They had hoped to host it two weeks prior, but when they discovered the clubhouse had already been scheduled for another event that could not be changed, they conceded.

When the dates for the party and wedding had been set, it became abundantly clear there would be no peace, since Callie had permitted the women full rein. When Mrs. Townsend insisted upon taking her to Biscayne to be fitted for a wedding gown, she didn't object. When Mrs. Bridgeport insisted upon purchasing items for her trousseau, Callie didn't object. When the two older women decided upon the decorations, flowers, and food for the engagement party, she didn't object. Each skirmish turned into a losing battle.

Mrs. Bridgeport had quieted Callie's objections by insisting that Mr. Bridgeport would have it no other way. He could think of nothing upon which he'd rather spend his money — a statement Callie found difficult to believe. When she raised her objections to Mrs. Townsend, the older woman immediately pointed out that she and Wesley would be leaving the country and the couple should indulge the family by permitting all of them this time of special celebration.

There seemed nothing Callie could do but give in. Still, this wasn't going to be the type of wedding she desired. Had her own mother remained a member of society and been living in the country, what would she have wanted for Callie's wedding? Callie couldn't even imagine what her own mother might suggest. They'd been apart for too long, and they'd never spoken of weddings. Although the letters from her mother helped a bit, they didn't create the closeness that Callie had developed with Mrs. Bridgeport over the past years. If her grandmother were still alive, there was little doubt what would have happened with the wedding plans. Grandmother would have sat her down and asked what Callie wanted — and then she would have set about making certain her granddaughter's wishes were fulfilled.

"And that's what I should do, as well." Callie whispered the words into the quiet of her bedroom, where no one else could hear. She would need to gather her courage if she was to have the wedding ceremony she desired. Most of all, she would need an ally, and there was only one choice: Wesley. He could help her explain to his family, while she hoped she could handle any objections from the Bridgeports.

With her thoughts settled on the possibility of taking control of the ceremony, Callie sat down at her desk and penned a letter to her parents. She doubted they would receive the letter before her wedding, but she wanted to tell them of her engagement and approaching marriage. Her excitement mounted as she told them about the wedding. She waited until the very end of the letter to tell them that God was directing both her and Wesley to join them in Africa.

I hope you will consider all of this joyous news. I know it was your earnest desire that I join you, and I hope you will feel the same about Wesley. He is a wonderful man, and although he has experienced great difficulty since beginning his medical career, he now believes

God plans to use his talents and abilities in Africa. We are excited at the prospect of joining you and lending our assistance and skills to the Lord's work.

I only wish you could be here for our wedding, but if this letter should reach you prior to our marriage, I know you will be with us in thought and spirit.

Your loving daughter and soon to be son-in-law,

Callie and Wesley

She hadn't gone into the details of Wesley's problems in Texas. There would be time enough for that once they arrived in Africa. For now, she simply wanted her parents to know of her impending marriage and their plans to go to Africa. She reread the pages she'd written on both the front and back of each sheet. There had been so much to tell them. A flutter of excitement filled her as she sealed the envelope. Callie tried to imagine what her parents would think and feel as they read her letter. She hoped they would feel the same excitement and joy that she'd experienced while writing her letter to them.

CHAPTER 30

Callie, Mrs. Bridgeport, Thomas, and Lottie were on the front porch the following day when Mr. Bridgeport returned to Fair Haven. He waved a letter overhead as he approached and spoke to them. "I picked up the mail at the clubhouse on my way." A slight frown creased his forehead. "Where is Daisy?"

Mrs. Bridgeport gestured to the chair beside her. "No need for concern. She's taking a nap. Wesley said he'd stop by to remove the bandage and look at her leg. She still tires easily, and the doctor in Biscayne said rest was the best cure at this time."

"I recall what the doctor said, Eunice." He grinned at his wife. "After all, I was there at the hospital with you."

Ignoring his comment, Mrs. Bridgeport pointed to his hand. "I see we've received mail."

"A full report on the damage from Samuel. I asked him to go to our house, and even though we had an earlier report, I asked him to check on your grandmother's house, too, Callie." He leaned forward and looked at Callie. "Samuel Broderick is one of my business partners. I think you've met him at the house, haven't you?"

"Yes, I remember him quite well. Tall with a long nose and dark mustache?"

Mrs. Bridgeport chuckled. "That's a very good description, Callie."

"I don't think Samuel's nose is particularly long. Do I have a long nose?"

"Goodness, Luther. Let's not spend our time talking about your physical attributes. What does Samuel's letter have to say?"

Callie folded her hands in her lap. The servants had already sent word that her grandmother's home had been destroyed, and Callie had accepted the loss. There was no reason to send someone to survey the area once again and tell her what she already knew.

"He says there is water damage in the basement, but it didn't reach the upper floors of the house. Our losses won't be as substantial as many have suffered." He glanced at Callie. "The news regarding your grandmother's home remains the same. It's a total loss, but Samuel says in his letter that the folks who were renting the house managed to save some of your grandmother's personal belongings that were stored in the attic."

"That was most kind of them. I know there were several trunks that contained some of her china and silver service, but I don't think I'll have need of those items in Africa. Perhaps I should consider selling them. I'm sure the money could be put to good use by Mother and Father."

Mrs. Bridgeport gasped. "You don't want to do that, my dear. You don't know — one day you and Wesley may return to live in this country, and you'll be glad to have a few of your grandmother's belongings." Mrs. Bridgeport tapped her husband's arm. "When you write to Samuel, tell him to have the trunks taken to our house. We can store them for you, Callie. There's no telling what may be in those trunks."

Callie conceded. Perhaps Mrs. Bridgeport was right. One day she and Wesley might have children of their own, and it would give her great pleasure to share those items with her children and tell them stories about her grandmother. Callie's thoughts returned to the special teas her grandmother would prepare for the two of them, using her silver tea service and one of her many lace tablecloths. Callie smiled. One day she might do the same with a daughter of her own.

Mr. Bridgeport nodded his agreement. "No need to worry yourself over the trunks, Callie." He handed the letter to his wife. "Samuel says it's good we didn't attempt to come home. Train service is at a standstill in and out of the city, and many of the roads remain closed." He leaned back in the chair. "I intensely dislike the circumstances that have kept us here, but it would seem this is exactly where we should be right now."

The older woman agreed and patted Callie's hand. "And it has proven best for Callie, as well. We're having great fun planning the engagement party and wedding, aren't we?"

Callie forced a smile. "I'm not sure I would call it fun, but —"

"Oh look! Wesley's coming." Mrs. Bridgeport pointed toward the road. "I'll go tell Jane to make some lemonade. Once Wesley has seen to Daisy, I'm sure he'll want to remain and visit a while."

Callie hoped so. If not, she'd accompany him to the golf course. They needed to talk. If she was going to have the kind of wedding she preferred, they needed to assert themselves to both Wesley's mother and to Mrs. Bridgeport as soon as possible.

The moment Wesley approached the front porch, Callie stood and greeted him. "I'll go upstairs with you, and we can see if Daisy is awake. She's been taking a nap."

Wes shook hands with Mr. Bridgeport before following Callie inside. He caught her hand before she started up the steps. "You appear unhappy. Is something wrong?"

"It's about the wedding. We'll talk after you see to Daisy." She tugged on his hand and moved toward the steps.

"Wait! You're not changing your mind about marrying me, are you?" His forehead creased and apprehension shone in his eyes.

She gently pressed her fingers against the creases that lined his forehead. "Of course not. You can stop frowning." Glancing about, she lowered her voice. "I want to change some of the plans your mother and Mrs. Bridgeport have made, that's all. Nothing to cause you alarm."

He loosened his hold so that she could ascend the steps. "You may think it's nothing to cause alarm, but I don't think those two women are going to agree."

She glanced over her shoulder. "That's exactly why we need to talk."

Daisy roused from her sleep as the two of them entered her room. She smiled at Wesley. "Mama says I get to wear a special dress when you marry Miss Callie. As soon as my leg gets a little better, she's going to take me and Lottie to Biscayne to the dressmaker." Daisy looked up at Callie. "Isn't that right?"

"It is, so you must continue to get your rest so your leg will heal. Mr. Wes is going to take off your bandage, and we'll see how it looks. Would that be all right with you?"

Daisy bobbed her head and extended the bandaged leg. " 'Cept he's a doctor now, so he's Dr. Wes."

Callie nodded and Wesley chuckled. "Dr. Wes at your service."

Daisy's cheery expression changed to a frown. "My dress got all wrinkled while I was sleeping."

"When a little girl is as pretty as you, no one notices a few wrinkles." Wesley carefully unwrapped the bandage. An indentation remained in Daisy's leg, but the wound had ceased oozing and had healed over. "It is looking much better, Daisy. You are an excellent patient."

The child beamed at him, caring not at all about the lingering irregularity in her leg. "Can I go outside now?"

"*May* I go outside now?" Callie said.

Wes chuckled. "You both have permission to go outside as soon as I put a fresh

467

bandage on your leg." When he finished, he lifted Daisy off the bed. "Can you make it down the stairs or should I carry you?"

"My leg is good enough to walk and go down the steps, but I can't skip yet." Daisy grasped Wes's hand and walked beside him while Callie followed behind.

"I think Jane is making some lemonade if you can stay, Wes."

"A new guest arrived at the lodge and has signed up for an afternoon lesson, so I don't think I'll have time. Want to walk along and we can talk?"

She nodded. "Absolutely. I'm not letting you out of my sight until we make a few plans of our own."

He winked at her. "I like the sound of that. And I like the idea of planning our honeymoon even more."

As they walked down the porch steps, Callie slipped her hand into the crook of his arm and laughed. "We can make those plans later. Right now, we need to plan our wedding, and I need your help."

"What do you have in mind?"

While Wesley listened, she explained her ideas, pleased when he nodded his agreement. "I think it sounds perfect. Now you need only convince Mother and Mrs. Bridgeport."

Callie shook her head. "*We* need to convince your mother and Mrs. Bridgeport. I told you I need an ally, and that ally needs to support me both in word and deed. You will be right alongside me when I speak to them." She hesitated a moment. "Won't you?"

"How could I say no to someone as beautiful and sweet as you?" He took her hand and tugged her off the path until they were hidden by the low-hanging branches of a huge live oak.

"Then why don't we plan to meet with them later this afternoon when you're done with your golf lesson? I'll send a note to your mother and ask her to come over to Fair Haven at three."

He pulled her close, and she gazed into his eyes. That was all it took. One glance, the slightest touch, and her heart raced. She lifted her arms and placed them around his neck. The butterflies in her stomach took flight. She'd never been so forward in her life. "Why don't we seal our agreement with a kiss?"

His lips curved in a slow, rakish smile. "I'd like nothing better."

The moment she returned to the cottage, Callie went in search of Mrs. Bridgeport

469

and suggested they host a private tea with Mrs. Townsend later in the afternoon. Gaining Mrs. Bridgeport's agreement hadn't been difficult, since she'd been slow to fill her social calendar following their return to the island. With Daisy still recuperating from her spider bite and the unexpected wedding plans, Mrs. Bridgeport declared she had more than enough to keep her busy without attending card parties and afternoon teas with the ladies.

Callie penned a quick invitation to Mrs. Townsend, and one of the gardeners agreed to deliver it to the clubhouse and wait for her future mother-in-law's response. Fortunately, it didn't take long before he'd returned with a note saying she'd be delighted.

As the time for the tea approached, Callie's bravery wilted like a vase of week-old flowers. She watched the road, hoping Wesley would arrive before his mother. Callie's invitation had stated she wanted to discuss the wedding plans further. Knowing Mrs. Townsend and Mrs. Bridgeport, they wouldn't want to waste time with polite conversation. They would want to talk about the wedding. If this conversation was going to go as she hoped, she needed to take control immediately. But without Wesley by her side, she doubted she'd be able to ward off the objections that were sure to come from both of the older women.

Callie's stomach tightened at the sound of an approaching carriage. Where was Wesley? She stepped onto the porch as the carriage came to a halt in front of Fair Haven. The driver jumped down and assisted Mrs. Townsend. Callie glanced in the opposite direction and sighed with relief when she caught sight of Wesley loping toward the cottage.

He lifted his arm overhead and called to his mother. Mrs. Townsend stopped and looked at him and then at Callie. Confusion shone in the older woman's eyes when Callie walked down the porch steps toward her. Mrs. Townsend remained by the walkway leading to the house.

Wesley slowed his gait to a long stride as he approached his mother. "It's good to see you, Mother. I'm glad you're able to join us for tea."

She narrowed her eyes, obviously attempting to calculate what was happening. "I didn't realize you were in the habit of taking tea, Wesley." She gave Callie a sidelong glance. "And my invitation didn't say that you would be attending our discussion."

He chuckled. "I thought that since I'm an

important member of the wedding party, it might be time for me to get a bit more involved." Without giving his mother a chance to voice her opinion, he offered his arm. "Sorry, but I didn't have an opportunity to change after my last golf lesson."

His mother didn't immediately take his arm. "I don't think any of us would object if you went back to the clubhouse and cleaned up. Grooms don't usually take part in the wedding arrangements."

Callie inhaled a deep breath. "I asked him to attend, Mrs. Townsend. Wesley and I have agreed upon some changes, so I thought he should be present."

Mrs. Townsend's shoulders stiffened. "Then I suppose we should go inside so that I can hear exactly what the two of you have come up with." She grasped Wesley's arm. "And is Eunice already aware of these possible changes?"

"No. That's why I suggested we have this tea. So Wesley and I could explain to both of you — together."

Callie swallowed the lump that had lodged in her throat. Had Mrs. Townsend noticed the tremor in her voice? If she didn't gain a bit of courage, the two older women would win the upper hand before the tea was served.

The moment the threesome entered the house, Mrs. Bridgeport descended the stairs and greeted Mrs. Townsend. "I'm glad you were free this afternoon, Blanche. There are always so many activities at the clubhouse, I worried you might have another engagement scheduled." Mrs. Bridgeport directed them into the parlor.

Mrs. Townsend approached one of the wing chairs and sat down. "Even if I'd had prior arrangements, I would have canceled them. Nothing is more important than the wedding, though I'm surprised to hear that these two have been doing a bit of scheming behind our backs." Her lips stretched in an exaggerated smile.

"Mother!" Wes frowned as he led Callie to the sofa. "We are not scheming. After all, this is our wedding. I believe we have a right to our say in the matter."

"Well, of course you do, so long as you realize that Eunice and I are far more experienced in such things." She preened at Mrs. Bridgeport. "Don't you agree, Eunice?"

Jane entered the room and placed the tea tray on the table near Mrs. Bridgeport. "Since I haven't had a child marry yet, I doubt I have your experience, Blanche. I did help plan my sister's wedding a number of years ago." She poured tea into one of

473

the cups and looked at Mrs. Townsend. "Cream and sugar?"

Wesley squeezed Callie's hand. Clearly, he expected her to speak up before the discussion went much further. "Although I understand you both have more experience than the two of us, Wesley and I have agreed that rather than a large wedding, we would prefer to have a very small sunrise wedding on the beach."

Mrs. Townsend gasped and immediately paled. "That won't do at all. The chapel is what we decided, isn't it, Eunice?" She reached for her fan and snapped it open. "The guests wouldn't be comfortable, and the river can have an odor in the early morning."

"The ocean side of the island, not near the river," Callie said.

"What? We'd have to transport guests to the other side of the island and then have them witness your wedding while standing on the beach. Just think of the discomfort. We couldn't seat anyone. The chairs would sink into the sand. Dear me, Callie, how did you ever come upon such an idea? It is totally unacceptable." She flapped her fan back and forth. "It simply will not work."

Callie accepted the cup of tea from Mrs. Bridgeport.

"I think Blanche is correct, Callie. A wedding on the beach presents innumerable problems. I think you need to reconsider."

"We don't want many guests at the actual wedding ceremony. Just Wesley's family and all of you. I'd like Jane and Lula to be there, of course. I think it will work. I'll wear a simple dress for the ceremony. When we were in Biscayne the other day, I saw a white lace dress that I think would be perfect for a beach wedding."

Mrs. Townsend snapped the fan together and tapped it on the arm of the chair. "We have already ordered your gown. Your measurements have been taken, and I am sure the seamstresses have begun their work. Simply stated, it is too late to cancel the order. I thought you had agreed that you wanted all of us to experience the joy of a beautiful wedding since you and Wesley will be leaving for Africa in the near future."

"If I could finish, I think you'll understand that I don't plan to completely eliminate what you've arranged."

Mrs. Bridgeport took a sip of her tea. "I don't believe I understand, Callie."

"We want a very small wedding, but we are willing to celebrate with other guests at a reception following the ceremony or the following day — whichever you believe is better. I will change into the more elaborate gown for the reception." She blurted out the suggestion without giving either of the women time to interrupt.

Wesley squeezed her hand. "I think we've arrived at a plan that will please everyone, don't you?" He looked back and forth between the two older women.

"Well, I'm not exactly sure. You've dropped this on us without proper time to consider all of the possibilities. I'm not sure the guests will understand that they aren't invited to the actual wedding ceremony." Mrs. Townsend removed a handkerchief from her reticule. "I simply do not see the necessity of this beach wedding idea. I'm not attempting to be overbearing, Callie, but it makes little sense to me." She set her gaze on Mrs. Bridgeport. "Do you see any merit to the idea, Eunice?"

Mrs. Bridgeport took a sip of her tea. "The idea is a bit unconventional, but it is their wedding, Blanche."

Callie inched forward on the sofa. "I wasn't presenting the plan as an idea in which I thought you might find merit. Rather, I was presenting it as what Wesley and I want. We prefer a simple ceremony with only family present. I have given this a great deal of thought. As you both know, my parents can't be present when we are married. However, standing near the ocean will bring me as close to them as possible." Her voice cracked. "I would very much like to feel a bit of their presence on my wedding day, Mrs. Townsend."

Wesley's mother settled back in her chair. "When you put it like that, I don't suppose I can refuse." She glanced at Wesley. "I'll send word to your brothers in Massachusetts so that they can make plans to attend." She gave a firm nod. "Yes, I do believe a beach wedding and a grand reception at the clubhouse sounds perfect."

From the tone of Mrs. Townsend's voice, one would have thought she'd devised the entire plan on her own. Callie squeezed Wes's hand and forced down a threatening giggle.

CHAPTER 31

May 3, 1913

Wesley adjusted his tie for the tenth time. Sunlight was just touching the horizon, and in a matter of minutes he would leave for the beach to marry the woman he loved.

"Are you ready?" Howard Townsend strode into the room without knocking. "Everyone is waiting."

His father appeared unusually anxious, and Wesley couldn't help but smile. "You look more nervous than I feel, and you're only the best man."

His father gave a shrug. "I've never held this position before."

"Just imagine you're conducting a board meeting at the textile mill." Wes tugged his suit back into place and chuckled. "You're always comfortable there."

His father cleared his throat. "Son, I may owe you an apology."

"And why would you say that now?"

Wes's father came forward and reached inside his gray suit coat. He pulled an envelope from his pocket and handed it to Wesley. "All of my life I've placed my focus on accomplishing great things."

"And you have." Wesley glanced at the envelope and wondered if it contained something beneficial or harmful.

"But the greatest things I accomplished were the very ones I didn't acknowledge. At least not in the proper manner." He looked away momentarily. "I've wronged you, Wesley, and I know that now. Your mother has a way of helping me to see the truth of a matter. And frankly, God uses her in ways that I would sometimes just as soon avoid." He glanced up and smiled.

"Callie does that for me," Wesley admitted. "She's like an anchor in some ways, and in other ways . . . well . . . she's more like a cornerstone. Her faith in God, when added to my own, makes me feel invincible. I know beyond doubt that God has great things planned for us."

"I do, too. And as much as I hate to admit it, I know those things aren't inside the walls of a textile mill." His father pointed to the envelope. "I also know that I am supposed to give you this small gift to help you on your way."

Wesley lifted the flap of the envelope and looked inside. His eyes widened at the sight of the bank draft. "This sum is more than a small gift."

His father nodded slowly. "Wes, I'm proud of you. What you and Callie are about to do will take not only faith in God and in each other, but it will also take money. I want you to have the things you'll need in Africa to minister to those people and to care for your bride. Believe me, I know that will not come cheap."

"But, Father —"

He held up his hand to silence Wesley's protests. "I have a few other things arranged, as well. I have friends who will help, too. We are well acquainted with people who deal in a variety of merchandise, and I have associates involved in shipping who will do their part when called upon. I'll arrange for you to transport anything you feel you will need. Most importantly, I promised your mother I would arrange for us to be together at least every two years. Otherwise she's threatened to drag me to the mission field to teach textile weaving to native Africans."

Wesley laughed. "I could just see her doing that, too."

His father placed his hand on Wesley's shoulder. "I'm proud of you, son, and I

480

want the best for you."

"I don't know what to say." Wesley met his father's eyes. "I know you haven't approved of my choices in the past."

"Let this be a way of showing my approval for them now. I was wrong to ever try to lead you away from God's calling on your life. I won't make that mistake again."

"Are you two coming or not?" Helena called from the open doorway.

Wesley laughed and tucked the envelope into his pocket. "We're ready, sister dear. Please lead the way. Gracious, but you'd think you were the bride instead of her attendant."

"Either way, I won't be late."

By the time Wesley and his family arrived at the wedding site on the beach, the sun had peeked above the horizon and cast breathtaking shades of golden-orange on the water. It was a gloriously painted divine canvas that made the perfect backdrop to their wedding.

The chatter of children announced the arrival of Mrs. Bridgeport, Lottie, and Thomas. Daisy, who had fully recovered from her spider bite, skipped ahead, tossing petals on the sand. Wes turned to his father. "How do I look?"

"You look fine, son." His father adjusted

Wes's suit lapels. "Besides, everyone, including you, will have eyes only for the bride."

Then, as if to prove this statement true, Callie appeared on the arm of Mr. Bridgeport. Wes stared at her in wonder. Clad in an unpretentious white muslin-and-lawn gown, Callie wore her hair in a simple arrangement, graced only by a few flowers.

The violinist Mrs. Bridgeport had hired began playing strains of Beethoven's "Romanza" while Wes's heart hammered against his ribs. Callie was a vision, and she was about to become his wife. His life seemed to flash before him, reminding him of the hopes and dreams he'd had — the mistakes he'd made. Suddenly, nothing seemed quite as important as this woman and this moment.

The music faded as Mr. Bridgeport brought her to stand before the preacher. Wes stepped forward and took her hand.

"Do right by her, son," Mr. Bridgeport admonished. "I may not be her father, but I care dearly for this child . . . uh, this young woman."

Wesley smiled and nodded, but his gaze never left Callie's radiant face. "I promise I will." He took Callie's small gloved hand in his, and this time the words were uttered as a pledge only to her. "I promise."

A gentle sea breeze stirred the wisps of hair around Callie's face. She seemed not to mind, however. Her eyes were fixed on Wesley's. He lost himself in her dark brown eyes. She was everything he had ever wanted in a mate — the completion of his very heart. He was filled with awe and thanksgiving as the preacher began to speak of the solemn institution of marriage.

"We are gathered here today in the sight of God and in the presence of this company to witness the union of Callie and Wesley in Christian marriage," the preacher declared. "May our heavenly Father look down upon this event with His smile of approval. May the Lord Jesus Christ be present and add His blessing. May the Holy Spirit attend and seal these vows in love. For marriage is a gift given by God."

Wesley looked at the gift he'd been given in Callie. God had known what he needed even when he couldn't imagine it.

"Jesus tells us to *keep* his commandment of love. The Greek word translated *keep* does not mean to obey. It means to hold in high esteem, to honor, to trust ultimately, to value above all else." The minister paused to look first at Wesley and then at Callie. "What he is calling for is that we trust His love for us even when we don't see it or embody it — that a husband and wife cleave to His love even more than they cleave to each other."

"Amen," Callie murmured and gave a quick look to Wesley. He nodded his agreement that he felt as strongly about this statement as she did.

Callie saw the love in Wesley's eyes and felt as if her heart might burst. She longed to remove her gloves and touch the fresh-shaven smoothness of his cheek. She could smell the scent of his cologne and wanted only to promise to love him forever and to seal the promise with a kiss.

Her cheeks warmed at the thought of their wedding night, and she briefly lowered her gaze. Then, as the preacher charged those gathered to attend the ceremony to guard this sacred trust, Callie raised her face and beamed a smile. This was the happiest day of her life and she intended that everyone should know it. They exchanged their vows, and when it came time for the ring to be placed on her finger, Callie pulled the glove from her hand and presented her fingers to Wesley. To her surprise he raised her hand to his lips and placed a gentle kiss upon the back. Then he turned her hand gently in his and caressed the palm.

"With this ring, I pledge to you my life and my love," he said, his gaze reaching deep into her soul. "I pledge not only to you, however, but I commit this marriage to our heavenly Father. . . ." He placed the lovely diamond and sapphire ring on her index finger. "And to the Son . . ." He moved the ring to her middle finger. "And to the Holy Ghost."

The ring slid gently onto her third finger, and Callie trembled at the impact of the moment and all that Wesley had just done. This wasn't just a promise to each other. This was a commitment to God, and she would never take that lightly.

With the ring in place, Wesley kissed it against her finger. Callie stared at the vision and then lifted her eyes once again to Wesley's loving gaze. Her vision blurred from the tears that rimmed her eyes.

"Wesley, you may now kiss your bride."

Wes cupped her face with such reverence that Callie couldn't help but melt against his touch. The sun's warm rays seemed to burst around them as their lips joined together. The gentle sound of the waves against the shore was muffled by the cheers of the audience who watched. But lost in the moment, Callie heard only the beating of her heart — a heart that beat for Wesley

Townsend. A throat was cleared nearby, and Wes broke their kiss with a grin. She had no idea how long the kiss had lasted, but Helena seemed more than a little anxious. She stepped forward and handed Callie and Wesley each a long-stemmed white rose. A light breeze brushed a stray curl against Callie's cheek as Wesley led them hand in hand to the water's edge.

She raised her eyes in question to Wesley.

"I wish your parents were here so I could thank them for raising such an incredible daughter. However, your mother and father are just on the other side of this water. I thought we could send these roses to them, as our way of making them part of our special day."

Tears pricked Callie's eyes. She looked across the vast expanse, her heart swelling with love and pride. Was it possible to love this man even more? "I suppose it's impossible, but I have a feeling they know exactly what is happening. I feel them here with us now."

"With God all things are possible." Wesley slipped his arm around her waist and pulled her close.

Callie tossed her rose into the water, and Wesley did likewise. "I'd like to think these roses could travel all the way to Africa and find their way to my parents." She looked at Wesley and saw the love in his eyes. "But no matter, I feel their love and yours, and I know that Africa isn't that far away after all."

He drew her ever so gently into his arms and kissed her. The kiss was once again lingering and left Callie breathless.

"I suppose they're gonna kiss all the time now." Daisy's voice was loud enough for everyone to hear.

The wedding audience burst into laughter, and Callie and Wes couldn't help but join in.

"I do plan to kiss her all the time, Daisy dear," Wesley declared. "But since we are to have a great party in a few hours, I will settle for one more kiss now." He gave Callie a quick peck and turned back to Daisy. "There you are."

Lottie and Daisy ran forward and wrapped their arms around Callie. "You look like a fairy princess," Lottie said.

"I feel rather like a princess." Callie looked up into Wes's face. "And the handsome prince has rescued me."

"Rescued you from what?" Daisy looked around the beach. "There aren't any dragons here."

Callie touched her finger to the tip of

Daisy's nose. "No indeed, Daisy. They wouldn't dare to show their faces here, but Wesley has rescued me from more harmful things than dragons." She squeezed her husband's hand and knew he understood.

For a moment they had eyes only for each other, but soon the bridal party surrounded them with well-wishes and congratulations. Callie knew there would be very little time for privacy or intimate words in the next few hours, but in that solitary moment, when she looked into her husband's eyes, she saw everything she had longed for but hadn't dared hope would come.

Hours later, following a bridal luncheon with the families, Callie donned the luxurious white silk gown Mrs. Townsend had ordered for the wedding. It was a marvelous creation of draping silk and white seed pearls. An incredibly lavish concoction, but Callie had to admit the luxurious material against her skin felt decadent. Besides, Mrs. Townsend grew teary eyed at the sight of her in it, saying it pleased her no end to see her new "daughter" in a proper wedding dress.

One of the Townsend maids, Ella, dressed Callie's hair, rearranging it in a full-bodied bun atop her head. Hot irons were applied to create delicate ringlets that fell in a fashionable style around her face. When the young woman finished her ministering, she applied dozens of seed pearls to Callie's coiffure and smiled approvingly.

"You look like a queen." The maid stepped back and surveyed her handiwork.

Callie caught sight of her reflection in the mirror. "Thank you, Ella. You did a wonderful job.

"You're beautiful," Mrs. Townsend declared as she and Helena entered the room. "Just look at her, Helena. Isn't she lovely?"

Callie looked at her new sister-in-law, expecting to see some remaining concerns or doubt in her expression. Instead, Helena stepped forward with tears in her eyes. "You are beautiful, and I know that you are exactly the right woman for my brother. I hope you'll forgive me for seeming . . . well, for not being very supportive in the beginning."

"There was never anything to forgive." Callie took Helena's hands. "But I have your blessing now?"

"I wish you nothing but God's blessings. I hope one day we might be the dearest of sisters."

Callie smiled and kissed Helena's cheek. "We already are."

Mrs. Townsend clapped her gloves hands. "Come, girls. Our reception guests await us."

The party was already in full swing by the time Callie descended the grand staircase. With the exception of soft strains of music from the twelve-piece orchestra, the room went quiet at her approach. When Callie reached the bottom step, Wesley stepped forward, decked out in the same grand style he'd worn at the masked ball. Only this time, there were no masks or pretenses between them.

"Mrs. Townsend, I presume," he said in a teasing tone. "Although I must admit, you look very little like the woman I married this morning."

Callie giggled. "Well, you'd best remember that I'm a woman full of surprises."

He chuckled and tucked her gloved arm against his waist. "I have a few surprises of my own, but I'm afraid you'll have to wait for those until we're alone. In the meantime, I'll have to endure sharing you with others."

"Indeed." Callie gave him a sly grin. "But I hope we shan't be all day at this party. I have it on the best authority there is a small hidden cottage — a cabin really — on the far north side of the island that is in want of residents."

Wesley raised a questioning brow. "Sounds rather intriguing."

She nodded quite innocently. "I thought so, too."

He laughed. "Then let us be about our duties as the guests of honor quickly." He pulled her forward into the gloriously decorated room before adding in a whisper, "So that we might be about our pleasures in a leisurely fashion."

He swept her into his arms for a first waltz as man and wife. Swirling the dance floor in the arms of her husband, Callie's heart was so full, it felt as if it might burst.

"Do you realize how happy you've made me?" His warm breath against her ear sent shivers along her spine.

She lifted her gaze to meet his. "I have an idea."

Once the waltz ended, they cut the tiered wedding cake and then began to accept congratulatory messages from the well-wishers. After a while, the two were whisked away from each other. Daniel, Charles, and Richard then playfully conspired to keep the couple separated as much as possible, pretending to have need of Wesley's help for a variety of reasons. From across the room, Callie would catch Wesley's eye, and she chuckled at the exasperated expression on his face. She knew better than to make a fuss about the matter, finding herself just as occupied with one Bridal Veil guest or another. Everyone wanted to admire her gown or offer their advice and suggestions on where to take a proper wedding trip. A few women had heard of the couple's plans to head out to Africa and admonished Callie to take plenty of mosquito netting.

"We went on safari last year." The woman gave a slight shudder. "I have never seen so many insects and snakes in all my life. I don't think the place very appealing at all — so much dirt and so many animals."

Callie smiled and accepted the comments with few replies. It wasn't important that these people understood her heart. They were far too concerned with issues that had little value in Callie's life.

"I would think a young woman like you would prefer Paris," another wealthy matron said. "It's lovely any time of the year. The fashions available there would delight you no end and would take you fashionably into any setting."

Callie wondered if that included poor African villages and sickrooms, but she said nothing. She didn't really need to speak. The women around her were quite capable of carrying on the conversation without her comments.

To her surprise, Helena interrupted the onslaught. "Callie, I need to speak to you for a moment. Ladies, if you'll please excuse us." She pulled Callie along, not even stopping when another cluster of elderly matrons called out.

"Whatever is the matter?" The brisk pace Helena set sent prickles of fear through her body. "Is something wrong?"

Just as they reached a long hallway, Helena pushed Callie to the right, a broad grin across her face. "There will be if I don't get you out of there."

Callie looked at her sister-in-law and shook her head. "What do you mean?"

"My brother has lost all patience with this affair." She smiled and pointed to the end of the hall. Wesley stepped out from the shadows. "He felt it was time for you two to make an escape, and I wanted to help."

Callie stopped and turned to the woman. "Thank you. You are already proving yourself to be a dear friend."

"Be on your way. I'll deal with the others." She winked at her brother. "I'm sure Mother and Mrs. Bridgeport will help, as well."

Callie moved down the hall as quickly as she felt proper. Wesley wrapped his arm around her waist and headed down a side hall toward an exit.

"I thought I might never have you to myself." His breath tickled her ear. She laughed, glancing over her shoulder to make certain they weren't being followed. Wes helped her into a carriage waiting by the side entrance and then signaled the driver to leave. "Exactly how did you manage this?"

"You're not the only one full of surprises." Wesley winked and pulled Callie into his arms. "My dearest wife," he murmured and settled his lips upon hers.

As the carriage transported them along the overgrown path toward the cottage, Callie lost herself in the wonder of his kiss and the warmth of his embrace.

"I love you," Wesley whispered against her ear before placing light kisses along her neck and jaw. "And I promise to love and cherish you for all time."

Callie wrapped her arms around his neck and sighed. "And I will honor and trust you . . . with my heart . . . my dreams . . . and my life."

ACKNOWLEDGMENTS

No book is written without the help and support of many people. The entire Bethany House staff constantly amazes me with their creative talents and ability to make each book shine. Special thanks to editors Sharon Asmus and Charlene Patterson for their encouragement and assistance. It is a genuine privilege to work with such talented editors as well as every member of the Bethany House family.

Thanks to Mary Greb-Hall, Lorna Seilstad, and Mary Kay Woodford for their prayers, critiques, expertise, and friendship.

Thanks to Gretchen Greminger, curator of the Jekyll Island Museum, for her speedy replies and helpful responses to my questions.

And special thanks to you, dear readers, for your e-mails and letters of encouragement, your expressions of kindness and love, your prayers, and your eagerness to read each book.

Above all, thanks and praise to our Lord Jesus Christ for the opportunity to live my dream and share the wonder of His love through story.

~Judy

ABOUT THE AUTHORS

Judith Miller is an award-winning author whose avid research and love for history are reflected in her bestselling novels. Judy makes her home in Topeka, Kansas.

Tracie Peterson is the bestselling, award-winning author of more than 80 novels. Tracie also teaches writing workshops at a variety of conferences on subjects such as inspirational romance and historical research. She and her family live in Belgrade, Montana.

For more information on Tracie and Judith's books, including behind-the-scenes details and photos from the BRIDAL VEIL ISLAND series, check out the Writes of Passage blog at *writespassage.blogspot.com*.